DEADLY
SUMMER

Other Titles by Denise Grover Swank

Rose Gardner Mysteries

TWENTY-EIGHT AND A HALF WISHES
TWENTY-NINE AND A HALF REASONS
THIRTY AND A HALF EXCUSES
FALLING TO PIECES (Novella)
THIRTY-ONE AND A HALF REGRETS
THIRTY-TWO AND A HALF COMPLICATIONS
PICKING UP THE PIECES (Novella)
THIRTY-THREE AND A HALF SHENANIGANS
ROSE AND HELENA SAVE CHRISTMAS (Novella)
RIPPLE OF SECRETS (Novella)
THIRTY-FOUR AND A HALF PREDICAMENTS
THIRTY-FIVE AND A HALF CONSPIRACIES
THIRTY-SIX AND A HALF MOTIVES

Rose Gardner Investigations and Neely Kate Mysteries

FAMILY JEWELS
TRAILER TRASH
FOR THE BIRDS

Magnolia Steele Mysteries

CENTER STAGE
ACT TWO
CALL BACK
CURTAIN CALL

EMERGENCE (Novella)
MIDDLE GROUND (Novella)
HOMECOMING (Novella)

Blood Borne Series

SILVER STAKED
WOLF BITE

On the Otherside

HERE
THERE

Stand-Alone Novels

ONE PARIS SUMMER

DEADLY SUMMER

DARLING INVESTIGATIONS

DENISE GROVER SWANK

Montlake
Romance

Published by Montlake Romance, Seattle

www.apub.com

Amazon, the Amazon logo, and Montlake Romance are trademarks of Amazon.com, Inc., or its affiliates.

ISBN-13: 9781542048217
ISBN-10: 1542048214

Cover design by Faceout Studios

Printed in the United States of America

To Trace: you've always been too devious for your own good.

CHAPTER ONE

This felt a lot like rock bottom.

I was sitting at the bar in Magnum, an upscale Vietnamese and Portuguese fusion restaurant, sipping a glass of white wine while I tried not to dwell on the fact that the restaurant was named after a condom. Okay, so it probably wasn't named after a condom, but it might as well have been. I hadn't had a decent job in almost eight years, and I was trying to decide whether to accept a nude photo shoot or star in my own personal version of hell—a reality TV show. I'd been looking for signs everywhere, and this seemed like a flashing billboard.

My grandmother was the one who'd gotten me into the habit of looking for signs. As a lifetime member of Sweet Briar, Alabama Calvary Baptist Church, I was positive she would tell me to run far away from the photo shoot, regardless of the name of the restaurant. It didn't matter that I hadn't talked to my grandmother in years—nine, to be exact. She always seemed to pop up in my head when I needed tough love.

But morals and principles didn't pay the bills, and I was drowning in them.

While I was finishing my backstroke in my Olympic-size pool of self-pity, I heard a woman shout in excitement, "Oh, my *God*! It's Isabella Holmes!"

It didn't matter that my name was Summer Butler, and Isabella was a character I'd played in a teen show called *Gotcha!* nearly a decade ago. As far as the world was concerned, we were one and the same.

Maybe if I ignore her, she'll go away. Sometimes it worked.

The bartender stopped in front of me and leaned his elbow on the counter, lowering his face to mine. "Want me to get rid of her?"

I studied him, wondering what he wanted. Everyone wanted something. The woman behind me probably wanted a selfie with me. The producer I was supposed to meet wanted to capitalize on my notoriety—former teen-superstar actress, now nearly bankrupt and unemployable, her life in the gutter. *Alpha Magazine* wanted to use my good-girl persona to sell lots of copies after they slutted me up. Justin, my manager, wanted to milk the little that was left of my career.

Ah. Judging from the gleam in his eyes, the bartender in front of me wanted in my pants, or up my dress, as the case may be. Men *loved* to screw Isabella Holmes.

At least I knew where I stood.

"No," I said, holding his gaze, "I can handle her." I had to admit he was a good-looking guy, but the perfectly styled hair screamed wannabe actor. I'd met more than my fair share who were hoping to use me as a launching pad to a career, which I found amusing given that *my* career was currently in the shitter.

He winked. "She's heading this way. Let me know if you want me to intervene."

"Thanks." I glanced over my shoulder as two women in their thirties charged toward me.

"Oh, my God," one woman said in a gush with her phone in her hand. "You're Isabella Holmes!"

I offered her a polite smile. "Actually, I'm Summer Butler. But yes, I *did* play Isabella several years ago."

"Whatever," she said, waving her hand in dismissal. "I can't believe it's you. TMZ said you were homeless."

I forced a laugh. Talk about bad acting. No wonder I couldn't get a job. I lifted my brow into a playfully amused expression. "Don't you know you can't believe everything you read in those tabloids?"

I was pretty proud of how I'd delivered the line, but the girl's friend didn't look convinced. "But Perez Hilton said your house is in foreclosure."

2

I lifted my wineglass to my lips and took a sip, giving the woman a patient look even though I was seething inside. Perez Hilton was right—or at least he would be soon enough. But my house was the least of my worries. I was desperate to save my family's legacy, but that was something you'd never learn about on a gossip site. Not even my grandmother knew.

Before my grandfather had died nine years ago, he'd swallowed his pride and asked me and my mother to cosign a loan to bail out the family farm. Only he'd asked us to keep it from my grandmother and my extended family, making me swear I'd never tell.

Several months later, my grandfather, aunt, and uncle had died in a fire, my fifteen-year-old cousin, Dixie, was charged with arson and three counts of manslaughter, and I had a major falling-out with my mother. When she headed back to our hometown of Sweet Briar, Alabama, under the guise of helping her mother and her dead brother's children, she ran off with most of my money, leaving me with the tatters of a career she'd spent the previous two years sabotaging in her greed for *more* money. Oh, and the responsibility for the loan my grandfather had taken out on the nearly two-centuries-old family farm. Now I was broke and nearly homeless, and there was an upcoming balloon payment on the farm, which I had no means of paying.

So it was pose nude or embarrass myself on TV. Either way I lost.

But at the moment, I needed to shut down this conversation. "My attorney is currently determining what legal action we can take for the defamation of my character."

They eyed me up and down, and even though it irritated the shit out of me, I let them look. My long blonde hair hung in loose waves, and I was wearing my size 1 thrift-store-find ivory Prada dress and Louboutin pumps; I'd dressed to impress. Small victories. I took them anywhere I could. I daintily set my wineglass on the bar. "Like I said, you can't always believe what you read."

"Like those photos of you in *In Touch Weekly*," her friend said, staring at me with wide eyes. "You looked *terrible* in those."

Everyone had fat rolls in a bikini if you were positioned the right—or wrong—way. To make matters worse, my body had been covered in a blotchy rash due to an allergic reaction to a new moisturizer. But I'd been stupid enough to let my best friend, Marina, talk me into going to the beach because "sunshine and vitamin D are nature's cure for blotchy skin."

"The paparazzi haven't followed you for months," Marina had said. She would know. She'd stopped working as my paid assistant a year ago, but she still hung out with me often enough as a friend.

Lucky for me the paps had followed Cameron Diaz, who'd ended up as the "star" in their beach-body roundup, and photographed *me* with a fat roll *and* blotchy skin. A designer who had been considering hiring me as the face of their new line canceled my lunch with the director of marketing the same afternoon the photos posted.

I lifted a shoulder into a shrug. "Photoshop. You wouldn't believe what tabloids do to have the latest scoop . . . even if it's a lie. Gossip sells."

And that was the true name of the game in la-la land. Selling—movies, TV shows, magazines. Popularity. It didn't matter what you were selling, as long as people wanted it. And no one had wanted me for nearly eight years.

"Can we take selfies with you?" the first woman asked.

I smiled even though I wanted to tell her no. I didn't need any more bad press, although a small part of me wondered if the executive producer I was about to meet would have welcomed it. Bad press made for great reality TV.

I plastered on my fan-photo smile as the first woman sidled up next to me and held her camera up over our heads, presumably to minimize her double chin. She lowered her phone and checked the image.

"Can we take that again?" she asked.

I gave her a gracious smile even though I was feeling anything but—I was nervous about meeting the producer, and I needed a few minutes to get myself together. But the sooner I got this over with, the sooner I'd be done with them. "Of course."

After half a dozen tries, she finally decided the first photo was the best. Her friend was less picky. She snapped a quick selfie of the two of us and then started to furiously tap on her phone.

"Hey," a middle-aged man said from behind her. He wore a button-down shirt covered in tiny palm trees and coconuts that screamed tourist. "You're Isabella Holmes."

"Summer Butler," I said with a forced smile.

"You were really a bitch when you turned that guy down when he asked you to prom. He went to a lot of trouble to ask you."

I stared at him in disbelief, sure he was joking. But he stared right back, waiting for me to respond. "That wasn't me," I said patiently. "That was in a TV show."

"It still wasn't nice."

"Maybe so," I said, "but I was following the script I was given." Not that I would have accepted had the actor asked me. I couldn't stand Connor Blake, my former costar on *Gotcha!* Never content playing second fiddle to me, he'd gone out of his way to make my life hell—on the show and off. He'd loved every minute of pretending to be my boyfriend during our fifth and final season, especially since it had been the final blow to my relationship with my then-boyfriend Luke Montgomery.

"You were much too sassy to your parents."

"Again," I said, trying to remain calm and stave off a building headache, "I was following the script."

I turned back to my drink, resisting the urge to chug it down to calm my nerves. The last thing I needed was my photo on the cover of the *National Enquirer.* I could see it now—a photo of me with my head tilted back to drain the last of my wineglass, plastered beneath the headline: "The Downfall of America's Darling—Drugs, Booze, and Wild Orgies." If only I had the courage to consider attending one of those wild orgies.

"Can I ask you for just one more thing?" the first woman asked.

Knowing what was coming, I lifted the wineglass to my lips to stall, muttering, "My firstborn child?"

"What?" she asked in confusion.

I set down the glass. "What do you need?"

"Will you say it?"

I knew my smile had to look forced, but I couldn't find it in myself to care. I decided to play dumb. "Say what?"

"You know," she said in a tone that suggested I was an idiot. "The line."

I took another sip of my wine. "And which line is that?"

"You know the line, sweetheart," the palm-tree guy said in condescending tone. "The line from that show."

I knew I should just say it and get rid of them, but if they had any idea how many times I'd said that line over the last fifteen years . . .

I shook my head, still playing dumb. "Which show?"

"You know," the man said in exasperation. He thrust his hips to the side, pointed his right index finger at me, and winked as he said, *"Gotcha!"*

The hostess was making her way to me, so I stuck my credit card in the black folder to pay for my drink. The bartender knew I was waiting on a table, so I wouldn't need to stay here for it to be returned. "That was really good," I said enthusiastically. "Have you considered trying out for the remake?"

One of the fans squealed. "There's gonna be a remake?"

There wasn't, but it didn't stop me from shrugging and offering a mischievous grin. "You didn't hear it from me."

"They're gonna find someone twenty years younger to play you, right?" the guy asked.

My eyes widened, my tongue stuck to the roof of my mouth. *Let it go, Summer.*

But dammit, I was tired of letting everything go.

I ignored him and walked toward the frazzled hostess, leaving the two women to their excitement.

"I'm sorry, Ms. Butler," she said, cringing, "but your party's been seated for five minutes. I forgot you were at the bar."

"That's okay," I said. The clenching of my stomach made me wish I had time to go to the bathroom, but if Scott Schapiro was already at the table, I couldn't keep him waiting.

The hostess led the way to a semicircular booth. A good-looking man in his forties, wearing a dress shirt and tie, sat on the opposite side. The way he impatiently tapped his finger on the table was a not-so-subtle sign that he was pissed.

"I told your manager one sharp," he said in a cold tone. "I'm on a tight timetable."

"I'm sorry, Mr. Schapiro," the hostess said. "It's all my fault. She was in the bar, and I forgot."

"Uh-huh." He looked up at me like I was an ant he was considering squashing. "How much did you pay her to say that?"

My mouth dropped open in shock, and before I could respond, he gestured to the seat opposite him.

"Well, don't just stand there. Sit down so we can get this over with."

The hostess shot me an apologetic look, but I was more concerned with the man glaring at me. I slid into the booth as gracefully as I could manage in my tight dress and set my purse on the seat beside me.

"I'm so sorry about the mix-up," I said with a smile as I folded my hands on the table in front of me. "I've been in the bar for the last fifteen minutes. The staff said they'd notify me when you arrived."

"Are you drunk?" he asked hopefully.

"What? No! I didn't even finish my glass of wine."

He rolled his eyes in disgust. "That's too bad."

"*What?*"

"Whatever," he said dismissively. "You're here. I'm here. Let's dispense with the niceties and get this started."

"Okay." I let out a tiny breath and waited for him to speak, which resulted in a five-second staring match.

He glanced down at his phone, then back up at me. "Well? I don't have all day."

He was really starting to tick me off. "And I'm ready to listen."

"Listen to what?" he asked. "You haven't even pitched me anything yet."

"Excuse me?" I asked, trying to cover my shock.

His eyes narrowed. "Your manager told me you were pitching me a few reality TV shows."

"He did *what*?" Justin had pushed me into taking this meeting, and I'd finally agreed because one, I was desperate, and two, Justin had said I would only have to listen to the producer's pitches.

Disgust washed over Mr. Schapiro's face. "So you're not prepared." He lifted a hand to flag down the waitress. "My time is valuable, Ms. Butler."

"Of course it is," I said, my mind scrambling. "You want ideas from *me*."

"Isn't that what I just said? Did I stutter?"

"No, it's just that . . ." How was I going to come up with ideas in a matter of seconds? I was an intelligent woman. I could do this.

The waitress walked over, and Mr. Schapiro lifted a credit card. "I need to settle my bill."

"Already?" she asked, taking his card. "You haven't ordered your food yet."

"And I won't be. Just the drink."

The waitress walked away, and I said, "I have ideas."

"Then you have about three minutes to pitch—the time it takes her to bring my receipt and for me to sign it."

"Okay . . ." *Crap.* Why hadn't I paid more attention to reality TV? "You could follow me to auditions."

"And when was the last time you had an audition?" he scoffed.

Score one for Scott Schapiro. "I'm considering renovating my house. You could follow that." *Oh, shit.* I hoped he didn't pick that one. Before long, I wouldn't even own a house.

"This isn't HGTV, Ms. Butler," he said in disgust. "It's E! Didn't you do your homework?"

Dammit. The waitress was heading our way.

"I don't have a boyfriend," I said. "You could follow me on some dates." When he looked unimpressed, I added, "I could do one of those dating sites." What the hell was I thinking? Had I really sunk this low?

I imagined myself posed on a school desk, naked from the waist up, wearing my character Isabella's plaid school-uniform skirt, my leg hiked up enough to give viewers a peek underneath it. Because that was probably my only other option if I didn't come up with something. And quick.

The waitress set the black bill folder in front of him, then scurried away. He lifted the flap and picked up the pen. "What else do you have?"

"I take yoga. Maybe I could teach classes."

He grunted and signed his name.

Crap! I was so pissed at Justin for doing this to me. Pissed at Scott Schapiro for treating me like I was worthless. Pissed at the people who still expected me to be Isabella Holmes, amateur teen sleuth at the made-up Roosevelt High School, who solved small mysteries for her friends and family. I was pissed at my mother for making me do the damn show at all and for stealing most of my money.

"Fine," I said in a snotty tone. "How about this? I'm a private investigator like my character in *Gotcha!*, only I solve real-life crimes. You like that one any better?"

He set down his pen and looked me in the eye. "Do you want to know what your trouble is, Summer?"

"Why do I think you're going to tell me whether I want to hear it or not, *Scott*?"

He grinned—slightly. "Your problem is that you're vanilla. You were a nice girl in a nice show, aimed at the tween demographic, and you're *still* nice. You don't drink to excess. You don't party. Hell, I don't think you've had a boyfriend in two years."

Three, but I wasn't about to correct him.

"Sure, you were embroiled in some controversy with your costar." He circled his finger. "Whoop-de-doo. You were nineteen fucking years old. What actor hasn't slept with a costar." He put his card into his wallet. "You're boring, Summer. Boring with a capital *B*. No one would want to watch your show because no one gives a shit." He stood. "Frankly, I was shocked to see a little bit of fire from you a moment ago, but a lit match isn't enough to make viewers watch. You'd be better off giving up the ghost and getting a real job."

I stood, getting really ticked off now. "Do you think I haven't tried? I'm too recognizable to get a normal job." I'd taken a managerial job at an upscale boutique, but the customers had all seemed more interested in getting autographs and selfies than in buying the merchandise. The owners had fired me for being too distracting.

"Not my problem, sweetheart . . ." He grinned. "Or should I say, *Darling*?"

The hostess slinked toward me with a nervous look. "Uh, Ms. Butler. Your credit card was declined."

Jesus, Mary, and Joseph. Of course it fucking was.

Scott Schapiro laughed.

Palm-tree guy from the bar walked past our table and headed straight for me, wobbling a little.

"Hey!" he said, wandering over to us. "Isabella! You didn't say your line."

Scott Schapiro glanced back at the man and let out a bark of a laugh. "You better give it to him, Summer," he said with a weaselly smile, "because this is about as good as it's going to get for you."

Those words were still echoing in my ears as the tourist came to a stop in front of me. "I want my line," he said, invading my personal space with his pointer finger. "Some America's Darling you are." Then he poked his finger at me, aiming for my chest before he wobbled and got a handful of my boob.

Everything welled up inside me—the debt, my mother's betrayal, my frustration at being the butt of everyone's jokes, and years and years of failure.

"You want the line?" I shouted, pulling back my arm. "Here's your *fucking line*!" I screeched as I punched him in the eye. *"Gotcha!"*

The man fell to his knees, covering his face with his hand. "Isabella Holmes just punched me in the face!"

I leaned over him and sneered, "How do you like America's Darling now?"

CHAPTER TWO

"Shit. This is bad," I said as I watched the video phone footage on TMZ while balancing a bag of frozen peas on the knuckles of my right hand. Lucky for me, I'd been captured on half a dozen camera phones, all showing me from various angles punching Richard Abbott, a forty-three-year-old mechanic from Omaha, Nebraska, in the face.

My front door opened, and I whipped around to see Marina walk in carrying a brown paper bag. I pushed out a breath of relief. I was so tightly wound, I wasn't sure I could handle this alone. I hadn't called her, but I wasn't surprised she'd come anyway even though she was supposed to be working.

"What in the hell happened?" she asked, walking toward me.

"I just snapped," I said, turning back to the TV as the host discussed what had led to my emotional breakdown.

"I'll say," she said in awe. "Have you been taking kickboxing or self-defense classes on the sly? Because that was quite a punch."

"No." I groaned and began to pace again. "Just hot yoga."

"Don't discount the Pilates," she said with a grin. "Your solid core helped with your follow-through." Then she imitated the punch that was replaying on my TV screen.

"Not helping."

She cringed when she saw the peas. "What in the hell is on your hand?" She stuck her finger into her mouth and made a gagging sound before she grabbed the package and tossed them across the room. The peas hit the wall and bounced to the tile floor, but before I could put up a fuss, she handed me a small container of gourmet ice cream. She winked. "You deserve it, America's Slugger." Her eyes widened. "Hey! Maybe you can get a job on one of those women's wrestling shows. Or roller derby."

I shot her a glare and muted the TV.

"What?" Marina asked in fake innocence, her hands wide. Her grin spread. "Too soon?"

I moved over to the front window and peered through the blinds. There were multiple cars parked up and down the street, and the paparazzi were standing on the sidewalk. "Did you see the police out front?" My neighbors were going to get pissed if the photographers blocked the street.

"Surely they're not going to arrest you for this," she said. "What two-hundred-and-fifty-pound man is going to admit to getting punched out by a tiny woman? He's more likely to file a civil suit."

Great. One more thing to worry about. "I can't afford a lawsuit. You can't squeeze blood out of a turnip."

She studied my face. "I know things are bad, Summer, but how bad are they?"

"I'm losing my house."

"What? *How?*"

I stopped pacing and ran my fingers through my hair. "Two words: my mother." The source of pretty much everything that had gone sour in my life.

"*That bitch.* What did she do now?"

I'd called my mother much worse names after discovering the extent of her thievery. "Nothing new. Just the same old shit cropping up anew."

"How much do you owe the bank?"

"Three million dollars." For the second mortgage on my house.

Marina's eyes bugged out of her head. "Oh. *Shit.*"

I sat the sofa. "*Shit* is right."

"I told you to go after her when she cleaned you out and ran."

"I couldn't."

The dark look she shot me suggested she strongly disagreed, but I didn't expect her to understand. Marina had run off to LA fifteen years ago and left her family behind. While I'd left mine in the past too, Marina was actually glad to be rid of hers. I hadn't wanted to be estranged from my grandmother and my cousins. But it was my fault their scandal had hit the tabloids. My fault the tragedy of the fire had been compounded by the coverage of it. And I had plenty of other things to feel guilty about too.

Suing my mother would have dragged what remained of my family into closer scrutiny, something she'd counted on. I'd decided to do my part to protect my cousins. And, even though she hated me—Meemaw. Any more drama from me would have kept them—especially my little cousin, who would have never purposefully set that fire, charges notwithstanding—in the spotlight. So I'd sucked up the multi-million-dollar mess, reasoning that I'd soon earn it back.

But I'd already spent so much money by then—on this house, on the furniture, on a wardrobe that had quickly gone out of style—and I hadn't booked any major jobs since then. The money from re-airings of *Gotcha!* brought in ridiculously low royalties, again thanks to my mother, who'd insisted on more money up front.

"You could sell your story about what happened," she suggested with raised eyebrows.

I shook my head. I couldn't risk it.

"Then you have to do the nude photos, Summer," Marina said. "You need the money."

"Tell me something I don't know," I groaned in frustration.

I put the ice cream in the freezer, grabbed the phone, and moped all the way to the high-end sofa my designer had insisted I buy. Something so uncomfortable no sane person would want to sit on it. "I was desperate enough to consider a reality TV show." I leaned my head back and moaned. "That's why I was at the restaurant taking a meeting with Scott Schapiro—to pitch ideas to him."

"Reality TV?" she asked, sounding hopeful.

I sat up and gave her a look of disbelief.

"Wait. *You* hate reality TV. You must be rock-bottom desperate." She sat down sideways beside me and crossed her legs. "Jesus, Summer. Why didn't you tell me?"

Utter embarrassment? Or maybe it was plain denial. But I wasn't copping to either one. "What good would it have done? It doesn't matter anyway. Schapiro told me I was too vanilla for people to care about. This probably blew the *Alpha* deal too. They wanted a good girl gone bad, but the effect would kind of be ruined now that I'm plastered on all the gossip sites."

My phone began to ring, and I glared at the screen when I saw Justin's name. I considered letting it go to voice mail, but this was all his fault, and it was time for me to fire his ass for good.

"You have a lot of fucking nerve," I said as soon as I answered.

"Summer, *darling.*"

"You set me up. Did you *want* me to fail?" I demanded, moving to the window and peering through the blinds. There were a couple of news trucks and more paparazzi now.

"No, of course not. If you'd known you would have to pitch, you never would have gone at all."

"Justin, I looked like a fool! It was so obvious I was unprepared . . . Besides, it was a waste of time. Schapiro said I was too boring."

"That's why I'm calling."

"To gloat?"

"No! To tell you that Schapiro changed his mind. He's offering you a contract, but you have to move fast."

I froze. "Wait. *What?*"

He laughed. "Schapiro is offering you a contract for a limited-run series. Kind of like a test series."

"What made him change his mind?"

"I don't know . . . probably watching you beat the shit out of that old man."

"He wasn't an old man, Justin. And it was one punch."

"For all I care, you could have used Rip Van Winkle as a punching bag. Schapiro is offering fifty thousand dollars per episode for six episodes. But you have less than twenty-four hours to sign and seventy-two to show up on set."

"That fast? Is it possible?"

"He's using the negative publicity to help grab an audience." He paused. "Are you sure that guy wasn't old? Only old guys wear palm-tree shirts."

"You're watching the videos?"

"Of course I am. I have to know what's going on." He let out a groan. "Damn, girl. I should have been trying to get you parts in action movies."

"Justin."

"My advice? Take the deal. You're not going to land anything that pays better."

I put my hand on my chest to slow my racing heart. "I don't even know what the reality show's about."

"Schapiro's assistant was fuzzy about the details, but I know there's travel involved."

"Travel?"

Marina gave me a thumbs-up sign, then handed me a glass of wine. God bless her.

"His producer is headed to your house right now with the contract. She'll give you all the details."

"Aren't you going to read it first? Aren't you going to *come over*?"

"Sorry, Summer. I'm tied up, but you're in good hands. Besides, you're a pro at this. Congrats, darling! You're back." Then he hung up.

I was back. I wasn't nearly as excited as I'd hoped I would be.

"Travel?" Marina asked. "Can I be your assistant again? I've always wanted to go to Greece. All those men wearing togas and wreaths on their heads." She made a roaring sound.

"*That* is Rome, Marina, and you're about two thousand years too late."

"Huh. Too bad." She grinned, and I shook my head.

"So what's the premise of the show?" she asked.

"I have no idea."

"He didn't give you any clue at your lunch?"

"There was no lunch," I said, flopping down on the sofa. "There was only a stolen glass of wine, and then I was whisked out the back."

She sat next to me and quirked her eyebrow. "Stolen wine?"

"Declined credit card."

She made an exaggerated grimace.

"And it turns out that I was the one pitching to him. Justin totally threw me to the wolves."

"*What?*" She sat next to me, sloshing the wine in her glass.

"I threw out a few random ideas. Maybe he picked the dating one. Maybe I get to date guys all over the world." That might not be so bad, come to think of it. My dry spell had been so long, my body felt like the Sahara.

"Maybe you get to cook all over the world."

"God, let's hope not. I can't cook."

"All the more reason to do it . . ."

Marina continued to throw out ideas, each one crazier than the last—including herself in each of the scenarios, of course—until the doorbell rang. I looked at the security-camera app on my phone. There was a woman in a trench coat on my front porch, and she looked *pissed*. Great.

"Reporter?" Marina asked.

I opened the door a crack, hoping she was a reporter, because if this was the producer, she looked even more intimidating than Scott Schapiro. "Can I help you?"

Trench-coat woman glared. "Let me in." She stood nearly a foot taller than I was in her three-inch heels. It didn't help that I was standing on my bare feet.

She started to walk in, but I blocked her path. "You're not coming in until I know who you are and what you want."

Trench-coat woman barely rolled her eyes, but that half gesture was enough for her to get her point across. I got the impression that she was used to getting her way without pushing for it.

"Lauren Chapman. I'm apparently the showrunner of your new show, so you better let me in or I'll make your life a living hell."

Holy crap. And here I'd thought this day couldn't get any worse.

I backed out of the way, and Lauren stormed past me.

"Summer!" photographers shouted from the street. "Why'd you hit your fan?"

"Summer! Is it true you're entering rehab?"

I grunted and slammed the door shut.

Lauren stood in the center of my living room, glancing around. "Not bad. You've got a great view of the ocean."

My house was incredibly small but ridiculously expensive because of its location. Right on the Malibu shore. It was going to kill me to lose it, but eight years of little income had taken their toll.

Then it hit me. They would probably expect to use this place for the show.

Lauren sat in my midcentury-modern Mies van der Rohe Barcelona original chair—another must-have according to my pushy decorator—and plopped a folder on my coffee table. "Just sign these and let's make it official so we can get started."

"Justin said I had to be on location within seventy-two hours. But he didn't say what the premise of the show would be."

Lauren groaned and shook her head. "You've got to be kidding."

I just stared at her. To my surprise, Marina, who stood behind me, remained completely silent. That was so unlike her.

"You'll be a PI, solving real cases." She opened the folder and slid a stack of papers toward me. "Now sign on the dotted line so we can proceed. We have a lot to do between now and Thursday morning. I want to get an early start."

"Wait." I held my hands up in protest. *"What?"*

"Schapiro said it was your idea," she said, winging a brow up. "Now sign."

"I wasn't serious," I protested. "It was supposed to be a joke."

She gave me a look so dry it would make a cactus thirsty. "I don't joke."

That much was obvious.

"Look," I said emphatically, "I'm not really a private investigator."

"No shit," Lauren snapped, crossing her legs and looking at her phone. "Why do you think we're scrambling? We're trying to work out the PI-license situation. So, ticktock, Summer. You're wasting many people's valuable time, especially *mine.*"

I picked up the multipage legal document and quickly scanned it, surprised to see a "Created by Scott Schapiro and Summer Butler" listed. I couldn't see

Schapiro adding that, so maybe Justin had done *something* to earn his percentage. "It says the location is TBA."

"As I said, we're working out the PI license. Schapiro insists you have to do this on your own and not shadow someone, but there are conditions that need to be met in order for you to get a valid license. They don't just let anyone with bad-acting experience get a license." One side of her mouth tipped into the hint of a smile.

Marina's head jutted back, and her typical attitude finally reengaged. "*Bad acting?*"

"Really, Marina?" I turned toward her. "That's what you pick up on?" Still, I couldn't ignore the warmth of gratitude spreading through my chest.

Lauren stared my friend down. "Why else has she gone a decade without a major project?"

"Hey!" Marina pointed her finger at her. "Just a few weeks ago, she was offered *Dancing with the Stars!*" It was a lie, but a flattering one.

"Trust me," Lauren said, her tone dripping with disgust, "I wish she were dancing her little heart out, but here we are." She turned her deadly gaze on me. "Sign the damn papers and stop wasting my time. Schapiro insists we have something ready to air in three weeks, which means we should have started this three months ago, not three days from now."

"But a real PI?" I asked. "I don't have any real-life experience."

Lauren pushed out a sigh so loud and long it could have inflated a bouncy castle. "I heard you weren't bright, but I'd hoped you were at least a little sharper than a Popsicle stick." She leaned forward and widened her eyes. "I *know* you don't, but don't you worry your pretty little head about that. We've got it covered."

"*Excuse me?* Who says I'm not bright?"

"Everyone."

I gave Marina a bewildered look, but she just shrugged. What the hell?

Lauren groaned. "Look, Dumpling—"

Marina lifted up her hand in a halt sign. "Darling." The producer shot her a stern look, but Marina held her ground. "Darling. Not Dumpling. America's *Darling.*"

18

Lauren narrowed her eyes. "Are you sure?"

Oh, for God's sake. "Yes!" I shouted. "*I'm* America's Darling! And I realize I'm supposedly not very bright, but I'm smart enough not to sign this contract until I know what's going on."

Lauren's back straightened, and she gave me an icy glare. "Fifty K an episode is insane for someone who hasn't proven she can bring in the ratings, but Schapiro has sharp instincts. He thinks this opportunity is so golden he's offering you a one-hundred-K bonus if we hit a one-point-oh rating or higher in the eighteen-to-forty-nine demographic. They're talking about putting us on Thursday night, typically death row for most shows, but Schapiro thinks he can pull in your previous viewers from *Gotcha!*—especially since you trashed your squeaky-clean image this afternoon—and I know how to do that. But to make a dent in the ratings, we have to bring our A game, and damn it, I plan on bringing it, Summer."

Stunned, I asked, "One hundred thousand?" It wouldn't help me save my house, but I could save the farm. I could do one thing right.

"That's right, *Darling*, keep up. I know what I'm doing, but I need to make sure you're willing to take direction, because that's the only way this will work."

I bristled. "Of course I'm willing to take direction!"

"Then we'll get along just fine." She leaned closer and lowered her voice. "Because, Summer, I don't let anyone get in my way. You need to reinvent your career, and I want my own show, which means it's in our best interest to work together. I can either be your best friend or your worst enemy. It's all up to you."

I narrowed my eyes. I had a feeling that statement would be tested.

"Do the smart thing," Lauren said in a patronizing tone. "Sign the damn papers."

Part of me wanted to shove the papers in her face and tell her to jump into the ocean that was right outside my windows. Justin had told me the same thing about Scott Schapiro's instincts, which meant I was probably worth a lot more than this hastily thrown-together offer, but I was desperate enough to forgo negotiating. No need to be greedy.

I grabbed the pen, flipped to the back page, and signed my name.

Lauren snatched the papers out of my hand, and a Cheshire-cat grin spread across her face.

Shit. Why did I feel like I'd just signed a deal with the devil?

"Great. My assistant will handle your flight arrangements, but plan on flying out Wednesday so you can be at your new office bright and early Thursday morning to start shooting." She started walking to the front door.

"Wait!" I called after her, her long legs outpacing me. "Flying out? I thought you didn't know where we were filming yet?"

She burst out the door and I followed, immediately accosted by a barrage of questions from the reporters.

"Is it true you have a drinking problem?" one of the photographers asked. "Witnesses say they saw you drinking heavily at Magnum before the incident."

"She's a lush!" Marina shouted over my shoulder. "Check her trash! You'll find more wine bottles than you can count!"

"Marina!" I protested.

"What? Just trying to help with your new bad-girl rep."

But I was more interested in where we were filming. I grabbed Lauren's forearm just as she reached the driveway. She tried to pull loose, but I dug my fingers in and held tight.

"Where are we going?"

Her grin turned devious. "You're right, we *have* settled on the place, as it happens. It's somewhere you'll recognize. Sweet Briar, Alabama. See you Thursday morning."

Horror washed over me. How could they have put all this together in only a few hours? If they knew where I was from, then they obviously knew about the fire and my cousin's juvenile conviction. They were probably planning to play up the notoriety, and now that I'd signed the damned contract, there wasn't a thing I could do about it.

I'd just cursed them to save them.

"I am *not* going to Sweet Briar," I insisted.

"Too late, *Darling.* You already signed the contract." She jerked free and then walked around the hood of her car in the driveway, cool as could be.

"Did you see her attack that woman?" a photographer called out to the others. Their cameras kept snapping away.

Dammit!

Lauren opened her car door, then shouted at me over the top of her car. "Congratulations!"

Congratulations? There was nothing to congratulate. I *couldn't* go back to my hometown. My mother and stepfather were there, along with my grandmother, who'd forbidden me from darkening her doorstep, and my cousins, who probably believed the reason I hadn't been back since I was seventeen was because I thought I was better than they were.

Add in the boy whose heart I had broken, and I was walking into a real-life reality TV drama.

Just like they were counting on.

CHAPTER THREE

Two days later, the production company put me on a red-eye from LA to Atlanta. Marina had pouted big-time when she'd realized she couldn't come with me, but I'd promised to call her often and fill her in on the details.

My plane was supposed to land around six in the morning, and Lauren's assistant, Karen, was scheduled to pick me up on the curb at six thirty. Instead, my plane had mechanical issues that delayed our takeoff, and Karen picked up my two bags and me at seven thirty.

She gave me a strained glance when I got in the car. "Lauren's going to be *pissed.*"

"She can't be angry over something that was out of your control," I said, fastening the seat belt as she punched the gas pedal and tore away from the curb.

"She's not going to be angry with *me.*" Her sympathetic look told me all I needed to know.

"I presume we'll start filming soon after we get to Sweet Briar," I said, leaning my head back on the seat. I'd barely gotten any sleep on the plane.

"Everyone will be ready and waiting . . . in about an hour." It would take two to get there.

"I didn't purposely sabotage the armrest on row twelve," I said. "I can't help it if it took them so long to get the part."

"Lauren won't care."

Karen didn't say another word for an hour other than to refuse to go through a Starbucks drive-through for a much-needed cup of caffeine.

The lack of sleep, paired with the movement of the car, soon had me dozing. The next thing I knew, Karen was pulling into a parallel parking space in downtown Sweet Briar.

"We're here," she said. "Isn't it quaint?"

I sat up, and a mixture of relief and anxiety washed through me. I'd lived in this town until my mother moved us out to LA when I was fourteen. It was funny that a lot of people born and raised in Sweet Briar were desperate to escape. I'd spent six years of my youth desperate to come back, but no amount of begging had swayed my mother. She'd insisted I was ridiculous to want to give up a very lucrative contract at a major kids' network to return to a backward southern Alabama town that everyone else was dying to escape from. What she really meant was she didn't want to give up my seven-figure income. How ironic that she'd run straight back home about two minutes after stealing most of my money.

What was I going to do if I saw her while I was here?

The chances of running into her were pretty high. Sweet Briar had a population of 2,731, as of the most recent census. Then again, last I'd heard, my mother had built a huge house out on Highway 10, halfway between Sweet Briar and the Alabama/Georgia state line. Maybe she wouldn't come into town.

Who was I kidding? The moment she heard there were cameras in the vicinity, she'd be looking for the spotlight.

I got out of the car and breathed in the air. It smelled different here—fresh and clean—bringing on my nostalgia full force. It was the middle of April, and the tulip trees along Main Street were covered in pink blossoms. I sucked in a deep breath trying to put a name to the scent, only coming up with one:

Home.

I quickly stuffed that notion away. I suspected my return would be met with cool disdain. I wasn't welcome here. Not by the people who truly mattered.

But if I could deal with Lauren, I could enjoy the two weeks I was here. I would let myself imagine a life different from the one my mother had forced upon me.

"Come on," Karen said, gasping as she checked her phone. "Lauren's *furious.*"

Great. But pissed or not, Lauren wasn't going to rush my reacclimation. It was like jumping into a pool of freezing water. I was still trying to work up the courage.

Downtown consisted of one-and-a-half blocks of shops and restaurants, and Karen had parked at about the halfway mark, giving us a wide view of both ends. I stood next to the open car door, trying to steady my nerves as I studied the storefronts. Not much had changed. There were several new places—a coffee shop, a yoga/fitness studio, and a nice-looking restaurant, but everything else was the same—the beauty shop, barbershop, a vintage-goods store, a clothing store, a small pizza place, a café, and a pharmacy. The chamber of commerce had an office on the corner in what used to be the bank years ago, but it was the retail space sandwiched between the yoga studio and the pizza place that caught my attention or, more accurately, the *sign* over the space . . .

DARLING INVESTIGATIONS

She'd named it after that stupid nickname the press had given me a decade ago.

Oh, hell no.

Lauren might be furious, but she was about to face my own fury. I slammed the car door shut and marched up the sidewalk to demand she change the name.

"Summer!" Karen called after me. "Wait!"

There was a small crowd of people out front, and it sounded like they were in a shouting match with a police officer who stood with his back to me. There was something to be said for the view. His broad shoulders stretched the fabric of his black uniform shirt, and his pants hung on his backside in a way that made me reconsider my usual apathy about men's butts. His dark-brown hair was trimmed close to his head, and he was tall enough that he towered over some of the women in the small group carrying signs that read **THE SUN SHINES WHEN SUMMER'S HOME** and **WELCOME BACK TO SWEET BRIAR, AMERICA'S DARLING!**

"We have every right to be here!" a woman shouted, raising her sign. A Lab-mix dog sat at her feet, and each time she lifted up her sign, she yanked his leash tight. "And just because you don't want them here doesn't mean you can make us leave!"

"That's right!" another woman yelled. "It's our God-given right to assemble."

"You're blocking the sidewalk, Sonya," the officer said with strained patience. "You can assemble, but Hugo's pissed because people can't get around you to the barbershop."

Sonya's righteous anger faded some. "Oh."

He made a sideways motion with his hand. "Now if you'd just clear a path for the passersby, you would make my life a hell of a lot easier."

His voice was familiar, and horror washed through me when I realized why. It just figured that the first person I'd run into was my old boyfriend.

This was *not* how I wanted him to see me again . . . in yoga pants and a T-shirt stained with coffee from when the plane had hit a pocket of turbulence. My hair wasn't so bad, but I wasn't sure my breath was ready to be up close and personal. Not that we would be getting up close and personal, of course.

The women had noticed I was standing to the side. Letting out squeals of excitement, they rushed at me, signs raised like they were going into battle. Luke spun around to face me, surprise filling his eyes, and the women pushed him toward me in their eagerness to greet me.

The dog had burst forward in excitement the second his owner joined the surge, and he ran around our legs, wrapping the leash line around them and pulling us closer together.

I started to lose balance and fall forward—straight into Luke's broad chest. He was losing balance too, and it became painfully evident we were going to crash into the brick building. Wrapping his arms around me and pulling me closer, he twisted and slammed into the wall, taking the brunt of the impact on his right shoulder and side. He'd gripped me tightly enough that I only crashed into the muscles on his arms.

I stared up at him in disbelief, unable to breathe.

In all the ways I'd imagined seeing him again, this particular scenario had never come to mind.

I would have recognized him anywhere . . . same dark-brown hair, same dark-brown eyes. He seemed taller now. His shoulders were broader, his arms thicker. He'd had a commanding presence when we were teens, but now he *demanded* attention, and damned if I didn't comply.

"You okay?" he asked, concern in his eyes.

"Yeah," I said, caught up in nostalgia.

Luke Montgomery had been my first love. My only love. I'd known losing him would hurt, but I hadn't expected it to hurt for so long. Seeing him face-to-face, it was impossible not to think about those lazy summer nights wrapped up in his arms, staring into those eyes . . .

My body responded to him the way it always had—a combination of comfort and passion I'd never found with anyone else. The way he was holding me close suggested he felt the same way.

"I heard you were still in Sweet Briar," I said softly.

But then a slight hardness crept into his eyes, layered with something even worse: disappointment. "I always told you I wanted to become a cop and stay in Sweet Briar."

A sad smile lifted my lips. "Sometimes we say things when we're kids . . . but then reality sets in."

"That's you, Summer, not me. When I say something, I mean it."

There was nothing I could say to that. I'd been young and naive and stupid. Maybe I deserved his contempt.

"Summer!" the women shouted, shoving papers and pens in my face. "Will you sign this for us?"

I'd completely tuned out the fact we'd been surrounded by a mob of about ten women, but they'd all watched our reintroduction with keen interest, as if my life had already become an episode of reality TV.

"How about I get untangled first," Luke said, trying to bend down to unwrap us. "Fredericka. This is your doin'! Take care of it."

Fredericka was still gawking at us, but she finally had the sense to make her dog stop running around, and between her and the other women, they worked us free from the leash line.

"Jesus Christ, Tony!" Lauren shouted from the doorway of the office. "Are you seriously telling me you didn't get a single minute of that on film?"

I could see her through a gap in the women, along with a glimpse of a man holding a camera.

"*Ladies!*" Lauren shouted like a PE teacher in a dodgeball game gone awry. "While I'm sure Summer is eager to see you all again, I really need her to get to work." She waved her hands in a shooing motion. "Go on, now. Go on."

The women sent her scathing looks, but they didn't seem to hold Lauren's bitchiness against me as they dispersed.

"Stay strong, Summer!" one woman said.

"Welcome home, Summer!" another woman shouted.

I thanked them as they wandered off.

Fredericka left with a wave after getting the last of the dog leash free, and as soon as Luke was no longer forcibly attached to me, he took off down the street. He didn't once look back.

I wasn't going to think about him either. *Right.*

"Well, don't just stand there," Lauren said, jostling me out of the shock of the encounter. "Let's get to work." Then she disappeared into the office.

I started to follow her but stopped to look in the window, hating myself a little for thinking it was cute. The outside had a vintage feel with its wood frame, glass door and windows, and the pale-green canopy hanging over the entire fifteen-foot length of the setup. But it was the inside that really caught my attention.

Sure, there were a few crew members gathered around, but the open room they stood in looked classy, not like the nightmare setup of an old film-noir PI office I'd feared. I had to say that Lauren had gotten one part right, or rather her set crew had. This would have been something I picked out myself. The lower walls were painted a sage green, and the top was a pale yellow. There was the map of Bixley County on the wall as well as our business license. The door was on the left side of the building, the same side that had a hallway leading to the back. A wide two-drawer legal file cabinet was along the left wall, beneath several pieces of artwork.

There were two desks in the remaining fifteen-by-twelve-foot space. The desks were covered with the typical objects you'd find in a working office. Each desk had a laptop, a short stack of manila folders, and a phone. The desk parallel to the wall on the right had a lamp and pencil cup filled with assorted writing utensils. The second desk was closer to the door and faced the windows. The only noticeable difference was that it held a small vase with daisies. Two chairs were arranged between the desks, which I presumed were for my clients.

Who was the other desk for?

But the **DARLING INVESTIGATIONS** painted on the window reminded me of my initial reaction.

Karen grabbed my arm and dragged me toward the door. "Come on!"

A bell on the door clanged when she opened it, and all eyes rose to us. A couple of the crew guys looked amused.

Lauren came bustling down the hall. "Well, look who bothered to show up."

I could have offered some snotty retort, but I decided to focus on the important issues. "Darling Investigations?" I asked. "Really?"

She lifted her eyebrows as though that one gesture was enough to communicate an entire paragraph of explanation. I had to admit—it kind of was.

"I'm trying to rise above my past, Lauren."

"Sorry, *chica*," she said, turning back to the screen. "America's Darling— Darling Investigations works. Besides, your past is attached to you like stink on a June bug. The sooner you accept it and make the most of it, the better off you'll be." She looked over her shoulder at the small group behind her. "That's how you say it, right? Stink on a June bug?"

One of them nodded.

She grinned. "God, I love the South. So many little sayings to exploit." Lauren pushed out a sigh. "Summer, I realize we never discussed wardrobe. I figured it was self-explanatory."

Out of instinct, I glanced down at my stained T-shirt that said I WAKE UP LOOKING LIKE THIS and dark-gray yoga pants. "This is what I flew in."

"Could have fooled me. You look like you came by wagon train."

A few of the crew members chuckled behind her.

I was fuming. "I had no idea I needed to follow a dress code *before* I was scheduled to show up on set. I planned on getting dressed here. I literally got off a plane, got in a car, and then drove two hours to get here."

"Okay," Lauren said in a mock-patient tone. "What do you plan to wear?"

This had been an hours-long discussion with Marina. What does a PI wear? We ultimately decided on jeans and T-shirts, low-key business attire, and both casual dresses and dresses for church. "Jeans and a T-shirt."

"Make it low-cut and we're good."

"Excuse me?"

She was clearly frustrated with me now. "Summer, what do you want? One minute you're pissed that I've named the place after your *very* recognizable nickname; the next you're pissed that I suggest you dress like you're not a teenager anymore." She flung a hand up. "Hell, most teenagers dress more provocatively than you do."

"Do you want me to throw on a bustier?" Jeez. I'd considered posing nude, and here I was pitching a fit over a low-cut shirt. Obviously, I never would have gone through with it.

Excitement filled her eyes, replaced by a scowl when she realized I didn't mean it. She walked over to me, and I had to repress the urge to take a step back. "For some reason, you seem to be struggling with this very simple concept, so let me explain it to you," she said in slow, carefully punctuated words. "Isabella Holmes is all grown up, sweetheart. She's sexy and confident and ready to kick ass and take names." She pointed down the hall. "Can you do that?" she asked, lifting her eyebrows again. Based on her forehead mobility, she hadn't had any recent Botox injections.

"No," I said, straightening my back. I tried to meet her eyes without looking up, but they only reached her shoulders.

The crew tensed.

"No?" she asked in disbelief.

"No. I am *not* Isabella Holmes. I'm Summer Butler, dammit, not a character from a teen show."

Her face started to turn red.

"But if you want a sexy version of *me*," I said in a tight voice, "that's what you're going to get."

"I better see at least four inches of skin on your chest from the base of your neck to the top of your shirt."

I was tempted to keep arguing, especially since I was starting to have major buyer's remorse, but to what end? Instead, I decided to ignore my growing mortification that this exchange had taken place in front of the entire crew and focus on what needed to be done. "I need to get my suitcases so I can change."

Karen brought in my luggage, and I dug out a pair of jeans and a plain teal scoop-neck T-shirt. I put back on the athletic shoes I'd worn on the plane. I washed my face and applied a light layer of makeup with a hint of blush and low-key eyeshadow, then ran a brush though my hair.

Karen was waiting outside the bathroom door, staring at her phone. Her gaze jerked up, but she wouldn't meet my eyes. "We have to get you fitted with a mike, but Lauren says you should come out for the team meeting. Chuck can hook you up while she talks."

"Okay."

She took my stack of clothes and the makeup bag from my hands, then gestured for me to head back into the office.

Lauren, standing regally at the front door, waved her hand at the first desk. "Summer, I take it you remember your assistant."

I turned to face the platinum-blonde woman who had a to-go coffee cup in her hand. Excitement filled her big blue eyes as she set the cup down on the desk.

I gasped. "Dixie?" I hadn't seen her since she was thirteen, but I would have recognized her anywhere. She was the spitting image of her mother.

My cousin was wearing a pair of denim shorts and a white eyelet three-quarter-sleeve shirt with a deep V that showed off the generous cleavage that had obviously come from her mother's genetics and not from our side of the family. Cowboy boots finished the ensemble. Her long hair hung past her shoulders in loose waves. Dixie was beyond cute, and the way Lauren smiled—like a shark who'd found some tasty new bait—set me on edge.

"Summer!" she exclaimed as she pulled me into a hug.

"I can't believe it," I said. And while I was thrilled to see her, it was hard to ignore the very real possibility that Lauren intended on exploiting Dixie's past and my family drama. "How's my favorite cousin?"

She leaned back and grinned, her entire face lighting up with happiness. "I'm gonna tell Teddy you said that."

I laughed. "Somehow I doubt he'll mind."

She laughed too. "You're right. He's the same ol' Teddy."

"You're my assistant?" I asked, hugging her again.

"Yeah, after Ms. Chapman came out to the farm to talk to Meemaw, she asked me if I was looking for a job. And oh, my word! I'm all official. Look at this, Summer!" She picked up a small plaque from the first desk and held it up. "This has my name on it!"

Sure enough, it read **DIXIE BUTLER, PERSONAL ASSISTANT**.

"That's not her name," I said, shooting a glare at Lauren.

Lauren looked down her nose at me. "We're selling her as your cousin. Would you rather we call you Summer Baumgartner?"

Cringing, I turned to Dixie. My mother had changed my name years ago, and while I didn't necessarily want to bring that into the spotlight, I didn't want Dixie to feel coerced into changing hers. "You don't mind that they've changed your name?"

She lifted her shoulder into an ambivalent shrug. "I can live with it."

One of the men walked over to me with a black box and a small microphone attached to a wire. "I'm Chuck, and I'm going to get you miked up."

A few people had regrouped outside the window, gawking. Dixie kept waving at some of them, and I was sure I recognized a few as well. I figured Lauren might pitch a fit, but she didn't seem to mind.

I stood next to my desk as Chuck clipped the box to the back waistband of my jeans, then ran the mike up the back of my shirt and clipped it to my neckline.

While he hooked me up, I leaned over my desk and lifted the flap of the top folder in the stack at the corner, revealing several blank pages of copy paper. Props. But next to them was a little wire container filled with pale-yellow business cards with **DARLING INVESTIGATIONS** at the top and my name and a phone number I didn't recognize at the bottom. I picked up a handful and stuck them in my jeans pocket.

"If we could get started . . . ," Lauren said in a snide tone. "We're on a tight schedule, and we need to leave to meet with your first clients in a few minutes."

I wondered how they'd managed to find clients in less than three days.

"We have nine hours to get everything in," she continued. "Your first case is a missing person."

"A missing person?" I asked as an arrow of fear shot through me. I was so not qualified for something like that. "Shouldn't we start with something smaller?"

Lauren put her hand on her hip and gave me a scathing look. "This is our big case for the season, so we need to get started on it right away."

"What do you mean *big case*?"

Her jaw clenched. Apparently asking the simplest of questions was akin to being needy or disagreeable. "We'll have one big, overarching mystery that you'll be investigating over the entire six episodes, and then each episode will feature a smaller case to fill out the twenty-two minutes." She took a breath. "You'll be interviewing Gretchen McBride this morning. Her brother, Otto Olson, is the person who's gone missing."

"Otto?" Dixie waved a hand in dismissal. "I know him. He goes on drunken sprees and then turns up a couple of days later."

"He's been gone nearly a week."

Dixie's mouth pursed. "That *is* longer than usual. So what are we doin'? Lookin' for him?"

"That's the plan," Lauren said. "We'll film at the McBrides', then we'll break for lunch at noon." She turned to me. "Summer, your truck is out front, and you and Dixie will ride together. Bill, one of the cameramen, will film you driving to their house."

"My *truck*?"

"Your grandmother had an old truck she said we could use."

I gave Dixie a questioning look.

Her smiled faded a few megawatts. "Pawpaw's."

Meemaw still had Pawpaw's truck . . . and now I would be using it. It felt like a blow right to my solar plexus. "That old truck still runs?"

"It was actually in good shape, according to your cousin Teddy. We put some cameras on it."

I nearly protested, but I had agreed to this whole venture. This was a reality show, which meant there were probably cameras everywhere. "Where else do you have cameras?" I glanced up at the ceiling. "In here?"

Lauren's mouth turned down. "There are some up here, but I doubt we'll ever need them." She spread her hands wide. "Let's get going."

I already had a feeling I was going to regret this.

CHAPTER FOUR

Bill, another cameraman, hopped into the back of a pickup truck and filmed us as we drove the ten blocks to the McBrides' house. As soon as we were alone together, Dixie turned in her seat to face me. We were going about ten miles an hour—apparently it was easier to film us that way—so I was able to shoot a glance at her every now and then.

"So," she said, "Maybelline started a Facebook page for Sweet Briar gossip—"

"Maybelline? The one who owns the café downtown?"

She laughed. "How many Maybellines do you know?"

Touché.

"She hears all kinds of things at the café and then posts about them online," Dixie continued. "People tell her things, knowin' she'll post their stories without usin' their names."

"I don't think I'm gonna like where you're going with this . . . ," I said.

She grinned. "Today, she posted about your encounter with Luke. Someone called it a reunion of star-crossed lovers."

I rolled my eyes and groaned.

"There's even a photo. Looks like there's still a spark, Summer."

She held up the phone as I pulled to a halt at a stop sign. The photo showed me with my side to the wall and Luke pressed to my front. I was looking up at him expectantly while he stared down at me with a dazed expression.

"I'm here to make this show," I said as I drove through the intersection. "Not rekindle my love life."

"So no boyfriend back in LA?"

I shot her a look of warning, but she only laughed. "I'm gonna take that as a no. And just so you know, Luke's currently single and has been for a good six months."

"I don't want to talk about Luke," I said. It wasn't exactly true, but I was trying to ignore the impulse. "I want to talk about *you*. I'm sorry I haven't been back, but Meemaw . . ."

"Made it pretty clear you weren't welcome?" she filled in. "I don't blame you one bit. She barely agreed to take me back in after I got out of juvenile detention."

"*Dixie*," I said in horror. I'd assumed everyone in the family believed in Dixie's lack of ill intent as much as I did. But Meemaw was one tough customer.

"You know Meemaw," she said, echoing my thoughts. "But Teddy told her if I wasn't comin' back, then he was leavin', and no one would be runnin' the farm, and that was that. She got over it. She's not happy with you bein' here, but Teddy pulled his threat again, and it's all good."

"Teddy wants me here?"

"Of course he does! We Baumgartner cousins need to stick together. We're family."

"Meemaw doesn't think so. She told me I was disowned. That I was as good as dead to her."

She scowled. "Meemaw's a cranky old woman who holds a grudge like her life depends on it. But I know she wants you here. Something in her changed when she found out you were comin' home. Give her time."

I was pretty sure there wasn't enough time in the world for her to get over it.

"I wanted to come back . . . ," I said, thinking this was the wrong time to bring this up, but not sure when the right one would be. "But I let other people talk me out of it. I was told I was too stupid to know what to do with my career and my life, and I listened. I let other people have more influence on my life than I should have. When Pawpaw and your parents died, I was in the middle of filming that stupid movie in Thailand—"

"Summer, you don't have to explain."

35

"I *do*. I had the director in one ear telling me the movie was depending on me to shoot those scenes. If I left, I would inconvenience a lot of people and cost the producer thousands of dollars. I'd never work again. And then I had my mother in my other ear, telling me I needed to stay. That Pawpaw and your parents were already dead, and it would do no good for me to drop all my responsibilities to go home." My voice broke. "I wanted to come, Dixie, but I was weak. I will never forgive myself for that, and apparently neither will Meemaw."

"Summer."

"No. It's okay. I understand. I don't blame her, and I'm surprised you don't hate me too. Especially after everything you went through."

"Hate you?" she asked in disbelief. "How could I hate you? That summer you came back to Sweet Briar, when Meemaw had cancer, you were already this big star, but you were so nice to me. And when you found out that Juliette Benson was giving me a hard time for having a flat chest, you found her at the pool and told her that Baumgartners were late bloomers, and everyone knows late-bloomer breasts were the best."

"You were my little cousin," I said. "Of course I had your back."

"And now I have yours."

My chin trembled. "You have no idea how much that means to me, Dixie."

"We Baumgartner girls need to stick together."

But it didn't ease my guilt for not being there for Dixie in her time of need. The letters I'd sent while she was in detention now felt like such an insignificant gesture, and the few phone calls we'd exchanged later had been cursory. I was the oldest out of the three of us. I should have made more effort. I should have stopped feeling sorry for myself and lamenting my problems long enough to realize the other people I cared about were hurting too. That Meemaw wasn't the only one who got a say in who was family.

I swallowed hard—and changed the subject because I needed to stay collected on the shoot. "Say, Dixie, can you tell me what you know about Otto? It would be good to have some idea about what we're walking into."

"I used to work at the Dollar General, and Otto and his buddies like to hang out in the grassy area next to the parking lot."

I shot her a glance. "Wouldn't it be easier to go to a bar?"

"The closest is the Jackhammer out on West Highway 10. Otherwise, you have to go up to Edna." She pushed out a breath. "Otto's a cheap drunk anyway. He wouldn't pay bar prices. He and his friends, Al and Fred, sit in lawn chairs around the picnic table and drink."

My mouth dropped open. "I find it hard to believe Luke would allow three guys to drink in public like that."

She grinned. "They're pretty good at hiding it."

"Still . . ."

"Everyone loves Otto. Sure, he's a drunk, but he's a friendly one, and honestly, he doesn't have much else. So people look out for him."

"Huh."

"Like I said, he usually hangs out next to the Dollar General, but he goes missing every so often. His health's not the greatest nowadays, so that might have something to do with it. Hasn't stopped his drinking any. I noticed he wasn't there last weekend, but I haven't been over there since then."

"Maybe his sister will have a better idea about how long he's been missing. Do you know anything about her?"

"No. I didn't even know he had a sister until Lauren mentioned her. He never talks about his family."

Ten minutes later, after Bill finally got the footage he needed, I turned onto Gretchen McBride's street, pulling up in front of the second house from the corner.

We were met by the crew when we got out of the truck. Lauren told Tony and Chuck to go set up in the house and then turned to me and Dixie.

"Here's the list of questions you need to ask," she said, handing me a paper. "When we finish here, we're running by the Dollar General to talk to two of Otto's acquaintances."

I took the list and glanced it over. "Dixie already knows a lot about Otto Olson that's not on this list. We should combine that with what we learn here and then decide where to investigate."

Anger flashed in Lauren's eyes, and she opened her mouth to say something before promptly closing it and pursing her lips together. After she took a deep breath, she said, "While I appreciate you taking some initiative, Summer, we have things planned out for this case. Every lead or clue we plan to have you look into has already been scheduled over the next two weeks, so I would appreciate it if you would just follow the script. We'll do multiple takes to make sure we get plenty of angles and expressions."

My mouth dropped open. "Let me get this straight—is everything scripted and coordinated? I thought this was a reality show."

Lauren burst into genuine laughter. "What part of *you* being a private eye is reality?"

I wasn't sure what annoyed me more—her tone or the fact that she had a point. "So you just want me to *pretend* I'm investigating?"

Lauren patted my cheek. "Now you've got it, *Darling*." She offered me her best interpretation of a warm smile. "Karen interviewed the McBrides last night and put together a plan. But we have a lot of places to go today, which means we're on a very tight schedule. We need to get in there and film this interview ASAP." Her smile looked like it hid sharp teeth. "Please."

I smiled back, just as fake. "Well, since you said please . . ."

Lauren spun on her heels and marched into the house.

This was going to be a long two weeks. I read over the short list of questions. Most of them looked pretty bland, but there were a few sensational ones, such as *How long has your brother been the town drunk?* I was definitely rephrasing that one.

Dixie leaned over and glanced at the paper. "Looks easy enough."

I handed it to her. "Make sure I stay on track."

"Don't you need the paper to remember the questions?"

"I memorized them already." Then I saw her look of surprise. I added, "I'm used to memorizing pages of scripts . . . or at least I used to be. I've got this."

When we entered the small ranch house, the McBrides were sitting on a sofa that had seen better days. Gretchen McBride looked like she was in her late forties. She was wearing a pair of khaki pants and a white shirt covered in flowers that washed out her complexion. Karen really should have spent part of her time last night helping Gretchen pick out her clothes. Nevertheless, she looked plenty put together considering that her brother was the town drunk. A slightly older man sat next to her, his eyes wide and his hands shaking with nerves.

I walked over to the couple and offered my hand. "Mr. and Mrs. McBride? I'm Summer. Thank you for letting us into you home."

Mr. McBride wiped his hand on his jeans, then stood and shook my hand. "I ain't never done nothing like this before, and I sure ain't never met a real TV star before."

"That's not true, Pete," Gretchen said in a patient tone. "You met Pipsqueak, the clown on that show that used to air on the local access channel."

"He wasn't a real star."

"You sure thought so." She lifted her hands in the air and performed her own interpretation of jazz hands. "You were all spazzy then too." Gretchen lowered her voice and winked. "He's nervous."

My eyes shifted quickly to Lauren then back to Mr. McBride. I was pretty sure my career had just been compared to the status of a D-star clown named Pipsqueak. "I'm not sure what Karen told y'all about how this works, but we'll be being doing a couple of takes. So how about we try a take or two with you with your wife, Mr. McBride, and then we'll see how everyone feels?"

He nodded. "Okay. But call me Pete."

"Okay, Pete, let's get started."

The crew had already arranged the living room furniture, and they indicated that I was to sit in the chair to the side of the McBrides' sofa. Lauren said Dixie could stay out of sight for the interview. Chuck performed another sound check, and then we started to shoot.

After our on-camera introductions, I rested my elbow on the armchair, leaned closer to Gretchen, and said, "I hear your brother is missing. When was the last time you saw him?"

"Last Friday." She sniffed and dabbed her nose with a tissue. "He's known to disappear for a few days at a time, but never for so long."

"Have you notified the police?"

"I called Luke, and he said Otto was probably off fishing and that I needed to wait longer before involving him."

"Is that what he does when he takes off?" I asked. "Does he go fishing?"

"He used to," she said. "Over at the creek that runs through the Masseys' land." Then she hastily added, "They gave him permission."

I nodded. "You said *used to*. He hasn't lately?"

"No. I don't think so. A few weeks ago there was a big storm comin' in—they were threatenin' a tornado—so I sent Pete out there to look for him. Otto doesn't have a car—just his bike—and I was worried sick he'd get blown away, but he wasn't out there."

"Where was he?"

"That's just it, I don't know. I mentioned it to Otto the next time I saw him, and he blustered about and wouldn't give me a straight answer." She pinched her lips and turned more serious. "Something is goin' on with him the last couple of weeks. He hasn't been himself."

"How so?"

"He's been nervous, you know? Like extra jumpy. I think he's hidin'."

I lifted my eyebrows. "Hiding from what?"

"I don't know. That's why I hired you."

I took a moment—both to build dramatic tension and because her words had put an actual lump in my throat—then nodded again. "Can you give me a list of his friends? Who he hung out with? Also, do you have a key to his house or apartment? It would be great if we could check it out."

"Yes, of course," she said, then pulled a list out of her pocket. The paper got stuck, and she had to buck her hips up a few times before she worked it loose and handed it to me. "I made it last night."

I opened the paper and saw a list of names and addresses, only it was a copy of her handwritten note. I could only presume that Karen had the original.

I summoned up Karen's list in my head, making sure I'd touched on all the questions. I handed her one of the business cards from my pocket, then grabbed a pen from the table next to the sofa and scribbled down my cell number. "This is my number. If you think of anything else that will help, give me a call or text. I'll let you know when we find something."

I stood, and she and her husband stood too.

"Thank you," Pete said, shaking my hand. "I know most people in this town think Otto's a joke, but he means something to us."

"I'll do my best to find him." I dropped his hand, and Lauren yelled "Cut."

We set up to reshoot the whole thing, and I couldn't help thinking how Pete's description of Otto, and how the town saw him, differed from Dixie's. The interview went pretty much the same, although it seemed much less natural on Gretchen's part, which wasn't a surprise. She did all the talking, but after I finished asking her Karen's questions, something occurred to me, and I turned to her husband. "Earlier you said that the town thinks Otto's a joke. Could you explain that? What has given you that impression?"

He blinked, looking like a raccoon caught in a flashlight beam while it raided a garbage can, but to his credit, he didn't contradict my lie about how I'd heard the information. "People say things."

"Like what?"

"They think he's simple. You know, slow-minded. But he's not. He's sharp as a tack. I think he likes to play dumb because nobody expects anything from him. He doesn't want that to change."

I leaned forward, feeling like I was onto something. "Why not?"

"On account of his wife and kids."

Gretchen shushed him and lightly swatted his arm. "She doesn't want to hear that."

"Actually," I said gently, "I do."

Gretchen released a heavy sigh. "Otto was married once. A long time ago. His wife and kids . . . they were in a fire. They didn't make it."

I gasped. "I'm so sorry." I reached over and put my hand on her knee. "How long ago?"

She covered my hand with hers. "About fifteen years now. It happened while everyone was asleep."

"But Otto got out?" I asked, pulling back my hand and sitting up again.

Gretchen hesitated. "Otto and Cheryl had had a fight. He was stayin' over at his friend's house."

"Oh, dear."

"He was never the same after that." She shook her head, her mouth turning into a frown. "He was a suspect for a while before they cleared it up. He had a drinking problem even back then—that was the reason for their fight—but his reason for sobering up left with them."

"I'm so sorry."

She nodded, wiping a tear from her eye. "Otto's a good man—flawed, but good."

"Everyone is flawed," I said. "There's no judgment on my part."

"Just find him. Please."

"We'll do our best."

Lauren yelled "Cut" and immediately wanted to start the scene again, but Gretchen was quietly crying. I looked up and realized Dixie wasn't next to Karen anymore.

"Where's Dixie?"

Karen shrugged. "She went outside just a few moments ago."

I stood to go after her, but Lauren grabbed my arm. "Where do you think you're going? We have another scene to shoot."

I gestured behind me. "Poor Gretchen needs a moment to get herself together, and I'm worried about my cousin."

"What on earth for?"

"Because both of *her parents* died in a fire nine years ago."

CHAPTER FIVE

I found Dixie sitting on the porch step, staring out into the backyard.

I sat down beside her and wrapped my arm around her back. "How're you doin'?"

"I'm fine," she sniffed out.

I leaned my head into hers. "I've been a really crappy cousin, but I want to be a good one now. If you ever want to talk about your parents or anything, I'm a pretty good listener." I bent down to catch her tear-filled gaze. "And I'm pretty good at opening a wine bottle too. Even my friend Marina says so."

Dixie laughed and swiped an escaping tear. "It's so stupid. I have no right to these feelings."

"What feelings? Grief?" I asked in disbelief.

She didn't answer for a moment. "Even if I *was* entitled then, they've been gone nine years."

"You lost your parents, Dixie, and Pawpaw too. You're entitled to your grief." I paused, then decided to address the elephant in the room. "Momma didn't tell me much, but I know you didn't intentionally start the fire. It was an accident."

"Accident or not, they're still dead."

"Your momma loved you. It would kill her to see you so upset this many years later."

She glanced over at me, swiping tears from her cheeks with her fingertips. "How do you know? Other than the summer you were home, you hadn't seen her in years."

I could have been hurt by that, but it was a fair question. I gave her a soft smile. "You're forgetting I had fourteen years with Aunt Merilee before I left. Who do you think I turned to when things got bad with Momma? Aunt Merilee was always there for me, no matter what." I grinned. "Even in the rare times I was wrong."

She smiled.

"My mother was a difficult woman to live with, and her expectations were sometimes too much for me to handle. All I had to do was turn to your momma, and she made everything better." I leaned my head on her shoulder. "Did I ever tell you that I used to daydream that you and I were sisters, and your momma was mine too?"

"No."

"Well . . . I did. I'd be upset if something happened to my mother, but it wouldn't be the same situation. Aunt Merilee was special. The kind of special you spend a lifetime grieving." I turned to look into her face. "But she would hate to know you were wallowing in guilt."

To my horror, Dixie broke into tears. "I don't know how to let it go, Summer."

I hugged her tight and let her cry. "I know." I was still wallowing in my own guilt, and my burden was a hell of a lot lighter than hers.

I felt movement behind me and caught Karen standing at the storm door. The glint in her eye told me she was about a second away from grabbing one of the camera guys, so I gave her a warning look. I'd let Dixie down for years. I'd do everything I could to make it up to her now. No cameras involved.

After a minute, my cousin sat up and wiped her face. "I had no idea about Otto."

"You were just a kid when it happened."

"Still, I would have . . . I don't know . . ."

"Treated him better?" I asked. "You always had a pure heart, Dixie Belle Baumgartner. I suspect you were as kind as you could possibly have been. And when we find him, you can talk about your shared experience. But we have to find him first."

She nodded.

"And we will find him. I promise."

"But Lauren . . ."

I suspected Lauren would purposely drag out finding him to make it last over the entire six episodes, and Dixie must have thought so too. "Yeah. I know. We'll figure it out." I stood and pulled her to her feet. "I love you, Dixie. We'll do this together."

"Thanks, Summer."

I went back inside and ignored the irritated looks from Lauren and Karen. "Let's give this another go."

The third take was the worst yet, but finally Lauren called it good. "Time to head to the Dollar General to interview Otto's friends."

The Dollar General was part of an L-shaped strip mall. It was on the short side that faced the street while the longer portion consisted of the payday loan place, a nail salon, a Chinese takeout restaurant, and a pawnshop. The intersection of the two sides was a surprisingly nice grassy spot with a picnic table, shaded by the surrounding trees. It was easy to see how Otto and his friends got away with hanging out there all day.

After everyone got out of their respective cars and the crew prepared for the shoot, Lauren rolled her eyes and said, "Let's go talk to a couple of drunk old farts."

"They don't seem very drunk," Dixie said, leading the way across the parking lot. "They look like they cleaned up."

"What?" Lauren stopped on the sidewalk, taking in the two older men sitting at the picnic table. They were dressed in short-sleeve, button-down shirts and ties. Their hair was combed, and they looked like two respectable members of Sweet Briar . . . the exact opposite of what I'd expected, and from the look on Lauren's face, not what she expected either. "What in the hell?" She turned her accusatory glare on Karen. "What did you tell them?"

Karen's eyes flew open in horror. "Nothing . . . nothing . . . ," she stammered. "I told them we'd be interviewing them, and asked them not to be late."

Lauren leaned her head back and let out a loud groan. "Let's go find out what happened." She marched over and stopped in front of them, putting her hands on her hips. "Gentlemen, I see that you've cleaned up."

"Yep," one of them said with a big toothless grin. "We wanted to look our best on TV."

"I got this shirt from the thrift store right over there," the other man said, pointing to the building across the street. A long scar ran down the side of his face.

Lauren gave them a look of strained patience. "We were hoping you'd look more like yourselves."

"We *do* look like ourselves," the toothless guy said.

"Fred," Dixie said, putting her hand on his shoulder, "I think they mean like you did yesterday when you talked to them."

"This won't work," Lauren said, throwing up her hands and spinning to face Karen.

They walked several feet away, and Dixie and I followed.

"What do you want me to do?" Karen asked in dismay. "Do you want me to mess up their hair and smear dirt on their faces?"

Lauren pursed her mouth as she turned around and studied them, and for a half second, I was sure she was going to take her up on it.

"How about we ask them questions and you can either blur their faces or we can come back later," I suggested.

"Or we could just ask them to look . . . more like themselves," Lauren said, waving to them.

"You're seriously going to ask two old men to make themselves look like bums?"

"Yes!"

I stared at her in disbelief. "That's insulting, Lauren. They're excited that they're dressed for TV. I say we come back tomorrow or a few days from now and catch them off guard. But we can ask them questions now."

"We don't need to ask them questions," Lauren spat out. "Karen already spoke with them yesterday." She shook her head. "Everyone go to lunch and we'll meet back at the office in an hour.

I pushed out a sigh as we headed toward the truck. If this morning was any indication of how this show would go, I was going to need to stock up on plenty of wine.

CHAPTER SIX

After I parked on Main Street, we walked the half block to the café. Dixie opened the door and motioned for me to go in first. Walking into Maybelline's Café was like stepping into the past. I'd spent a lot of time here when I was a kid, and even more on my trip home the summer I was seventeen. I'd gotten to know Maybelline pretty well, so I wasn't surprised when she called out my name.

"Summer!"

"Hey, Maybelline."

The elderly woman with shockingly orange hair waddled toward me and pulled me into a bear hug. "I was wondering how long it would take you to show up here. You've been gone too long, girl."

"I know," I said. "But I'm back now, and I'm starving for one of your country-fried steak dinners. We have to be back in about thirty minutes. Should I order something else?" Perhaps I should have for the sake of my figure, but I wasn't doing the *Alpha* photo shoot, so maybe it didn't matter too much.

A mock scowl scrunched up her face, and she pointed to an empty booth. "*Order something else?* You get your ass over to that booth right now. No more sass outta you."

I laughed. "Yes, ma'am."

Dixie grinned and motioned to the back wall. "Maybelline still has your autograph hangin' up."

I walked over to the wall and noticed my headshot photo from *Gotcha!* when I was seventeen, along with a small board tacked with pictures cut out of magazines and newspapers.

I read the autographed message on the headshot. *Maybelline. You make the best biscuits this side of the Mississippi. XOXO Summer.*

"You were in so much trouble with Meemaw when she read that," Dixie said, shaking her head.

"*Read* it?" I laughed. "You ran home to tell her all about it that very afternoon."

"Well, you knew she was gonna find out anyway."

"I guess." To the right, I saw some photos of another woman I didn't recognize. "Who's that?" I asked.

"Magnolia Steele," Dixie said, looping her arm through mine and pulling me over to the booth, but I resisted, trying to get a closer look.

"Who's Magnolia Steele?"

"You know, that Broadway star who showed off her boobs to the world onstage."

I made a face. "That happens all the time in Broadway plays."

"This wasn't planned," Dixie said. "She was the lead in a new musical, and she got into a brawl with one of the actresses. It was a big thing about a month ago. Didn't you hear about it?"

I shrugged. "Yeah, I guess . . ."

"You guess?"

"Okay. I did. Everyone did. What's she doing on Maybelline's wall?" *Next to my photos?*

"Her momma is from here. Lila Brewer, Lila Steele now. She's Celia Brewer's daughter."

"Huh." None of those names meant anything to me. "So what's she doing up there?"

"The town's divided on it," Dixie said. "Half of them want her up there, and half of them don't. And now Mayor Sterling invited Magnolia to be in the

Boll Weevil Parade next Tuesday." She paused. "But last I knew, he hadn't heard from her yet."

"The Boll Weevil Parade?"

Maybelline walked out of the back with two glasses and gestured toward the booth. "What are you doin' gawkin' at those photos? Get in your seats."

Dixie and I hurried to our booth like we were chicks being chided by their mother.

She set two glasses of tea on the table in front of us.

"Is that sweet tea?" I asked.

She gave me a look that suggested I was an idiot. "What else would it be?"

"I'm gonna have to buy all new clothes by the end of the week," I teased.

"You could stand to put a little meat on your bones," Maybelline scolded. "You're too damn skinny."

"I definitely need to spend more time here with you, Miss Maybelline. But I'm worried I'll end up looking like a beach ball."

"As if . . ." She waved her hand in dismissal. "It's good to have you back, girl. I hope you stick around."

"Thanks."

I turned back to my cousin and smiled. I couldn't believe that not only was Dixie sitting across from me, but she was actually happy that I was here. "I want to know what you've been up to," I said. "Do you have a boyfriend? Did you ever go to college?"

She grimaced. "I broke up with Ryker Pelletier about a month ago." She paused. "Or I guess he broke up with me."

"I'm sorry."

"I'm better off without him," she said, but I could see the pain in her eyes. "Teddy's happier. He couldn't stand him. He tried to convince me that Ryker was cheating on me, but I never saw it."

"You know what, Dixie? You *are* better off. You deserve better than someone who cheats on you."

She looked down at the table, then back up at me. "What about you? I bet you date all kinds of movie stars."

I snorted. "I haven't had a boyfriend in three years."

"I can help you with that," said a guy standing next to our booth. The glimpse of a police uniform out of the corner of my eye made my heart speed up—I remembered being wrapped in Luke's arms that morning, his face inches from mine—but this wasn't Luke.

"Cale Malone," Dixie said. "What do you think you're doin'?"

He laughed. "Tryin' to hit on a TV star, Dixie. Luke got first shot with her the summer she came back when we were in high school. Now's my chance." I could tell from the glint in his eyes he was teasing. Mostly.

"Don't you have something important to do?" Dixie asked. "Like find a doughnut somewhere?"

"Very funny," he said good-naturedly. "You know I prefer bagels. I'm just pickin' up some lunch. Luke's got his panties in a wad over Summer's new show, and he's havin' a staff meetin' on how to deal with it."

"Deal with *what*?" Dixie asked in disbelief.

"The chaos from everyone bein' here."

"It's not my intention to stir up trouble, Cale," I said. "We'll only be here two weeks."

He grinned. "Oh, *I* don't have a problem with you bein' here, and neither does most everyone else. But Luke . . . he's another story . . . and I suspect it has something to do with your personal history."

And didn't that feel like a punch in the gut? Earlier, it had almost seemed like he still cared about me, but maybe seeing me had just thrown him off guard.

He turned to Dixie. "I bet you didn't know that Summer and I go way back. Even more so than her and Luke. We were a year ahead of her in school, but the PE teacher combined the fourth-grade and third-grade classes for square dancing. Summer was my partner. She talked me into doing one too many do-si-dos, and I threw up on her shoes."

"You're lyin'," Dixie said.

"Nope," he laughed. "All she had to do was bat those baby blues and most boys would do whatever she wanted. Even back then. I was no more immune to her charm than anyone else."

51

I shook my head and grinned. "You always were full of bullshit, Cale. Remember how you handled ruining my shoes in PE?"

A smile spread across his face. "I think I told you that you were too good for worn-out shoes."

"I told my mother the same thing, but it didn't work," I said. "She just hosed them off outside, then tossed them into the washing machine."

I had entered my first pageant when I was nine months old. They'd been my mother's way of trying to break me into Hollywood. She'd thought nothing of spending thousands of dollars on pageant dresses and talent costumes, hairpieces and mouthpieces, but her habits hadn't left much of anything for everyday clothes—not that I'd minded. Jeans and shorts and scuffed-up shoes had been fine by me.

Orneriness filled Cale's eyes. "You gonna say the line for me?"

I gave him a haughty grin. "The only line I'm gonna give you is *Fuck off.*"

He laughed and turned to Dixie. "I spent that whole summer she was here trying to get her to say that line." The smoldering look he gave me probably worked on half the town, but it did absolutely nothing for me. "One of these days, I'm gonna get you to say it and a whole lot more. Just you wait."

Maybelline brought out our lunches and cast a glance at Cale. "Your order's not ready yet. Have a seat and it will be in a few minutes."

He started to slide in next to me, but she shooed him away. "You let these girls eat in peace, Officer Malone."

He grinned. "She brought out the *officer*, so I know I'm in trouble." He lifted his shoulder toward the back. "I'm gonna use the bathroom."

Maybelline pursed her lips as he walked toward the hall. "That boy . . ." Then she set the plates in front of us. "I better not see any food left on this plate, Summer Baumgartner," she said. "Or no more country-fried steak for you."

"Yes, ma'am."

We were too busy eating to talk more, and Maybelline's steak, mashed potatoes and gravy, and green beans were so good I didn't even consider talking. Dixie's phone started to ring, and she glanced at the screen. "I need to get this. It's Teddy."

"Okay."

I expected her to take it at the table, so I was surprised when she got up and walked out of the restaurant. I hid my hurt feelings. I'd hoped he'd called to tell me hi. But as she went through the door, an older man wearing dress pants, a dress shirt, and a tie walked in. He saw me at the table and strolled over, wearing a bright smile.

"You don't remember me, do you?" he asked, but he didn't seem slighted.

"Sorry." I stood and brushed some crumbs off my lap. I dropped my hand when I realized he was watching the movement with more interest than seemed polite. "I left when I was fourteen, so I've forgotten quite a few people."

"That's not entirely true," he said. "You came back the summer you were seventeen. When Viola was ill."

I froze, feeling uncomfortable that he knew personal details about my grandmother and me. Maybelline was one thing—I'd spent countless hours here—but I didn't know this man at all.

He laughed. "Sorry. I just realized how that sounded. I'm Mayor Sterling. I've been mayor for about fifteen years, so I knew when you were in town back then. We had to deal with a few paparazzi situations."

"Oh," I said, feeling like a bitch. "I had no idea."

"That was the plan," he said. "We made sure they never found their farm. Your grandfather wanted to make sure you were never aware of the situation."

"Wow." How had that slipped past me? I'd probably been too wrapped up in Luke. "Thank you."

"We take care of our own in Sweet Briar," he said.

It should have sounded friendly, but the way he said it sounded totally skeevy. I nodded, trying to hide my discomfort.

"If there's anything I can do for you while you're here, Summer, please let me know. And ignore the naysayers, especially the police chief. He had his say about your show, and he was outvoted." He frowned and shook his head. "Some people are just resistant to change."

I cringed.

"Aww . . . I shouldn't have said anything. I don't want to go spoilin' your homecoming. Almost everyone wants you here. In fact, we're plannin' a parade. We're just tryin' to work out the logistics of havin' it so close to the Boll Weevil Parade next week."

"Dixie mentioned the Boll Weevil Parade. That's new."

"Sweet Briar's gotten a whole lot more festive since you left." He smiled and patted my shoulder. "But we may have to combine the two. Maybe make you the guest of honor."

Good heavens. "Mayor Sterling, please," I said, emphatically, "don't go to any trouble on my account. Besides, I heard you already invited Magnolia Steele to be the guest of honor."

"She hasn't answered yet, so we need to come up with an alternate plan."

"As excited as I am about the generous offer," I said, trying to sound polite, "I'm afraid I must regretfully decline. We don't have a regular schedule, so I'm hesitant to commit. And maybe Magnolia will come through."

"Aren't you a sweet girl? Same old Summer." He nodded in approval. "It's good to have you back."

"Thanks . . ."

"Mayor Sterling," Maybelline said, walking out of the kitchen with a stack of plates balanced all over her arms, "you here for my mac and cheese?"

His face lit up and he winked. "It's Thursday, isn't it?"

She laughed. "So it is."

Cale emerged from the dark hall. "That order ready yet, Maybelline? Luke's gonna tan my hide if I'm not back soon."

"Give me a minute," she said, bustling off to the kitchen.

Cale and Mayor Sterling locked eyes, and I felt the mood shift.

"Mayor," Cale said with an air of formality that sounded strained.

The mayor didn't answer, just nodded, then sat down in a booth.

That was weird.

Cale headed up to the register to pay for his food, and I glanced down at the time on my phone. We only had a few minutes to get back to the office. Since we'd gotten off to a bad start, I didn't want to press my luck.

After I asked Maybelline for the bill, I decided to make a quick stop at the restroom. Who knew when Lauren would give us a bathroom break? For all I knew, she'd decide we filmed better if we were kept in a constant state of slight discomfort.

The single bathroom was available, thankfully. As soon as I finished my business, I walked out, intent on paying, gathering up Dixie, and heading out posthaste, but something caught my eye. Someone who looked just like the mayor had walked out the back door.

I told myself it was nothing, but the way he'd looked behind him—as if making sure he hadn't been seen—seemed strange. Add in his encounter with Cale . . . I decided to follow him.

Mayor Sterling had left the back door propped open with a brick. I stood out of sight in the dark shadows of the hallway, close enough to see but not be seen. The mayor and another man were standing next to a dumpster behind the pharmacy, one shop down. From their body language and their angry voices, they were in a heated discussion.

Mayor Sterling was talking to a guy who looked like he was in his late twenties, but the two of them seemed incredibly mismatched. While the mayor was wearing his fancy dress clothes, the other guy had on jeans and a dark T-shirt. His arms were covered in tattoo sleeves. While his artwork didn't bother me—I could appreciate a man with nice tattoos—his demeanor set me on edge. He looked downright rough and cocky. He said something I couldn't hear that made the mayor straighten his back.

Was this some kind of drug deal?

I was curious. Truth be told, I had more in common with the character I played on *Gotcha!* than I liked to let on—we both tended to be too curious for our own good. I knew I needed to get back to Lauren, but I wasn't ready to move on yet.

Their unintelligible conversation lasted about ten more seconds before the tattooed man stalked off toward the motorcycle parked in the alley. The mayor turned around and headed toward the back door, toward *me*.

I spun around to run back to my table, but I plowed right into Dixie.

"What are you doin'?" she asked.

"I was just going to the bathroom."

"It's not out back, silly," Dixie said, then opened the bathroom door. "It's right here."

"Oh . . ."

Mayor Sterling walked in, wiping sweat off his brow with a cloth handkerchief. He looked startled to see us. "Summer. Dixie. What are you two doin' back here?"

That was odd. He'd sounded polished and professional earlier, but now he seemed nervous.

Dixie didn't seem to notice. She waved her hand and laughed. "Poor Summer forgot how to find the bathroom. I guess she's been gone a little too long."

He didn't look so convinced.

I rolled my eyes and played the clueless blonde, a role I hated but found useful all too often. "I got turned around."

Dixie continued to hold the door open. "Are you goin' in?"

I shook my head. "I think I'll just go back at the office. Sorry to be blockin' your way, Mayor Sterling."

"Not a problem," he said, wiping his brow again. There was a deep frown etched into his face; he was looking a whole lot less friendly than he had ten minutes ago.

I followed Dixie back to our table, surprised to see the check along with a ten-dollar bill.

"I took care of it," Dixie said when she saw my confusion. "She only charged for my meal. Maybelline said the first one was on the house as long as you promised to come back and let her fatten you up."

I chuckled. "That likely won't be a problem." We had already waved goodbye to Maybelline and were well on our way back to the office by the time I remembered her phone call.

"Everything okay with Teddy?"

She frowned. "He worries too much." I didn't say anything, and after a moment, she added, "Ever since I started dating Ryker, he's been a worrywart, callin' multiple times a day to check on me. I thought it would stop after we broke up, but if anything, it's gotten worse."

"What's he worried about?" I asked.

"He thinks Ryker is low-life scum, so when we were together, he was always worried something would happen to me."

"And after?"

"I think he's worried I'm gonna go back."

I considered her words for a moment, wondering what had Teddy so concerned. "Does Teddy have something to be worried about?"

She gave me a long, hard look and then walked into the office without a word.

CHAPTER SEVEN

We were a few minutes early, but Lauren must have put the fear of God into everyone, because we were the last to arrive.

At 1 p.m. sharp, a woman showed up at the door. I was sure she was just another gawker, but Karen rushed out to greet her.

Lauren looked up from her tablet. "Okay. Let's not waste any time. That's our next client, Mrs. Peabody."

Dixie looked surprised. "What's Summer investigating for Nettie?"

"She's looking for proof her husband is a philanderer."

Dixie burst out laughing. "The whole dang town knows that."

Lauren shot her a withering glare. "We're still lining up cases. We'll need some easy ones too, to help round out the episodes."

Dixie turned to me. "I thought the whole point was to solve mysteries."

I shrugged, still trying to figure out the real point of this show. I was beginning to think Lauren and I had two entirely different expectations. I knew some reality shows were scripted, but if Dixie was right about Mr. Peabody, this bordered on ridiculous.

Lauren ignored her. "Mrs. Peabody will come through the front door. Dixie, you're going to say 'Welcome to Darling Investigations,' and then you'll step in. Summer, you'll ask her what she needs, and then ask any follow-up questions you need to figure out where to investigate."

Sounded easy enough.

Dixie and I got settled in the chairs behind our desks, then one of the guys moved in front of Tony's camera with a clapperboard and said, "Scene three, take one, Darling Investigations." Then he lowered the arm with a loud clack and stepped out of the way.

Lauren pointed to the door, and Nettie Peabody swooped in dramatically, but the intended effect was ruined when she stopped short of Dixie's desk and did a double take. "What the hell is *she* doin' here?"

Dixie's eyes grew as wide as quarters.

I stood and clenched my hands at my sides. "You have a problem with my cousin?"

"I sure as hell do! I don't want to be talkin' to no crackhead arsonist who killed her own folks."

That would have pissed me off on the best of days, but I'd just seen firsthand how much guilt Dixie carried over the accident. How dare this woman talk to her like that?

I walked around my desk and said with plenty of attitude, "Excuse me?"

She moved closer, with a sneer on her face. "Y'all may have kept it all hush-hush on account of Trent Dunbar, but we all know what happened, and two damn years in juvie for killing three people ain't near long enough."

"I don't know what the hell you're talking about," I said, "but you—"

"Summer," Dixie said, sounding defeated. "Stop."

"*Dixie!*"

Dixie shook her head and looked up at Nettie. "If you don't want me here while you talk to Summer, I'll go, but don't hold what I did against her."

Oh, my God. Why wasn't Dixie defending herself? It didn't surprise me one bit that everyone in the town knew about the fire, but Nettie's accusations didn't match the basic-as-bones story I'd heard. While I knew Dixie had been incarcerated for setting the fire, this was the first I'd heard about drugs (as far as I knew, she'd always been clean as a whistle) or her then-boyfriend being Trent Dunbar, the son of the owner of Dunbar Lumber, the biggest employer in the county.

Then I realized this was all being captured on film . . . and Lauren was standing beside the camera with a gleeful look in her eyes.

I could either throw a fit and yell "Cut," or try to salvage this, but one thing was certain, this entire incident would be aired on national TV. There was no stopping that now.

I wrapped an arm around Dixie's back, cupping her upper arm with my hand and pulling her to my side. "I'm sorry you feel that way, Nettie, but Dixie and I are a team. That incident happened nine years ago, when my cousin was fifteen years old. We all do stupid things when we're young, and thank God most of the time no one gets hurt for it. Dixie just happened to fall into that small percentage of bad luck. If you can't find it in yourself to let bygones be bygones, then maybe we're not the right agency for you."

Nettie cast an eye toward the camera and lost some of her bluster. "Well . . . you can't blame me for my concerns."

"You are definitely entitled to your concerns, and you're also entitled to find someone else to help you, but if you hire us, then you need to know up front that Dixie is my partner."

Belatedly, I worried that this had been the wrong tactic. Here we were, shining a spotlight on Dixie's past, the very thing I'd hoped to avoid. A quick glance to Dixie confirmed that she was shell-shocked. Dammit. Why hadn't I warned her this was a possibility?

Still, by handling it this way, we could have some impact on the way the story was slanted. I'd rather do that than leave it wholly in Lauren's hands.

"Fine," Nettie huffed.

I blinked, surprised she'd conceded so quickly. I'd known she would agree—the hungry glance she'd thrown the camera had convinced me she'd do *anything* to be on this show, even publicly embarrass herself by admitting to her husband's infidelity—but I'd expected her to put up more of a fuss.

I motioned to the client chairs. "Why don't you have a seat."

I walked around and sat at my desk. "What can we do for you, Mrs. Peabody?"

"Call me Nettie. I need to hire you to find out if my husband is cheating."

Dixie leaned back in her chair and gave her a snide look. "The whole dang town knows the answer to that, Nettie Peabody. Whatcha doin' wastin' your money and Summer's time?"

Nettie sputtered, surprise covering her face. She'd thought her insults had given her some sort of control over Dixie. Thank God, my cousin had gotten her spunk back.

"Are you gonna look into it or not?" Nettie asked.

Dixie gave her a shrug full of attitude, then motioned toward me. "It's your checkbook."

Nettie turned back to me. "I remember you from dance class," she said with a sneer. "You always thought you was something back then. You ain't no better now. You're stuck back here just like the rest of us."

Apparently the pretense of civility had flown out the window. "Maybe so, but you've shown up on my doorstep asking for my help. So what can I help you with?"

Tony the cameraman walked closer to get both of our faces in the shot.

Nettie looked fit to be tied, but God love her, she kept plugging along. "It seems like Dixie's got it all figured out."

"I'd like to hear it from you," I said patiently.

"My no-good husband's hookin' up with the town harlot, and I need proof so I can get his fishing boat in the divorce."

I made a face, then said, "Well, okay . . . so you need photos?"

"And video if you can get it."

"Video of . . . ?" I asked, afraid of the answer.

"Them doin' it. What do you think I want video of? Goin' fishing like he claims to be doin' whenever he's with her?"

"Uh . . . ," I said, taking a quick peek at Dixie.

"We can do that," Dixie said, nodding her head.

I realized that Bill was filming too, getting shots of Dixie.

"Really?" Nettie asked, sounding surprised.

"Sure," Dixie said. "I can't guarantee what quality it will be, but we can do it."

"I'm goin' to need a name and address, if you have it," I said, opening my desk drawer. "Have you noticed a pattern to his goin' to see his mistress?"

"Mistress?" Nettie said. "You're makin' it sound all fancy. He's screwin' the town harlot."

Grimacing, I pulled a stenographer's notebook and pen out of the open drawer. "And who do you think he's havin' an affair with?" Belatedly, I heard my accent slip. *Dammit.*

"Yeah, he's screwin' Becky MacDonald—with an *M-A-C*, not an *M-C*." She got up and looked at my notebook. "Yeah, that's right."

"Do you have an address for Ms. MacDonald?"

"Shoot," Nettie said in a snide tone. "You should have it already. Your guys have already been over at her house, makin' sure it looks okay for shooting."

"Cut!" Lauren yelled, then scolded Nettie for letting the audience know this wasn't all in the moment. "Let's try it again," she said. "We'll take it from Dixie telling Nettie to have a seat."

Sure enough, we took multiple takes, each one more stilted than the last.

Finally, a little more than an hour after we started, Lauren called it good and told Chuck to remove Nettie's mike. "So this next case is insurance fraud," Lauren told us as Nettie walked out the door. "The case is going to be called into the office. Dixie, I want you to take it, then put the caller on hold and let Summer find out what they want. After that, the two of you will discuss when and how to investigate."

"Okay . . . ," I said. "What kind of insurance fraud?"

"Worker's comp."

"Are you going to give me any more information than that, or am I supposed to just make it up as I go?"

It was an innocent question, but Lauren didn't take it that way. Glaring at me in a way that promised future pain and suffering, Lauren held out a piece of paper. I refused to take it.

"Look," I said, "I get that reality TV is scripted, but do you really want me to fake a phone call? Won't Chuck pick up the voice on the other line through my mike? Even if he fuzzes out the other voice, it seems like it would play more naturally if there's someone on the other end."

Chuck took a breath, then said hesitantly, "She's got a point, Lauren."

"Fine," Lauren said, shoving the paper at Karen. "You have two minutes to study that paper enough to answer any questions Summer asks you."

Karen took the paper, her eyes wide with fear.

Lauren ignored her and turned to face the rest of us. "We'll take several shots of this call before we head for our next location. After that we'll go to Dr. Livingston's office." She turned to Karen. "Are you ready?" But when she saw her assistant's fear-stricken face, she jerked the paper out of her hand. "I'm going to make the call."

Karen looked close to tears.

Lauren pulled her phone from her pocket. "Start the damn scene." The camera guy started to roll film as she stalked outside. She stood there, watching us through the window like a murderer waiting to strike, and then lifted her cell to her ear. Tension filled the room as the phone on Dixie's desk started to ring. Dixie jumped, startled by the sound. I expected Lauren to cut the scene, but she gave me an evil smile.

Somebody was cranky.

Dixie answered the phone. "Darlin' Investigations."

She listened for a second, seemingly unnerved, and glanced over at me. "Let me get Summer on the line for you." Then she pushed a button on her phone and said, "There's a Ms. Dearborn on line one wantin' to hire you to investigate a workman's-comp fraud case."

"Thanks, Dixie," I said, picking up the receiver and pressing the blinking button.

"Summer Butler. How can I help you?" I said. *That's how an investigator would answer, right?*

"I need more drama, Summer," Lauren said. "We're paying you a lot of money, and so far, you're not delivering enough."

I hid my shock. I'd expected her to give me something to use for my side of the phone call. "Yes, we do investigate workman's-comp fraud. Can you explain the situation?"

"This afternoon was better, but I needed you to ask the McBrides more sensational questions this morning. We need a hell of a lot more drama."

"Yes," I said, sitting up straighter. "I personally handle everything, including the investigations."

"If you can't deliver, we'll have to drag Dixie's past into the show. And there's plenty of material to use there. Maybe more than you know," Lauren said.

I'd expected as much, but it felt worse to have it confirmed. For Lauren, it turned out, a threat was the same thing as a pep talk. "So why don't you give me details about the case?"

"You're too nice. You're here because you punched an old man in the face. We need more of that."

"You said this was workman's comp?" I asked, trying to hide my horror. She wanted me to punch more people?

"You're not a good girl anymore. So bring out the sexy. Bring out your inner bitch. I need more of the fire I saw with you defending Dixie or I'm bringing in the *other* fire."

I took a breath, trying to keep myself under control. I couldn't risk my cousin getting wrapped up in this. I'd suck it up and do whatever Lauren wanted from me. "Yes, ma'am. I'll be happy to help you."

"I knew we could come to an agreement."

"So this is a back injury, you said?" I asked.

"That's right. He claims to have a back injury, but you're going to catch him in his lie. When you hang up, tell Dixie I'm e-mailing you a file. Don't fuck this up, Summer. Both of our careers depend on it." She hung up and moved toward the door.

I still held the phone pressed to my ear. "I'll send you the rates. I look forward to working on your case." Then I hung up. Lauren held my gaze as she strutted into the room with a triumphant smile.

Score one for Lauren. I'd been intimidated into submission.

For now.

CHAPTER EIGHT

We spent the next two hours at the house of the town harlot, aka Becky MacDonald, because Karen had arranged for Nettie's husband to be there. I took the camera Lauren had provided and snuck around the house, peeking into the windows and taking photos. Then I got multiple shots of Nettie's husband running out the front door toward his truck. Thankfully, Becky and Earl supplied plenty of drama, from her running out in her lingerie to him tripping over a tree root as he tried to pull a shirt over his head, so I didn't catch any more grief from Lauren for being too boring. The topper was the policeman who showed up claiming someone had turned me in for being a Peeping Tom. Since he put a pair of handcuffs on me, I suspected that *someone* had been Lauren.

The next stop was staking out the disability-claim guy in his doctor's parking lot. That was a whole lot less interesting, so either Lauren had some surprise planned, or I was going to have to come up with something fast.

Karen gave us the address, and we headed to the office and parked in the back lot.

"What are we lookin' for?" Dixie asked.

I grabbed my phone out of my pocket and pulled up Lauren's e-mail. "Tommy Kilpatrick, twenty-seven years old. He's five-ten, one hundred and eighty pounds, and has brown hair and brown eyes." I held out my phone screen so she could see his photo. "He lives here in Sweet Briar and works for Acme Concrete. He hurt his back on the job. He's been on disability for three months and claims he's still too injured to work." I looked up at Dixie. "We need to prove he's lying."

My cousin nodded. "Got it."

They'd want footage of us scoping the place out, so I rolled down the window and picked up the camera, aiming the lens at the entrance to the doctor's office.

"What kind of car does he drive?" Dixie asked.

"The paperwork didn't say."

She pursed her lips. "I think he just got out of a brand-new Range Rover."

"*What?*" She pointed in the direction she'd spotted Tommy, and I held up the camera and zoomed in on him. "I think you're right."

Dixie reached for the camera. "Let me have a look." She held it up and focused on the man walking into the office, remembering to snap several photos—something I hadn't done. "Yep. That's gotta be him."

As he disappeared into the office building, I turned to Dixie. "How much do you think Tommy makes at Acme Concrete?"

"Not enough to buy a new Range Rover."

"I wonder if he's married. Or if his parents have money," I said, forgetting, for a moment, this was all make-believe.

"I think I'd know if his parents had money. Only a handful of people have that kind of money here. The Dunbars, a couple of doctors . . . your mother."

My mother. I'd deal with that issue later. Hopefully *off* camera.

Right. And I had a bridge to sell on QVC during my next gig.

"Maybe he got some kind of settlement," Dixie said.

I pulled up his file on my phone, which actually looked like a real case file. "Um . . . I don't think he did. He's on temporary leave until he gets better." I glanced back up through the windshield. "Maybe he borrowed it from a friend."

"Or he's up to no good."

We were supposed to be private investigators. Shouldn't we have access to license-plate information? "Can you make out his license-plate number?"

She looked through the camera lens again. "It's parked at an angle. I can't make it out."

I reached for the door handle. "I'm going to find out what it is." It wasn't until I was out of the truck that I realized I'd forgotten I was supposed to be doing this on camera, but Lauren didn't stop me. It didn't take me long to figure out why. Tony stood next to his truck with his camera aimed at me.

I walked over to the SUV and pulled out my phone. "It's a Georgia license plate," I said to myself, taking a few photos of the vehicle and the plates. The sound of a motorcycle caught my attention, and I saw a big Harley pulling into the parking lot of the strip mall next door. That lot was nearly empty other than a white cargo van parked on the opposite side. When the driver parked the Harley and took off his helmet, I realized it was the guy who'd been talking to the mayor in the alley outside the café. Acting on impulse, I lifted my phone and snapped several photos of him as he walked into a dry-cleaning place—an odd choice given that he wasn't taking anything in, and it hardly seemed practical to carry dry cleaning home on a bike.

I'd made it across the small grass strip separating the two parking lots before Lauren started shouting at me like a mother rounding up a disobedient child. "Summer! Get back here!"

I planned to ignore her, but the guy walked out seconds later with a brown paper bag tucked under his left arm.

"Summer!"

Dammit. I took several more photos, pretending to take photos of the entire parking lot as I watched him stuff the brown paper bag into the side-saddle pouch on his bike. Which was why I saw the brown bag tumble out onto the pavement as he drove off. He didn't appear to notice.

That curiosity kicked in again, and I sent Dixie a text. Distract Lauren.

Seconds later, Dixie started screaming inside the truck cab. The crew ran over to her to see what was wrong. I took advantage of the distraction to make a grab for the brown bag. It held a rectangular wad, and a quick peek inside revealed it to be a stack of money.

Holy crap.

"What the hell are you doing?" Lauren screamed after me. "The show's in *this* parking lot!"

Denise Grover Swank

I heard Dixie shouting something about a spider.

I held the bag at my side, hiding it as I turned. "Just looking around."

"Get over here!"

What was I going to do with it? Take it into the dry-cleaning store? Put it back on the ground? What would Lauren do if I told her? Keep it?

Who dropped a bag full of money?

A police car pulled into the parking lot, and I saw Cale through the window. He parked in the space next to me and got out. "Are you a hobbit goin' for your second lunch?" he asked as a grin spread across his face. "You must have a hollow leg."

"It's not a lunch," I said with a snort. "It's a bag full of money."

"Where'd you get a bag of money?"

"I found it here in the parking lot. A motorcyclist just peeled out of here, and it dropped out of his bag."

"You don't say," he murmured as he reached for it. I handed it over, and he whistled when he glanced inside. "I'll take this down to the station. Anyone who drops a bag of money's gonna go lookin' for it."

"Okay."

He leaned down and tossed it into the passenger seat of his police car.

"What are you doing here anyway?" I asked.

His grin grew even bigger as his eyes twinkled with mischief. "Luke's got us takin' turns keepin' an eye on all y'all. He assigned us shifts at our meeting."

"So that's why Officer Hawkins showed up at our last location."

"I guess it seems less like harassment if we take turns," he said with a laugh that suggested he thought the task was ridiculous. There was a sinking feeling in my stomach. Luke was doing his level best to boot me out of town.

"What exactly does he think we're going to do?"

"That remains to be seen."

"Well, tell Chief Montgomery that he should do his own dirty work."

He laughed again. "There's no way in hell I'm telling him that. You can do it yourself." He glanced over at the crew behind me. "That one woman looks pissed as hell. If Luke asks, I harassed the shit out of you all. Otherwise, I'm out of here." He got in his car and gave me a little wave before he backed up.

As he pulled out of the lot, I realized I hadn't given him any details about the guy who'd dropped the money. I turned around to deal with the pissed-as-hell woman.

"What was that all about?" Lauren asked as I approached her. "Why did you go over there in the first place?"

"You said you wanted drama, and this case seems dull as dirt, so I went lookin' for trouble."

"How did you come across a bag of money?" she asked with a hand on her hip.

"How . . . ?" That damn microphone. "I found it in the lot. The guy on the motorcycle dropped it, and I went to see what it was."

"Why in God's name did you give it to that police officer?"

"Because it was lost money, Lauren. He can try to give it to the rightful owner. I couldn't very well refuse to hand it over."

"You deviated from the plan. I never told you to get out of the truck. I never told you to go pick up a bag of money. You need to clear things with me first."

"Is Tommy Kilpatrick even a real case?" I asked.

She shrugged. "They're all varying degrees of real."

"So Acme Concrete really thinks he's faking his injury?"

"They gave us two weeks to prove it."

Strangely enough, that made me feel better. "So what do you have planned for the rest of the afternoon?"

She checked her watch. "I think we'll send Bill to get some B-roll of Kilpatrick's house, and Tony will get some B-roll of you and Dixie working at the office this afternoon."

"How will Bill explain taking footage of Tommy's house if he sees him?"

She shrugged. "He can tell him he's filming for Google."

I had to admit that was a good idea, but plenty of other things weren't adding up. "That should have us finishing up between five and six. I thought we were pushing ten-hour days."

Lauren hesitated. "I have everyone on a special project tonight."

Oh, Lord. I wasn't sure I wanted to know, but if the wicked look in her eyes was any indication, I was going to find out—and soon.

When I got back in the truck, I could see Dixie was dying to find out more about the money, but I didn't dare tell her in the bugged-up cab. It was bothering me that I hadn't yet told Cale about the connection between the guy who'd dropped the money and the mayor. I knew in my gut they were related somehow. I just wasn't sure how.

We spent another half hour doing retakes of Dixie and me in the truck cab talking about the case, then Tommy Kilpatrick walked out, got into his Range Rover, and drove off.

I was dying to follow him, but Lauren insisted we head back to the office, which included more grueling, slo-mo filming of us driving and then parking in front of the office.

Karen had gone back and put cones in an empty spot to save it for us, and the cones had caught some attention, so there was a small crowd outside the office. Karen blocked the sidewalk off with the cones, and Lauren, who clearly thought she was a paragon of generosity, told the gathered people they could cross our shot one or two at a time (possibly getting some screen time in the process) so long as they agreed not to stop and dawdle . . . which was like asking them to walk past a spaceship. They kept gawking and even waving at the camera. Lauren was fit to be tied by the fifth take.

She balled her hands into fists at her sides, and her face turned red as she screamed, "Can you morons get *anything* right?"

That didn't exactly earn her any love, and an earsplitting fuss quickly rose up. It was interrupted when a now-familiar man's voice shouted, "Everyone calm down!"

The crowd quieted, and Officer Hawkins, who'd almost arrested me for peeping earlier, passed through them with his thumbs hooked in his waistband and a grin on his face. This had to be his most exciting day in ages. "Ms. Chapman, do you have a permit to be blocking the sidewalk?"

"No, but—"

He held up his hand, his smile widening. "There are no buts in the law, ma'am."

"No," she sneered, practically nose to nose with him, "but apparently, there are plenty of *asses*."

Oh, crap.

"She's gonna get this show kicked out of town, ain't she?" Dixie asked, her voice tight. We were in the truck, having returned to the cab after the last disastrous take.

"It sure looks that way." I wasn't sure which outcome to hope for.

Dixie and I got out and tried to sneak into the office, but a few people in the crowd saw me and asked me for autographs. Since I didn't have anything to hand out, I signed two receipts and a church program from a month ago before we slipped inside.

Lauren and the officer's disagreement ended in a spectacular shouting match before she stomped into the office and down the hall. She was back moments later with a bag slung over her shoulder. Heading for the door, she barked at Bill, "Stay here and get the B-roll of Summer and Dixie at the office, then send Dixie home and get some footage of Summer alone."

"Okay."

"Tony and everyone else, come with me to the farm."

The farm? "Wait? My grandmother's farm?"

Lauren paused at the door and turned only long enough to give me an evil smile.

Shit.

I nearly attacked Dixie as she walked in the door. "Why are they going out to the farm?"

She gave me a blank look. "For the family dinner."

The blood rushed to my feet, leaving me light-headed. "What family dinner? Who's coming?"

"Just me and Teddy. And Meemaw, of course. And you. Didn't they tell you?"

I stumbled backward, resting my butt on the edge of my desk. "Oh, thank God."

"Who did you think would be there?" Her mouth formed a perfect O. "Your mother."

I nodded.

"We haven't seen her in ages. She came back to town actin' like you'd taken her for a ride, but it smelled mighty fishy after she started buildin' that big house. As far as I know, she and Meemaw haven't talked in a couple of years."

"Really?"

Her lips pursed and she gave me a half shrug. "Yeah."

I looked up to ask Bill what he wanted us to do to start the B-roll, but he was already recording. I was horrified anew. "Tell me you didn't record that."

"Sorry, Summer. Part of reality TV is catching the candid moments."

I snorted. "After a whole day of scripted filming."

"*Some* part of it has to be reality."

Part of me wanted to flee. To pick up and move to some remote country where no one would recognize me. While everyone suspected my mother and I had had a falling-out, neither of us had publicly confirmed it. Still . . . as much as I hated the thought of people knowing the truth, maybe it was time. If this got out, it might even put some of the worst rumors about me to bed.

I sat down at my desk. "We're supposed to look like we're working, right?"

"Yeah. I'm going to be moving in and out of the office. Just pretend I'm not here."

Yeah. Right.

He kept filming as I opened my laptop and booted it up, seeing what programs were loaded. It was pretty bare-bones, not that I was surprised. I'd actually expected the computers to be props.

"We need to run that license-plate number," I told Dixie. "There has to be a program we can use. Can you do a search to see if we can get one now that I'm an official PI?" I almost laughed, but the business license on the wall assured me that Darling Investigations was in the business of private investigation.

"On it."

"Are there many serious crimes around here?" I asked.

Dixie seemed to understand what I was getting at. "No. Burglaries, of course. A lot of DUIs. Some drug possession and dealing. The occasional assaults, but few rapes or murders. There've been a few drug overdoses over the last few months. That seems to have Luke on edge."

I started doing an Internet search for Tommy Kilpatrick in Sweet Briar, Alabama, coming up with a couple of hits about his years on the Sweet Briar High School baseball team and an arrest for a DUI. There was also a post in the *Sweet Briar Gazette* about his accident at Acme Concrete, but it didn't go into much detail. I jotted down some of the names of his fellow baseball teammates, hoping they'd kept in touch and could give me some information. But all the while, I kept wondering about that bag of cash. What was it for? How much money was in there? And what did the mayor have to do with any of it? I really needed to call Cale.

I was snared up in my thoughts by the time Bill returned to the doorway. "Okay, that's enough with you, Dixie. Lauren wants you out at the farm."

"Okay." Dixie closed her laptop and stood. "You okay being here on your own, Summer?"

I smiled. "I'll see you at dinner."

She left and Bill spent the next twenty minutes taking more shots of me alone from varying angles before he said we were done.

"Do you mind if I head out there by myself?" I asked. "I need some time alone."

"Yeah," he said. "No problem. It's probably hard being thrust back into it all after being gone so long."

"Yeah. It is." I grabbed my phone and keys. "Okay. See you out there."

He gave me a wave as he started to pack up his camera.

When I got out to the truck, I noticed that my two suitcases were in the truck bed. It occurred to me that they'd never told me where I was staying. *Crap.* It would have been nice to go to my hotel and freshen up before dinner, especially since I hadn't seen Meemaw for so long. I considered calling Karen, the only one who'd given me her number, but the sun was already low on the horizon, and there was a stop I wanted to make before I went to the farmhouse.

I got in the truck and started to head out of town. I was passing the police station and thinking of Luke when I saw flashing lights in my rearview mirror.

Great. This was harassment, plain and simple. I'd been going the speed limit—a couple of miles below, actually—and I'd broken no traffic rules.

I pulled into the empty parking lot of a sign business, which looked to be closed since it was after six. Shifting the old truck into park, I leaned over to get the registration paperwork from the glove compartment.

"License, registration, and proof of insurance," Luke barked, for all the world like he hadn't been wrapped around me eight hours earlier. I started sifting through the mess of papers, but I couldn't find what I needed.

"I'm looking," I said, straining against the seat belt.

"I'm goin' to need you to step out of the truck."

"I'm trying to find it!" I insisted.

"*Now.*"

After my crap day, he was about to catch the brunt of my wrath.

CHAPTER NINE

"This is harassment, Luke," I snapped. "You've had officers watching us all day, and now this. You know I didn't do anything wrong. I expected better from you."

Guilt flashed in his eyes, but his anger flared up as quickly as an Alabama thunderstorm. "You're disrupting my town. You blew in like a tornado and disrupted my life twelve years ago, and here you are disruptin' it again."

I searched deep for an ember of anger to stoke, anything that would overtake the pain that was about to make me burst into tears. "I have no intention of disrupting your life again. That's not why I'm here."

"I'm the damn police chief, Summer. You're disruptin' the town, which means you're disruptin' me." He turned away. "If I had my way, I'd kick your whole damn circus out of the city limits, but your producer promised something to Mayor Sterling and swayed the whole city council, and now I'm hamstrung."

That perked up my interest. "Promised what?"

"Probably money for that stoplight he's wanting on Oak Street, but that's not the point . . ."

I cocked my head, wondering if I was onto something. "Is he open to bribes?"

He winced and gave me a look that told me exactly what he thought of me nosing into the town's affairs. "*What?*"

"Is Mayor Sterling open to bribes? Or likely to be involved in something shady? I saw him doing something suspicious behind Maybelline's Café today, then this afternoon I saw a guy drop—"

"Am I on your damn show?" He spun around and glanced over his shoulder, then back at me. "I told that damn producer I wanted no part of it. She does *not* have my permission to put me on camera."

"What are you talking about?"

He took a step closer to me, his jaw clenched tight as he glared at me. "Am I being recorded right now?"

My eyes widened in shock. "No. I just—"

"This is not your town anymore, Summer," he said. "For all your pretty words about leaving your Hollywood life behind, *you never came back*. You have no business being here, and you certainly have no business stirrin' shit up."

"I don't want to be here any more than you want me to be," I said, finally finding my temper and hanging on to it like a drowning woman. I advanced toward him, looking up into his anger-filled eyes. "But this is where I was born and raised for the first fourteen years of my life. This is my damned town too, so you can stuff it!"

His eyes narrowed as he took several steps backward, but sorrow had replaced most of his anger. "You never wanted to be here. Not even when you claimed you did. So why are you here now? After all these years?"

"I didn't have a choice," I said, nearly cringing when I realized how pathetic I sounded. "I know that doesn't help, but there it is."

He glanced toward the police station. "So you really *don't* want to be here."

While I'd staunchly resisted the idea of coming back, now that I was here, I was ready to face everything I'd done wrong head-on, and the way things had gone down with Luke was one of my biggest regrets.

I started to contradict him, but he turned back to face me, and the pain in his eyes stole my breath. "For nearly two years, I waited for you." He moved closer until he was standing over me, his anger returning, blending with his pain. "Then your grandfather died, and I was sure you'd come back for his funeral, but hell no, you were too damned selfish for that. I believed you, Summer. I fell for it hook, line and sinker. For all your talk, you're no different than your mother."

I gasped. We might have broken up almost a decade ago, but he obviously still knew how to hurt me. "I was young and stupid, and I did a lot of things I deeply regret."

"Save it for the camera. The sooner you leave Sweet Briar, the better. I plan to do everything in my power to get you out of here before you cause any lasting damage."

"Damage to you or the town?" I asked in a strangled voice.

He shook his head. "You have no power to hurt me anymore. I gave up that ghost nine years ago." But the look on his face suggested that was a lie.

I stood there, watching in shock as he got in his police car and drove out of the lot. This felt like one embarrassment too many, and I was sure there were plenty more humiliations to come.

I will not cry. I will not cry.

I got back in the truck, turning onto County Road 95 out of a habit I hadn't used in twelve years. It was time to face my grandmother. But first I was going to see Pawpaw.

Until I was six, my mother and I had lived with my grandparents. We moved out after she married Burt, but I'd still spent a lot of time with Meemaw and Pawpaw while Momma and Burt were in their "honeymoon stage." Not that I'd minded. My headstrong, stubborn mother had always been challenging, and my whole life had been driven by the sheer force of her personality. Until Momma moved us away when I was fourteen, my grandfather had been my rock, my lifeline— the one thing anchoring me.

I'd never seen his grave, but my mother had told me that he was buried in the family cemetery on the land his family had owned since 1823. Most people weren't buried on family land these days, but my grandfather and the land had had a symbiotic relationship. I couldn't imagine him leaving it, even in death.

The family cemetery was off the lane to the farmhouse, about fifty feet from the country road but still far enough from the house that I could stop and pay my respects without being seen by anyone inside.

One homecoming at a time.

I parked on the side of the gravel road and got out of the truck, then leaned my butt against the side of the closed driver's-side door, closing my eyes and breathing deep, taking in the sweet fragrance of the magnolia tree next to the graveyard. When I was seven, Pawpaw told me why he'd planted it: It was so beating hot in the summer, the people buried in the earth used to get up at night and walk to the creek that ran through the Baumgartner property about two hundred feet to the north for a cold drink of water. He figured if he could cool off the graves, they'd stay put. According to him, it had worked . . . for half the occupants. The ones remaining in the sun still made their nightly trek.

His story had scared me half to death, and that night I had refused to go to sleep, terrified a ghost would get confused and come into the house looking for a drink of water. Meemaw, fit to be tied, had made him tell me the truth—that he'd planted it to have a cool place to sit and rest a spell while working in the cotton fields next to the cemetery.

Whatever his reasons for planting it, the tree had thrived. It was now at least fifty feet tall and a good thirty to forty feet wide. I wondered if it covered Pawpaw's grave, or if he'd joined the wanderers in their search for water. There was only one way to find out.

I walked across the gravel drive, trying to figure out the best path. Pawpaw had been faithful about keeping the grounds maintained, but Teddy was clearly not as discerning. Weeds had sprouted up around the markers, some of which were so old the names and dates had worn away. But Pawpaw's was easy to spot—a red-and-black granite headstone topped by a cherub . . . obviously the work of my mother. Pawpaw would have hated it.

I allowed myself a little laugh when I realized his grave was in the sun, especially since the two graves next to it were in the shade—Stanley and Merilee Baumgartner. I wasn't surprised to see that their headstones were much simpler. My mother never could stand her sister-in-law and had been mostly estranged from her brother because of it.

I stomped on the weeds, trying to make a path to the graves. As I got closer, I noticed a bundle of yellow tulips tied up with twine at the base of Merilee's headstone. Dixie had always loved yellow tulips.

I ran my fingers over the etched stone on Pawpaw's grave. It still haunted me that I had missed their funerals. I had my mother to blame for that too, but that decision had been the beginning of the end. Soon after, I told her no for the first time and stuck to my guns. *That*, I couldn't regret.

I knelt on the ground, ignoring the fact that I was probably staining my jeans. I closed my eyes and summoned up his memory, this man I'd dared to love more than my own mother. His death had been my greatest loss. No one else had shown me such unconditional love. Once, I had believed my grandmother loved me that way too, but she'd been quick to turn her back on me in the end. Pawpaw was the only one who'd understood that the life my mother had picked for me was not of my choosing—a reality that had caused a huge rift between the two of them.

I sucked in a deep breath, the scent of the magnolia blossoms overhead filling my nose with a sweet scent better than any perfume, and told myself that wallowing never did any good. I could wallow all I wanted, but my problems would still be waiting for me. I needed to suck it up and face the music.

The farmhouse was another couple hundred feet farther down the gravel lane. Even though I hadn't been back here since the summer I was seventeen, it still felt so much like home. I knew I was close when the trees began to line the road. Pawpaw had planted those too—forty poplar trees, twenty on either side—saying the Baumgartner House rivaled any plantation in *Gone with the Wind*. In truth, my grandparents' home more closely resembled a sharecropper's house, but that hadn't deterred my grandfather's visions of greatness.

Instead of bolstering the home's image, the trees seemed to mock it, to draw the eye to how small and worn it looked.

This house had been built in 1864, rebuilt after the original had been burned down in the Civil War. Pawpaw said that before the war, the house had been finer, but there hadn't been enough money to rebuild it to its previous glory. Now it was a four-bedroom, two-bath home that hadn't seen a remodel this century . . . unless it had happened since my last visit, which seemed unlikely, as I was making the mortgage payments due to hard times.

I parked in front of the house, cringing when I saw the cars and trucks belonging to the production staff. I was probably going to see my grandmother for the first time in years in front of cameras.

Great. Still, there was no denying it was this show that had drawn me back home, and now that I was here, I could use this opportunity to try to fix things. Or at least apply a few patches.

I got out and walked up to the porch. The amount of blooming bulb flowers near the front door could have rivaled Holland; it looked like the pansies had exploded. My grandmother had never been one to waste time on planting flowers, so I couldn't help wondering who'd taken the trouble to buy and arrange them.

When I reached the front door, I hesitated, then reached out and rapped loudly.

Dixie answered with a huge grin. She'd changed out of her shorts into a simple sleeveless blue dress. "You made it."

The smell of Meemaw's cooking rolled out of the door, and nostalgia stole my breath, reminding me of the happiest moments in my life—living here. "Yeah."

"Dixie?" a woman called out from the kitchen. "Is that her?"

My grandmother.

My stomach seized with nerves. Meemaw had always had a temper, but Pawpaw used to cool her down. Had anyone taken over that responsibility after his death?

"Yes, ma'am," Dixie hollered back. "I'm gonna help her with her bags."

"My bags?" I asked in confusion.

"Lauren says you're stayin' here, so I figured it would be easier to bring your stuff in now."

Staying here. That made sense, especially if the producers were looking for drama, but the thought made me quake in my shoes.

"I think I should go in and say hi to her," I said.

Dixie shook her head and stepped outside, shutting the door behind her. "She's in the middle of cookin'. You'll just tick her off."

Meemaw had always hated people coming into her kitchen when she was cooking. Dixie was right. If I wanted to start out on the right foot, I needed to wait . . . even if my heart ached a bit that she hadn't rushed out to greet me.

We walked down the steps and toward the back of the truck. I gestured to the multiple cars parked by the side of the house. "Why is Meemaw allowing all of this?"

"Well . . . she's none too happy, but Lauren promised her a new fence along the western property line. Seein' how we couldn't figure out how to scrape up the money for it, she agreed."

I started walking again. "Is she pissed at *me*?"

Dixie's mouth pursed, and she gave me a long look before she said, "We sure are havin' some great weather. Should be good for stakeouts, huh?"

Shit.

Two weeks. That's all I had to endure, then I could go back to . . . what? My salary for the show would help out, certainly, but it wouldn't save my house. So, I'd return just in time to pack up my life and go . . . where? One step at a time.

We lugged the suitcases up the few steps on the porch. They weighed close to fifty pounds each, but Dixie carried the second one with hardly any trouble at all.

Once we rolled them across the threshold, I noticed the production crew in the living room setting up for another shoot. Dinner.

Dixie practically pushed me toward the hallway off the living room. "Teddy and I have the bedrooms upstairs, so you get the bedroom in the back."

"You haven't considered moving out?" I asked. Dixie was twenty-five, and Teddy was a year younger than I was.

She gave me a look of surprise. "Why would we leave? Teddy runs the farm, and I help Meemaw with the house. Plus, the pay at the Dollar General was crap. I can't afford to live anywhere else." She pushed me down the short hall. "Meemaw's still in the front bedroom, so you two will share a bathroom."

We walked into the living room, which was on the front left side of the house, and at first glance it looked like nothing had changed. I could see into the dining room and hoped to catch a glimpse of my grandmother through the swinging door into the kitchen, but Dixie headed me toward the right. The main living areas took up the west side of the house, but the two bedrooms and a bathroom took up the east side.

My grandmother's bedroom was in the front, and I almost gasped aloud when Dixie steered me past the bathroom and into the back bedroom. It hadn't changed one bit. It was big enough to comfortably hold a full-size bed, a chest of drawers, and a chair. Just like I remembered, the white wrought-iron bed was covered in a pink-and-white quilt with multiple images of a girl wearing sunbonnets. I used to love that quilt when I was a kid.

Truth was, the back bedroom had been *my* room.

Tears stung my eyes. My grandmother had kept everything exactly the same. If she was pissed at me, why hadn't she changed it? Was it because she'd always hoped I would come back or because she was too frugal to get new bedding?

"Dixie Belle Baumgartner!" I heard my grandmother shouting on the other side of the door. "You two need to come out to dinner."

I found it interesting that she hadn't used my name yet, not once. Maybe she was waiting until she saw me face-to-face. But if I heard her so clearly, that meant she was out of the kitchen.

Dixie grabbed my hand and squeezed. "You ready?"

"As I'll ever be."

I followed my cousin into the dining room, my breath coming in shallow pants. Half of me was dying to see her, and the other half was terrified of being rejected. Again.

I heard my grandmother before I saw her. She was shooing the crew out of the way as she set out the food.

"If you're gonna film this, then you better be ready to get on with it," she said in a no-nonsense tone. "My food's about to get cold."

"We're waiting on our other camera guy," Tony said.

"Well, he better get here fast," she snapped.

I didn't have time to prepare myself, but maybe there *was* no preparing for some things. Either way, she was there in front of me before I was ready for her. I was surprised by how much older she looked. She was only sixty-eight, but the deep wrinkles on her face made her look well into her seventies. All that sun from working out in the fields with her husband. Her salt-and-pepper hair was silver now, and she looked shorter, probably because she was slightly stooped over. Still, her gray eyes were just as alert as I remembered them—never missing a thing.

"Summer Lynn," she said, looking me up and down, "you're too skinny."

That was such a Meemaw thing to say I would have laughed if I hadn't been so nervous. "I suspect one night at your dinner table will fix that."

She remained in place, looking like she was about to say something before she pressed her lips together.

"I missed you, Meemaw," I nearly whispered. "It's good to be home."

She made a guttural sound and waved to the table. "Dinner's getting cold. Sit down." Then she disappeared into the kitchen.

All in all, this could have gone worse. I was going to call it a win.

I glanced at the table, not surprised to see a spread. My grandmother was known far and wide for her cooking, and she'd always relished the opportunity to cook for other people. I counted the place settings and glanced at Dixie. "Four. Teddy's coming, right?" I asked hopefully.

"He wouldn't miss it. He ran to the feed store for a bit. He's eager to see you."

My aunt and uncle had lived in a mobile home on the farm, and since I had spent so much of my own childhood here, Teddy and I had practically grown up together. We'd been close up until I left when I was fourteen. We'd tried to keep in touch, but Teddy had never been one to talk on the phone, and we'd soon grown apart. Being here made me realize how much I had missed him. "I'm eager to see him too."

It felt like I was sitting in a spotlight, all my failings and worries, hopes and fears exposed. Then I looked up at the ceiling and realized that was literally true. It was a tangle of steel beams and wires holding up lights.

"Those damned lights," Meemaw said as she pushed through the swinging door with a plate of what looked like country-fried steak. Had she made it because she knew it was my favorite? She set it on the table next to the bowls of mashed potatoes, gravy, and collard greens.

"For the show?" I asked in surprise.

"Yep."

I wanted to apologize, but she'd already disappeared into the back. It occurred to me that it wasn't right for Meemaw to run back and forth from the kitchen while we stood around like toads on a log. She'd always put us to work when we were younger. "Shouldn't we help her?" I asked my cousin.

Dixie lowered her voice. "She won't let me help. She says the kitchen is her kingdom."

My grandmother returned a few seconds later holding a white ceramic pitcher. "What in the Sam Hill are you two doin' still standin' there? *Sit down.* Are ya deaf?"

"No, ma'am," Dixie said, sounding contrite, but she shot me a surreptitious grin.

"Is there a particular place you want me to sit?" I asked, glancing around the table. It had been built by my great-great-grandfather and was designed to hold fourteen people comfortably. The four place settings were on the end closest to the kitchen—two spots facing another two. The end of the table was left empty.

My grandfather's spot.

Meemaw set the pitcher on the table and gestured to the side of the table opposite her.

"You can't start dinner yet," Lauren said, walking through the front door. "We're still waiting on our other cameraman. You said you were serving dinner at seven, and it's only six fifty-five."

Meemaw's eyes narrowed. "This is *my* house, and we eat when I say we do. If you don't like it, then tough." She glared at Dixie before shifting her gaze to me. "*Sit.*"

I quickly took my seat while Dixie sat across from me. Meemaw sat next to her.

"Let's say grace," Meemaw said, lifting her hands.

"Don't start without me!" I heard a man call out from the kitchen.

The guy who rushed in from the swinging door looked like a much younger version of my grandfather. My mouth gaped open when I saw him, but a huge grin spread across his face.

Teddy was all grown up and extremely good-looking, but he didn't have the arrogant air a lot of good-looking guys had.

"Summer!" I stood, and he pulled me into a bear hug. "I can't believe you're home. I hope you're considering stayin'—the Baumgartner cousins all together again."

He wanted me to stay? A lump filled my throat, and I cast a glance toward Meemaw, but she waved her hand. "We're not talkin' about that. Not tonight." She shot a glare at Lauren.

But Lauren was too busy grinning at Teddy to notice. Probably because his good looks would be great for ratings. I suspected she would figure out ways to insert him into the show any chance she got.

"Teddy," she said in the nicest voice she'd used all day, "would you mind coming back into the room just like you did a moment ago?"

"Why?" he asked in confusion.

"So we can film it."

Bill hurried through the front door. Lauren looked furious with him, but her expression completely transformed after he walked over to her and whispered something in her ear. After a couple of seconds, she shot me a pleased glance.

What was that about?

"Get set up, Bill," Lauren said. "We're rolling."

Teddy made his entrance two more times before Meemaw started cursing about her dinner getting ruined. Lauren gave the all clear for dinner to carry on.

Meemaw said grace—with everyone holding hands—and we had finally started dishing food onto our plates when a knock landed on the front door.

Dixie gave Teddy and Meemaw a questioning glance. "Did you invite someone else?"

"Don't look at me," Meemaw barked.

Teddy shook his head. "Wasn't me this time."

"Hello," a voice called out from the living room. "Did you start without us?"

I froze. *No. It can't be.*

But it was. Standing in the dining room doorway was my mother.

CHAPTER TEN

"Summer," my mother said in a snippy tone, "you're back in town and didn't bother to tell me."

I pushed out a breath. I was going to kill Lauren. And all this was being captured on camera. If Lauren expected us to reshoot Momma's grand entrance, I would walk right out of this house.

"Momma," I said, trying to keep my tone civil, "I just arrived this morning."

"I hear you got a new business," she said, walking into the room. "You're a detective now. A real one."

My stepfather followed, staying multiple steps behind her. His black hair had gone mostly gray, but he still had the same browbeaten look he'd worn since shortly after he'd married my mother. "Hello, Summer," he said softly, unable to look me in the eye.

"Hi, Burt."

"What in the Sam Hill are you doin' here, Beatrice?" Meemaw asked while slapping a spoonful of potatoes onto her plate.

Momma lifted her chin. "We've dropped by for dinner."

"No one invited you."

My mother laughed. "Invited? But we're family." She pointed to the table. "Burt, you sit there. I'll go get us plates and silverware."

Burt walked around the table and sat next to me. "How've ya been, Summer?"

Deadly Summer

My mouth dropped open, and some choice words came to mind before I remembered everything was being captured on video. "Just fine, Burt. How about you? Enjoying that huge house?"

He had the good grace to look embarrassed. "Yeah. You should drop by for a visit."

"I'm sure I'll be too busy," I said.

"Too good for the likes of us?" my mother asked as she came out of the kitchen with two plates in one hand and silverware in the other. "You always had an attitude, Summer. Thinkin' you knew better than everyone else."

I almost protested, but her question was a trap I refused to fall into. She wanted me to argue. She wanted me to fuss. And I wouldn't do it. I was done making a spectacle of myself for my mother. I'd decided that the day she'd walked off with my money. Based on the giant diamond rings on her hands, she was living large while I was struggling to save the farm. Had I made the wrong decision back then? Should I have slapped her with a lawsuit?

A quick glance to Dixie reminded me of my reasons. But I couldn't forget that Dixie still wasn't safe. Not while I was here, and certainly not while we were shooting this show.

"We haven't seen you in a while, Aunt Beatrice," Teddy said with a smirk. "What a funny coincidence that you showed up *tonight*."

Everyone at the table knew Teddy meant the coincidence was that her sudden reappearance coincided with that of the cameras, but my mother, of course, chose to pretend otherwise. "I haven't seen my daughter in ages, Teddy. *Of course* I came around."

"And why haven't you been around to see *us*, Aunt Beatrice? What's it been? Two years?"

"It's just so *far*, Teddy," she said, pressing her fingertips to her chest with a dramatic flair. "We're practically in Georgia. And then there's my busy schedule . . . coaching all those pageant girls."

"I'm sure all those living Barbie dolls keep you busy," he said. "As for the drive here . . . well, I do understand. The last nine minutes of that ten-minute drive are the hardest."

87

Dixie released a giggle, and even Meemaw cracked a smile. My mother's mouth dropped open before she quickly shut it.

While I was loving every moment of my mother's discomfort, I was smart enough to know that if our family dinner was drama-free, it would be less likely to make the final cut—and we wouldn't be subjected to too many more of them. "So, Teddy," I said to change the subject, "Dixie says you work on the farm."

He reached for one of Meemaw's yeast rolls. "That's right."

"Are you planting cotton?"

"Of course, he's plantin' cotton," Meemaw snapped. "It's a damn cotton farm. What else would we be plantin'?"

"Well . . . ," Teddy said, turning to me, "I've been thinkin' about expanding. The Johnsons are gonna start raisin' organic chickens."

My grandmother shot him a glare. "Not that nonsense again."

"Meemaw," he groaned in frustration, "Cotton's not enough. Even Pawpaw saw that."

She pointed her fork at him. "This has been a cotton farm for nearly two hundred years, and that's not about to change. Organic chickens . . ." She shook her head. "Over my dead body."

He scooped a huge bite of mashed potatoes onto his fork. "I'm not *tryin'* to change that, Meemaw. We'll just take some of the land for the chickens."

"No." She shot me a glare. "We're not discussing this in front of company."

There was that word again. *Company.* And she made damn sure I knew she was referring to my mother and me, not the production crew.

But Teddy decided to use the audience to his advantage. "The farm's hurting, Meemaw. We need the money."

"Not in front of company," she said more firmly.

I was reeling from the news that the farm was still in financial straits. I'd bailed it out before—hell, I was still bailing it out. I couldn't afford to do anything more. How bad off were they?

My mother picked up on the tension right away—and, as was her way, stuck her finger in it. "Are you going to lose the farm?"

"Of course we're not going to lose the farm," Meemaw mumbled.

"But Teddy said—"

"Teddy's a fool who needs to learn to keep his trap shut."

My mother turned to me. "Are you still—"

I needed to change the topic quickly. Pawpaw didn't want my grandmother to know about the loan and had made me swear to keep it secret. Sure, he was dead now, but he'd taught me that swearing an oath meant something, even if the world no longer thought so.

"Meemaw," I said loud enough to interrupt my mother, "what do you know about Mayor Sterling?"

Her head jutted back. "Garner Sterling? What about him?"

Part of me hated to bring this up while filming, but I had an idea for how to ensure this didn't make it on the air. These kinds of shows liked to pretend that their cameras didn't exist. I couldn't see them using anything that specifically called out the filming process. "I saw Luke Montgomery earlier, and he thinks the mayor was bribed with a stoplight to let the production crew film in town. Do you think the mayor's on the up-and-up?"

Teddy sat up straighter, irritation radiating off him. "You saw Luke Montgomery?"

"Yeah," I said, wondering why he was riled up. "This morning outside the office dealing with a crowd, then he pulled me over this evening."

"Pulled you over?" Teddy said, turning to face me. "What for?"

"Nothing, really. I think he just wanted to tell me off."

Teddy shook his head, looking like he was madder than a hornet. "With all the issues goin' on in this town, he's wasting his time pullin' you over?"

"What issues?"

Dixie leaned over the table and lowered her voice. "Now's not the time, Teddy."

"Now's the perfect time," Teddy said, dropping his fork on his plate with a clang. "How about there've been two overdose deaths in just as many months, and he's not doin' jack shit about it."

"That may not be true," Dixie said, imploring him with her eyes to be quiet.

"There's something brewing in this town, something ugly, and Luke's turned his back on the whole thing."

My mother decided she needed to jump in. "That man's part of the reason we live outside of the city limits. I could only take so much of his harassment."

"Harassment?" I said. "Over what?"

She shook her head in disgust. "I know that boy still harbors a grudge against me for talking you into some common sense about your contract for *Gotcha!* He plans to use his position to punish me for it." She angrily stabbed her green beans. "I can only imagine what would have happened if you'd stayed. That boy was after your money and your fame. He was never interested in you."

Of all the things she could say. Luke had never wanted any of it—the money, the fame. He'd *only* wanted me. My mother was the one who'd used me. But that wasn't the kind of drama I was willing to give Lauren.

Meemaw's eyes narrowed. I remembered this look from when I was a girl. This was a warning of an impending explosion. "Beatrice, are you actually suggesting that Luke Montgomery abuses his position?"

My mother shrugged. "It's a small town. People talk."

Meemaw slammed her fist on the table, making the dishes rattle and several of us jump. "Luke Montgomery is just what this town needs, someone who doesn't fall for all the nonsense that other people do." She turned her attention to me. "Like that damn Garner Sterling. Throwing ridiculous parades, thinking he's going to rebuild this town with tourism. He's lost his fool mind." She pointed her fork at Teddy. "You've got a vendetta against that man, and you need to let it go. It's poisoning you, boy."

Teddy's hands balled into fists on the table. "Why is Luke Montgomery a man in your eyes, but I'm a boy?"

"Maybe because he acts like one."

Deathly silence hung over the table until my mother broke it.

"You never had good sense when it came to men," Momma said to me with a wicked look in her eyes. She was determined to switch the conversation from her failings to mine. "Especially where that Luke Montgomery is concerned.

Please don't tell me you're doing something desperate like trying to relive your youth with your high school crush."

"He was more than a crush, and you know it, Momma," I said before I could stop myself.

"You claimed it was love," she scoffed. "What could you possibly know about love at seventeen?"

"I obviously didn't learn from you," I snapped back. "You still haven't learned what real love is at forty-six."

"Did you just say *my age* on TV?" my mother asked in horror.

It hadn't escaped my notice that she'd objected to my use of her age, but not what I'd said. "I'm shocked you haven't told the cameramen what angle you want to be filmed at to hide your double chins."

Momma gasped and lifted her hand to her neck. "I do not have double chins! My plastic surgeon gave me a five-year guarantee!"

"Cut!" Lauren shouted, her face red. She marched over to me. "What are you doing? You can't mention the cameras. Now we have to start over again and have your mother and stepfather come back in."

"Like hell you will," Meemaw said with a curled upper lip. "We're gonna eat. I'm too old for all this pretend crap."

"Fine," Lauren huffed. "Just carry on your conversation."

Somebody clapped the clapperboard and there was dead silence. We all ate, looking down at our plates. After nearly thirty seconds, Lauren yelled. "What the hell is this? Talk!"

Obviously Lauren didn't know this family very well if she thought we were going to talk. Baumgartners didn't talk. Ever.

My mother and Burt left an hour later. Momma had tried to plug her pageant business multiple times and Burt's accounting business twice. She'd also tried to coerce Meemaw into selling the farm—and had nearly gotten herself kicked out of the house. But as soon as dinner was over, she stood and looked down at her husband. "Burt, I think we should go. It's such a long drive, and I need to prepare for the Little Miss Peach Pageant in Athens this weekend."

"Of course, dear," he said, pushing his half-finished strawberry pie to the middle of the table.

I realized he hadn't said much more than "yes" or "of course" since he'd walked in and invited me to their house.

"Viola," he said to my grandmother, "thank you for a lovely dinner."

She harrumphed but didn't meet his eyes.

"Summer . . ." His voice trailed off when my mother gave him a deadly look.

Momma turned around and walked toward the door, Burt trailing on her heels. I kept thinking she would have some parting words for me, if nothing else than for the cameras, but when she finally stopped at the front door, one of the cameras on her and the other aimed at the table, my mother said, "Oh, Momma. I forgot. I have a group of girls coming to get headshots by the magnolia tree in the graveyard next week. So don't go doin' something foolish like callin' the police." Then she was gone.

Only she wasn't really gone. Chuck had set up several lights, and my mother was now in her coveted spotlight, telling Lauren and Bill about her evening, and probably that she was sure Suzie Jenkins was going to be crowned Junior Miss Supreme this weekend.

Dixie glanced up at me with a frown, and I knew what she was thinking: *Poor Summer.*

I was tired of people's pity and their scorn. Tomorrow, I was taking charge of my life. I was going to make sure this show worked.

CHAPTER ELEVEN

The next morning after we got into the truck to head into town, I saw that Dixie was glued to her phone.

"Everything okay?"

"There's been a murder," she said with her eyes still fixed on the screen.

"In Sweet Briar?" I asked in shock.

"Yeah. It's on Maybelline's Facebook page."

"Who?"

"She doesn't know. Only that a body was found behind Ruby Garwood's garage. Cale found it while he was driving home last night. Luke's keepin' it all hush-hush."

"When was the last time there was a murder in this town?"

"The county has 'em from time to time, but I can't remember the last time someone was killed in city limits." She paused for a moment. "So what's that mean for our show?"

"I don't know," I said. "Nothing, I suppose. Otto's disappearance seems to be the only real thing we're investigating if you don't count the workman's-comp case, and honestly, I'm not convinced *that's* real." I gasped. "Do you think it could be Otto?"

"Oh, golly," she said. "I hope not."

She continued to look at her phone, then squealed. "Oh! There's something about you!"

"On Maybelline's Facebook page?" *Great.* Had someone seen Luke pull me over last night?

"No! Reality Jane."

The website devoted to reality TV shows? "What?" I jerked my gaze over to her, trying to see her screen. "Is it about me punching that guy?"

"No." She glanced up at me with wide eyes. "It's about you and your mother."

"*What?*"

"'Trouble in Summer Land?'" Dixie read. "'Rumor has it that Summer Butler's split with her mother wasn't so sweet after all. Summer's in her hometown of Sweet Briar, Alabama, filming her new reality TV show, *Darling Investigations*, and a source tells us that Summer had a family reunion with her mother, and sparks flew. Their parting may not have been as amicable as we were led to believe.'"

"Who told them that?" I asked in horror.

Dixie shook her head. "I don't know."

I was still fuming when I pulled up in front of our office a few minutes before eight thirty. Lauren and Karen were waiting for us outside.

"Don't get settled," Lauren said through the truck window. "We're shooting a bunch of location shots today, so we're heading out after Chuck mikes you up."

"Did you tell Reality Jane about me and my mother?" I demanded.

Her eyes widened. "What? No. Why?"

"There's a post about it on the website!"

Excitement washed over her face. "Really?"

"Lauren! Someone who was at the dinner last night leaked my fight with my mother. Aren't you going to reprimand your crew?"

"Hell, I wish I'd thought of it, but who says it was the crew? It could have been someone in your family. It could have been Dixie, for all I know."

Dixie's eyes flew wide. "It wasn't me, Summer. I swear."

"I know." If it was a family member, I knew exactly which one it had been. My mother. She'd do anything for the chance to get publicity for her stupid pageant school.

"If we could get back to our actual work today," Lauren said in a dry tone. "We're staking out the insurance-fraud case. We have another location to catch Nettie's wayward husband with girlfriend number two, and we're heading back to the Dollar General to have another go at the old drunks."

We got out of the truck so Chuck could put on our mikes, and Karen gave us Tommy Kilpatrick's address. I entered the address into the map app on my phone, and we headed for the door, but something just felt *wrong*. Like we were a bunch of frauds.

I'd realized how next to impossible it would be to solve real cases. Granted, I was new to the whole *real* sleuthing thing, but it was kind of hard to sneak up on people when you had an entourage, including a camera guy in the back filming your every move.

We drove in a circle two times with Bill filming before we finally pulled up in front of Tommy Kilpatrick's house to "stake it out."

"This is ridiculous," I said as I shifted the truck into park. "How are we supposed to sneak up on him? And yes, I know you can hear me, Chuck."

I looked in the rearview mirror. Chuck was sitting in the front seat of the camera truck, and he lifted his hand in a one-finger salute while a big grin spread across his face.

Laughing a little, I reached for the messenger bag on the seat between Dixie and me. I'd brought my own laptop today and quickly hooked it up to the hot spot on my phone.

"I did some research last night before I went to sleep, and it looks like this guy went to Sweet Briar High School," I said to Dixie. "He graduated in the class ahead of you. Do you remember him?"

Dixie's face looked strained. "No."

God, I was so stupid. Dixie hadn't graduated. She'd missed her last two years of high school. "Dixie, I'm so sorry. How thoughtless of me."

She shrugged, then changed the subject. "I think you should do the Boll Weevil Parade."

I snorted. "And be second choice to Magnolia Steele?"

Dixie cocked her head. "Magnolia hasn't said diddly, and besides, the mayor didn't know you were coming back to town. So, all in all, you better get ready to ride on the big float."

"Oh, my Lord. There's a big float?" I asked in dismay.

"Well, *of course* there's a big float. It's a parade, ain't it?"

I grimaced. "I thought maybe it was the Sweet Briar High School marching band and Doug Frasier leading his miniature goats down Main Street."

"We'll have those too, but there will be plenty of floats. There's contests too."

"How many contests are there?"

"That's a good question . . ." Dixie leaned forward and squinted her eyes. "Hey. I think Tommy's comin' out of his house." Then she added, "Oh, by the way, I told Mayor Sterling you'd do it."

I started to protest, but sure enough, the front door opened and a guy walked out. "Is it him?" I asked. "He's in the shadows, so I can't tell."

Dixie picked up the camera and peered through the viewfinder. "I can't see his face. It looks like his body build . . . scrawny."

She was right, but if I remembered correctly, that description fit about one-third of the Sweet Briar population. "Where's he goin'?" I asked. "There's no car in the driveway."

"Good question," Dixie said.

The guy walked down his driveway, heading toward the street. As he entered the sunlight, I could see that it was Tommy Kilpatrick looking like he was coming down off a heck of a bender. He stopped in front of his mailbox and pulled out a stack of mail, then turned toward us and waved.

Dixie and I waved back. Some super sleuths we were.

He walked into the road, moving closer to us. "Are y'all lost?"

"No," I said, sneaking a glance at Dixie before shifting my gaze to Tommy. "We're just hanging out on your street, enjoying the fine morning."

He glanced back at the truck behind us. "Hey, I think I saw all y'all in Dr. Livingston's parking lot yesterday."

I considered denying it, but honestly, how could I hope to deny my entourage? "Yeah. We were there."

"Cool." Then he grinned, his face lighting up. "Oh! *Hey!* You're Summer Butler!" He smacked the side of his head, then winced. "You're doin' that show . . . Hey! Can I be on it?"

Little did he know . . . "We got some footage of the parking lot yesterday, so I bet you turned up on the screen."

"Awesome . . . Can I get an autograph? My sister *loved* your show."

"Yeah . . ." I glanced around the truck cab, but Dixie was already handing me a receipt from Maybelline's Café along with a pen. "This is all I have," I said. "I hope it's okay. Who do I make it out to?"

"Deidre." He put the heels of his hands on his temples. "Her birthday's next week. She's going to shit her pants when I give her this!"

"Make sure she has a change of clothes," Dixie said in a sweet voice.

"I will," he said as he took the receipt from me. He pulled his phone out of his pocket. "Hey, will you do that thing?"

"What thing?" I asked, playing dumb.

"You know, that *gotcha* thing." As he said the word, he winked and pointed his finger, thrusting his hip to the side.

I cocked my head and gave him a wry grin. "I can't compete with that. You do it for her instead. I'll even take the video." I grabbed the phone from him and held it up. "Do it again."

"Wouldn't it be better if *you* did it?" he asked.

"No way . . . ," I said. "You do it so much better than me. Come on . . . Let me see it."

He repeated the move, and I got him to do it several more times before he decided he'd had enough.

"Well, we need to get goin'," I said. "But you have a nice day, Tommy."

"How'd you know my name?"

"Uh . . ." I cringed. "Everyone knows *you*, Tommy Kilpatrick. You're like a Sweet Briar baseball legend."

"Summer Butler knows who I am?" he asked, jerking his head back. "This day is totally awesome!"

"Say," I said as I opened my door, "since you're already out here, and you're being so sweet and all, I just thought of something else we could do for Deidre."

"Really? What?"

I'd looked over Tommy's file again last night. He'd claimed he couldn't lift more than fifty pounds, so if we could prove otherwise, I might have a hope in hell of solving this case. "I was thinking you could pick me up and hold me. Dixie here can take a picture, and you can give it to your sister."

His smile fell, and he rubbed his stubble-covered cheek. "I dunno."

"Your sister would totally love it." I slid out of the car and stepped onto the sidewalk next to him.

"It's just that I hurt my back at work a few weeks ago. That was why I was at the doctor's office yesterday. Gettin' a steroid shot."

I grabbed his scrawny bicep and squeezed. "What? A beefcake like you has a back problem? No way." I wrapped my hand around his neck and turned to face Dixie. "Can you snap the photo?"

"You betcha." She slid across the vinyl seat and hopped out of the still-open door.

Tommy made a face that suggested he wasn't so sure this was a good idea, but the glazed look in his eyes and the strong stench of pot on his clothes made me believe I could convince him.

"I bet Summer would print it up and sign it too," Dixie said. "You could show all your friends."

"Okay . . ." But he didn't sound convinced. Still, he bent his knees to pick me up. I expected him to scoop me up—one arm beneath my knees and one behind my back, like he was carrying me over the threshold—but instead he threw me over his shoulder, my hand dangling down to his legs and butt.

Tommy's feet faltered, and he was still bent at the knees. I could tell he was about to fall, so I scrambled for something to hold onto and found the closest thing—his butt.

"Summer Butler's holdin' my ass!" Tommy shouted in triumph right before he toppled over . . . thankfully onto the side I *wasn't* hanging over.

I scrambled up as Tommy started moaning in pain. "I can't move! My back!"

Oh, shit.

"I guess he wasn't pretendin'," Dixie stage-whispered to me behind her hand.

I grimaced. "I guess not."

"What do we do?" Dixie asked.

"I don't know." I shot a glance back to Lauren in the car behind the truck, but her face was expressionless. The guys, however, were all laughing, and Chuck looked like he was actually crying through his laughter. My only comfort was that Bill was shaking so hard the footage might be shit, but then again, that wasn't really good either. "We can't just leave him here."

"Can we help you into the house, Tommy?"

"Just help me up."

Dixie and I got on either side of him and helped hoist him to his feet. When we dropped our hold, he put his hand to his right lower back—the side I'd been on.

"Did you get the shot?" Tommy asked.

Dixie opened her photo app and scrolled through the few photos she'd snapped. "None of them show Summer's face."

No. They were all of my butt, and the angle made my ass look huge.

"They're perfect," Tommy said. He pointed to the screen. "Look, that one shows her coppin' a feel of my buns of steel."

I choked on a snort. More like doughy buns.

Dixie tried not to laugh. "Give me your number and I'll text it to you."

"No, you won't!" I protested.

Dixie turned to me with an innocent look. "You have to give him his photos, Summer."

Dammit. I'd injured the guy, so it was the least I could do. "Fine."

My own phone rang, and I wasn't surprised to see Lauren's number.

"If you're done playing carnival freak show up there," she sniped, "then how about we head across town to catch Earl Peabody with his newest lover?"

I turned away from Tommy. "I can't just leave him here in the street."

"Yes. You can. Let's go."

I hung up, stuffed the phone into my pocket, and turned back to Tommy. "You gonna be okay?"

"Yeah . . ."

"Should we call your doctor or somethin'?" Dixie asked.

"Nah. I'll just take some hydrocodone I got from a friend." He started ambling across the street, then glanced back at me and grimaced. "Thanks for the autograph."

"Yeah, anytime." Now I felt a little guilty for not doing the *Gotcha!* move for him.

"Well," Dixie said in a long drawl, "I guess we solved our first real case."

"Yeah. He wasn't faking."

"But at least they know the truth."

"I guess."

A car horn blared out. Tommy tripped over something in his yard and landed flat on his back, his arms and legs flailing around like a turtle turned topsy-turvy. A murder of crows flew out of a large oak tree, screaming in protest.

Tony walked up behind us, still laughing as he watched Tommy struggle to get up. "We're gonna have to haul his ass inside, aren't we?"

"Yeah . . ."

He shot me a grin. "Taken down by Summer Butler. That'll make for great ratings."

"Can you keep that off the show?" I begged.

He chuckled as he started across the street, then glanced back at me. "Not a snowball's chance in hell."

Chapter Twelve

We spent another hour staking out Earl at his next honey's house. This one was less eventful, which I wasn't sure was such a good thing given Lauren's push for drama, and afterward we headed back to the Dollar General in the hopes of catching Otto's cronies off guard.

I wondered if they would even be there at eleven in the morning, but sure enough, they were lounging at the table, looking less clean-cut than the day before and already three sheets to the wind. Since Karen and Lauren weren't surprised to see them, and each of the guys had a half-empty bottle of Jim Beam, it wasn't hard to deduce what Karen had been up to when she'd disappeared for a while an hour earlier.

Chuck didn't want to risk hooking microphones up on two drunk guys, so he pulled out the overhead mike, and Dixie and I started questioning Al and Fred.

I held out my hand. "Hi, I'm Summer, and I want to ask you a few questions about your friend."

Fred shook my hand with a wicked glint in his eyes. "Tiny?"

"No," I said, squinting in confusion. "Otto."

"Too bad," Fred said with a leer. He reached for his crotch. "Tiny wanted an introduction."

"Eww!" I said, taking several steps backward. What man would willingly name his pecker Tiny?

"What?" Fred asked. "I may be old, but I ain't blind, and you're one foxy lay-dee."

"Did you eat some of Big Dave's jambalaya again?" Dixie asked him like he was a naughty five-year-old.

"Maybe . . . ," he said in a pout.

"I keep telling you to leave that shit alone, Fred. It's gonna ruin you for life."

"Whiskey done ruined me for life."

"Nevertheless," she said, "that jambalaya's gonna get you arrested for indecent exposure, and then you'll have to dry out in jail."

I had so many questions for Dixie when we were done.

"We wanna ask you a few things about Otto, but you be sure and leave Tiny where he is," Dixie said, putting her hand on her hip. She gave Fred a death stare, and he finally put his hands on the table. "When was the last time you saw him?" she continued.

"I don't need to see 'im," Fred said with a leer. "But he'd like to see you, Dixie."

"I've seen enough of Tiny to last a lifetime," Dixie said.

"I think we're gettin' off track here," I said.

"So when did you last see Otto?" Dixie prompted again.

"Sunday morning," Al said. "He was in a bad way."

"How so?" I asked.

"He don't usually come around on Sundays," Al said. "He tends to go to church, but when I asked him why he wasn't at church, he said he'd seen something bad, and he was a bad person for not tellin' Luke what it was."

Dixie shot me a worried look.

"Did you ask him what he saw?" I asked.

"Of course we did," Fred grunted. "I wanted to be the first to tell Maybelline so she could put it on her Facebook page. But he was buttoned up tighter than a nun's habit."

I was tempted to point out the shortfalls of his analogy, but I didn't want to digress down another raunchy path.

"Did you notice anything else about him?" Dixie asked. "What was he wearin'?"

"His church clothes," Al said. "He said he'd planned to go but chickened out at the last minute. Falene stopped by to pick him up, but he hid in his house." When he saw my confusion, he said, "Falene's picked him up every Sunday morning for the last six months. She takes him to church on account of him losin' his driver's license, and his car, years ago."

"So Falene came by to pick him up, but he changed his mind and came here still in his church clothes?" I asked.

"Yeah. But he was already well on his way to bein' drunk by the time I saw him. Then something spooked him, and he took off back home."

"What spooked him?" Dixie asked.

"No idea," Al said. "But he beat it outta here."

"And you haven't seen him since?" Dixie asked.

"Nope," Fred said, "but tell him he still owes me five bucks."

"Yeah, we'll be sure to tell him when we see him," Dixie mumbled, walking over to me.

I clasped my hands in front of me. "Thank you, gentlemen, but we've gotta be goin'. We may be back to ask more questions."

"You know where to find us," Al said.

Fred just snickered.

Lauren called "Cut," then told the crew to pack up and head toward the First Baptist Church downtown so we could interview the minister about Otto.

I told Lauren I needed to go to the bathroom and then slipped inside the Dollar General. Dixie came with me, and we asked the employees if they had seen Otto since Sunday. No one had information for us, and they couldn't remember anything remarkable.

Lauren and the crew had left by the time we went outside, but I wasn't worried since they had to set up at the church.

When we got into the truck, I looked at Dixie. She'd been a little quiet and subdued since our interview outside. "Do you think Otto was really scared, or do you think his pervy friends were making it up to be on TV?"

"Call me crazy, but I think he saw something. He always goes to church. Something must have happened to make him skip it."

"What do you think Otto saw?"

"I have no earthly idea."

"Do you think the minister at the church would know?"

"Maybe . . . ," she said, twisting her mouth to the side.

"What we need to do is ask his neighbors if they saw anything," I said. "If something scared him, then he probably went home, like Al said, don't you think?"

"Yeah."

"I don't know about you," I said, "but I'm getting a bad feeling about this."

She frowned. "Yeah, me too."

"Have you heard anything more about the body that was found this morning?"

"Nothing."

"You know, it's been bugging me that I didn't describe the motorcyclist who dropped that money to Cale. I think I should call him. And maybe tell him what Al and Fred just told us about Otto. Who knows, he might let something slip if this is related to Otto."

"Lauren's gonna be pissed," Dixie said.

"She might not realize it was us. We can pretend it was an anonymous source, like whoever contacted Reality Jane."

Still parked in the Dollar General lot, I got out my phone and looked up the number for the police station.

"I have Cale's number," Dixie said. "If that's what you're lookin' for."

I cast her a questioning glance, and she shook her head. "We went out on a couple of dates. There was no spark, but I still have his number. It would probably be the fastest way to reach him."

"Okay."

I saved the police-station number for future reference, then put in the number Dixie gave me.

"Malone."

"Cale, it's Summer."

"Summer," he said in surprise, "what can I do for you?" He paused, then said, "Please tell me you haven't been snooping around the murder we're investigatin.'"

"God, no," I said. "I know this is a bad time, but I'm calling for a couple of reasons. Did the owner of the money I found turn up at the station? I realized I should have described him a little better."

He hesitated for several seconds. "Sorry. I had to switch gears there. Yeah, as a matter of fact, he did. He was grateful someone as honest as you found it."

"Wasn't that an awful lot of money to be carrying in a paper bag?"

He laughed. "You really have been gone awhile. A lot of people deal in cash here. Ed works on bikes, and he sold one to the guy working the counter at the dry cleaner's."

"Oh."

"You're actually taking this reality show seriously, aren't you?"

"Well . . . I don't know about my producer, but yeah, I am. In fact, I know that Luke talked to Gretchen McBride about Otto being missing, and I have some new information."

"On Otto?" He paused a second. I heard someone calling Cale's name in the background. "Otto runs off from time to time, Summer. He always comes back."

"But something scared him, Cale."

I heard him push out a breath. "Sorry, Summer, I know you're worried, but he'll turn up. Right now we're tryin' to deal with a real case." Then he hung up.

His attitude pissed me off, but I also understood. I told Dixie Cale's explanation about the money, and she didn't look surprised.

"Sounds like Ed Reynolds. He owns a motorcycle shop, and he does like to deal in cash. But he's usually not so careless."

"You didn't recognize him in the parking lot?" I asked. But then again, he'd worn a helmet. Maybe she hadn't.

"I never even saw him. I was too busy trying to distract the crew pretending to be attacked by a giant spider. I sure as Pete hope they don't put that in the show." She motioned to the dashboard. "We better get goin'. Lauren's gonna tan our hides."

Chapter Thirteen

The moment I met the elderly Reverend Timothy Miller, I knew he was a patient man. Lauren was pacing his office with a scowl on her face, but Reverend Miller sat at his desk quietly drinking tea while everyone scurried about his office. Tony had his camera set up behind one of the guest chairs, and Bill's camera was to one side of the desk, practically pointed at the other one.

"Where the hell have you been, Summer?" Lauren snapped.

"I got lost," I said, crossing the room to the minster's desk. "Hi, I'm Summer. Thank you so much for meeting with us today." With Lauren's tight schedule and need to follow everything by the script, I had a feeling she wouldn't approve of our questioning the Dollar General employees. Better to keep it to ourselves, especially since we hadn't discovered anything.

"You got lost in the Dollar General?" Lauren asked in disbelief.

"Have you *been* inside the Dollar General?" Dixie asked. "There's miles and miles of discounts."

Lauren stared at her blankly for a second, then shook her head. "Never mind."

Karen handed me another piece of paper. "We're all set up for you to talk to the reverend. After we finish up, we're going to talk to one of the people in Otto's Sunday-school class in the classroom. We're on a tight schedule, so we're going try to do this in two takes with both cameras rolling."

"Okay." I noticed two chairs in front of Reverend Miller's desk. "I want Dixie sitting in on this one."

"That's not necessary," Karen said.

"Actually," I said, starting to look over the questions, "it is." I held the paper out to Dixie and leaned close to her ear. "What do you think?"

"There's nothing about what happened Sunday," she whispered.

"Exactly," I said with a knowing smile. I sat in one of the chairs, and Dixie sat in the other.

"Reverend, I'm sure Karen and Lauren filled you in on what we're doing, but just to be clear, Dixie and I are going to ask you some questions about Otto Olson. Tony and Bill will be filming, but we're going to pretend they aren't here."

He nodded slightly and set the teacup back down on the desk.

After Karen started the scene, I smiled at the minister. "How long have you known Otto Olson?"

"Many, many years," Reverend Miller said. "I married him and his wife. She'd attended since she was a child."

"Has he always attended church here?"

"He stopped coming for a long while after his tragedy, but he's been in regular attendance for the past three years now. He lost his driver's license several years ago, so different parishioners take turns picking him up. Lately, Falene Able has been picking him up, but he wasn't there when she stopped this past Sunday."

"Do you know why?"

He shook his head. "No."

"Does he miss very often?"

"No. Hardly ever."

"Your parishioners," I said. "They don't mind that Otto drinks?"

"Some do, but most of them hope he'll see the light."

"And you?" Dixie asked. "Do you think Otto will give up drinking?"

He hesitated. "Of course I join my parishioners in their hope, but I'm also a realist. Otto Olson drinks because he's heartbroken. He's biding his time until he can be with his family."

"That's so sad," I said.

"And yet I fear it's true."

Lauren called "Cut," and as we started the scene again, I couldn't help thinking how odd this was. We were discussing a real missing man, yet we were treating the show like a scripted sitcom. We were using Otto's possible tragedy as entertainment, which suddenly felt very wrong.

When Lauren called "Cut" and told everyone to pack up and move to the classroom, I excused myself to go to the restroom, needing a moment to pull myself together. I leaned the back of my head against the wall and took a breath. There was something sinister going on with Otto Olson, and I didn't trust Lauren to let us do a thorough investigation. Cale had blown me off, but I had someone else to try.

A sign I was truly desperate.

Before I could change my mind, I placed a call to the police station.

"Sweet Briar Police," a young woman said. "This is Amber."

"I need to speak to Luke Montgomery."

"Who's calling?"

"A concerned citizen."

She sighed. "If you're calling because of that fit Luke threw at the emergency city council meeting, you'll need to come into the office and fill out the form."

What? "No. That's not why I'm calling. I need to talk to him about a missing person."

"Is this about the dead man who was found behind poor Ruby Garwood's garage?"

She wasn't telling me anything I hadn't already heard, but hearing it from someone at the police station made it more real. "Is it Otto Olson?" But as soon as the question left my mouth, I knew it couldn't be him. If it had been, surely Cale wouldn't have told me Otto would turn up.

"Otto? I forgot that he was missin'. Holy Toledo! This is Summer Butler, isn't it? I know y'all are lookin into Otto's disappearance."

"Yeah. How'd you know?"

"Betty Green knows Gretchen McBride. Your show bein' here is the biggest thing to hit Sweet Briar since Priscilla Trout heard Sherry Baker yelling for help in her bedroom. Willy found her naked as the day she was born and tied up to the bed. He thought something devious had happened, but Sherry fessed up that her boyfriend, Herbie, had tied her up for some kinky sex. He got pissed and left her like that after she compared his performance to Jimmie Dale's."

"I'm not sure we're as exciting as that," I said. "But I am worried about Otto. That's why I'm calling."

"If it makes you feel any better," she said in a low voice, "the dead man's not Otto. I don't know who it is—they won't tell me because they think I'll blab it—but Luke would be more upset if it were Otto. Now, you didn't hear that from me."

I pushed out a sigh of relief, but something she'd said stuck out to me. "Why would Luke be upset?"

"He has a soft spot for Otto. He's a champion for the underdogs in this town like—" She cut herself off. "Like lots of people."

That was weird, but I didn't think now was the time to address it. "I have some information that I should tell Luke."

"Well, he's still at the crime scene, but I can give you his cell number."

"Really?"

"Yeah. Just don't tell him where you got it." Then she quickly rattled off a number I repeated twice in my head.

"Thanks." I was having second thoughts about calling Luke, so I entered his number before I could change my mind.

"Montgomery," he grunted into the phone when he answered.

I closed my eyes when they started to burn with tears. There was something seriously wrong with me if hearing him grunt his name in my ear could make me heartsick. It had been a decade, for God's sake. We'd been no more than kids.

"Hello?" he said when I didn't answer.

Pull yourself together. "Luke, it's Summer."

"What the . . . How you'd get this number?"

"It doesn't matter. I'm calling about something important. Otto Olson."

"I don't have time to get dragged into your show's nonsense, Summer. There was a very real murder in the middle of the night, and I'm trying to figure out who did it."

"I know, and I'm sorry," I said in a sympathetic voice. "But I think something bad happened to Otto."

He paused. "Why do you think that?" he finally said, sounding less antagonistic.

"Because Fred and Al said he was scared on Sunday. Scared enough to not want to go to church."

He paused. "You found that in your investigation?"

"Yeah. We're at the church now, but my producer is treating this like it's a joke, and I have a really bad feelin' about it."

"Okay . . . Look, I really am busy right now, but I hope to be free in a couple of hours. Maybe you can call me then to tell me what else you've found out."

I was shocked he was taking this seriously. "Okay. Thanks."

The next interview didn't take long. The woman tried to convince us that Otto had hidden gold on his old property, then plugged her housecleaning service by saying Otto would have used it if only he'd dig up that gold and start spending it.

After we stopped filming, I pulled Lauren to the side. "Is this the angle we're taking? That Otto has gold hidden on his property?"

"You have to have a few false leads," Lauren said. "Otherwise finding him would be too easy. We'll have a couple of other interviews this afternoon."

"Please don't tell me you've hidden him somewhere to prolong our search."

Her eyes lit up. "I don't, but that's actually a good idea in case he does turn up."

I shook my head in disgust.

Dixie was busy talking to Bill, so I left the room to give myself a chance to think.

I paced the hall for a few minutes and was about to go back to the classroom to see where we were headed next, when a twentysomething man with short brown hair and a scruff of a beard stepped out of a dark classroom and blocked my path.

After all the cloak-and-dagger nonsense, I nearly screamed—then I noticed the broom in the man's hand. *Get a grip, Summer.* He was the janitor, but his plain blue T-shirt and jeans had thrown me off.

"I know you're lookin' for Otto. I know something." His voice shook and he looked nervous.

"What do you know?"

He grabbed my arm and pulled me into the dark classroom he'd just left. "Otto hasn't been right for the last couple of weeks. He's been nervous and on edge. I asked him if everything was okay, and he told me he didn't know."

This fit with what Fred and Al had told us.

"But there's more." He looked uncertain, then said, "I went fishing out at Lake Edna yesterday, and there's a path that leads into the woods. I saw a bike there, and I could swear it was Otto's."

"How do you know it's Otto's?"

"Sometimes his rides to church flake out, or he needs to go to the store or somethin' and his sister can't bring him. It's pretty recognizable. It has big ol' tires and a basket in the front, and the color's all messed up. It used to be red, but one day he was drunk and spray-painted it blue, only it didn't stick very well. The bike I saw at the lake looked just like it."

"Lake Edna?"

"Yeah, at the Sunny Beach rec area. Out on the walking trail. It was chained off, but I saw the bike out there." I knew the place well. Luke and I had gone there together countless times over the summer I'd spent in Sweet Briar.

I nodded, feeling sick to my stomach. "Thanks, but how do you think his bike got out there? That has to be twenty miles. That would probably take him all day."

"Dunno. That's why I wasn't sure it was his, but the more I think on it, the more I wonder."

Now I had to convince Lauren to go out there.

Everyone was almost done packing up by the time I got back, and Lauren announced we were breaking for lunch before we started investigating a new case in the afternoon.

"I thought you said we had more interviews about Otto's disappearance," I said.

"Two of them flaked out," she snarled. "Now we're scrambling. This show is cursed."

"Dixie and I are gonna run out to Lake Edna."

Dixie's eyes widened.

"What in the hell for?" Lauren asked.

"I haven't been out there since I was seventeen," I said. "I want to see it for old times' sake. Besides, it's our lunch break, so as long as we're back before call time, what does it matter?"

Her brow furrowed and she studied me for several seconds. "Fine. But take Bill with you to get some B-roll of the place."

"Hey!" Bill protested. "It's *my* lunch break too."

This was working out better than I could have hoped. If we found his bike, we could have Bill film it. "We'll feed you," I said. "There used to be a really good chicken place on the way. Is it still there, Dixie?"

The way Dixie was watching me told me that she knew I was up to something. "Yeah, Mama Jane's has the best Southern fried chicken south of the Mason-Dixon Line." Then she gave him a flirty smile. "You can ride in the middle. There's plenty of room. No need to be ridin' in the back like you do with Tony."

His gaze dipped slightly to her generous cleavage. "Okay."

I scowled. I wanted Bill to come with us, but I didn't like Dixie using herself like that.

"Okay, get going!" Lauren said, waving her arm in a big sweep.

Bill picked up his camera case and started for the door.

I started after him, then stopped. "What about Chuck?"

Lauren's face scrunched up in irritation. "Why do you need him? Bill's only getting B-roll."

"Okay."

Dixie and I trailed Bill to the truck, leaving the rest of the crew in the poor reverend's office. Dixie reached over and turned off my mike, then pulled off hers and turned it off as well. "What's really goin' on?" she whispered while Bill put his gear in the back.

I told her about my call to Luke and what the janitor had said. She was silent for several seconds before she said, "I'm surprised you called Luke."

"Well," I said, sounding defensive, "he was the one Gretchen talked to in the first place. I thought maybe that gave him automatic possession of the case."

"You might be right, but you should have called Willy." She shook her head. "No, you should have told me, and we could have figured it out together."

"You're right. I'm sorry."

My apology caught her by surprise. She finally said, "Okay, now that we have that established, what's your plan? Obviously you want Bill there."

"I do, but not at the price of using you to get it."

She waved her hand, and I grabbed it and pulled her to a halt. "Don't do it, Dixie. Don't use your body and your looks to get men to do what you want."

Horror filled her eyes and she jerked loose. "You think I'm a slut?"

"That's not what I mean at all." I ran a hand over my head, frustrated that this was coming across wrong. "Look, Dixie, although I've done a shitty job of showing it over the last few years, I *love* you. I don't want you to get hurt. I know firsthand that letting men use you and treat you like an object chips at your soul little by little. Don't do it. It might seem like it's worth it in the short run, but you'll hate yourself for it later."

The hardness in her eyes faded. "Is that what happened to you with your costar from *Gotcha!*?"

Little did she know. "Something like that. But he was only one of several. Just don't do it, okay? We'll always find another way."

She threw her arms around my neck and pulled me into a hug without saying a word.

I squeezed her back, then noticed Bill standing at the back of the truck and looking like he was having second thoughts.

"What's wrong?" I asked as I released Dixie and headed back toward him, prepared to do a lot of sweet talking.

"I don't have anything to tie the camera down, and I don't want it sliding around."

"Do you need to sit back there with it?" Dixie asked. "Because it's a beautiful day, and I would be happy to sit back there with you."

I sucked in an angry breath, pissed that we'd just had that conversation and she was doing the exact opposite of what I'd told her, but she turned her back to him as he lowered he truck gate to climb in.

"I know what you're thinkin'," Dixie whispered to me, "but I wanna do this. He's actually a nice guy."

"He's a lech," I hissed back. "I saw him checkin' out your boobs, Dixie."

"So what? Men check women out." Then, before I could protest more, she spun around, her long platinum-blonde hair swinging with her. "Can you help me up?"

I nearly snorted. She'd grown up on a farm. She'd been crawling in truck beds before she could walk. And I would know. I'd been there with her. But I got into the truck and turned over the engine, telling myself that Dixie was a grown woman, capable of making her own decisions.

So why did I suddenly feel so responsible for her?

CHAPTER FOURTEEN

Dixie was right—it was a beautiful day. It was the middle of April, and being so close to the Gulf of Mexico, Sweet Briar and Bixley County heated up a lot faster than the rest of the country. But we were enjoying a good spell—the expected high was in the midseventies, and the sun was shining.

We stopped off at Mama Jane's, a hole-in-the-wall restaurant that only sold fried chicken and the fixings out of the window of what looked like a dilapidated shack. Dixie had called ahead, and they had a huge bucket of chicken, mashed potatoes and gravy, green beans, and rolls waiting for us when we pulled up. I realized too late that I only had fourteen dollars in my wallet—not nearly enough to pay for the twenty-five-dollar lunch, and my credit cards were mostly maxed out. But Bill, in his effort to impress Dixie, was already hopping out of the truck to pay for it. The looks my cousin was giving him suggested that she was actually into him, but I worried that acting was in the Baumgartner family blood. I'd have to interrogate her later.

Ten minutes later, I pulled into the Sunny Beach rec area and drove all the way to the end, parking close to the trail by the picnic shelter. This was where the janitor claimed to have seen Otto's bike, but I didn't make any mention of it when we got out, instead suggesting that we all go sit on the pier and enjoy the sunshine and the view. I'd figure out an excuse to investigate after we ate.

The restaurant had included plates and plasticware, so we filled our plates and dove in.

"Oh, my word," I said through a mouthful of chicken. "I'm gonna get so fat while I'm here."

"Please," Dixie scoffed. "Maybelline was right. You need more meat on you. I'd never work out in Hollywood because I like to eat too much." To prove her point, she took a big bite from the chicken leg in her hand.

"I think you look perfect just the way you are," Bill said, giving her puppy-dog eyes.

Frowning, I scrutinized him closely. He'd come off as a player earlier, but I had to admit he seemed pretty smitten with her.

Dixie laughed and waved her hand. "Oh, come on. Summer's the star. Not me."

"You're just as pretty as she is," he said, then lowered his voice and added, "if not prettier."

"Sittin' right here," I said in a dry tone.

Bill laughed and turned to me. "I'm just kiddin', Summer, but I have to say you're not like what I'd heard about you."

My back stiffened, but I tried to hide my unease. "Oh, really. What did you hear?"

He cringed. "Never mind. I shouldn't have said anything."

"I'm not sensitive," I said. "I know what people say—or used to when everything went down with Conner Blake and the contract dispute with the show."

Still, he hesitated.

"Here's what I know people were saying—that I was a self-centered diva who didn't like to share the limelight. How'm I doin'?"

His cheeks reddened. "Summer . . ."

"I know that Lauren warned you all about me. Did she regurgitate the same old stories?"

He sat up straighter, looking pissed. "Is that why you agreed so quickly to bring me with you guys? So you could quiz me about Lauren?"

"Really?" I laughed. "I don't need to quiz you to know she tried to poison you all. And I don't even really need to know what she said. All I can do is be me and try to prove whatever she said is a lie or a misinterpretation of the facts." I hesitated, wondering how much to tell him, then decided I didn't trust him yet.

"So why didn't you fight Lauren when she told me to come along?" he prodded.

"Because we're gonna be workin' together for another two weeks, and I figured the best way to get to know me and Dixie was one-on-one. Nothing sinister about that, right?"

"Yeah . . ." He didn't sound convinced.

"Look, I know a lot of what we're doin' is as fake as a three-dollar bill," I said, realizing my Southern accent was creeping in. "But I think the Otto Olson case is real. So why's Lauren wasting our time with crazy nonsense like buried gold?"

"Filler," Bill said with a shrug. "And false leads, like Lauren said. She's right. It can't be *too* easy."

"The police aren't very interested in this case, so we could make a difference. We could help Gretchen get some peace."

"What exactly are you suggesting?" Bill asked. "Renegade sleuthing?"

I hadn't gotten that far. "I don't know," I admitted. "But I don't want to be the butt of people's jokes anymore. I want people to take me seriously, and we both know that's not Lauren's goal."

"Summer, I sympathize, I really do, but I'm not sure what I can do about it." "I know."

He and Dixie spent the next ten minutes making small talk. Turned out Bill had grown up not too far from Sweet Briar, but on the Georgia side, and was living in Atlanta now. After I finished eating, I stood and said, "I need to walk off this food or I won't fit in my jeans tomorrow. You two can stay here if you want."

Dixie gave me a worried look. "Are you sure?"

"Yeah. I'll text you if I get into trouble."

"What kind of trouble could you get into?" Bill asked.

Dixie winked. "You just never know with Summer."

I threw my trash into a metal bin by the picnic shelter and then jogged to the truck. I grabbed the camera in case I saw something useful. I knew I only had about ten minutes before we needed to leave if we were going to be back in time, and while I was tempted to say screw it and not worry about showing up late, I really did need to choose my battles.

I headed toward the trail, stepping over the metal chain blocking the path, ignoring the sign that said CLOSED FOR MAINTENANCE. The trail went into the woods for about ten feet before curving right, away from the lake. It curved again after about twenty feet and then continued on for another hundred feet or so. I was definitely heading away from the lake.

I was just about to turn back, sure I was on the wrong trail, when the path broke out into a clearing surrounded by dense trees to my right. My eyes adjusted to the shadows, and I spotted a bike on the far side of the clearing—blue and red, just as the janitor had described it. I started snapping photos as I approached. Glancing around to take in my surroundings, it struck me how remote this place was. The janitor said he'd found the bike while he was out here fishing, but this path twisted *away* from the lake. It didn't make sense.

I heard a tree branch crack in the patch of trees to my left, and I froze, wondering if this had been a setup. The hair on the back of my neck stood on end, and I held my breath.

God, I was an idiot. I had followed a remote path into the woods, looking for a man I had begun to suspect had met with foul play. So here I was, alone and certain someone was out there watching me, and I was completely defenseless. Well, not completely . . . I'd learned a few self-defense moves, although I couldn't think of a single one at the moment. The camera was heavy, so I could use it as a weapon, but Lauren would kill me if broke it—not that she planned to use any of the photos I had taken.

Get it together, Summer!

There was another crack, this time more directly in front of me. Common sense told me that it was nothing—probably an animal that was more scared of me than I was of it—but instinct told me the noise was from a human, and they were watching me now. What was the smart thing to do? Call 911? Over a broken tree branch? Luke would *never* listen to me, then. Maybe it was just some (mostly) harmless drunks or a couple of kids skipping school. This land was supposed to be closed to the public right now. Neither of us was supposed to be out here; maybe *they* were hiding from *me*.

"Hello," I called out. "Who's there?" I took a step forward to investigate, then stopped abruptly. I was acting like every stupid woman in a horror movie.

I pulled out my phone and texted Dixie.

I found Otto's bike in the woods. I think someone is here watching me, but no proof. Bring Bill.

If the noise was in front of me, then I needed to escape the way I'd come, but I didn't like the thought of turning my back to whoever was out there. I started taking slow steps backward, trying not to look like I was running away, which was stupid. It was a lot slower this way. Then I heard another sound in the trees to my left, immediately followed by a succession of crunching sounds to the right.

Oh, my God. Was there more than one person out here?

Run.

I spun around and started to take off, only to immediately trip. My arms windmilled to keep me from falling, but I ended up in the woods to my right, away from the parking lot. The camera hanging from my neck hit me hard in the abdomen, nearly knocking the wind out of me, while my forehead smacked hard into a low tree branch. My vision began to darken and tunnel.

Oh, crap. I couldn't pass out.

I blinked hard a couple of times, trying to regain my sight. The branch had stopped my fall, and I'd ended up on my knees.

Get up. Run!

But my coordination was off, and I fell forward, landing on my hands, the camera swinging wildly between my arms. Something sharp pricked my palm, and I started to crawl, but which way was the path?

Calm down, Summer. Think. I stopped and sucked in a deep breath as I tried to make sense of my surroundings.

More broken tree branches snapped behind me, but the same sound was also coming from my left—there were definitely two people chasing me. I started crawling frantically, pretty certain I was crawling *away* from the trail.

"Summer?" Dixie called out, but her voice was distant.

"Here!" I shouted, but I still hadn't regained my full breath, and it came out hoarse and weak. "Here!"

The noise behind me was getting closer, so I continued crawling. I was moving away from my cousin, but now I was worried I'd put Dixie in danger too. The woods were dense, even this close off the trail, and between my fuzzy vision and the tears now filling my eyes, I was struggling to see where I was going.

I heard what sounded like a man's grunt to my left. I scrambled forward, my hand hitting something cold and damp. When I looked to see what it was, my mouth dropped in horror. I was face-to-face with a very dead Otto Olson.

I recoiled in horror and started to scream. The camera swung and smacked into my ribs. It was then I saw movement in my still-fuzzy peripheral vision. Suddenly pain filled my head and everything turned to black.

Chapter Fifteen

I woke to Dixie's voice. Something soft was under the back of my very sore head. "Summer? Oh, my God, Summer? Do something, Bill!"

"I've already called 911," he said, sounding uncharacteristically serious.

I blinked my eyes open and saw Dixie's tear-streaked face staring down at me. I realized the something soft was her legs. My head was on her lap.

"Oh, thank God," she said in a broken voice. "She's awake."

"Otto," I gasped.

"He's over there." She tilted her head to the side. Several tears fell down her cheeks. "We moved you away from him once we realized you'd fainted."

Was that what had happened? It all came rushing back, along with the horror of the final seconds before I blacked out. I sat upright, then winced and grabbed my head as sharp pain shot through it. "There's someone out there."

"What are you talking about?" she asked, her eyes full of concern. "There's no one out there. Bill looked."

I glanced back and forth between them, trying to piece everything together. "But I was sure . . ." I felt like I was forgetting something.

"You have a huge lump on your forehead," Dixie said. "How'd you get it?"

"I heard someone in the woods. I tried running away, but I stumbled into the trees and hit my head. The back of my head hurts too." Everything seemed to be in slow motion, and I felt *so heavy*. All I wanted was to fall asleep. "I'm gonna lie back down and take a nap."

"No," Bill said, reaching for my arm. "Help me, Dixie. We should get her to the clearing."

"Then I can take a nap," I said, my eyelids drooping. Dixie grabbed my other arm, but I could hardly get my feet to work.

"No falling asleep, Summer," Bill said in a sharp voice, giving me a shake. "You have to stay awake."

"Is she okay?" Dixie asked.

"I'm sure she has a concussion. We need to keep her awake until the ambulance gets here."

We finally made it to the clearing, and I fell to my knees. I felt like I weighed a thousand pounds, and I was exhausted from the effort of standing. All I wanted was to lie down and rest.

"Summer," Bill said, pulling me back up into a sitting position, "no, no you can't lie down. Stay awake." He leaned into my face. "Look at me. Keep your eyes open."

"Your breath smells like chicken," I murmured, then blinked hard. Bill was right. I needed to get myself together. "Where's your camera?"

"Over there." He motioned to the camera lying in the dirt. "I dropped it when we heard you screaming. Lauren's going to kill me."

Focus. We had a job to do. "You have to get it, and film before the sheriff gets here."

"What are you talking about?"

"Otto's bike is over there by the tree," I said. "The janitor at the church told me he saw it out here. That's why I wanted to come . . . to look for it."

"What bike?"

I blinked again. Sure enough, there was no bike. "It was there. I swear. I took photos of it." Then I glanced down and realized the camera wasn't around my neck. "Where's the camera?" I turned to my cousin, starting to panic. "Dixie, where is it?"

"I don't know. I didn't see it."

"It must have fallen off when you fell," Bill said.

"No." I shook my head and instantly regretted it. "It didn't." I wasn't sure how I knew, but I felt certain I was right. My ribs ached and I tenderly touched them. "You need to find it. It has photos of the bike and the woods. Whoever was out there might be in the shots."

"Summer," Bill said, "there's no one out there. You just suffered a concussion. You're confused."

"I'm not confused, at least not about the bike. It was there." I struggled to get to my feet, but Bill gave me an impatient look and tried to push me back down.

"Summer, you need to wait for the EMTs to check you out. You probably have to go to the hospital."

I shoved his arm away. "Dixie, help me."

She glanced up at Bill as though asking for permission.

"No," I barked. "Don't look at him. Look at me. I'm not crazy, and I'm not confused. I saw it. I need you to help me over there."

"Summer."

The first wail of sirens filled the air, and I knew we didn't have much time. "Dixie, *please.*"

Dixie grabbed my arm and helped me up, then we stumbled closer. My vision was still off—I was now seeing double—so I squinted to try to focus. "It was there."

Dixie let go of me and moved closer. Suddenly, her body jerked upright. "I think I see a tire track." She spun around to face Bill. "Get your camera. We need proof."

He leaned over to look and then glanced up at me. "Jesus. You're right."

Before I could process what was going on, he had his camera out and pointed at me. "I'm not sure how this will turn out. It's pretty dark back here, but we'll give it a go." He lifted his hand and counted down with his fingers— three, two, one—and then showed me a fist, or at least I thought he did. I was having trouble seeing it.

"Summer," he said in a clear voice. "Tell us what happened."

"I was in the woods on a trail here by Lake Edna. The trail opened into this clearing," I said, sweeping my arm to indicate the area around us. A wave of nausea rolled through me, but I ignored it as Bill slowly panned the camera around.

The sirens were becoming louder. We didn't have much time.

"I found the bike over there," I pointed in that direction, and Bill did a slow pan. "But then I heard a sound in the woods. While it could have been an animal, I just *knew* it was a person. I texted Dixie to bring Bill, the cameraman. But I couldn't wait for them—I felt like I was in danger, so I started to run. I tripped and stumbled into the woods, still being chased. Then I fell. Everything went a little hazy after that. I vaguely remember finding Otto Olson's body, I . . . I think someone hit my head from behind"—Dixie gasped, but Bill didn't stop filming—"and the next thing I knew, I woke up. Dixie and Bill had found me, but the bike and my camera—which I'd used to take photos of the bike—were gone."

"How'd you know the bike was out here?" Bill asked.

"I met the janitor at the First Baptist Church in Sweet Briar earlier, and he told me he'd seen Otto Olson's bike off this path. He was here yesterday, fishing at the lake, when he spotted the bike. So when we broke for lunch, I decided to come check it out." I paused. "I'm sorry, Bill."

We could hear the voices of the emergency personnel now. Bill pointed his camera at the ground and looked me in the face. "It's okay. I believe you now."

"Believe what? That I wasn't trying to trick you?"

"That too, but also that you really want to do this . . . solve crimes, not just be on camera."

"I do."

"Then I'm all in."

I didn't have time to ask him what he meant, because the sheriff's deputies entered the clearing.

"Where's the victim?" one of the deputies asked. He was young and cute, and Dixie instantly perked up.

I wondered how Bill was going to handle that.

"Which victim?" Dixie asked. "The one with the concussion or the dead one?" Then she gave him a soft smile. "I bet you want the live one." She wrapped an arm around my back. "She's right here."

The deputy's gaze shifted to Bill, who had just put his camera down.

An older deputy followed behind him. "Hey, you're that girl from *Gotcha!* Are you filming that show here?"

Bill headed over to the other deputies, presumably to tell them about poor Otto.

I grimaced. "Yes and no . . ."

"Shouldn't you pick her up and carry her to the ambulance?" Dixie asked the younger one, giving him a coy look.

His mouth quivered with the hint of a grin. "That's not how it's typically done."

"She was passed out on the ground not more than ten minutes ago, and she was out for a good five minutes. I don't think she should be standing around like this."

Concern washed over his face.

"She has a point, Ms. . . ." The older deputy said, looking at me as though searching for my real name.

"If either of you call me the *Gotcha!* girl, you're the ones who are gonna need to be carried out of here."

The older deputy grinned. "You're Summer Butler. And the fact you're so feisty is a good sign. I'm Deputy Robinson, and this is Deputy Dixon."

Dixie beamed at the younger deputy.

This hardly seemed like the time for matchmaking.

Deputy Dixon moved closer and motioned to the side of the clearing. "Do you want to sit down?"

"No. Staying here is creeping me out. Can I go sit on the tail bed of my truck until the ambulance arrives?"

"Yeah," he said, sounding surprised. "I'll walk with you."

"You don't have to," I said. "I'm sure you have other things to take care of here."

"You were the one to find the body, right? The caller said you'd passed out after finding a body."

"I didn't pass out. I was chased into the woods, and I think someone hit me in the back of the head and knocked me out." My memories of what had happened between finding the bike and waking up were all fuzzy.

Both deputies did a double take.

"Someone attacked you?" Deputy Robinson asked.

"Yeah, and before we leave the clearing, I need to point out that when I got here, there was a bike right here." I gestured to where it had been. "Now it's gone, and the camera I used to take photos of it is gone too."

Deputy Dixon turned serious. "Now I really need to stick with you."

The ambulance arrived moments after I sat on the tailgate. Deputy Dixon talked to the EMTs for a while and then returned to me. "I need to go check on what's going on in the clearing, but you'll be in the EMTs' capable hands."

"Thank you, Deputy."

He nodded, then headed off.

The EMTs gave me a quick evaluation and said I needed to go to the hospital in Sweet Briar to be seen by a doctor.

"I need to tell my cousin Dixie first," I said. "She'll be worried if I just leave." I pulled out my phone and sent her a text to meet me at the hospital.

Just as I got into the back of the ambulance, I was certain I saw a white van driving off.

Where had I seen one before? My head was too muddled to figure it out.

A half hour later, I was in the Sweet Briar Hospital ER, wearing nothing but a hospital gown and what little was left of my dignity. But Lauren quickly dispatched of the latter after she and Karen walked into my exam room.

"If you're going to cause drama, couldn't you have the good sense to get it on camera?" my producer demanded.

"Lauren . . ."

"Don't *Lauren* me. You ruined everything!" she shouted at the top of her lungs. "Finding Otto Olson was our entire season!"

I couldn't believe her. A man was dead, and she was pissed that she'd lost her overarching story. "But we don't know how he died, Lauren. We can find out who killed him."

"No," she said. A blood vessel throbbed on her forehead. "You will do absolutely nothing unless I tell you to." She pointed her finger at me. "You don't even shit unless you have permission from me."

"Lauren . . ."

"Do you understand?" she forced through gritted teeth.

"We can use this," Karen interrupted with a fearful look.

Lauren turned toward her, some of her anger fading. "Go on."

"Obviously we need a new, big mystery, but this is going to create a huge buzz. People are going to want to see the episode where she finds the body. Besides," Karen added, "people are already talking about her rift with her mother. This could make national headlines."

"We don't have any film of it," Lauren said, her brow furrowed.

"Bill's still out there. We can have him get a bunch of footage and then have Summer do a voice-over of what happened."

Lauren threw up her hands in excitement. "Oh, my God. You're brilliant."

The door opened and a nurse forced her way around Karen. "What in the Sam Hill is going on in here?"

Neither of them said anything.

"Ms. Butler has a concussion," the nurse said. "This shoutin' could be causin' her harm, not to mention you're disturbin' the other patients."

"How soon until she can get out of here and get back to work?" Lauren asked.

"She's had a concussion, ma'am. Do you realize how serious that is?"

"She's talking and sitting," Lauren said. "That's all I need. Ticktock. Time's wasting. Where are her clothes?"

The nurse gasped in shock, then said, "The doctor is considerin' keepin' her overnight."

"What?" I asked.

Lauren shook her head. "Nope. That won't work with her schedule."

"Even if she wanted to leave without the doctor's permission, we aren't allowed to let her go until the deputy takes her statement."

"Because she found a body?" Lauren asked in disbelief. "Surely they don't think she killed him."

"Not just that, ma'am," the nurse said, starting to get pissed. "She was attacked."

I'd hoped for more sympathy from Lauren at the mention of my attack, but I wasn't prepared for the gleam of excitement in her eyes.

"Really?" she asked me.

"Yeah . . ."

"Bill said you got the concussion from running into a tree just before you saw the body."

"Well, that was the first one," I reluctantly conceded. Why hadn't he told her the whole story? Maybe he'd texted her while I was passed out. "I was running from whoever was stalking me in the woods. After I found Otto, I think someone hit me on the back of the head and took my camera."

Lauren turned to the nurse. "She can't leave, but can she have visitors?"

The nurse narrowed her eyes. "Within reason."

Lauren's grin turned wicked. "I'll be right back."

The nurse watched her leave and said, "We can ban her from your room, you know."

I sighed. "That will only make it worse. Maybe she'll get it out of her system."

The pitying look the nurse gave me confirmed it was wishful thinking.

Lauren and Karen were back about five minutes later with Tony, Chuck, and Troy the lighting guy in tow.

"I suspect the nurse will try to kick us out," Lauren told them as they entered the room, "but let's get what we can."

Chuck quickly hooked me up with a new mike since my other one was in the truck, while Tony and Troy talked about camera angles and lighting.

"I want you to look more injured," Lauren said as she squinted at me. "It's too bad we don't have a makeup artist to give your bruises more definition."

"What?"

"We can get that tomorrow," Karen said. "Plus, they'll naturally look worse anyway."

"Good thinking," Lauren told her. Turning to me, she said, "We're going to play up the angle that you were out there working on the case. You got attacked because you got too close to the murderer."

"Or a rapist," Karen added, sounding a little too hopeful for my liking.

My shudder sent a new wave of pain through my brain. "I'm not going to suggest either of those things. We don't know what happened yet."

"The truth is what we present," Lauren said. "And if we repeat it enough, people will believe it."

"That's wrong."

"And yet it's what you signed up for," she said in a short tone.

"I'll tell you what happened, but I won't say the person who attacked me was a murderer for certain."

Lauren remained surprisingly quiet.

A few minutes later, Tony and Troy were ready, and Chuck said the sound was good. I felt exhausted. I eased myself down on the gurney—the back semireclined—suddenly feeling every ache and pain in my body.

"Summer," Lauren said, her voice full of sympathy, "tell us about your vicious attack."

"I was chased through the woods, and then I found poor Otto. I . . . I was looking at him when I think someone hit me on the head and stole my camera," I said, pretty much repeating what I'd just said to her off camera.

"Cut!" Lauren shouted. "What the hell, Summer? You know how this goes. You need to drag the story out and play it up for the camera."

"So that's how it's done," I heard Luke say in a dry voice.

I instantly shot upright. The room spun and a strong wave of nausea rolled through me. I swallowed the taste of bile. "I need a bowl."

Lauren looked at me like I'd lost my mind, but Karen's eyes filled with horror. She clearly knew why I needed the bowl, but that hadn't translated to her getting it for me. She seemed frozen in place.

Luke had entered the room, and he was casting a contemptuous gaze on the crew.

"What are you doing here, Officer?" Lauren asked. "I thought this incident was being handled by the sheriff's department."

"It is, but it involves the death of one of my residents, so I thought I'd check in with the person who stumbled upon his body."

The room was spinning and my stomach was churning. I closed my eyes, hoping everything would settle down, but after two seconds it was only getting worse. "I need a bowl," I repeated in a strained voice.

No one paid me any attention, though Karen was still looking at me like I was about to explode.

"That's so sweet of you, Officer," Lauren said.

"That's chief," Luke said, his tone so cold I could feel the bite several feet away. "Chief Montgomery. I'm the police chief in this town."

"Nice to finally meet you," Lauren said in a low, sexy tone I wasn't used to hearing from her.

I cracked an eye, surprised to see her trying to give him a come-hither look. Apparently, even Lauren Chapman wasn't immune to Luke's questionable charm. But opening my eyes only made the nausea situation worse. At this point, I was positive I was going to barf; it was only a matter of how quickly it occurred.

"Let's not beat around the bush," Luke said. "Your entire production is disrupting my town. I haven't had a murder in three years, and now there have been two within a twenty-four-hour period. Don't think it's lost on me that they both happened after you and your circus came to town."

I had to admit he had a point, and I might have said so, but I was too busy trying not to vomit. I was past the point of repeating my request for a bowl. I slid off the gurney to find one myself.

"Are you insinuating this is my fault?" Lauren asked in disbelief. "Let me remind you that Otto Olson was found out by the lake, which is out of your jurisdiction."

I couldn't figure out where I was going, but opening my eyes made everything worse. I cracked them slightly, and my stomach churned in protest. *Oh,*

Lord. If I could make it to the sink on the other side of Lauren and Luke . . . But everything was spinning, and I was weaving like a drunk person.

"Summer," Karen said from the other side of the room, "maybe you should sit down. You're about to fall."

Luke's eyes widened slightly when he saw me. He rushed over and grabbed my arm to steady me, but the sudden change in my balance released the tenuous hold I had on my stomach.

I barfed all over his shirt.

The entire room gasped in horror, but I was too busy falling to the ground to care. Luke's grip on my arm tightened, and his free arm slid around my back, the only thing holding me up.

"Summer!" Lauren cried out, stepping back from the puddle on the floor, but when I turned to face her, I threw up again, hitting from her thighs to her shoes.

Lauren screamed.

The sound split my head, and everything went black again.

Chapter Sixteen

There was a cold rag pressed to my head when I woke up, but my eyelids felt too heavy to open. My head was still killing me, and the smell of vomit made me nauseated all over again. I released a moan and tried to sit up.

"Whoa," Luke said in a soothing tone as he gently pushed me back down. "You need to lie still."

"What happened?" I croaked out.

"After your amazing reenactment of Linda Blair's scene in *The Exorcist*, you passed out." The amused tone in his voice made me feel more relieved. He didn't hate me.

"And Lauren?"

"She ran out screaming, and the rest of them ran with her."

"That almost makes it worth it." I cracked an eye, relieved to see he'd changed into a scrub shirt. "You should let your momma see you wearing that," I said. "She always wanted you to be a doctor instead of a cop."

"Momma died a couple of years ago."

I cringed. "Luke, I'm so sorry. I know how close you were to her."

He didn't say anything, but I could tell his guard was back up.

"And your dad?"

"Still as ornery as ever." He paused. "But Momma got her doctor. Levi graduated from med school a couple of months before she died."

"Was it an accident?" I asked.

He cracked a grin. "We all think he paid someone to take all his exams, so you could say it was an accident." Then his grin faded. "Pancreatic cancer. By the time she found out, it was too late. It all happened fast."

"I'm sorry," I repeated.

He remained silent, then after several seconds he asked, "What happened out there, Summer?"

"I was lookin' for Otto," I said, feeling defeated. Sure, I'd found him, but I hadn't found him in the way I'd hoped. "I have to tell poor Gretchen. She's going to be so upset." My voice broke. I'd failed her, just like I'd failed everything else in my life.

"You really care about her," he said more to himself than to me. "Don't worry about tellin' Gretchen. I went to see her as soon as I got the news."

"Thank you. How's she doin'?"

"She's upset . . . and grateful to you for finding him. He could have been out there for a while before someone stumbled upon him."

I may have found him, but I hadn't found him alive. It seemed like a hollow consolation.

I turned to look up at him, surprised to see the worry on his face. When his brown eyes caught mine, an electrical current flowed through my veins, filling me with a yearning I hadn't felt in years. We'd built separate lives, but all it took was standing in his orbit for me to realize no man had ever come close to making me feel what I'd felt with him years ago. Still, I couldn't ignore that we'd been kids then. What if I'd idealized our connection? And even if I hadn't, there was no denying we were different people now.

His hand lifted to my face, tenderly caressing my cheek as his eyes searched mine. "Who attacked you, Summer?"

"I don't know," I said. I tried to hold his gaze, but my eyelids felt like they had tiny weights on them. I told him everything, including someone chasing me in the woods, then looked up at him, finding it difficult to open my eyes enough to see him. "When I came to, my camera was gone and so was the bike."

His hand now rested on my arm, and he squeezed it slightly. "What camera? What bike?"

I explained it to him, and his face was so unreadable, I couldn't tell whether he believed me or not. "I still need to give Deputy Dixon my statement."

He wove his fingers with mine, taking care with the IV lines sticking out of the top of my hand. "I'll tell him what you said so they'll know what they're workin' with, but he can get your official statement when you're feelin' better. Probably tomorrow."

"Tomorrow? I'll be back to work tomorrow."

"Back to work? Summer, you suffered a serious concussion. The doctor was worried about bleeding in your brain until the CAT scan said you were okay."

"But we only have two weeks . . ."

"Two weeks to what?"

"To film the show."

"Summer." His voice was tight. "That show almost got you killed."

"I signed a contract, Luke."

His body tensed. "And again with a fucking contract."

This was déjà vu from twelve years ago. From when I returned to Hollywood at the end of the best summer of my life.

Part of me screamed to tell him that I was doing this to save the farm, but I knew there were people eavesdropping. I couldn't risk Meemaw finding out through Maybelline's Facebook page. Still, his attitude was pissing me off. "Are you kidding me?" I asked, trying to sit up, but my head hurt too much to follow through with the plan. "You of all people should understand the concept of following the law."

He sighed. "We're never going to agree on this. You're going to insist on following through on your contract, and then you're going to leave. Just like last time."

"I don't know what I'm going to do when I'm done," I said. "I'm just tryin' to make it through the next two weeks."

"If you survive the next two weeks," he grunted.

"How did Otto Olson die?"

"They don't know yet."

"Surely they have some idea."

"He had a bottle of whiskey with him. They think he drank himself to death, but we'll need to wait on the autopsy to confirm it." His eyes narrowed. "That information needs to stay between the two of us. I only told you because you found him. I know your imagination . . ."

"Runs wild." He'd always teased me about it when we were together.

"Are you happy out there, Summer?" he asked quietly.

"Do you want the truth or the answer you want to hear?" I asked, sounding more tired than snotty. Oddly enough, they were one and the same, but I couldn't handle him gloating over my loneliness and unhappiness. "Are *you* happy *here*?"

He didn't answer for several seconds, then he stood. "I've got to get back." He sounded gruffer, and I wondered if he regretted being nice to me.

"Why did you really come, Luke?"

"I wish I knew." Then he turned and walked out the door.

I'd been moved to a hospital room on the second floor by the time Dixie came by. She'd already heard about my barf-fest.

"Who told you?" I asked. "Lauren?"

"Nah, I read about it on Maybelline's Facebook page."

I groaned. The whole damn town knew. "You've got to be kidding me."

She laughed, but she seemed nervous. "You know how gossip flies here in Sweet Briar."

"I guess. Tell me what you found out at the lake."

She grimaced. "Not much."

Still, her expression didn't look disappointed, exactly. I got the impression she had some news she didn't want to share with me. "What?"

"Have you talked to Deputy Dixon yet?"

"No. Luke said he'd be by tomorrow. Why?"

"Well . . . I saw him out in the hall, so maybe he's gonna talk to you today." She made a beeline for the door. "Sure enough, he's at the nurse's station and heading this way."

"What's going on, Dixie?"

"I think Deputy Dixon should be the one to tell you."

That sounded ominous, and I would have argued with her, but the deputy walked into the room with a sweet but guarded expression—the kind you'd give your grandmother with dementia.

"How are you feeling, Summer?" he asked as he moved close to my bed.

"I've been better."

"I need to get your official statement about what happened at the lake."

"Okay, but why am I suddenly worried to give it to you?"

His smile turned more compassionate. "The memory is a tricky thing. Especially with head injuries."

The back of my bed was already elevated to a near-sitting position, which made it easier for me to sit fully upright. "What's that supposed to mean?"

"Nothing, Summer. Just tell me what you remember."

I repeated the story of someone chasing me, but this time I felt like my every word was being weighed for truth. And this time I more distinctly remembered someone hitting me on the back of the head. When I finished, I glanced over at the grim-faced deputy. "Am I a suspect in Otto Olson's death?"

"I wouldn't say that . . ." He shifted in his seat, looking like he'd developed hemorrhoids. "Can you tell me when you got into town?"

My eyes darted to Dixie, something I instantly regretted—one, because pain shot through my head, and two, she had a weird expression too.

"What's goin' on here?" I demanded, realizing I'd slipped into a full-on Southern accent. *Dammit.*

"Summer," the deputy said, looking up from his notebook, "I just need you to answer my questions so we can get this all cleared up."

"*What* cleared up?"

"They think you did this, Summer," Dixie blurted out.

"You just said I wasn't a suspect!" I cried out to the deputy.

"No," Dixie said. "He said he *wouldn't say that*." She used air quotes for emphasis.

I scooted back a bit in the bed and wrapped my arms across my chest, dragging my IV lines with me. "Do you think I injured myself on purpose too?"

Deputy Dixon lifted up his hands. "Summer, calm down. Gettin' all excited and flustered won't help anything."

"Gettin' excited and flustered? You're accusing me of murderin' some poor innocent man!"

"I'm not accusin' you of murder," he said, getting to his feet. "But some things aren't adding up, which looks a little suspicious given the way he was found. Now tell me when you got into town."

I swallowed hard, feeling nauseated again, but for an entirely different reason. "Yesterday morning. I flew into Atlanta, and Karen—the producer's assistant—picked me up from the airport. We arrived around ten, I think, and got right to work."

"And how long did you work yesterday?"

I shot another glance at Dixie, who now looked furious, before returning my attention to the deputy. "Nine? I left the office and headed to Meemaw's house, and they filmed our dinner. It's all kind of fuzzy right now."

He gave me a look that said, *How convenient*.

"I have a head injury!" I protested. "And besides, I have people who can account for what I was doin' up until around nine o'clock last night."

"And who are these people?"

"The crew . . . then Officer Hawkins saw me in the afternoon. He hung around Becky's house, and we saw him again around five when we went back to the office. Then Bill, one of the cameramen, took some footage of me and Dixie working. After that, I left and went to the farm."

"With your cousin?"

"No. Alone."

He pursed his lips and nodded.

"The chief of police pulled me over on the way home. He can account for some of that time."

"You sure had a lot of encounters with the Sweet Briar police in a very short period of time. Why did the police chief pull you over?"

I frowned. "It's personal."

He gave me a look of surprise.

"That's all I'm gonna say about that. If you want to know the details, then you should ask him if he filed a police report."

He studied me for a moment. "You went straight to the farm after that?"

I doubted he needed a minute-by-minute play of my activities, but just to make sure he knew I wasn't hiding anything, I said, "I stopped at the family cemetery to pay my respects first."

"Respects to who?"

My mouth dropped open. "It's a *family* cemetery, Deputy."

"So you stopped to pay your respects to some guy who died a hundred years ago?"

"No! I stopped to see my grandfather and my aunt and uncle. This is the first time I've been back to Sweet Briar since the fire." My voice clogged with tears. "Not that that's any of your business."

"Actually, it *is* my business," he said, not unkindly. "I'm trying to make sure you have an alibi."

"If you don't think I murdered him, then what on earth do I need an alibi *for*?"

"He thinks you moved Otto's body," Dixie said, sounding even more pissed.

Deputy Dixon turned to face my cousin. "Miss Baumgartner, you need to leave."

Dixie was at my side in an instant, snatching up my hand and clinging to it. "I'm not leavin' my cousin."

His back stiffened and he pressed back his shoulders, puffing out his chest. "I can *make* you leave. This is official business."

"And Luke said you weren't gonna question her until tomorrow. In fact, I'm pretty doggone sure he told the nurses not to let you in to see her today, so if you kick me out, I'll be calling 911 and askin' him to come over and get this all sorted out."

"You realize this is makin' you all look guilty."

I shook my head, instantly regretting it. "Guilty? Why would I move poor Otto's body, and where would I have found it in the first place?"

He pressed his lips together. "What happened after you left the cemetery?"

"I went to the house, and the crew filmed a family dinner. I was tired after it was over, so I went to bed."

"At nine?"

"Around there. I slept until six thirty, then took a shower and headed into town with Dixie so we could meet our eight-thirty call time. I've been with the crew all day."

"And no one can account for your whereabouts from nine last night until six thirty this morning?"

"I was sleeping."

He scribbled something in his notebook. "Uh-huh."

"You seriously think I moved his body? I barely saw the guy, but there's no doubt he outweighs me by a good fifty pounds."

He pursed his lips and shrugged. "Maybe you had help."

"Maybe you need to up your dose of antipsychotics," I snapped back.

Dixie dropped my hand, moved between us, and started pushing the deputy toward the door. "My cousin's suffered an ordeal. Maybe you should question her later."

Deputy Dixon dug in his heels.

I leaned to the side, facing him, as a new thought struck me. "If you think I moved his body—which insinuates I faked the whole thing—then how do you explain someone chasing me?"

His eyebrows rose. "*Did* someone chase you? You admitted that you ran into a tree branch."

"And how do you explain the lump on the back of my head?" I asked, getting furious. "You think I grabbed a tree branch and hit myself?" I was becoming hysterical. "And where's the camera? And the bike?"

"Was there a bike? And we only have your word that you had the camera in the first place, not to mention you freely admit your recollections are still hazy."

"Dixie knew I had the camera."

The deputy turned to Dixie. "Did you see her take the camera into the woods?"

Her silence was answer enough. She'd been sitting on the pier with Bill.

A wave of fear washed through me. I wasn't sure what they'd found in those woods, but they clearly had it out for me. "Do I need to hire a lawyer?"

"I don't know, Ms. Butler. Do you?"

Dixie had had enough. She resumed her mission to shove him out of the room. "Get the hell out of here, you Yankee bastard."

"Yankee! Who the hell are you callin' a Yankee?"

"I can sniff out your bad accent a mile away," she said, giving him one last shove into the hall. "And if you come back in here, I'm calling the police!"

"I *am* the police!"

Dixie spun around to face me, putting her back to the door to hold it shut. "A lot has been goin' on while you've been sleepin' and barfin.'"

I sank back into the pillows. "Oh, my God. Do you think Lauren had anything to do with this?"

"If she did, Bill doesn't know anything about it."

"Are you sure you can take his word for it?"

She gave me a cocky look. "I'm like a human lie detector."

"Yeah, right."

After glancing back at the door, Dixie walked toward the bed. "No. Seriously. I can figure out bullshit faster than you can shake a stick."

I narrowed my eyes. "How?"

She shrugged. "I dunno. But why do you think I've never stayed with a guy for very long? I always know when he's bullshittin' me."

Terrible cousin that I'd been, I hadn't known that—any of it. Still, I had serious doubts about the whole bullshit-meter thing. I suspected she could just read through a guy's crap, but then again, it probably came down to the same thing. "Well, then, I obviously have the best assistant in the world for a job like this."

She grinned.

"I wonder if I should hire an attorney." *Dammit.* I didn't have money for that kind of thing. "Maybe Lauren moved the body. Who knows? She could have convinced the janitor to tell me about the bike."

She shook her head. "I don't think so. I was with Bill when he talked to her, and I'm sure she was just as surprised by the accusation as we were."

"So they think Otto was murdered?"

She shook her head. "No. They're sure he died from alcohol poisoning."

"Did they have time to run his blood alcohol level?"

"They're still working on it, but I heard them say there weren't any signs of trauma." She paused, moving closer and lowering her voice. "But none of this make sense, Summer. I saw a bottle of Jim Beam sticking out of his jacket pocket, and he hated Jim Beam."

"Maybe he wanted to be drunk bad enough he didn't care."

She shook her head. "No way. He almost died from Jim Beam once. He swore he'd never drink it again. Just ask Fred and Al."

Ugh. I'd rather not. "So why would he have a bottle of Jim Beam?" I asked. "Did he commit suicide?"

"And move his own body?"

She had a point.

"I think someone murdered Otto Olson, and they're settin' you up."

CHAPTER SEVENTEEN

We spent the next five minutes trying to make heads or tails of it, but murder was the only conclusion that fit.

"It can't be anything else," Dixie said. "One, there's no doubt he was scared last Sunday. Everyone's said so. Something had him spooked. Two, he would never drink Jim Beam. Three, even if he died at the lake, how'd he get out there?" She narrowed her eyes. "You said the janitor at the church told you about the bike, right?"

"He told me he saw it there when he was fishing yesterday."

She cocked her head, scrutinizing me. "Old Pete doesn't fish."

"Old Pete? Why would they call a guy in his twenties Old Pete?"

"Old Pete's seventy years old."

My mouth dropped open, then I leaned my head back into the pillow, staring at the ceiling. "Then who did I talk to?"

"Are you sure you talked to anyone? You hit your head pretty hard, and your memory is hazy."

I shot her a look. "Dixie, I told you about him before we even left the church."

"True." She tapped her chin. "So someone was setting you up."

"The guy told me about the bike to lure me there, but why take the bike?"

"I don't know."

Something nagged at my mind, a half-formed memory that wouldn't surface, but what? "I'm forgetting something important," I said, tears filling my eyes. "It's right there, but I can't reach it."

"Oh, Summer. Your head was hurt pretty bad. Maybe you just think there's something."

"No. I *know* there is."

Tears flowed from my eyes, pissing me off. How had I gotten here? In this ridiculous situation. I always tried to do the right thing, and yet I always seemed to get screwed over.

Maybe I should just give up.

"I think I want to be alone right now."

"Summer . . ." Her voice broke. "I'm sorry."

I opened my eyes. "I'm not mad at you, Dixie. I'm just really tired."

"We'll figure this out. I promise."

I tried to focus on her face so it wasn't so blurry. "I think I'm going to quit the show."

"What?"

I shook my head, tears flowing from me like a faucet now that I'd let them loose. "I hate it. We're messing with people's lives and faking so much. No wonder they think I moved Otto's body. Why wouldn't they? We've faked everything else."

"Summer. You're hurt and tired. Just think about it."

I started to cry harder. "I know you're counting on me so you don't have to work at the Dollar General, and Meemaw and Teddy are counting on me for the farm, but I don't think I can do this anymore."

Her voice sounded strained. "Why are Meemaw and Teddy countin' on you for the farm?"

Oh, crap. She didn't know about that part. I needed her to leave before I told her everything. "Just go."

"Summer . . ."

"*Please.* Just go."

"I'm comin' back later to check on you," she said, rubbing my arm.

Then she turned around and left me alone.

Alone. I'd felt alone ever since I'd left Sweet Briar twelve years ago. And I was so weary of it.

I slept most of the rest of the afternoon, waking up only when the nurses came to check on me. I was surprised Lauren hadn't come back, so I mentioned it to the nurse who came in to scold me for not eating the disgusting dinner of instant mashed potatoes and meat loaf that tasted like cardboard. She looked like she was Dixie's age, so I had a hard time taking her seriously.

"Oh, she's been by a few times," the nurse said, checking my IV line. "But we were given strict orders not to let Ms. Chapman in."

"By the doctor?"

She laughed. "Oh, no. By Luke."

"The police chief? Why?"

She shrugged. "Beats me, but honey, when Luke tells you to do something, you don't argue." A naughty grin lit up her face. Great, another Luke lover. She picked up a single red rose I hadn't noticed before from the bedside table. She sniffed it and grinned as she set it back down.

Where had that come from? Luke?

Then another thought floated to the surface of my jumbled mind: *I've got plenty of competition.*

I was tempted to physically shake the notion away, but I'd probably only puke on *her* shoes. There was no *Luke and Summer.* Not anymore. We'd been kids, and now we were adults. We were different people. There was no picking up where we'd left off—not that I would want to because the end had been ugly. But I was a fool if I thought I could pretend I wasn't still attracted to him. I just needed to remember I was leaving when this was over.

I just needed to remember why I was leaving.

"When can I get out of here?"

Deadly Summer

"Unless you have some major setback, tomorrow morning. You probably could have gone home tonight, but the doctor wanted to make sure you didn't fall into a coma."

My eyes flew wide. "What?"

She waved a hand dismissively. "Nothin' to worry about. Just a precaution."

"And if I want to go back to work?"

She turned to look at me. "You'll have to ask Dr. Livingston about that tomorrow."

"But what's your best guess?"

"I guess it depends on how bad you want to do it." She grinned. "You know us Sweet Briar folk don't let much hold us back."

I knew it all too well. "Thanks."

She started to leave, then turned around to face me. "But if it were me and I decided to start filmin' a show again, I'd probably take it easy for a couple of days. No crazy stunts. Lots of sittin' around."

I gave her a smile. "Thanks."

"Honestly, I'm surprised Luke's not here with you."

"What? Why?"

"Everyone knows he rushed to the hospital as soon as he heard you were here."

"That was an official visit."

She snickered. "You keep tellin' people that, but we know all about it from the town Facebook page."

It was time to see that Facebook page for myself. "Do you know where my phone is? It was with my clothes."

She waved a hand. "You let me get it. You shouldn't be gettin' out of bed unless you have someone helpin' you. In fact, while I'm in here, do you need to pee? You've had a lot of fluids goin' through you with the IV."

"No. Just my phone, please."

She opened a cabinet and found my phone, then handed it to me with a wink. "Look up Sweet Briar News."

I cracked a grin as I took my phone from her. "How much is actual news?"

145

She chuckled and gave me a lazy shrug. "I guess it depends on what you call news."

I opened my Facebook app and quickly found the page. There had been lots of posts today, but there had also been lots of actual news. The post at the top was about how the Bixley County sheriff's department had moved Otto's body to the Sweet Briar Hospital for an autopsy.

Otto's body was in the same building I was in. I shuddered. Maybe I should go home and risk the coma.

Below that was a post about my *Exorcist* reenactment, and from the glee over Luke getting plastered, it was obvious the person who'd written the post (presumably Maybelline) had already filled in Amber's protest form at the police station. But there were lots of comments about how worried Luke had been and how he'd stayed by my side until I came to.

Did that mean he really did care about me?

The post below that was about Otto's death. Maybelline was setting up a fund in the café to help pay for the funeral.

Below that was a post about the sheriff's office being dispatched to Lake Edna, and a note that, rumor had it, Dixie and I had gone out there. People were instructed to watch for more information.

Did Maybelline have a police scanner, or had someone else told her?

Before that, there was a post about Dixie and me chatting up Fred and Al, who were back to their usual appearance by the Dollar General.

There were plenty of posts about other things we'd done around town, but I was more interested in the one post about the murder. The only new information was that Ruby Garwood had heard a scuffle out back before calling the police. Cale had thought he was about to tuck in for the night, but he'd found a body instead. The alley was completely blocked off, and no one other than the cops knew who had been killed.

My gaze jerked up when I heard a soft rapping on the door. Dixie walked in holding a pie covered in whipped cream.

"I came bearing gifts," she said with a soft smile.

"I owe you a huge apology, Dixie. I totally overreacted earlier."

"Hush now. I don't blame you one bit, Summer, so don't you go worryin' about anything."

"I wasn't very nice."

"Bull hockey. And you'd just had your head bashed in."

I cringed. "I wouldn't say it was bashed in . . ."

"True. Your brains weren't leakin' out . . ." Then a huge grin broke out on her face. "Ready for some strawberry pie? Looks a little like brains, right?"

"Oh, my word. That's so tacky." I shook my head and started laughing, immediately regretting both. I squinted while I waited for the pain to subside. "I hope you brought forks."

Dixie beamed while she set the pie on the bedside tray and then fished two metal forks out of her purse.

"Where'd you get those? Meemaw's silverware drawer? She's going to kill you," I said as I took one.

"What Meemaw doesn't know doesn't hurt her." She dug a fork into the pie. "Just like she can't know we ate like this. She'd call us heathens."

I dug my fork into the middle. "She already thinks the worst of me, so why not." The words were pathetic, so I tried for a light tone.

"She loves you, Summer. I suggested moving to your old bedroom, but she wouldn't consider it. She's been waitin' for you to come back even if she won't admit it."

"Does she know I'm here?"

Dixie made a face that suggested she did.

"What did she say?"

"Nothin'."

What did I expect? In the grand scheme of things, I wasn't dying . . . unless I fell into a coma. I was still counting on the nurse's assurance it was unlikely. But Meemaw's silence still hurt.

I took a bite, embarrassed when I released an involuntary moan. "Who made this?" I asked through a mouthful of pie.

She grinned and wiggled her shoulders back and forth. "I did."

I scooped out another bite and released another moan. "This is orgasmic, Dixie."

She chuckled and pointed a pie-filled fork at me. "You must be havin' some pretty bad sex if you believe that."

"It's been three years, but my last boyfriend wasn't too bad in bed," I said with a wicked grin.

Dixie squealed. "Oh, my word. Which movie star was it?"

I lifted my eyebrows. "No one you'd know."

"Try me."

"Aiden Clay."

She scrunched her nose. "Who's that?"

"Exactly." I scooped a smaller bite. "And it was short-lived." I grimaced. "Let's just say I could have used your bullshit detector."

"Aww . . . Summer."

"I'm over it." I set the fork on the bedside tray. "This pie is delicious, but I can't eat anymore."

Dixie took another bite. "Are you really quittin' the show?"

"I don't know. I hate being a quitter. But I really do hate what we're doing."

She gave me a sly look. "What if we found Otto's killer?"

"What?"

"Bill and I talked it over, and we both support you in this."

"What does that mean?"

"Bill already tried to convince Lauren to investigate Otto's death. She said it was a dead end with little possible payoff. She's already got a new big case lined up but won't tell anyone other than Karen what it is."

"More lies," I said in defeat.

Dixie was silent for a moment. "Someone killed Otto. I believe it with all my heart," she said quietly. "He blamed himself for the fire that killed his family, and it drove him to drink, but he wouldn't have killed himself out of the blue. He would have done it a long time ago."

"Dixie . . ."

She turned quiet. "There's something else, Summer. Something you need to know."

The seriousness in her eyes scared me. "What?"

She pulled up a screen on her phone. On a national gossip site, there was a post titled "America's Darling Not So Darling?" There were several photos of me looking like I was yelling and chewing people out—Lauren, Officer Hawkins, Becky in her front yard. Somehow someone had gotten a photo of me talking to Luke last night, and they'd caught me poking his chest.

"How . . . ?"

"I don't know," she said, "but Lauren's ecstatic, so she probably had something to do with it. And I bet you she's putting some of this in the show."

Crap. Dixie was right.

"All the more reason to quit, Dixie. She's gonna ruin me."

She shook her head. "No. If you quit now, you know you'll look like you're guilty of bein' a diva."

"So I'm supposed to go along with it?"

"No!" She sat on the side of my bed and grabbed my hand. "Bill has a plan to find Otto's killer and restore your reputation, but you have to be all in." She paused and searched my face. "Come on, Summer. Let's bring Lauren to her knees."

Part of me was tired. Someone had attacked me for trying to find out the truth about Otto, and now I was catching hell for trying to do my job. Did I really want to risk my life? But there was no denying it felt good to feel like I was doing something real. Only the job had been left half-finished. I'd promised to find Otto for Gretchen, and while I had fulfilled that promise, I was certain she'd never be at peace until she knew what happened to him. We had the chance to give her closure.

"Okay," I said. "Let's do it."

CHAPTER EIGHTEEN

"Now what exactly are we going to do?" I asked.

Dixie grinned. "When we're not shooting with Lauren, Bill's gonna sneak his camera out of the supply room at the office and follow us while we go around askin' questions about Otto's death."

"Everyone knows everyone else's business in this town. How are we going to keep it a secret from Lauren?"

"Nobody likes that Yankee," she said with a snort. "They won't tell her out of spite."

"If Lauren finds out . . ."

"She won't. And just think how satisfying it would be to find out who killed Otto and shove it in that deputy's face."

"True . . ."

"But to find out who killed Otto, we need to find out how he died, and I know his body is in the morgue."

I sucked in a breath. "You better not be thinkin' what I think you're thinkin'."

"I'm not suggestin' we go do the autopsy ourselves."

"Then what *are* you suggesting?"

"We should go down there and see if we can find the report."

"I don't do dead people, Dixie."

"No crap. You passed out when you found Otto."

"I passed out because someone whacked me in the head." I rubbed my scalp for emphasis.

"Look, I'm not asking you to start readin' toe tags," she said. "But if we go down to the morgue, we might stumble upon the report."

"Because you think it will just be lyin' around?" I asked in disbelief.

She shrugged. "You never know. This *is* Sweet Briar."

Unfortunately, she had a point.

"You don't even have to go in," she said with a cajoling look on her face. "But if I push you in a wheelchair, we can say we were wanderin' around because you were feelin' cooped up in your room. Easy enough to pretend we got lost."

"Dammit," I grumbled. She was right. It was the perfect excuse. "I really hate dead people, Dixie."

"You already said that, and you already met your dead-person quota for the day. You just sit in the chair and film me while I'm snoopin'."

"Film you?"

"Yeah." She reached into her oversize purse and pulled out a small video camera. "Bill gave me this to use when he's not with us."

I gave her a stare of disbelief, which strained my eyes and made my head hurt worse. "I'm gonna film us in the morgue? Breakin' the rules?"

"See, that's your problem," Dixie said, touching the tip of my nose with the end of her index finger. "You're too much of a stickler for the rules. Sometimes you've gotta break 'em."

"I guess you would know," I said, then instantly regretted it. "I'm sorry."

She shrugged, trying to look like it didn't bother her, but her smile slightly fell.

Part of me wondered if she had a point. Scott Schapiro had called me boring and vanilla. Dixie was right—I did follow the rules. I'd already started shaking things up. Maybe it was time to ratchet it up to an earthquake.

"Okay."

Her mouth formed an *O*. "Really?"

"Yeah."

"I'll get a wheelchair." Then she ran out the door.

She was back within a few minutes, pushing the chair into the room. "I told the nurses I was takin' you for a spin." She helped me get situated in the chair with the stupid hospital gown I was wearing. I was still hooked up to the IV, so she unhooked the bag and attached it to the pole on the chair. After she grabbed a blanket from the cabinet and spread it over my lap and legs, she handed me the video camera.

"You can hide it under the blanket."

"Good idea."

She walked over to the bed tray and scooped another huge bite of pie, popped it in her mouth, then said with a full mouth, "Let's go."

She pushed me past the two nurses who were waving at us from the nurses' station.

"If she starts to feel nauseated, bring her right back," said the nurse who'd checked on me earlier.

"No worries there," Dixie laughed. "I heard all about what happened earlier, and I want no part of that."

I scowled. "Hey. I couldn't help it."

I'd been in the Sweet Briar Hospital a few times when I was younger, but I wasn't familiar with the layout. Dixie, on the other hand, seemed to know exactly where she was going. She headed straight for the elevator and pushed the button marked "B."

The hospital was two stories, with the patient beds on the second floor and the ER and a bunch of doctors' offices on the first floor. I had no idea what was in the basement, but I imagined it was a good place for a morgue.

Once we were enclosed in the elevator, I said, "How do you know the autopsy will be done? Or that there will be a report? On TV, those things take weeks."

"I suspect it won't be totally done, but rumor has it that Doc Bailey likes to get the jump on things, *and* he does everything the old-fashioned way—by hand. He refuses to use computers. He's probably jotted down notes somewhere."

"Wouldn't those be in his office?" I asked in a worried tone.

"It's next to the morgue."

The elevator dinged, and the doors opened to a dim hallway. We faced a dingy gray wall and a linoleum floor that looked like it was white under a decade's worth of grime.

152

"I'm having second thoughts," I said. "This place is giving me the creeps."

"Don't be such a baby." She pushed me out of the elevator into the hall, which got even darker.

"Dixie . . ."

"Got it covered. Hold this." A beam of light shone over my shoulder, and she handed me a flashlight.

"Why not just turn on the lights?"

"Rumor has it they don't work." She found a switch on the wall, and nothing happened. "See? Aren't you happy I came prepared? Besides, we don't want anyone seein' us."

There was little worry of that from what I was seeing. The hall was a graveyard of hospital beds and wheelchairs, which somehow didn't make me feel better about this whole enterprise.

"Shine the light down the hall," she said. "The morgue's at the end."

"Do I want to know how you know that?" I asked, but I did as she said, and the flashlight beam illuminated the curve of the shadowy hallway.

She was quiet for a moment. "It's where I saw Momma and Daddy."

I gasped in horror. *"They made you identify their bodies?"* I couldn't imagine any fifteen-year-old kid mature enough to handle such a thing.

"No," she answered in a raspy voice. "I snuck in to see them."

"Why?"

"I didn't believe it was true . . . that they were really dead, but no one would let me see them. They said I just had to trust that they were gone. I couldn't do that. I had to see for myself."

"Why wouldn't they let you see them?"

She paused. "Because they were unrecognizable. From the fire."

I jerked around to look up at her, an action that the pain shooting through my head made me instantly regret. "Oh, Dixie." Pain for my cousin filled my voice.

"It's okay. But I know where it is, and I know how to get in."

"Are you sure you want to do this?" I asked softly.

"Yes." Her voice was hard, and it brooked no argument.

I considered arguing with her anyway, but from the determination on her face, I wondered if maybe she needed to do this for her own reasons. "Okay."

"You should start filming," she said. "Maybe film yourself first, then turn it around to show what I'm doing."

"I'm sure I look like crap." I hadn't looked in a mirror since this whole ordeal had begun.

"That's okay," she said. "Makes it look more authentic, don't ya think? Less Hollywood and more like a real PI."

A soft grin lifted the corners of my mouth as I pulled the camera out from under the blanket. "Yeah. You're right."

"I know a thing or two."

I suspected Dixie wasn't used to people finding merit in her ideas. "You know more than a thing or two." After a few seconds of fumbling, I turned on the camera and flipped the viewfinder so I could center the frame on my face. Thankfully, I didn't look as bad as I'd expected, but Karen would no doubt be thrilled by the large bruise surfacing on the right side of my forehead.

"Three, two, one," I said, then launched into my reporting. "It's rumored that Otto Olson died from alcohol poisoning, but a few things aren't adding up. One, the sheriff's department thinks his body was moved. If he died from alcohol poisoning, who moved him and why? That's what my partner Dixie and I are trying to find out, and since I'm currently a patient in the Sweet Briar Hospital, we decided to take a ride down to the basement, which happens to house the morgue, in the hopes of finding someone who can give us a few answers."

I stopped the recording. "Dixie, we can't show us sneaking into the morgue. We could get charged with breaking and entering, along with a bunch of other charges I'm sure Luke would love to throw at me."

"Fine, but let's still record it all and figure out what to keep or delete later."

I wasn't sure that was so smart, but it might be good to have something to review later, especially since my head was still fuzzy. "Okay."

She stopped in front of a door with the numbers **0134** engraved on a plague. "This is it."

"It doesn't say *morgue*."

"It doesn't have to. Besides, no need to advertise it." She moved in front of me and pulled two hairpins from her pocket. After a few seconds, I heard the lock click and she opened the door.

"I'm scared to ask why you know how to do that."

"And yet it's a valuable life skill," she said with a grin as she pocketed the pins. "It's gotten me out of a few jams."

"Or *into* them," I teased.

She laughed. "Your brain damage must be improving."

My answering grin slipped away the moment she pushed the door open more and flicked on the lights. There was a sheet-covered body on a metal cart in the middle of the white sterile room, but we'd expected that. I'd forgotten about the *other* body, but of course it would still be in here. There it was on a gurney on the opposite side of the room, covered with another sheet, thank God.

I covered my stomach with my hand. "I think I'm gonna be sick."

Dixie turned around and bent at the knees to look in my eyes. "Oh, no, you don't! No barfin' and leavin' evidence that we were here."

I couldn't promise anything, so I said, "Just find what you're lookin' for, and let's go."

"It's probably in Doc Bailey's office, which is on the other side of the room." I shuddered. "I'll wait here."

"Summer."

"No. No way. I'm not goin' in there. I'm not maneuvering a wheelchair in there." I shuddered.

She pushed out a massive sigh and tried to open the door on the other side, then pulled out her pins again. This lock seemed to take longer, but she finally got it open, and I was surprised to see there was a light already on in the room She came back, grabbed the camera, and started filming as she walked toward the door.

My eyes kept drifting to the dead bodies, and my stomach twisted more and more, making me regret my attempt to eat that cardboard meat loaf—but not the strawberry pie . . . never regret pie. I closed my eyes, which proved a mistake because the smells hit me. Nearly a minute later, I was thinking about telling Dixie I was going to wait by the elevators when I heard it ding.

Shit.

Voices filtered down the hall.

". . . nothing unusual, Luke," I heard an older man say.

Double shit. There was a sound of banging metal down the hall, immediately followed by Luke's cursing. "Why don't you get the damn lights fixed, Doc?"

"It saves the hospital money," he grunted.

I had a sudden appreciation that the lights were out.

But I couldn't stay here or we'd be found out—and now that we were down here, it was painfully obvious we couldn't explain away our break-in as some sort of demented stroll. I got to my feet, flipped off the morgue light, and pushed the wheelchair close to the wall, letting it join the ranks of the other abandoned chairs. Where was I going to hide? My sole option wasn't a great one—I'd have to make a beeline through the damn morgue to join Dixie in the office. Our only real hope was if there was somewhere to hide in there. Or that they never went in.

I suspected my luck wasn't that good.

But I had another, more immediate issue—I still had an IV, and the bag was currently attached to the pole on the chair. I stood on my tiptoes to pull it off the hook, but I couldn't see what I was doing, and the voices were getting louder.

"It was all pretty cut-and-dried," the doctor said.

"Humor me," Luke said.

I jerked the bag again, to no avail, and I realized I had two options—stand there and be prepared to come up with some wacky explanation, or jerk out my IV and run into the morgue.

Not a fan of self-inflicted pain, I was tempted to go with the first, but where would that leave Dixie? I gave the bag one last try. It came unhooked this time, but the tubing of my IV got caught on the wheelchair handle, jerking the needle out of my hand.

I bit my lip in an effort to not cry out, already running across the hall into the morgue while clutching my now-useless IV bag. I shut the door behind me and had the sense to lock it, even though I was locking myself into a room with two dead men.

A soft glow still emanated from the cracked door through which Dixie had disappeared, so I hurried toward it, bumping into the wall as a wave of vertigo hit me. I'd just gotten into the office and shut the door when I heard the men's voices in the other room.

I glanced behind me and realized I wasn't in an office after all—I was in a lab, and the counters were lined with lots of buckets and plastic bags filled with what looked like body parts steeped in fluid.

I was definitely going to be sick.

No. No, I wasn't. I couldn't be.

There was no sign of Dixie, but I still had my phone in my hand, so I sent her a text that I was in the lab hiding from Luke and Doc Bailey.

Seconds later, she appeared in a doorway on the other side of the big room. She moved closer, and I held my finger to my lips and pointed to the door, then pressed my ear to the wood. It was a risk, but something told me we had to hear what they were saying.

Dixie stood next to me and did the same.

"No sign of trauma," the doctor said. "But here's the interesting part—you said he hadn't been seen since Sunday, right?"

"Yeah."

"He hasn't been dead for that long. My best guess is that he died sometime last night."

"Then where's he been?" Luke asked.

The doctor chuckled. "That falls under your job description."

"There wasn't anything on him that gave any hints as to where he'd been?"

"Nothing I can see, but I'm waiting to see if you want to send him to Montgomery for a forensic autopsy."

"I take it you ran a blood alcohol?"

"Yep. Three-point-one."

Luke was silent for a moment. "Otto was a drunk, but never that drunk."

"His tolerance was probably built up. But I can tell you that I'm ninety-nine percent certain he died from alcohol poisoning."

"But how did he get moved, and why?"

"That falls under your job description too," the doctor said with a grin in his voice. "Do you think it was Summer?"

"She can't weigh one hundred and twenty pounds soaking wet," he said. "She would have needed help."

One hundred and twenty pounds!

"You think her cousin helped her? She tends to be on the wild side."

"I don't know . . . ," he said. "My gut tells me no, but . . ."

"You're worried your past with Summer is clouding your judgment?"

"Yeah. And Dixie."

What did that mean? I shot a glance at Dixie. I couldn't make out her face very well, but I felt her body tense. I reached out and squeezed her hand. She squeezed back.

"Anything I don't already know about the other guy?" Luke said.

"Gunshot wound to the head from close range. Entry through the forehead and the exit wound out the back of the skull. Pretty clear-cut cause of death."

Luke sighed. "Now I just have to find out who killed him."

"Glad that's your job," the doctor said. "Still not ready to release his name?"

"He doesn't have any family here. We're trying to track someone down first. The guy he's known to hang out with is currently missing."

"You think his friend killed him and ditched town?"

"It's a working theory."

"Maybe Maybelline could ask about the friend on her Facebook page," the doctor said.

"Since when do you use Facebook?" Luke asked.

"I don't, but I know half this damn town does. They rely on it more than they do the newspapers."

"Can't do it," Luke groaned. "It's poor taste, Doc. Besides, as nosy as this town is, half of them will be callin' Amber to speculate about him being the murder victim. The town's in enough chaos with that film crew muckin' around."

"Nevertheless . . ."

"*No,*" Luke barked. "I'll figure out another way." Then his tone softened. "I'm done here. Thanks for meetin' me so late."

"Whatever I can do to help, Luke."

They had been silent for a moment when Luke said, "Why are there blood drops on the floor? You and your staff are meticulous for cleaning up, and this is fresh." His voice sounded strained.

"Good question."

"Shit," Luke said. "Do you think someone was down here tampering with the bodies?"

"The morgue door was locked," the doctor said. "And the bodies were undisturbed."

"What about the blood specimens?" Luke asked. "What if they were after them?"

"Why would they be? I could get new samples."

Luke was quiet for a moment. "Humor me and check anyway."

That was our cue to hide.

Dixie grabbed my wrist and pulled me toward the door on the other side of the lab, which turned out to be a small hallway. She darted into the first door to the right—a small supply closet—tugging me in with her and carefully shutting the door.

We heard the two men walk into the lab a few feet away.

"There's blood in here," Luke said. "By the door, and it stops in front of the evidence fridge. Shit."

"It doesn't look tampered with," the doctor said.

"You got a pair of gloves I can use so I don't get prints on the fridge?"

"Sure," he said, but he sounded like he was placating him. We heard the jangle of keys, and a few seconds later the doctor said, "See. It's all accounted for."

"So how do you explain the blood?"

"We have a new lab tech, and he's been known to be a little sloppy. I'll give him a talkin'-to tomorrow. Now let's get out of here. I'm gonna miss *Law and Order.*"

"You can DVR that, Doc."

"All those letters. VHS. DVR. CD-ROM. A bunch of alphabet soup." Their voices grew fainter, and I heard the door close in the other room.

Dixie and I waited for a good half minute before we opened the supply closet.

"Well, the good news is that Luke doesn't suspect *you*," Dixie said.

"That's true," I said. "*And* we know what killed Otto."

"Not necessarily. Luke's right. Otto was never shit-faced drunk. He always seemed to have a good buzz, and that was about it."

"So how do you explain his blood alcohol level?"

"I dunno," she said. "But if he drank himself dead on his own, how do you explain the Jim Beam? Or that he was moved? Where did he die?"

I sighed. "So basically we still know nothing."

"We'll start lookin' for more clues tomorrow," Dixie said as we walked into the morgue and shut the door behind us, plunging us into darkness. She flipped on the flashlight beam and started for the door—then stopped. "I want to see him."

"Who? Otto?"

"Nope. The mystery guy. I want to see if I know who he is."

"No. No way. He's got a bullet hole in his forehead."

She ignored my protests and walked around the center table to the one against the wall. Grabbing the sheet with one hand and holding the flashlight on the body with the other, she paused and then gave a good yank.

I inched closer and stood next to the side of the gurney, staring down at his face. I swallowed hard when I saw the red circle on his forehead. I'd seen him before.

He was the man who'd been talking to Mayor Sterling in the alley the day before. "I know him."

But Dixie was as stiff as a statue as she stared down at him, her face nearly the color of the off-white sheet covering his body.

"Dixie? Do *you* know him?" From the way she was staring at him, I was pretty sure she didn't just know him—she knew him *well*. "Dixie. Who is he?"

"Ryker Pelletier. My ex-boyfriend."

CHAPTER NINETEEN

I jerked the sheet out of her clenched fist and covered his face back up. Once his face was out of sight, she seemed to get ahold of herself.

Her arm snaked around my waist. "Let's get you back to your chair," she said quietly.

I let her guide me out of the room and back to the wheelchair while I cradled my stupid IV bag like a baby. It was then that she realized it was no longer attached to me.

"The blood was from you," she murmured, picking up the blanket that had been on my lap off the seat and then helping me into the chair. She took the bag, hung it back up, and stuffed the end of the tube under the blanket. The camera went in along with it.

"I saw him yesterday, Dixie," I said, looking up at her. "I saw him arguing with the mayor behind Maybelline's restaurant, and he was the one who dropped the money in the parking lot."

I couldn't tell Luke that I'd seen him before because I wasn't supposed to be down here. Still, the information I had was important. It was looking more and more likely that the mayor was up to something shady, but I couldn't just come out and accuse him of it. I was pretty sure most of the people in town loved him.

What was I going to do? But at the moment I was more worried about my cousin. "Do you have any idea what could have happened to him?"

Dixie started pushing the chair toward the elevator. "I know who Luke is looking for. Ed Reynolds. Ed was Ryker's best friend."

"*Ed?* Oh, my God." I tried to turn to glance at her, but the sudden motion sent a wave of nausea through my body. "Cale told me *Ed* showed up at the police station to see if anyone had turned in the money. But Ryker dropped that bag. I'm sure of it. Why would Ed pick it up?"

"Ed and Ryker have a shop together . . . or I guess *had* a shop together."

"Do you think Ed could have killed Ryker?"

"I don't know . . . maybe. He had a temper sometimes." Dixie stopped in front of the elevator and reached to press the button, but I grabbed her wrist.

"Dixie. Let's take a minute, okay? I know this is a shock. Do you need to sit down?"

She didn't answer.

"I'm not ready to go back to my room yet," I said, knowing she'd take my request more seriously if I pretended it was only for my benefit. "Let's go sit outside for a few minutes and regroup. Okay?"

She nodded and pushed the button. The elevator door opened a few seconds later, and Dixie pushed my chair inside. When we got out on the first floor, she wheeled me outside and parked me by a park bench next to a small flower garden. The sun had set, so it was dark outside, and I was slightly chilly in my hospital gown, but I breathed in deep lungfuls of air as I tried to clear my head.

Dixie sat down next to me, leaned forward, and closed her eyes. I reached for her hand and squeezed tight.

"You said you broke up a month ago?"

"Yeah," she whispered.

"Why did you break up?"

"I don't know," she said as a tear rolled down her face. "He never told me why. Just that he didn't want to be with me anymore."

"How long were you together?"

"Six months." She turned her head to look at me. "I didn't love him. I wasn't even sure if I liked him at the end. And like I told you, Teddy hated him. He didn't think Ryker was good enough for me, and he was probably right." She lifted her shoulder into a slow shrug. "Maybe that's why I stayed with him. To rebel against Teddy."

"Did he hurt you?" I asked.

She was quiet for a moment. "Not like you think. He never hit me or anything. He just wasn't very nice."

"Then why'd you stay? Surely not to piss off Teddy."

She didn't answer.

"Dixie, I know you're upset, and I hate to bring this up, but did Ryker know Otto?"

She gave me a wry smile. "Everyone knew Otto. But if you're asking if Ryker and Otto talked or hung out? That's a definite no. Ryker thought he was gross."

"I can't help thinking their deaths are related. I just can't figure out how." My head was killing me, and I was so tired I could fall asleep in my chair, but I didn't want to go back to my room. Truth be told, I was creeped out at the thought of Dixie leaving me here alone.

"I need to tell Luke or Cale that I saw Mayor Sterling and Ryker together behind the café, but I can't do that until they release his name."

Dixie pulled out her phone and opened her photo app. "We can say you saw him in one of my photos." She started scrolling and brought up a photo of Ryker next to Dixie in what was obviously a selfie. She was smiling, but she didn't look like her perky self, while Ryker's expression suggested he was granting her a huge favor for taking part.

"Isn't it gonna look like a huge coincidence if I call Luke after he was just in the morgue?" I asked.

"That's why you're gonna call Cale."

I felt better about calling Cale, but I was still overwhelmed by what I'd jumped into. This wasn't just a lame reality show. This was life and death, and I felt supremely unqualified to have any part of it. "I'm a coward," I whispered.

"You're *not* a coward, Summer."

I sat there for a moment, staring out at the cars in the parking lot. No. Dixie was wrong. I'd been a coward most of my life. I'd let my mother boss me around and put me in those stupid pageants. I'd let her strong-arm me into going to Hollywood. I'd let her get away with stealing all my money to avoid a scandal and a fuss. I could have figured out another way to deal with her than a public court battle. And now here I was back in Sweet Briar because I had eagerly accepted someone else's solution for fixing everything—money—rather than coming up with one of my own.

For twenty-nine years, I'd let circumstances rule my life because I was too scared to take charge and navigate. It was time to grab the steering wheel.

"Do you really think we can do this?" I asked.

"Figure out who killed them both?" She nodded. "I've been watchin' you when you interview people, Summer. You know what to ask and how to put someone at ease. You've got an instinct for this. I think you can." She grinned. "Maybe you were so good as Isabella Holmes because you're a natural detective."

Which meant maybe I wasn't a very good actress after all. But that was an issue for another day, because my brain felt like it had just finished a triathlon after a three-day fast. "Don't sell yourself short. You have a knack for this too." I gave her a small grin. "Maybe it's in the Baumgartner blood."

A soft smile lifted the corners of her mouth, mirroring mine. "Yeah."

Maybe Dixie was looking for a purpose too. I realized that's what I'd *really* been looking for—a purpose. I'd just been too stupid to realize it.

When these two weeks were up, what if I stayed and did this for real?

It was too soon to be considering something like that, and I sure couldn't mention it to Dixie and get her hopes up. "We need a plan for tomorrow. It's gonna be hard doing these side investigations along with the ones Lauren picks out for us."

"Yeah. Agreed." She stood and moved behind my chair. "But right now we're headin' back to your room. You look like you're about to pass out."

"I think I just want to go home."

"But you're still hurt. They want to keep you overnight."

"Just to make sure I don't fall into a coma, and the nurse said that wasn't likely to happen. Maybe you could check on me a couple of times to make sure I'm still breathing."

She stopped pushing. "I don't know, Summer."

"You don't have to check on me. I'll just set an alarm, and if you hear it goin' off, maybe check on me then."

"Not that!" she protested. "I don't mind checkin' on you. I just hate to bring you home if you need to be here."

"Look, I've been traipsing around the morgue, big as you please. Obviously I can walk. And I asked the nurse about goin' back to work, and she seemed to think it would be fine if I take it slow and sit a lot." When she still looked unsure, I said, "Please, Dixie? The thought of sleepin' in that hospital room, knowing those two guys are under the same roof, gives me the creeps."

She put her hand on my shoulder. "Okay. I'll take you home."

Getting the nurse to agree wasn't easy, but in the end, I told her that it was my decision, not hers. I was taking charge of my life, and this was the first decision made by the new me.

Dixie found my clothes in the cabinet, and I put them on, already feeling exhausted. I wondered if the nurse was right and I needed to stay and let them watch over me for one more night. But all I had to do was think about the two bodies in the morgue.

Nope. I was leaving.

I called Cale on the way home. A half hour wasn't going to make any difference, and we had no idea who'd be listening in the hospital. But when I placed the call, it went straight to voice mail.

"He's probably busy," Dixie said. "Or sleepin'. If he found Ryker in the middle of the night, he's been up for hours."

"True." But about two minutes later, my phone rang with a call from Cale's number.

"Summer?" he asked, sounding on edge. "Everything okay?"

"Yeah," I said. A wave of exhaustion washed over me, and I closed my eyes. "I just found out something that might help you."

"Whew. Okay. What?"

"I was just lookin' at Dixie's photos, and she showed me one that had her ex-boyfriend in it. The man who dropped the money was her ex, Ryker, not Ed. Are you sure Ed picked up the money?"

I knew Ryker was dead, but of course Cale didn't know that, so I wasn't surprised when he was quiet for a couple of seconds. Finally, he said, "So I was hoodwinked."

His voice was so full of self-recrimination, I almost felt guilty for telling him. "Maybe."

He was silent again, then groaned. "Can I ask you a huge favor?"

"Yeah . . ."

"Can you keep this to yourself? Luke's already lookin' over my shoulder with this murder like I'm a rookie cop, and if he finds out about the money . . ."

"You're asking me to lie to Luke?"

"No, of course not, but it's not like it would come up in normal conversation, right?" He groaned. "Never mind. I have no right to ask."

He was right. It wasn't likely to come up in casual conversation, not that we'd be *having* any conversations. "If he flat-out asks, I won't keep it from him, but otherwise I see no reason to bring it up. It's not like I'll be seeing much of him."

Cale laughed. "He's still got a thing for you, Summer. I asked him how he'd feel about me asking you out, and he nearly had a stroke. I wouldn't put it past him to stand guard outside your hospital room tonight."

"Well, he'd be wasting his time because I got an early discharge, and Dixie is takin' me home."

Cale chuckled then turned serious. "Thanks for your call, Summer."

"Yeah, no problem." After I hung up, I relayed everything to Dixie, but she'd figured out most of it already.

"Should I be worried Cale asked me to keep it from Luke?"

"Nah, those two are friends, but they are as different as night and day. Cale's more of a good ol' boy, while Luke's more by the book. They clash over it sometimes. And Ed and Ryker *did* deal in cash, so I can see why he just handed it over, especially if Ed showed up askin' about it right after you turned it in."

We were quiet the rest of the way home, mostly because I kept drifting off to sleep.

Meemaw was standing at the front door when we got back to the farm. She came out to the porch and stared at me with her eagle eyes.

When Dixie opened the door, Meemaw called out, "I thought you was supposed to stay overnight."

"Since when do Baumgartners do what they're told?" I answered back. My head was still pounding, and it took plenty of effort to make the response sound sassy.

She gave a curt nod, and a grin tugged at the corners of her mouth. "About damn time." Then she turned around and went back into the house.

What did that mean? Was she saying it was time I stood up for myself? Had she been waiting all this time for me to stand up to *her*?

It was a good thing she left, because by the time I got out of the car, I had serious doubts I would make it to my room. Meemaw had always hated any sort of weakness. I would have lost what little hard-earned respect she'd just given me.

I'd almost made it to the porch when Teddy came around the side of the house, wiping his hand on a rag. He stopped when he saw us.

"Summer?" He rushed over when he saw my faltering steps. "You're supposed to be in the hospital."

"The food sucks there."

He grinned, and before I knew what he was doing, he scooped me up in his arms and told Dixie to open the door.

"What are you doin', Teddy Baumgartner?" I asked, but I wrapped an arm around his neck and rested my head on his shoulder. It felt nice to be able to have someone to lean on . . . literally.

He grinned. "You're obviously about to pass out and fall on your ass, and I suspect it's easier to pick you up from a standing position than it would be to scoop you up off the floor."

"I'm not gonna pass out."

"You're just usually that pale," he said as he carried me into the house.

"Take her up to my room," Dixie said. "It's bigger."

"Dixie . . ." I wasn't sure why she wanted me in her room, but I wasn't about to put her out.

"You hush now. I'm being lazy. I don't want to traipse down the stairs to check on you when your alarm doesn't stop. I'd rather call 911 from the comfort of my own bed."

I grinned. That sounded like a Baumgartner explanation.

I missed being a Baumgartner.

Teddy got me settled on Dixie's bed, then looked down at me. "We didn't just get you back to lose you again," he said with a thick voice. "Be more careful, little cousin."

I grinned. "Little cousin? I'm a year older than you, boy."

"And I just carried you up the stairs without losing my breath. Who's the little cousin now?"

"Thanks, Teddy."

He nodded and left the room.

"He reminds me so much of Pawpaw," I murmured.

"He is a lot like him, isn't he?" she said, heading for the door. "He'll do anything and everything he can to make this farm work, even if it means defying Meemaw." She paused. "I'm gonna get your pajamas . . . and the strawberry pie out of the truck. Your clothes are covered in dirt."

"Okay."

She turned to walk out, and I heard her call Teddy's name from behind the partially closed door.

"Yeah?" he said.

"What do you know about Ryker lying dead in the Sweet Briar morgue?" she asked in a hushed but accusing tone.

Teddy was silent.

"I asked you a question, Teddy!"

His voice turned hard. "Are you seriously standing there asking me if I killed your ex-boyfriend?"

"No . . . I don't know . . ." She sounded far less sure. "But you called me yesterday and warned me to stay away from him."

"Maybe I knew he was wrapped up in something shady that was gonna get his ass killed. Did you ever think about that?"

"If he was, I never saw any sign of it. I told you that."

"Then he did a mighty fine job of hiding it from you, Dixie, because he was dirty as a pig in shit."

"How do you know that? Are you mixed up in it too? Where's that extra money coming from?"

"You don't need to worry about that. I promised you I'd save the farm, and I meant it." Then I heard him stomping down the stairs.

Did Teddy know about the balloon payment on the loan, or was this something new? And was my cousin mixed up in something dirty? I couldn't believe it, but my head was too groggy for me to think it through, and it felt too heavy to hold up anymore. I lay down on the bed, intending to close my eyes for just a moment.

I must have dozed off by the time Dixie came back because I woke up with a start. She was calling my name and giving my arm a hard shake. "Oh, my God. Summer!"

I blinked my eyes open. "I'm not in a coma. I'm sleeping."

"You scared me half to death!"

"Sorry."

"I have your pajamas." She tossed them on the bed. "Do you need help putting them on?"

My arms and legs felt like they were made from lead, and I was starting to wonder about the wisdom of leaving the hospital, but it was too late to change my mind now. "No."

Dixie left the room, and after a bit of a struggle, I managed to get changed. I climbed under the covers and was already dozing again by the time Dixie got into bed beside me.

"Dixie?" I murmured, sounding drunk to my own ears.

"Yeah?"

"Do you think Teddy killed Ryker?"

I heard her gasp, then felt her hand on my arm. "I didn't think you'd hear that, and no, I do *not* think Teddy killed Ryker. I was just . . . tired and frustrated. Teddy doesn't have it in him to kill someone. Now go to sleep."

It was as if her words had cast a spell on me. I was dozing in seconds, then I quickly drifted deeper into sleep.

The next time I woke up, it was even more abrupt. Dixie had burst out of bed. The clock on her nightstand said it was after midnight. I'd been asleep for several hours.

"What's going on?" I asked, sounding groggy.

She pulled a gun out of her nightstand, and I was instantly awake.

"Dixie?"

"You stay here. Someone's in the house."

"Have you called 911?"

She snorted. "We'll deal with it." Then she headed out the door, and I heard Teddy's voice too.

I grabbed my phone and called 911 anyway. Like Luke had said, there hadn't been any murders in town for three years, and now there had been two deaths in twenty-four hours. I wasn't taking any chances with my cousins and Meemaw.

"This is 911. What's your emergency?" the woman asked in a sleepy voice.

"I'm calling from the Baumgartner farm. Someone broke into the house."

"We'll send someone right away," she said, sounding more alert. "Is the prowler still there?"

"I don't know," I said, my stomach in knots.

There was more banging downstairs and then the indistinguishable sound of several rounds from a shotgun.

"Send someone quick," I said. "I just heard gunshots."

CHAPTER TWENTY

After I hung up, I bolted out of bed so fast the room began to spin. I put a hand on the sloped ceiling and waited for it to pass, but the sounds of more banging spurred me into action. I knew I shouldn't rush into something, especially if bullets were flying, but I couldn't hide in Dixie's room like some scared little girl.

Even if I felt like one.

I clung to the side of the wall as I descended the steps, hoping the dizziness would fade. I strained to hear any sounds, but the downstairs was oddly silent. As I reached the bottom step, I realized both my cousins had weapons, and I was defenseless. I peeked around the corner into the dining room and saw it was empty. I heard more noises out behind the house, and the sound of a car engine.

I left the staircase, grabbed a crystal candlestick from Meemaw's hutch, and entered the kitchen through the swinging door. It was quiet again, but the back door was open. An exterior light was on, and I saw three figures in the shadows near the barn. One of them took off running for Teddy's pickup truck.

Distant sirens filled the night air as I slipped out the door.

"Teddy!" Meemaw shouted. "Don't go doin' something foolish!"

But her words didn't even slow Teddy down as he climbed inside the truck.

"Is he goin' after the people who tried to break in?"

"Summer!" Dixie shouted. "What are you doin' out here?"

"Seein' what all the commotion's about. Is he goin' after them?"

"Yes."

The truck started, and he swung it in a wide circle, driving to the lane between the house and the detached garage.

I knew going after someone who'd broken into your home with a loaded shotgun was a recipe for trouble, so I ran over to the gravel driveway and stood in the middle as Teddy barreled toward me.

"Summer!" Dixie screamed.

Teddy laid on the horn, but I stood my ground, counting on the fact that the guy who'd carried me upstairs so sweetly a few hours ago wasn't about to mow me down now.

The sirens were close enough that flashing lights were bouncing off the garage.

Teddy hit the brakes, and gravel went flying as he skidded to a stop. Only he'd picked up enough speed that he wasn't going to stop in time to miss me.

Shit. I was in an unintentional game of chicken with my cousin.

I darted for the house, reasoning that he'd aim for the garage before damaging our century-old home. Thankfully, I was right—and I barely had time to wonder if I had saved him only to unintentionally injure him when he came to a stop before hitting the cinder-block garage.

"What the Sam Hill's goin' on here?" Luke shouted from behind me.

Teddy got out of his truck, ignoring the police chief and instead stalking toward me. "What the hell were you doin', Summer? I could have killed you!" He grabbed his head with both hands and bent over his knees. *"Fuck!"*

My heart racing like it was in a hundred-yard dash, I started to move toward him, but Luke blocked my path, lifting a hand to hold me back.

"What's goin' on, Teddy?" Luke barked. "Why did I pull up to find you nearly running down your cousin?"

He flung a hand out toward me. "She stood in the middle of the drive, blocking the path. I was goin' after whoever broke in."

Luke glanced over his shoulder at me as though waiting for me to disagree or concur.

"I've lost too many family members to tragedy." My voice cracked. "I wasn't going to risk losing Teddy too. Who knows what would have happened to him if he'd caught up to them."

Luke turned his attention back to Teddy. "She's right, man. What were you thinkin'?"

Teddy stood upright, his chest puffing out. "I was thinkin' that I was protectin' my family and what's mine."

"That's for me and my men to figure out, Teddy. Not you."

"Not if they're on my land!" he spat out while he clenched his fist.

"But you were about to chase 'em *off* your land." Luke dropped his hand and took a step to the side. "Let's just everyone take a breath, and then you can tell me what happened." He glanced toward the barn. "Dixie and Miss Viola, if you'd be so kind as to put away your guns, I'd feel a little better."

I hadn't noticed before, but sure enough they were both armed—Dixie with her handgun and Meemaw with a shotgun. The both lowered their weapons.

Luke shot a glance to the candlestick still in my hand. "And if you're planning to redecorate, you'll have to wait until I'm done."

I narrowed my eyes and put a hand on my hip.

His back stiffened, and he turned to me, giving me his full attention. "What the hell are you doin' here at all? Dr. Livingston said he was keeping you until tomorrow."

"I decided to leave early, not that it's any of your business!" I advanced toward him. "What's the doctor doing givin' you my personal medical information? Isn't that against the law?"

His jaw clenched. "I was checking in case I needed to give you protection in the hospital. And then I talked to Deputy Dixon."

"Oh, really? So you think I'm lying too?" I was standing in front of him now, and I had to lean my head back to look up at him. "You think I moved Otto Olson's body to the woods for a freaking TV show I hate?" I knew he didn't really believe that—he'd said as much in the morgue—but he'd also confessed our history might be clouding his judgment.

"If you hate it so much, quit!"

I wasn't having this conversation with him again. We'd started having it twelve years ago, and it never ended any differently, so why were we still wasting our time? "Don't you have other things to do besides berate me for my career choices, *Officer*?" I said in a snotty tone. "Like investigate the break-in?"

"*Was* there a break-in?" he asked in an equally hateful tone.

I gasped in pure shock.

His face fell. "Summer . . ."

Teddy took up the mantel of confronting Luke. "Are you seriously callin' my cousin a *liar*?"

Luke lifted his hands in defense. "Teddy, I was out of line."

"I'll say." His eyes widened, and he took a step toward Luke as he started putting things together. "Jesus Christ! You think she was lying about gettin' attacked?"

Luke took a step back, still holding his hands up in a defensive stance. "I didn't say that."

Teddy was standing in front of me now, putting himself between us. "Then why would you suspect her of movin' Otto's body?" He glanced over at me, then back to Luke. "How the hell would Summer be able to move Otto's body? Jesus Christ," he said in disgust. "I knew you hated her, but that's low even for you."

The words felt like a slap across the face. "Oh, my God." I walked around Teddy to face Luke. "You told people you hated me?"

"Summer. No."

Teddy balled his fists at his sides. "Get the hell off our land."

"Teddy," Luke said in a pleading tone as he extended his hand toward him, "tempers are short—"

"You're damn right they are."

"But if you had a break-in, we need to investigate."

"I don't trust you to investigate, Luke Montgomery," Teddy said, taking a step toward him. "You didn't see Summer when she came home tonight. She looked like a fuckin' ghost. I had to carry her upstairs for fear she'd pass out before she even got inside the house. I take great offense to you insinuatin' she's fakin' that."

Luke cast a concerned glance toward me. "Summer. Maybe you should sit down."

"Don't you talk to her!" Teddy pointed a finger at him. "You have no right to talk to her. In fact, get the hell out of here before I call the sheriff to haul your ass off."

"I know she's not fakin' it, Teddy. I talked to her doctor—"

"To see if she was fakin'?"

"No!" Luke took a step back and put his hands on top of his head. "I'm talkin' to you man-to-man now, Teddy, not as the police chief." He paused to make sure Teddy was listening. "I know Summer's not fakin' anything. We may have our differences, but she's incapable of that kind of duplicity. Was she attacked? I'd like to talk to her more about that. I thought she was spending the night in the hospital, and I planned to talk to her tomorrow, which is now today." He pushed out a breath when he realized Teddy was listening. "But I do know something happened to her in the woods, and I'm trying to figure that out."

Teddy took in two heavy breaths before he answered. "I thought the sheriff's department was handling Otto's death."

Luke took a step closer and nodded. "They are, but just like you take care of your own, I take care of my own too."

My chest froze. Was Luke calling me his own? While part of me took great offense, another part of me rejoiced.

"My sworn duty is to protect the citizens of Sweet Briar," he continued as he held Teddy's gaze, "and I take that very seriously. And since Summer's originally from here and temporarily livin' here again, she's included in that."

Oh. Of course. That buoyant feeling that had risen inside me sank, carrying the rest of my energy with it. I knew I wouldn't be able to remain upright much longer. "I've got to sit down."

Teddy snaked an arm around me, pulling me to his side. "I still want you gone, Luke."

"Teddy, listen to me. The sheriff's department is the one trying to pin this Otto mess on Summer. If you want to help her, then keep them out of it." He paused. "We're on the same side here."

"Fine, then no one's investigatin'. Matter of a fact, there wasn't a break-in."

Luke released a groan.

"Teddy," Meemaw said, "enough of this nonsense. The window on the back bedroom is busted out."

"Raccoons busted out a window last year," Teddy said in a gruff tone.

"We may grow coons big here," she said, "but I've never seen one get big enough to drive off in a truck."

Meemaw walked over to us, and her tone softened as she held Teddy's gaze. "Your Pawpaw and your daddy would be proud of ya, boy—standin' up for your family. But you have to know when to back down."

"Just like you've always backed away from anything to do with Summer?" he asked with a hard edge in his voice.

Her eyes narrowed. "That's enough, boy."

"Is it? You've been dancing around her bein' back ever since that woman came to talk to you about her stayin' here."

"This is a family discussion."

"Family . . . some family."

My grandmother looked so angry, I was sure she was going to snap his head off. "This is still my land, boy . . ."

"And you never tire of reminding me of that."

The pain in Teddy's voice broke my heart.

I tugged on his arm and whispered, "Don't do this on my account, Teddy."

He glanced down at me. "Family actually means something to me, Summer."

He made it sound like a conviction, only I was sure he wasn't convicting *me*.

Teddy glanced from Luke to our grandmother. "You two make me sick. Did you ever once stop and put yourself in Summer's shoes?" He shook his head in disgust. "You do whatever you want, Meemaw. You always do." He steered me toward the front porch, and I staggered along with him, hating that I was the source of this conflict.

"Teddy, I'm sorry," I whispered as tears stung my eyes.

"Don't you dare tell me that." Then he grinned. "Unless you plan to tell me sorry for almost makin' me run you down." He paused. "Jesus. I think I aged ten years."

I leaned my head into his chest. "I couldn't let you get hurt. I heard gunshots. What if they shot you?"

"I was the one to get off a few shots."

"Okay, then," I said as we started up the porch steps. "What if you caught up with the robbers and got so pissed you shot them? Luke wouldn't be able to get you out of those charges."

"Just like he didn't get Dixie out of her charges?"

The blood rushed to my feet, and I stumbled on the top step, but Teddy held me up. "What?"

I stood still on the front porch.

"Luke was the one who arrested Dixie for setting the old barn on fire." He studied me. "You didn't know?

I shook my head.

"Sorry, Summy. I thought you did."

I couldn't help the small smile that surfaced at his use of his childhood nickname for me, but it faded as soon as his words registered. "How can Dixie stand talkin' to him?"

"She doesn't blame him, but I do. My family had already been ripped to pieces, then Luke went and stole my sister too."

I closed my eyes, suffocating in guilt. "Oh, Teddy. I'm so, so sorry. I should have been here for you."

"You were livin' in your own hell."

My eyes opened and I glanced up at him. "What?"

"I'm not blind, unlike half the people around here, and I'm certainly not as stupid as Meemaw gives me credit for. I know Aunt Bea. She's a manipulator and a bitch. I remember how much you always hated those pageants. You never wanted that life. You wanted to live here and marry Luke and have a family of your own and live on Baumgartner land. Aunt Beatrice stole your life from you."

I gazed up at him in wonder. Someone finally understood.

"Ah . . . don't cry, Summy. Why're you cryin'?"

I hadn't even realized there were tears in my eyes. "Because I love you so much."

I threw my arms around his neck, and his wrapped around me. "I always have your back, Summer. *Always*. I take my responsibility as your cousin seriously. Just like my responsibility for Dixie."

I couldn't believe he was giving me the same status as his sister. "I was gone for so long."

"We were always more like siblings than cousins," he said with a crack in his voice. "The spell we spent apart doesn't change that. But you're back now. That's what matters, isn't it? Dixie came back and then you did. The Baumgartner kids are together again."

I started crying. "I'm so stupid."

"Why would you say that?"

"Because I was so scared to come back and face Meemaw. She made it clear that I wasn't welcome here, but I should have fought harder to stay in the family. I was missin' out on two something wonderfuls—you and Dixie."

"That's all water under the bridge," he said. "You're here now. That's what matters." Then he leaned back and searched my face. "Promise me you won't ever jump out in front of my truck again."

"No. I'll do whatever it takes to protect you, Teddy. We Baumgartner kids have each *other's* backs."

Chapter Twenty-One

Teddy and I went into the kitchen, and he made me sit at the small two-person table shoved up against the wall while he set the kettle on the stove.

"Maybe you should go back to bed, Summer."

I shook my head. "I could never go back to sleep." Which was a lie. I was about to pass out in my chair, but it didn't feel right to go to bed while Luke was here investigating.

"Then how about we go hang out in the living room after I get your tea made? I hate these old, rickety chairs."

"Okay."

About five minutes later, Dixie came inside and saw Teddy fixing my tea.

"I want a cup of tea," she said in a good-natured whine.

"Fine," he said. "I'll make you one too." But he turned back and grinned at me, and I felt grateful that I was here with them.

I started to cry again.

"Summer?" Dixie asked, sounding worried. "Why are you cryin'? Are you feelin' bad?"

"No. It's because I'm so happy."

"Happy? You're sittin' in Meemaw's chair that's about to collapse underneath you at two in the morning because someone tried to break into the room you've been sleepin' in, and then your own cousin tried to run you over, and then that same cousin got into a huge argument with your old boyfriend."

"That has to be one of the longest sentences ever." But Dixie was right. My feelings were crazy given the circumstances, yet there was no denying them. Maybe I'd suffered brain damage. I'd give it more consideration as soon as I could think straight. I grabbed a napkin from a wooden napkin holder decorated with a hand-painted design of a goat and a frog. I was pretty sure it was something Teddy had made in his woodshop. "And yes, I'm happy that I'm here with the two of you."

Dixie grunted. "I'm all for family time, but I prefer for it to be between nine a.m. and midnight."

"I'll remember that for future reference."

Teddy reached for my arm and helped me out of my chair. "Let's go into the living room."

"I'm not an invalid, Teddy."

"No, but you're supposed to still be in the hospital, so let us baby you." His eyes narrowed. "If you start cryin' again, I'm not gonna give you your tea."

"Yes, you will," I said with a huge grin as tears leaked from my eyes.

"Why couldn't God give me a boy cousin?" Teddy asked as he picked up my cup. "Or a brother?" he asked, pushing his way through the swinging door.

"Hush. You love us." Dixie grinned. "I made pie earlier. You get Summer settled, and I'll get you a slice."

"Deal."

Several minutes later, we were in the living room, with Dixie and me snuggled up on the sofa and Teddy in the matching love seat. I took a few bites of pie and a sip of tea and then, content and cozy, leaned my head back against the cushions.

I must have dozed off, because the next thing I knew, I was alone on the sofa, and Luke was saying something at the front door.

"Sh . . . ," Dixie said, hidden behind the short wall marking the entryway. "Summer's asleep on the couch."

"Why did she really leave the hospital, Dixie?" he asked.

"She was freaked out."

"You believe she was attacked?"

"Yeah, I do. And I sure as shoot know she didn't move Otto Olson's body. And before you can ask, I didn't do it either. I'm stayin' out of trouble, Luke. Just like I promised."

That got my attention. She'd made some kind of deal with Luke?

"Did you tell Teddy?" she asked.

"I told you I wouldn't tell a soul. Why?"

She paused. "Nothing. Right now we need to think about Summer and the break-in."

"I'll be honest, Dixie," he said. "I don't know what to make of any of this. Why did they break in to her window? Did it wake her up?"

"She was up in my room because I wanted her close to me. The only reason she was stayin' at the hospital was because they wanted to make sure she didn't slip into a coma."

"*What?*"

"Calm down," she said. "The chances were low, otherwise I wouldn't have brought her home."

"How many people know she's stayin' here?" Luke asked.

"The whole dang town."

They were quiet for a minute before Luke said, "Do you think someone's after Summer?"

"I don't know," she said in quiet voice. "But I can't help thinking someone is settin' her up."

"Teddy is sure the break-in happened because of him. He says he thinks they broke in to get money he'd won in a poker game. He claims he pissed a few guys off because of his winnin' streak."

"Then maybe that's the reason," she said. But I wasn't sure if he believed her—I knew I didn't.

"She's takin' it easy tomorrow, right?" he asked. "I don't have to worry about her traipsing around town?"

"She's going to work," Dixie said. "But if it makes you feel any better, she's planning on keepin' it pretty tame . . . lots of sittin' around and interviewing Lauren's lame clients."

"They can't be that tame if they almost got Summer killed."

"That was our doin'," Dixie said. "We followed a lead that Otto's bike was at the lake."

"Lead? What lead? Deputy Dixon never said a word about a lead."

"I guess that's because he was puttin' so much effort into makin' sure she looked guilty. People hate her just because she's Summer Butler. I know you try to pretend you hate her too."

"Dixie."

"Look, I'm just sayin' most people have a motive for doin' things to someone else, but Summer gets haters just for breathin'. You know there's a few people around here who are jealous of her. Isn't that why you broke up with Gina Matherson?"

Oh, my God. Luke had dated Gina Matherson? She'd been the queen of gossip in middle school, and the summer Luke and I had dated, he'd insisted she hadn't changed. Of all the people in town, she was one of the last I could see him dating.

"I don't want to talk about Gina. Tell me more about the lead at the church."

I knew I should tell them I was awake, but every conversation Luke and I had devolved into an argument. At least he was getting useful information from Dixie.

"After we interviewed Reverend Miller and a church member, Summer went to the bathroom and called you."

"Yeah . . ."

"Well, I guess this guy popped out of a classroom and told her he'd seen Otto's bike out on a trail near the lake. Said he was there fishin'. We went out there to see if we could find a lead on Otto. Summer thought the guy who told her was a janitor because he had a broom, but when she described him later, I knew she'd been tricked. The guy she saw was in his twenties, but Old Pete is the real janitor there—has been for years—and he's in his seventies."

"So who did she talk to?"

"Beats me."

"You didn't see him?"

"No. Only Summer."

"Hmm . . ."

"What's that supposed to mean?" she asked in an accusatory tone.

"Nothin'. Just tryin' to get the facts straight."

"Huh." Dixie didn't sound convinced.

"Look, if someone *is* settin' her up, it makes sense they'd wait until she was alone to give her the information. With no witnesses, it's easier to cast doubt on her story."

"But who set her up, and why would the sheriff's deputy believe she moved the body?"

"I don't know, but I aim to find out." He paused. "Just keep an eye on her, okay?" Luke asked in a soft tone. "And if anything looks amiss . . . call me."

"You still care about her," Dixie said.

"If I can prevent anyone from getting hurt or injured, I'll do it."

"So you're only doin' this because it's your job."

"You say that like it's a bad thing."

"It's just what every girl likes to hear."

"Dixie . . . ," he said in a warning tone.

"Just sayin'."

"I'm goin' home and goin' to bed. I have to be at the Rotary breakfast at eight. You still doin' okay?" he asked.

"Yeah."

"I'm a phone call away, Dixie. You know that."

"Thanks."

What was that all about?

"One more thing," Luke said. "When was the last time you saw Ryker?"

"I don't want to talk about Ryker."

"You're better off without him. He wasn—*isn't* a good man."

"I know," she said, her voice heavy with tears.

Dixie told him goodbye, then walked into the living room with her hand on her hip. "How much of that did you hear?"

I felt terrible. "Dixie . . ."

"Hey," she said, "no judgment here. I wouldn't have interrupted that conversation either." She paused. "He still has feelings for you, you know."

"No, he doesn't," I said, but my heart beat a little faster in my chest. To lighten the moment, I added, "Besides, how could I ever be with someone who slept with that gossip Gina Matherson?"

"You were with that scumbag Connor Blake."

I shuddered. "I never slept with my sleazy costar. He just made the world think we did." And Luke too.

"Well . . ."—she sat down beside me—"I'd bet the whole farm that Luke didn't sleep with Gina even though she tried to convince everyone it happened."

"Dixie . . . Luke and I are like oil and vinegar. You can throw 'em in a bottle and get them to stick together for a little bit, but they always separate. Always." And that knowledge made me sadder than I wanted to admit.

"Let's go to bed," she said, getting to her feet and pulling me off the couch. "You need your rest."

"Okay."

We went upstairs, and I was dragging by the time we got to the top.

"I should have had Teddy carry me back up," I joked.

"He probably would have done it too if he were here."

That caught my attention. "Where'd he go?"

"Beats me. He said he needed to think." She must have seen the concern on my face because she said, "Don't worry. It's his thing. You know how Pawpaw liked to walk the farm? Well, Teddy does too. He'll be back once he feels better."

"You're sure he didn't go after the guys he thinks broke in?"

"Honestly, I don't know."

"Don't baby me, Dixie," I said as I sank onto the bed. "I want the truth even when it's hard. He went after them."

After a moment of silence, she lay down beside me. "Maybe."

Worry slithered through my gut.

"Don't concern yourself about Teddy. He's the most level-headed of all of us. He's nobody's fool. If he went after them, he knows the odds are on his side. He'll be careful."

I was counting on it.

CHAPTER TWENTY-TWO

When I woke up the next morning, I was glad I'd sent Lauren a text saying we would be in late. In fact, part of me was sorry I said I'd go in at all. I was pretty sure I'd benefit from sleeping the day away. But I had a new incentive to make this show work—Teddy and Dixie had reminded me that we were a family. The show had to succeed so we could pay off that loan. Then I could figure out where I fit in here.

Still, I couldn't let go of the conversation I'd overheard between Teddy and Dixie the night before. I needed to talk to Teddy and find out what financial issues he was dealing with regarding the farm, but I was also worried about how he'd come up with the extra cash. I was particularly worried after Dixie had suggested his strategy might not be on the up-and-up.

After I showered and went into the kitchen, I was surprised to see my grandmother in front of the stove frying bacon. Dixie was still in the shower, and there was no sign of Teddy. I almost walked out, but the coffee smell was begging me to stay.

"Good morning," I said as I walked over to the cabinet and grabbed a mug.

She didn't answer while I poured myself some coffee and topped it off with milk. I tried to ignore my disappointment as I headed for the swinging door.

"Where you goin'?" she asked, her gaze still on the skillet. "I'm about to start the pancakes."

My mouth dropped open, but nothing came out.

She glanced up at me. "You're too damn skinny. Your momma always wanted you that way, keepin' pieces of pie and cookies from you . . . Well, you're home now, and Baumgartners eat."

Tears flooded my eyes. This was as close to a declaration of love as I was going to get from Meemaw. "Yes, ma'am," I croaked out.

"We still have ten minutes, so go tell your cousins."

I could still hear the shower upstairs, so I went out the front door to drink my coffee on the porch. I was surprised to see Teddy sitting on the steps with his own cup of coffee.

"Is there room for me?" I asked.

He glanced over his shoulder and grinned. "Summy, what are you doin' out of bed?"

"No rest for the wicked," I said, descending the steps. I squeezed in next to him, bumping him with my hip to get him to make room.

"Tell me about it." He chuckled as he scooted over, but all the laughter had left his voice when he asked, "Why were you and Dixie out at Lake Edna yesterday?"

I realized that he didn't know anything about our investigations—fake or otherwise. I told him about the cases Lauren had lined up, then said, "But Otto . . . he was really missing. And Gretchen was so upset. The Sweet Briar Police weren't lookin' into it, and Lauren saw no urgency in the matter, so I decided we could kill two birds with one stone—find Otto and help redeem my image on the show."

"It almost got you killed, Summer."

"I wasn't purposely lookin' for danger. No one thought anything bad had happened to Otto." Dixie and I hadn't bought that, but there was no need to tell him that. "The janitor told me he'd seen Otto's bike out there, so we went to look."

Teddy sat up. "What janitor?"

I told him what I remembered about the incident, then added his description. "He was average height and build, he had brown eyes, a trim beard, and short brown hair—nearly shaved—and he was wearing a blue T-shirt and jeans. Do you know who it could have been?"

He shook his head. "No. Not a clue." He turned to me, looking more serious. "You need to leave everything regarding Otto Olson alone."

"What?"

"It's obviously bigger than you and Dixie thought. You should step aside and let the police handle it."

"Teddy."

"I'm serious, Summer. Stick to your fake cases with Lauren or, if you hate it enough, quit."

"I can't quit."

"If the show's makin' you miserable, then do it. Ignore the whole Baumgartners-aren't-quitters motto. Meemaw'll get over it."

"It's more than that." I took a sip of my coffee, then turned to face him. "I need to be honest about something, Teddy. The reason I'm really here." I hadn't intended to say anything, but the secret had been weighing more heavily on me now that I was here with them. It was harder to ignore.

A grin twitched at the corners of his lips. "You're working for the cotton farmers in Dale County, trying to learn my secrets."

"I'm serious, Teddy."

He sat up slightly. "Okay."

"A few months before the fire, I was in Atlanta filming a commercial, and Pawpaw came up to see me."

Teddy watched me intently.

"The farm was having problems . . . there had been a huge rainy period, and the fields were too wet to harvest. Most of the crop was lost."

"I remember," he said. "I was in school up at Alabama A&M. I was concerned about the rain, but Dad and Pawpaw said there was nothing to worry about."

"Pawpaw asked me for a loan."

He turned to look out at the land in front of us. "So you gave him one?"

"Sort of." I pushed out a breath and leaned over my knees. "He needed three hundred thousand to tide him over to the next year, but he had two conditions. One, he wouldn't let me give him the money outright. He asked me to cosign a loan with a ten-year balloon payment. I was to make the payments for the first year, then he'd take over as soon as he got back on his feet. He was certain he could pay it off before it came due. But then he died, and Momma and I had our falling-out, and she took off with my money."

He did a double take. "Wait. *What?*"

"The loan—"

"Not the loan, Summer. The part about your mother taking your money. She said the money she had was from managing your career."

I gave him a sad smile. "I finally stood up to Momma, and my bank account was the price I paid."

"She stole your money? Why didn't you press charges?"

"Dixie. It would have caught the attention of the media, and I was doin' my best to lie low and let the news about the fire fizzle out. If I'd prosecuted or sued . . . especially since Momma ran back here . . ."

His eyes sank closed. "You gave up your money to protect Dixie." He sounded heartsick.

I glanced at the door behind me. "You can never tell her. Swear to me."

"Yeah, I won't. She would hate that. But I don't understand how this happened."

"Bottom line, Momma took most of my money, which meant I couldn't just outright pay off the loan. I've been making the payments ever since, but the balloon payment is coming due, Teddy. And that's why I'm here—I'll make enough money from this show to pay it off."

"Why didn't you tell me?" he asked, starting to sound pissed.

"That was the second part of the promise: I couldn't tell Meemaw."

He gave me a wry grin. "Uh, I know you had a head injury, but I'm still not sure how you've confused me with Meemaw."

"You were still in college when Pawpaw died, and then you dropped out of school, and you were dealing with the whole mess with Dixie and the farm . . . I didn't want to worry you. And if I'm being honest, I was sure I'd make the money back. I never expected to be nearly thirty years old and so flat-out broke that I'm on the verge of losing my house *and* the family farm." I grabbed his hand. "But I'm going to save the farm, Teddy. I promise you that."

"Jesus, Summer. You're losing your house? Don't you want to put the money toward that?"

"It's too late for that, and if I have to choose, I pick the farm."

"Where are you gonna live when this is done?"

"I don't know yet."

"Do you want to go back to California? You never wanted that life."

"I don't know. I don't know anything."

"I do. You have a home here, Summy. You belong here with us."

My eyes filled with tears, and I rested my head on his shoulder to hide them. "I heard you and Dixie talking last night. I take it the farm has more money problems."

His shoulder stiffened under my cheek. "I'm takin' care of it, Summer."

"But if we work together—"

"You have the loan covered. Leave it to me to handle the rest." He leaned down and kissed my temple.

"Why'd Dixie think you might know something about what happened to her old boyfriend?"

"I do. Ryker Pelletier was a drug-dealin' piece of white trash, and he got what was comin' to him." His voice was so hard he didn't sound anything like himself.

I sat up. "Did Dixie know?"

The screen door opened and Dixie asked, "Did Dixie know what?"

"About Ryker bein' in the Sweet Briar Hospital morgue," Teddy said, getting to his feet.

Did the abrupt change in subject mean Dixie *didn't* know about Ryker dealing drugs?

"I was with you when we found him," Dixie said. "Don't you remember? Maybe you shouldn't work today."

"I remember," I said, rubbing my eyes. "I'm just tired, but I *have* to work today." I looked up at Teddy for support now that he knew the stakes.

"She'll be okay, but if she looks too tired, tell that witch Lauren she's either taking a break or coming home."

"I'll have no problem keepin' Lauren in line," Dixie said, "but you need to keep the news about Ryker to yourself. Luke's still keepin' his identity secret, which means we're not supposed to know."

"Did Luke tell *you* last night?" Teddy asked.

"Definitely not."

Teddy's brow lowered into a scowl. "I still don't get why you're civil to the man who ruined your life."

Dixie groaned. "I'm not having this conversation *again*. Let it go."

My phone started to ring in my pocket.

"Get yourselves in here," Meemaw called out from inside the house. "Breakfast is ready."

I tugged my phone out, and my heart stuck in my chest when I saw it was Marina's number. LA was two hours behind, which meant it was close to seven in the morning there. Way too early for Marina to be calling me.

"I'll be there in a minute," I said. "My best friend is callin'."

"Don't take too long," Dixie said. "Meemaw will tan your hide if the pancakes get cold."

"Start without me."

I answered the phone while Dixie and Teddy went inside. "Marina, what are you doin' callin' me this early?"

"I just found out you were attacked! Why didn't you call me?"

"I'm sorry . . . yesterday was crazy."

"I had to find out on the news, Summer! They said you were in the hospital in critical condition with a head injury!"

"It's not as bad as it sounds. In fact, I'm sitting on Meemaw's front porch drinking a cup of coffee. I really am sorry."

She hesitated. "How's it going out there?"

I pushed out a huge groan. "Workin' with Lauren is just as difficult as we expected, but it's good gettin' to be with my family again."

"I hear your Alabama accent is coming back."

"Yeah . . ." I sighed. No use fighting it.

"Have you seen your ex?"

"Multiple times. It's gone better than expected."

"Is the spark still there?"

I wasn't sure what to tell her. In truth, the spark had never left. The real question was how smart it would be to consider fanning it into a flame. "It's complicated." I heard my grandmother yelling my name. "I have to go, Marina. I'll call you soon. Thanks again for house-sitting." Given how many paparazzi had staked out my house, we'd agreed it would be a good idea for Marina to stay there and keep an eye on things.

"You better . . . But, hey! Before you go, I thought you should know that those weird hang-up calls on your house phone have stopped."

After my right hook made national television, I'd gotten several calls to my landline from a blocked number. The caller would quietly say my name and then hang up. "Well, I guess that's a good thing, right? They must have figured out I'm not there right now."

"I guess, but I still have a bad feeling about it."

"You know weird things happen with me. But if they've stopped, then we have nothing to worry about. I'll call you later, Marina. Thanks."

"Be careful out there, Summer."

"I plan to."

By the time I finally joined my family at the table, Dixie and Teddy were nearly done, and I was full after a few bites. The nurse had told me not to operate any moving vehicles until my vision was fully repaired, so Dixie drove the truck into town while I dozed in the passenger seat. I woke up when she pulled into a parking spot close to the office, and I was beginning to question whether I could handle going back to work. My head felt like it was splitting in two, and my vision was fuzzy.

When we walked into the office at nine thirty, Lauren had a full-blown conniption.

"You're late!"

"I'm not supposed to be here at all, Lauren," I said, sitting in my chair. The room was hot, stuffy, and crowded with people. Her yelling wasn't helping my headache. "The doctor expected me to take time off, but I'll be fine as long as I don't overdo it."

She gave me her version of a death stare, but it was hard to take someone seriously after seeing them plastered with your vomit.

"I'm here," I said. "I'm gonna stick this out for as long as I can." I glanced over at the crew. "Is it just me, or is it hot in here?"

"The a/c's out," Tony said. "We're leaving the door propped open for now, but someone's coming to look at it."

Karen was studying me, looking pleased as she said to Lauren, "I told you her bruises would look worse today. It makes this whole thing more authentic."

Or it would make me look like a joke, depending on how Lauren decided to spin it. I wouldn't put it past her to play up the Summer-moved-Otto's-body-and-faked-her-attack angle to manipulate ratings. I had to earn my $50,000-per-episode salary, and she might decide this was how.

I sucked in a breath. We'd only been filming for two days, but other than Otto's body and my attack, there was absolutely *nothing* to justify the high price tag. Oh, Lord. What if she found out the other dead guy was Dixie's ex-boyfriend? And if he had been a drug dealer . . . I had to make sure she had plenty of other drama for the show. Even if it painted me in a bad light.

Then something else occurred to me.

Maybe she really *was* behind moving the body, only not how we'd thought. Maybe this was all some elaborate scheme to set me up and make me look like a fool. It was safe to say she didn't like me, and she seemed ambitious enough not to think twice about sabotaging people to benefit her own career.

Lauren threw up her hands. "Whatever. We're an hour and a half behind schedule. Let's get started."

I wanted to point out that I'd warned her in the text I'd sent the night before, but it would have been wasted breath.

"Okay," Lauren said, "to accommodate Summer's *special needs*"—she used air quotes to insinuate I was being a diva—"Karen has rearranged the schedule again. She's set up a series of interviews for most of the day so our 'star' can sit her pretty little ass in a chair all day."

I was past caring what Lauren thought of me, but I did want the respect of the crew. A quick glance assured me they knew what was going on. They all seemed sympathetic, all except . . . "Where's Bill?"

"You don't need to worry about Bill," Lauren said. "That's my job."

I shot a worried glance to Dixie, who was sitting at her own desk. Had Lauren figured out that Bill had offered to help us and fired him? But Dixie gave me a reassuring smile, and I was pretty sure she'd been in contact with him. He was probably out getting B-roll.

Lauren went through a list of six interviews, which ranged from a couple who thought their housekeeper was stealing from them to a husband and wife who questioned which neighborhood dog had impregnated their Yorkie show dog, and a follow-up visit with the adulterer's wife, Nettie Peabody.

"If you'll give me your spare outfits, I'll put them in the back," Karen said. I was taken aback when I realized she was addressing Dixie and me.

"What?"

She gave me a blank look. "You were supposed to bring two or three extra outfits to wear for the interviews." When I didn't say anything, she added, "We're filming all those interviews today, but we don't want it to look like they happened on the same day."

That made sense, but it was the first I'd heard of it. I glanced at Dixie again, and she gave me a sunny smile. "Got it covered." Then she reached down into her oversize bag and pulled out a smaller bag.

Karen took it from her and looked inside.

"How are you going to explain the bruises on my face not changing over multiple 'days'?" I asked, the sound of my own voice sending shock waves of pain through my head. I already needed another round of over-the-counter painkillers.

"Seriously, Summer?" Lauren groaned. "I thought you were a professional. *Makeup.*"

Of course. And any other time I would have realized that. *Maybe I should call today off.* "Sorry, Lauren," I sighed as I rubbed my temple. "This is my first foray into *reality* TV."

"Keep it up and your next reality show will be filming a porno."

"*Excuse me?*" Luke asked from the doorway.

My mouth dropped open when I saw him. What was he doing here?

"Can I help you with something, *Chief?*" Lauren asked dryly. "Because this is a closed set."

"Then maybe you should have closed the door."

She walked over to him, but something in her had changed. There was a certain swagger in her step that suggested she wasn't any less attracted to Luke after seeing him covered in vomit. "This is private property, *Chief.*"

The way she kept saying *chief* made me wonder if Lauren had a thing for law-enforcement officers.

"And I'm standing in the threshold."

Lauren tipped one shoulder higher and tilted her head just a bit to the side, a slightly dismissive gesture, but it was obvious she was coming on to him. "I might be able to invite you in if you're a good boy."

"Is that an invitation to be in one of your pornos?" he asked sarcastically.

She got flustered and took a step back. "*I* don't make pornos," she said, outrage filling her voice.

"And the last time I checked, neither does Ms. Butler."

Lauren put a hand on her hip and her gaze narrowed. "Is there something I can help you with, Chief Montgomery?"

He looked down at her with cool disdain. "You? No." His gaze lifted to me. "I need to speak to Ms. Butler, but it's not urgent."

"She'll be busy all day," Lauren said, glaring up at him.

"Surely she gets a lunch break. Isn't that union rules?"

My eyes widened in shock. I'd told him plenty about movie and TV-show sets during our summer together, but he'd never seemed particularly interested. This was proof he *had* paid attention. I knew he wanted to talk to me about Otto, but I was surprised he'd gone to the trouble of dropping by the office.

Lauren turned her glare on Karen.

"Yes," Karen said, getting flustered as she glanced down at her tablet. "But we haven't scheduled a time yet. We have two interviews to get to this morning, and we never know how long those will last."

Luke turned to my cousin. "Dixie, you're her assistant, right?"

She sat up straighter in her seat. "Yeah."

"Would you give me a call when Ms. Butler gets a lunch break?"

She gave me a glance as though asking permission, so I gave a tiny nod. She turned back to Luke. "Yeah. Sure."

Luke's gaze landed on me for a few seconds as though studying me to make sure I was okay. "Thanks." Then he headed down the sidewalk toward the coffee shop.

"What was that about?" Lauren asked.

"I have no idea," I said, not wanting to get into it. If she found out this was likely related to Otto, she'd probably figure out a way to film it.

"You need to keep your personal life out of the workplace." Then Lauren started barking orders to start the first interview.

The morning dragged on. Nettie came in to hear her report, and we explained that while we'd gotten plenty of proof of her husband's cheating, my camera had been stolen.

"You mean someone else has photos of my husband in his skivvies?" she screeched.

My mouth parted as I turned toward Dixie. The whole world was going to see him without a shirt, though they'd see every last bit of the couple's dirty laundry, and she was worried about a few tame photos.

Dixie quickly took over. "Don't worry, Nettie. He doesn't look all that great in them, so no one's gonna be pinnin' him up on their wall."

She only calmed down after we reluctantly agreed to get more photos. Lauren made us run the scene again, this time pretending to show Nettie photos on my laptop.

The next clients, Derick and Mallory Hinton, were the ones with the dog—which they'd brought with them. The Hintons were in their thirties and didn't look like they were from around Sweet Briar. They seemed too polished. Derick wore expensive dress pants and loafers and a silk tie he wore with his fitted (and probably tailored) dress shirt. Mallory wore a designer black dress and heels and carried a Prada purse.

Dixie greeted them and motioned the two to the chairs in front of my desk before maneuvering her chair closer.

Mallory cradled her Yorkie to her chest. The dog had a pink bow between her ears and studied me as though trying to decide if I was friend or foe. "Our little Fifi was violated."

"Now, Mallory," Derick cooed, rubbing his wife's arm, "Fifi doesn't seem the worse for wear."

Mallory turned on her husband with fury in her eyes, jerking her arm from his touch. "I wouldn't expect you to understand, Derick. You're a *man*."

"Oh, my God, Mallory. Not that again. She's a dog."

Mallory became even more outraged. "A dog? She's like a child to me! And our child was raped!"

While their argument would probably be good for ratings, it was making my head hurt even more. "Did you witness the event that led to Fifi's impregnation?"

She pressed her lips tightly together. "No. Well . . ."

"Mallory," I said, "before we know if we can help you, you have to give us something to follow up on. But first, let me ask you this: what do you plan to do when you find out which dog impregnated Fifi?"

"Stop saying *impregnated*. You make it sound . . . normal." She shuddered. "My poor dog was *violated*."

"Was she injured?" I asked.

She frowned. "Not that I know of."

"Y'all aren't from around here, are you?" Dixie asked in disbelief.

"No," Derick said, "we're from Atlanta, and we were told Sweet Briar is a bedroom community of Dothan."

"I see," Dixie said, then turned her attention to Mallory. "Mrs. Hinton," Dixie said, drawing out her name, "you do know how all that works, don't you?"

"What works?"

Dixie narrowed her eyes. "When a dog goes in heat."

"You mean when she's on her period?" Mallory asked.

"Okay . . . ," Dixie said with forced patience. "So you know that a lot of dogs in heat are lookin' for . . . a boyfriend."

Mallory's eyes widened. "*What?* Not my Fifi. She's a lady."

Dixie's eyes twinkled. "You know what they say—a lady on the street and a freak in the . . . alley."

Mallory gasped in horror and clutched her dog tighter.

"We're getting off track here," I said. "Back to my original question: What do you plan to do if you find out which dog . . . is the father of Fifi's puppies?"

"Sue for child support, *of course.*"

I blinked, sure my concussion had given me hallucinations. This was insane, but obviously Lauren knew all about this woman's brand of crazy. Hell, she probably already knew who the culprit was. Dixie and I had a part to play, and we were expected to deliver.

After we discussed all the possible ways Fifi could have gotten loose (Derick admitted he had let her out unsupervised while Mallory was enjoying a spa day), we told them we'd get back to them. Then we ran the scene two more times. Proving she was as tired with the takes as we were, Fifi got down, peed by the window, and snapped at Dixie when she tried to pick her up.

"Good riddance," Dixie said when they walked out the door. "Is it lunch-time yet?"

I gave her a suspicious look. I knew why she was so eager.

"Be back in an hour ready to talk to the Davises about their daughter," Lauren said. "And Summer and Dixie, you need to have already changed your clothes."

Dixie was busy tapping on her phone, but she glanced up at me. "You should change before you go to lunch, Summer. I bet the blue dress I brought for you will make your eyes pop on camera."

"She's right," Karen agreed, oblivious to the real reason Dixie was suggesting the dress.

"Fine," I huffed. "But I know what you're up to, Dixie Belle Baumgartner, and you're wasting your time." I refused to get my hopes up.

"Helpin' you look good on camera? I know I am; you already look great."

I snorted. "Suckin' up won't help you now."

Karen found the dress and handed it to me, along with a pair of nude flats that weren't mine. Dixie.

I went into the bathroom and changed. I was zipping up the back when Dixie knocked on the door. She opened it before I could respond and handed me a tube of lipstick. "Here. You need this."

I gave her a hard look in the mirror. "To be interviewed by the police chief about the pretend janitor?"

"Oh," she said, getting excited, "just like Sharon Stone in *Basic Instinct*." She grabbed the bottom of my dress and started to lift. "Quick. Take off your panties."

I slapped her hands away. "I will do no such thing! This is a professional . . . meeting. Dressin' me up like a Barbie doll isn't gonna change that fact."

"Lookin' like a Barbie doll did you good in all those pageants your momma put you in."

I pushed her out into the hall, getting grumpy. "The only thing that stuck with me from all those damn pageants was cupcake hands." Then I made a face and held my arms slightly out from my body, my fingers pressed together and curved inward as though I was carrying cupcakes.

"No wonder you won Junior Miss Supreme of Bixley County," Luke said from the office.

My gaze jerked up, and I flushed when I saw him. "It was Junior Miss Supreme *Princess*," I said. "And it was a long time ago."

"Your momma still has the trophy and the tiara," Dixie said.

I spun to face her, feeling dizzy from moving so fast. "What?"

"Yeah. In her trophy room. She has all of 'em."

I felt a pang of rejection and hurt. She had kept my trophies and tiaras, but she'd turned her back on me. Why did I care so much? It wasn't like I wanted them anyway.

I'd always been Momma's path to glory, and she'd left me behind when I'd stopped being useful. In the end, my mother had chosen the pageants over me. It hadn't come as much of a surprise, but there was still a big gaping hole in my heart.

Chapter Twenty-Three

"Summer?" Luke asked in a low voice, next to me now. "You ready?"

"Yeah."

"Don't forget she needs to be back by one fifteen," Dixie said, sounding a little too pleased with herself.

"Yes, ma'am," Luke said with a grin.

He put his hand at the small of my back as he guided me to the door. Karen gave him a long, appreciative glance, but Lauren scowled.

"You got yourself a new admirer," I teased when we were on the sidewalk.

"Your boss?" he asked in disgust. "I think I'd rather become a monk."

I laughed, and he looked down at me, a slow smile spreading across his face. "What?"

He shook his head. "Nothin'."

"No," I said, feeling self-conscious. "What?"

For a moment I thought he wasn't going to answer, but then he smiled, and his eyes lit up with warmth. "I always liked your laugh."

Heat spread through my body, pooling between my legs, and I resisted the urge to slap myself. *Really, Summer? You are so easy.*

But I wasn't, and I knew it. Not with other men anyway. Yet I always had been with Luke. All he had to do was give me that look that drove all the women crazy, and just like the rest of them, I'd come running.

I couldn't be that girl anymore. Because while we had undeniable, off-the-charts chemistry, after I'd grown up a little, I'd realized we would have never worked out. Luke was too dead set in his ways, and he expected me to fit into that pretty picture. He wanted a wife to raise his kids and devote her life to him. And while I'd wanted that when I was seventeen, I couldn't be that person now—nor did I want to be. Sure, I wanted the husband and the kids, but I needed more. I'd been forced to grow up quickly after Momma deserted me, and I'd learned to stand on my own, even if it looked like I was doing it badly. But one thing was certain: I needed a purpose other than being someone's wife.

Besides, I was tired of fitting into other people's pictures. I wanted to make my own picture, but I was beginning to think changing the scenery in it could be a good idea.

"You can't remember my laugh," I said. "It's been too long."

"No way I'd ever forget it," he said. "Hearing you laugh was one of the best parts of that summer . . . and the countless phone calls."

My steps faltered, and I wrapped my arms across my chest. What was he up to? "Where are we goin'?"

He glanced toward the courthouse, then back at me. "The police station."

I had a moment of panic, but as soon as I calmed down enough to think, I realized it made sense. He wanted me to tell him what I knew about Otto and the janitor who wasn't really a janitor. "Okay." I started walking again, setting off another wave of dizziness that made me stumble.

"Maybe walking's not a good idea," he said as he grabbed my elbow. "Why don't you wait at the office and let me get my car. I remembered how you liked to walk, so I thought . . ."

"That I'd want to walk. Yeah, I'd like that. Let's just take it slow." I started across the street toward the police station, Luke catching up with me a second later.

We were silent the rest of the way, and I was even more irritated by how utterly exhausted I felt when we walked into the air-conditioned building.

The young woman behind the desk brushed heavy auburn bangs from her eyes and jumped up when she saw me. "Oh! You're Summer Butler! You're even prettier in person."

"Thanks," I said with a weary smile.

"Amber, we're gonna be in my office. Hold my calls unless it's important." Luke wrapped an arm lightly around my back and steered me toward the short hall to the left.

Her eyes twinkled as her gaze dropped to his arm. "Sure thing, Luke."

Luke led me down a short hall to a door with a glass window that said **LUKE MONTGOMERY, CHIEF OF POLICE**.

I stopped for a moment to take it in.

"What?" he asked.

"Nothin'."

"You have to tell me," he said with a smile in his voice as he pushed the door open. Just as I expected, it was as neat as a pin, but there were several files stacked on a brown leather sofa on the wall across from his desk.

"This was your dream," I said. "And you did it. I'm just admirin' it."

He leaned over and picked up the files off the sofa, setting them on his desk. "Sit," he said, extending an arm toward it.

"This isn't what I expected," I said. "I thought we'd do this in an interrogation room."

"No," he said softly, "it's not like that. I just want to talk to you as a friend."

I looked up into his face, my body filled with so much longing I had to resist the urge to reach out and pull him to me. "Are we friends?" I asked in a tight voice.

"I think I'd like to be."

I leaned my head back on the sofa, refusing to let myself hope. Hope was for dreamers, and I'd learned to be practical years ago.

"I'll be right back."

I heard him walk out of the room and wondered where he was going. I must have dozed off because I heard crinkling paper, and when I opened my eyes, he'd rolled his office chair out from behind his desk and was sitting in front of me.

"Sorry," I said, sitting up.

"Don't be sorry. You obviously need sleep."

"How long was I out?"

"Only about ten minutes. Enough time for me to check in with Cale and then get lunch together."

"Lunch?" It was then I noticed he'd set two paper plates on the sofa next to me with sandwiches, potato salad, and pickles.

"It's your lunch break," he said, handing me a plate. "You need to eat."

"You got this for me?"

He grinned. "I'd hoped to eat what was on one of the plates, but if you want both, you're welcome to them."

I grinned back, staring at him. This was a dream. It had to be. Only Luke wasn't smiling at me in most of my dreams. "Why are you bein' so nice to me today?" I asked quietly.

"Because Teddy made a lot of sense."

"About what?"

"That maybe I haven't been fair to you."

My chest froze, and the vault locking away all my pain cracked a little, overwhelming me with emotion. I didn't have the strength to handle this, and I certainly didn't have the courage. "I can't do this right now, Luke."

"Can't do what?" he asked softly.

Get a grip. I took a deep breath. "I want to be friends too, but I can't deal with my past right now. I'm just tryin' to do what needs to be done so I can pay off my grandmother's farm."

Shit. Why did I tell him that?

He scooted his chair closer and leaned forward, his elbows on his thighs. "Wait. *What?*"

"Never mind. Forget I said anything."

"Oh, no. You can't just drop a bombshell like that and expect me not to ask you any questions. Teddy and Dixie have never said a word."

"I don't see what the mortgage on my grandparents' farm has to do with Otto Olson."

His gaze held mine. "But it's the kind of thing you tell a friend."

"A close friend," I said with more anger than I'd intended. "And you ruined that ten years ago when you decided to believe I was sleeping with Connor Blake."

His jaw clenched. He stood upright and moved to the window.

"I know I hurt you, Luke. I had every intention of comin' back as soon as I finished filming the next season of the show. But I didn't turn eighteen until June, and Momma renegotiated the contract that spring. I wanted out. I told you that. I would have done anything to get out of that contract. So I came up with a plan to get me out of it, and you went and believed the worst of me."

"You were naked in those photos, Summer. And so was he."

"You chose to believe a tabloid over me. My career was destroyed. I was kicked off the show, and I lost you."

"Then why didn't you come back home? That's what you swore you wanted to do. Yet when you had the opportunity, you stayed in LA."

"You seriously expected me to come back here and face you when I knew you believed the gossip about Connor?" I asked in disbelief. "Knowing how small this town is? You ruined that for me too."

He didn't answer.

"I made a mistake," I said, rubbing my temple in an effort to ease the pain. "The studio was making me pretend to date Connor that fifth season. His publicist told us we'd ruin our squeaky-clean reputations if we leaked the photos. He knew I wanted to get out of my contract, and Connor claimed he wanted out too. I was a year into the new three-year contract my mother had just signed me up for, and I was barely nineteen and desperate, which meant I was stupid."

"Why didn't you tell me your plan?" he demanded.

"You would have told me not to do it. But I wasn't naked; we were just topless, and I didn't even kiss him. We just made it look like we did."

"You were topless!" he shouted.

I stood and gave him a look of disbelief. We were rehashing a ten-year-old argument. Again. "Comin' here to talk to you was a terrible idea. I think I should talk to Cale or Willy."

"You can't talk to Cale," he groaned in frustration. "He's busy with the murder investigation."

"Why aren't you workin' on it with him?" I asked.

"Because I'm here with you!"

"Not anymore you're not." I headed for the door, but as soon as I reached for the doorknob, Luke was behind me, wrapping his hand around mine on the door. He placed our linked hands on my abdomen as his chest pressed to my back.

"Summer. Stop." His voice was low and sounded strained. He held me like that for several seconds. "I'm sorry. I'm doin' the shittiest job in the history of apologies."

I closed my eyes and leaned the back of my head against his chest, but the jarring sent another round of pain through my head.

He stiffened and loosened his hold. "You should sit down. You're still not well."

He put his arm around me to lead me back to the sofa, but I pushed his hand away and sat down, sinking into the cushions. "Were you planning to ask me questions about finding Otto?"

"Yeah," he said, sounding dejected. "Don't you want to eat first?"

"How about we talk while we eat?"

"Okay. Tell me about what happened in the woods."

I told him everything I remembered—seeing the bike, hearing a noise, running, then finding Otto, but everything from the first time I'd hit my head to the time someone had hit it for me was still hazy. "But I'm forgetting something," I said. "Something important. I just can't put my finger on what."

"It will come. Give it time." He glanced at my barely touched plate. "You aren't hungry?"

"My stomach's still not right."

"I want to ask you about the guy who approached you at the church. Are you up to it? Would you rather lie down and take a nap?"

"No. I want to tell you now."

"Okay." He leaned over and took my plate, then leaned back and set it on the desk. "I take it you didn't know him?"

"No, and he never gave me his name."

He picked up his half-eaten sandwich. "What did he look like?" He took a bite while he waited for my answer.

"Don't you need to write this down?"

"This isn't official." He tapped the side of his head with the finger of his free hand. "Besides, I've got a memory like a steel trap."

"Uh-huh."

He cocked an eyebrow. "You disagree?"

"I can think of a couple of instances in the past when you forgot a few things."

From the look in his eyes, he must have remembered something bittersweet. "I'm listening now, I promise."

"Thanks."

He nodded. "Now what did the guy look like?"

I launched into the same description I'd given Teddy, ending with, "And he was carrying a broom."

He scooped up a forkful of potato salad. "The big commercial kind or a small house broom?"

"Now you're making fun of me."

"No. I swear. It's a legit question."

"A house kind with a wooden handle."

"Oh." He took a bite, then said through a mouthful of food, "That could be significant."

I gave him a scorching look.

"No, I'm serious. Wooden-handled brooms aren't that common anymore."

"How do you know that? Do they have a class at the police academy titled Household Cleaning Tools and Products?"

He laughed. "No. Experience." He scooped up more potato salad. "And I bought a broom at Lowe's last week in Dothan. Almost all metal handles."

"It could have been a broom the church has owned for years that he picked up as a prop. I can't see him carryin' a broom around town."

He got a cheesy grin as he took a bite of a chip.

"What?" I asked, wiping my face in case I had crumbs.

"There's nothin' on your face. I was grinning because I was imagining the guy walking around town, carryin' the broom over his shoulder with a bag tied on the end."

I glanced up at him and grinned. "Looks like someone acquired some of my imagination."

"I learned a lot of things from you that summer." His tone was bittersweet. "I was so stupid, Summer. You have to understand what was goin' on in my head. I'd been waiting for two years, but you always had an excuse, and phone calls weren't enough," he said softly, his anger gone. "I thought you were stringing me along. It was hard enough knowing you were goin' to events with that bastard Blake, supposedly pretending to date him . . . then when I saw you in those photos . . . I lost my shit."

"You wouldn't even listen to my explanation, Luke," I said with tears in my voice.

"I was a twenty-year-old hotheaded idiot. It's no excuse, yet there it is. Cale told me I'd get over you, but I didn't. By the time I realized what a mistake I'd made, I was too proud to go to you and admit it. And then I convinced myself I was justified, that fame had changed you, but part of me always knew better."

I didn't say anything, in total shock.

"Then Thursday morning . . . the moment I saw you and then held you . . . I knew I'd never gotten over you, Summer. When I thought about you swooping in and just leavin' again . . ." He shook his head. "I was pissed, and then I took it out on you later."

He set his plate on his desk. "I've been a total asshole, and I'm more sorry than you could know." He hesitated. "You scared the hell out of me yesterday. When I heard you were in the hospital, I dropped everything and ran over to see you. And then when you passed out . . . Jesus, Summer. You turned so pale I thought you were dead."

I sat there in disbelief. I'd waited for years to hear him apologize.

"It made me start thinkin' about things, realizing you weren't the person I'd made you out to be in my head. That you were still you."

"But I'm not me anymore. Sure, there's part of seventeen-year-old Summer in me, but I've lived through a lot of shit, Luke. *A. Lot. Of. Shit.* And I've done it all alone. I can't just get over that, and I can't believe you can just get over it either," I said, my voice raising in frustration.

Contrition filled his eyes. "Thinkin' I might have lost my second chance with you made me get over a lot of things quick."

"I haven't caught up yet, Luke. I can't go from you hating me for years to . . . this." I got up and headed for the door, realizing that the hem of my dress was hiked up. Great.

"Summer! We're not done yet."

"Well, I am." I burst out of his office while tugging my dress down, Luke hot on my heels. I came to an abrupt halt when I saw we'd attracted an audience, then staggered from one foot to the other like a drunkard as a wave of dizziness washed over me. Amber, Willy Hawkins, and a familiar-looking older woman had gathered in the lobby, and all of them were staring at us.

Well, shit. This was going to end up in a tabloid somewhere.

"Don't y'all have something better to do than gossip like a bunch of fish-wives?" Luke bellowed when he saw them.

"But I *am* a fishwife, dear," the older woman said with a glint in her eye. "You know Ernie fishes up at Lake Edna."

"Nevertheless, Melba," Luke said in a stern voice, "anything you heard in that office is confidential information."

"Of course it is," Melba said, nodding enthusiastically.

"If I see this on Maybelline's gossip page, you're the first one I'm arrestin'." Then I realized why she looked familiar. She was Maybelline's sister.

"Arrestin' me for what, my dear?" she asked, reaching up to pinch his cheek. "Gossipin' isn't illegal."

"No, but allowing your dog to bark after ten p.m. is. I'll have Willy parked outside your house waiting for the tiniest of yips out of Parker Posey."

"Parker Posey does *not* bark."

"Parker Posey?" I asked no one in particular.

"That's her Chihuahua," Amber stage-whispered behind me. "She named her that on account of her shit smelling like a bouquet of flowers. And she loves *You've Got Mail.*"

Maybe Luke could have her arrested for outrageous lies.

But I realized this was my opportunity to escape. I quietly slid to the front door and walked out onto the sidewalk, squinting in the afternoon sun.

I'd made it twenty steps to the street before Luke caught up with me. I considered that a win.

"Summer, where are you goin'?" he asked.

"That is none of your business."

"You don't have to be back to the office for another half hour."

"So?"

He gently grabbed my arm and pulled me to a halt. "I'm probably gonna regret this, but I'm about to go to the Baptist church to talk to Reverend Miller. Do you want to tag along?"

I shaded my eyes to look up at him. "Why?"

"Why? I thought you were playin' private eye."

"Playin'?"

"Wrong choice of words, but we both know that this racket Lauren's runnin' is fake as a three-dollar bill."

"No kidding."

"Which is why you, Dixie, and that cameraman were out at the lake yesterday. You thought something was up, so you were trying to do a real investigation."

"And a fat lot of good that did poor Otto," I said bitterly. "He's still dead."

"He was dead before you even asked your first question, Summer. You are *not* responsible for his death."

"But you were right. Two people have been killed since this circus came to town. That can't be a coincidence."

"I still know it has nothing to do with you."

I wasn't so sure, and it wasn't because I was being narcissistic. My gut instinct told me there had to be some sort of connection.

"You may not have found Otto, but you can still help him. He may have died from alcohol poisoning, but given the way he was moved and the fact that he was found with a bottle of Jim Beam, I'm not buying it was an accident."

"You know he hated Jim Beam?" I asked in surprise.

"I knew a lot of things about Otto. I want to find out what happened to him. You can help me find out who killed him."

My mouth dropped open in shock, but I quickly closed it. "You're not even investigating the case. Deputy Dixon is in charge of it."

"I don't trust Boy Wonder's investigation."

"Boy Wonder?"

Luke scowled. "He trained up in Atlanta and thinks he's better than the rest of us homegrown cops."

"So this is personal."

"More so than you think."

I gave him a questioning look. "Why?"

"I think he's tryin' to pin part of it on you."

CHAPTER TWENTY-FOUR

It felt weird driving in a police car with Luke, but it could have been worse. At least I was sitting in the front seat.

"So if you aren't officially investigating this case, should you really be questioning Reverend Miller?" I asked as he pulled into the parking lot of the church.

"I'm asking questions about incidents that happened in my town. There's nothing wrong with that."

"So why are you really bringing me along? Because I don't believe for one minute you want me to help you investigate a real case."

"The truth?"

"Yes."

"Dixon thinks you're making up the guy you talked to here. If we can put an ID on this guy, then I can question him and hopefully find out why he set you up and what he knows about Otto's death. So I really want to find this guy, especially since Otto's time of death falls during the time you don't have an alibi."

Fear skated down my back. "You mean while I was sleeping? I thought he died of alcohol poisoning."

Luke leaned closer. "Doc Bailey thinks so—his blood alcohol was really high, but they're looking for a reason why his body was moved. I'm not sure it matters to the deputy one way or another. I stuck my nose into it, and Dixon and I don't get along. When he found out that you and I had dated . . . and the fact I was asking questions . . ." He paused, and the worried look on his face scared me. "The guy's got an ax to grind, Summer, and he's gonna use you to sharpen it."

I let that sink in. "Why didn't you tell me sooner?"

"I didn't want to worry you."

"Why are you telling me now?"

"I think you have a right to know. Dixon's focusing on the transporting of Otto's body, but I suspect it won't take long for him to start looking for a more sinister cause of death . . . just like we are. Even if he doesn't take it that far, he might make a bunch of noise just to prove a point." He paused. "But let's keep it between us for the time being. Dixon's having Otto's body sent to Montgomery for an official state autopsy. That'll take a few days, so he's gonna sit tight, knowin' that you're stickin' around for your show. He's poking around and dropping your name just to make us both nervous."

"Oh, my God, Luke . . . is he gonna arrest me?"

"He doesn't have any evidence to back up an arrest, and everything at this point is pure speculation on his part. But if he finds something to latch onto . . ."

"You won't be able to stop him."

"I can if I find enough evidence on my own. I can't help thinking the two deaths are tied together somehow. It's just too coincidental they died within twelve hours of each other."

"But what's the connection?"

He ran a hand over his face. "That's what I can't figure out."

Should I tell him I'd seen Ryker talking to the mayor—and that he'd later dropped the money? Cale had asked me not to, and Cale was officially in charge of the murder investigation, but I felt like this was important enough to tell Luke.

So why did I feel like I was betraying Cale?

He opened his car door and started to get out.

"Luke . . ."

He stopped and turned back to face me.

Better to start with the money. That was easier to explain. "The first day we started filming, we were in Dr. Livingston's parking lot, and I saw something strange."

He shut his door. "What?"

I grimaced. "I was checking out a license plate for a case we were working on—"

His back stiffened. "What do you mean checking out a license plate?"

"Do you want to know or not?" His reaction to something fairly innocuous didn't bode well for how this conversation would go. I reconsidered my decision, but I knew he needed to know.

He remained silent.

"We were investigating a guy who had hurt his back and couldn't go back to work at Acme Concrete. He was seeing his doctor."

"Tommy Kilpatrick."

"Yeah."

"He wrenched his back when a piece of equipment malfunctioned. We charged Acme with negligence, and now they're giving Tommy a hard time. What exactly were you doin'?"

I didn't want to admit to any of it. "Let's just say I saw a suspicious license plate, and I took a photo of it."

His brow lowered, suggesting he knew exactly whose license plate I'd photographed. "Go on."

"While I was taking the photos, I saw a motorcycle pull into the parking lot of the strip mall next door. This tattooed guy in a dark T-shirt got off, went inside the dry cleaner's, and then came back out about twenty seconds later. He was carrying a small, wadded-up brown-paper bag, and he put it into one of those leather side pouches. But it fell out before he took off. I went over and checked it out."

"What was it?"

I looked into his eyes. "A bag of money. Cash."

"And you didn't think to turn it in to the police?"

"As I stood there trying to figure out what to do with it, Cale pulled up. He said he was keepin' track of us after your lunch meeting the day we started filming." I gave him a dirty look. "You must have had him and Willy tag-teaming us."

He scowled.

"I gave the money to Cale. He said he'd take it back to the station in case the owner showed up for it."

"He never said a word to me."

Should I tell him about the connection to Ryker? I'd led Cale to believe I'd keep it secret, but I didn't want Luke to think I was keeping anything from him.

"How much money are we talkin' about?"

"I saw a five-dollar bill on top, but I'm not sure what the rest of the bills were. I asked Cale about it yesterday, and he said the owner had shown up to claim it. His name was Ed. Cale said he owned a motorcycle-repair shop and often dealt in cash." I watched Luke's face. "From the description, I knew Ed wasn't the one who'd dropped the money."

"Ryker Pelletier." He pushed out a breath of frustration. From the look in his eyes, I suspected that he wanted to tell me that Ryker was dead, but he held his tongue. "Was Dixie with you when you saw this happen?"

"She was in the truck. She didn't see anything. But Luke, there was something else." He waited with a worried look. "I saw Ryker talking to the mayor."

He looked even more torn. "Go on."

"In the alley behind Maybelline's diner, and it wasn't a friendly conversation."

He sat back in his seat and looked out the windshield. "Ryker had a zoning issue with the city. He could have been talkin' to Mayor Sterling about that."

"You don't look convinced."

"I don't know what's goin' on in this town right now." He sounded frustrated. "Did you tell Dixie about all of this?" The look on my face must have answered that question, because he followed up with, "Does she know what the argument was about?"

"How would she know? She and Ryker broke up a month ago."

"Are you sure?" he asked. "I saw Ryker headin' out to the Baumgartner farm last week."

I narrowed my eyes. "Dixie told me they broke up. In fact, she and Teddy had a small argument over it last night before we went to bed."

"Argument over what?"

"Teddy not approving of her datin' him." He didn't look altogether convinced, but I didn't want to talk it to death. I glanced at the clock on the dashboard. "If we're gonna do this, we need to hurry up so I can get back on time."

I opened the car door, knowing he probably wasn't done with me yet. He caught up pretty quickly.

He glanced around and lowered his voice. "Is it possible someone saw you pick up the money? The thief went for your window in the break-in."

I stopped walking. "First of all, how would they know about the money, and second, how would they know which window was mine?"

"I don't know, Summer," he said in frustration. "It's Sweet Briar. People talk."

"About which bedroom window is mine?" I asked in disbelief.

"When was the last time anyone tried to break in to your family's farmhouse?"

That question hurt, but I knew it was unintentional. "I don't know. I've been estranged from my family since Pawpaw, Uncle Stanley, and Aunt Merilee died."

"Well, I've been on the police force since I was twenty years old, and I've never once been out to a break in call at the farm before last night. Do you ever remember there being a break-in when you were growing up there?"

"No."

"There are a few too many coincidences piling up here. And a lot of them have some kind of link to you."

He was right, but I was about to tell him off for suggesting I had something to do with it when he lifted a finger and put it on my parted lips.

"I'm not insinuatin' that you've done anything wrong," he said in a husky voice.

I knew I needed to pay attention to his words, but nearly every part of me was focusing on his finger pressed against my lips. My body was on fire from a single touch, and from the look in Luke's eyes, he felt it too.

Focus, Summer.

I pushed his hand away, but I didn't put much force behind it. "Then what are you sayin'?"

"Dixie mentioned that you have people who hate you and would want to hurt you just because of who you are. Do you think that's true?"

"I don't have anyone pissed at me at the moment except for a forty-three-year-old man from Omaha who's sporting a black eye."

Luke grinned. "Amber told me all about that punch." His grin spread. "Let me guess. He asked you to say the *Gotcha!* line."

I gave him the stink-eye. He knew how much I hated it. "Maybe."

"Is it possible that someone's stalking you?"

"Why would someone be stalking me? I haven't been popular for years."

"Nothing unusual? Letters? Phone calls?"

"No . . . Wait." Surely there wasn't a connection, but I might as well mention it. "I was getting calls after I hit that guy. My friend Marina said they stopped after I left."

"What did the caller say?"

"My name. He'd kind of whisper it and then hang up."

"A man?"

"Yeah."

"Does he sound old? Young?"

"I don't know, Luke. He always whispered it. I couldn't tell."

"What did the police say?"

"I never called them. It was Malibu. What are they going to do about a bunch of hang-up calls? They would have told me to change my number."

His eyes darkened. "The calls came to your home phone? Not your cell?"

"Right."

"Listen to me. If you get even the hint of a similar call, I want to know."

"And what are you gonna do about it? Trace the number? You know you can't do that for an annoyance call."

He grabbed my arm and tugged me closer, his voice turning husky again. "Humor me."

My breath stuck in my chest being this close to him. "Fine," I forced out. "I'll tell you, but I don't anticipate getting any."

He stared into my face, and the way his lips parted made me wonder if he was thinking about kissing me.

"So let's say the calls are from some creeper," I said, feeling dizzy again. I wasn't sure if it was from my head injury or from being this close to Luke. I took a step back, out of his reach. "That doesn't explain Ryker or Ed or the mayor. And how would the creeper know about Otto? And why would he move him? That makes no sense."

He pushed out a long breath as he scanned the parking lot, then he shook his head. "There's a personal element here, Summer. Why else send you to find Otto?" Frustration filled his eyes.

"Let's go talk to the minister and see if he can shed any light on anything. Lauren will make my life miserable if I'm not back in time."

"Okay." He put his hand at the small of my back as we walked the rest of the way to the front door of the church. I remembered the way to the office, but obviously Luke had been here before too. When we got to the reverend's office, his secretary was sitting at her desk, greeting us with a wide smile.

"Hello, Chief Montgomery," she said. She looked a whole lot less friendly when she turned to me. "And nice to see you again so soon, Summer. Are you two here to see Reverend Miller?"

"Yeah," Luke said. "Is he in?"

"He's quite the popular guy. He's had a few people dropping in today. In fact, he's in there with a sheriff's deputy right now."

I glanced over at Luke. I wasn't sure if that news was good or bad—at least the deputy was doing his research? But the look on Luke's face told me it wasn't ideal.

"I see," he said. "Maybe we could ask you a few questions, Anabelle."

She smiled up at him, folding her hands on the desk in front of her. "Of course. Whatever I can do to help, *Luke*."

Luke ignored her insult toward me, but I frowned.

"When Summer was here with her crew yesterday, she talked to a man she thought might be the janitor. He had popped out of a classroom. This guy was about five-ten, short, brown hair, like a crew cut, and a little bit of a beard.

Blue T-shirt and jeans. Do you know who it could have been? Possibly a new temporary employee? Someone who was hired to help out with landscaping?"

She looked up at me with suspicion in her eyes. "This is about your mystery man, isn't it? That's what the deputy is talking to the reverend about now."

"Shows what a fool he is." Luke grinned. "Anabelle, we both know that you're the one to talk to, now don't we?"

She giggled, keeping her eyes on the chief of police.

"Who do you think the guy could have been?"

"The deputy thinks she made him up."

Luke's back stiffened. "Is that what he told you?"

"No, he didn't have to. I could see it in his eyes." She held her first two fingers up to her own eyes as though she was about to poke them out.

"And what do *you* think?" Luke asked. "I take it no one comes to mind who fits that description."

"No. No one." She glanced up at me with eyes full of judgment. "Deputy Dixon said she was makin' things up for that show, and Nettie Peabody confirmed it."

"That's the producer's doin'," I said. "And only for the cameras. There were no cameras around when I talked to the guy here yesterday, so there would be no reason for me to lie." Not entirely true, but the camera hadn't been rolling while I was running for my life.

Anabelle didn't look totally convinced. "Unless *you* moved his body there."

"But why?" I asked. "Why would I do that?"

"For your show."

It was obvious we weren't going to get any information here, but I wanted to plead my case anyway. "I'm not lying, Miss Anabelle. I've got no reason to lie, and I've got every reason to find the *very real* man I talked to yesterday, if for no other reason than to find out how he knew Otto was out there."

Luke added, "He might have seen something else to help us figure out what happened."

"Oh," she said, some of her antagonism fading. "I hadn't thought about that."

"If something comes to mind, will you call me?" Luke asked. "Tell Amber you need to speak directly to me."

"Okay."

Luke cast a glance toward the closed door, then gestured toward the hallway. I led the way, but when we got to the hall, he headed away from the exit toward the bathrooms.

"Where are you going?" I asked quietly since he kept glancing back to see if anyone was behind us.

"To find that broom."

"Why? To see if it exists?"

He ignored my questions and continued down the hall until he stopped in front of a door and opened it. "Bingo."

I walked up beside him. He'd found the broom closet, and sure enough, there were three wooden handles. One belonged to a mop, and the others were brooms.

"I know this sounds crazy," Luke said, "but is there any chance you can figure out if it was one of these brooms?"

"It was a broom, Luke. I was too busy listening to his story about Otto's bike. Unless you dust for prints, how is this goin' to help?"

"I *am* going to dust for prints."

My eyes widened. "Are you serious?"

"Yeah, but I don't want Boy Wonder to see us, so try to figure out which one it was."

I studied them both and finally pointed to the one on the left. "That one."

"Are you sure?"

"Yeah. I remember seeing that red splotch of paint on the handle."

"Okay." He glanced down the hall toward the office, then grabbed an unused cleaning rag from the cart. He opened it up, wrapped it around the handle, and pulled it out of the closet. "Let's go."

I felt naughty, like the time I snuck into Connor's dressing room and drew a mustache on a life-size photo of him some fan sent, then convinced my hairdresser to give me an alibi. That was Luke and me now as we hurried out of the church.

He stuffed the broom into the back seat of the squad car, and when we both got inside, I started to laugh.

"What's so funny?" he asked.

"I just stole a broom with the chief of police."

He grinned. "While it's true we might have appropriated it under dubious circumstances, and it probably wouldn't hold up in a court of law, I'm hoping your helpful *friend* left some decent prints. If he's been arrested before, I can find him in the system."

He pulled out of the lot just as Deputy Dixon came strutting out of the building.

"Do you think he saw us?" I asked.

Luke glanced in his rearview mirror. "I know he saw my car, but I'm not sure if he saw you."

We were silent during the short drive to my office. Luke pulled into a parking space and turned to face me. "I'll be out of the office this afternoon, but if Deputy Dixon shows up wanting to talk to you, call me straight away. Don't answer any of his questions until I get there."

"Okay."

"And if anything happens to make you feel unsafe, call me."

"Okay."

He leaned closer and lowered his voice. "I want to make sure this is perfectly clear. Call my cell phone. Skip Amber. And if you can't get ahold of me and it's an emergency, call Cale. I'll give you his number."

"I already have it. I'll be fine."

He gave me a stern look. "Summer . . . be careful."

"Thanks." When he was being protective and caring like this, it was easy to gloss over all the crap that had happened between us, but I was pretty sure ignoring it was a bad idea. Still, my brain seemed to have forgotten to tell my body.

He was watching me with his dark, worried eyes, and damned if my body didn't turn and lean toward him. My hand started to lift to touch him before I came to my senses.

Starting something with Luke was a very, very, *very* bad idea.

"I've gotta go." I scrambled out of the car, because at the moment, the *real* danger was sitting behind the wheel of the police chief's cruiser.

CHAPTER TWENTY-FIVE

By the time Lauren called it a day at six thirty, I was beyond exhausted. I'd forced myself to look attentive for the last thirty minutes while a woman told me her house was either haunted or her ex-husband was harassing her. We promised we'd get to the bottom of it. Since these cases all seemed to be preplanned, I'd bet good money that Lauren would have us insist it was the ghost, specifically the one that old-timers said roamed the streets of Sweet Briar. I suspected the legend was pure prime-time gold in her eyes.

"We have an eight-a.m. call time tomorrow, so everyone be on time," Lauren said as the crew began to pack up. "And, Summer," she said, turning to me, "your little staycation is over. You're going back out in the field tomorrow, so be prepared. We'll be lucky to finish filming on time as it is."

Only Lauren would consider working from a chair while recovering from a concussion a staycation, but I was too tired to argue with her. Besides, we both wanted the same thing—to not only wrap up the show, but to have it do extremely well. We just had two different ways of approaching it.

"And this look"—she waved her hand in a circle while pointing it at me—"is a good look for you. Wear another dress tomorrow."

I was certain I'd heard her wrong. "You want me to wear a dress to investigate cases?"

"Yes," she said with a snappy attitude. "Do you have a problem with that?"

"Actually, I do. A good PI blends in, and there's no way I'll blend in wearing dresses and flats. In case you hadn't noticed, no one dresses like that around here, with the exception of the Hintons, and they don't count because they aren't *from around here.*"

"Well, maybe if you were a real investigator, that would be a concern, but everyone knows that there's nothing real about reality TV. This is a good look for you, Summer, so you need to exploit it for as long as you can, because you don't *have* anything else. You are a talentless former teen star who was only popular because of her looks and her fake clean persona."

"Fake clean?"

"Stick to the point, Summer, and that is that you are a has-been, and we need to milk that well dry. And this look"—she waved her hand again—"is part of it. It's your shtick. So wear a new dress tomorrow, and have a few on standby. We'll let Karen tell you what to wear and when to wear it just like I'll tell you what to say and when. Do you understand?"

I was so exhausted I could literally lay my head down on the desk and fall asleep, so I was proud of myself for pulling it together and looking her in the eye. I was stuck, and we both knew it. I should have just agreed and been done with it, but Lauren was a bully. The first time you backed down to a bully, you set a precedent. I'd learned that lesson again and again from my own mother, yet I had no idea how to put my foot down now.

"Do you understand?" she asked in a biting tone. "Do I need to remind you what the consequences of not following my direction could mean?" When I didn't answer, she moved closer to my desk and sneered down at me. "Do you understand, Summer?"

I cast a quick glance to at Dixie, who was watching our interaction in horror. I had to keep Dixie out of this. Nevertheless, I didn't even have the energy to work up anything more than a spark of outrage. "Yes."

Triumph filled her eyes. "Good girl." Then she spun around and headed to the back to talk to the film editors who had arrived the day before, during my *staycation* at the hospital.

I had to get out of here.

But a wave of dizziness hit me as soon as I got to my feet. Closing my eyes, I dropped my fingertips to the desktop to keep myself from falling over.

"Summer," Dixie whispered next to me, "let's go."

I sucked in a deep breath and opened my eyes, horrified to see that everyone in the room was watching me with pity and concern.

I hated all of it.

Dixie reached for me, but I gently pushed her hand away. I needed to walk out of here on my own. Otherwise I'd never regain my dignity.

Grabbing my purse from the drawer, I concentrated on walking to the door. Once I got there, I'd make a new plan.

No one said anything as I left the office, but I heard them murmuring to each other as soon as I hit the sidewalk.

"Summer," Dixie said quietly into my ear, "I know you're tired, but Maybelline has something to tell us. She says it has something to do with Otto."

"What?"

"She refused to tell me. She insisted she'll only tell you in person. I promised we'd stop by after we got done filmin', but you look like death warmed over. We should talk to her tomorrow."

"When? Before our eight a.m. call time? She'll be busy with the breakfast rush. We need to talk to her tonight." I glanced behind us. "I thought Bill was supposed to be working with us."

"He's gonna meet us there. Apparently he needs to sit through some crew meeting before he can leave. Then he has to borrow a camera."

"So it could be a while?"

"Yeah."

"Then I'm taking a nap in the truck."

She grimaced.

"Dixie, I kid you not, I'm about to pass out right where I'm standing. I need to sleep."

"Okay. But the truck?"

"I don't know where else to go, so this will work in a pinch." Actually, a more tempting option *did* come to mind: the sofa in Luke's office. That, however, would be tempting fate on multiple levels. It was one thing to take me to steal that broom, but another thing entirely to endorse me investigating Otto's death without him. The presence of Bill—and a camera—would doubly put him off. There was no way he'd condone it, and I didn't want to think of a story to explain why I didn't just go home.

Thankfully, my truck was parked in front of Maybelline's diner, so Dixie went inside to wait while I settled in for a nap. I cracked the windows and then curled up on the seat, my head under the steering wheel. I was deep in a dreamless sleep when I woke up to Luke's frantic voice—*"Summer?"*—and his fingertips on my neck.

I groaned, feeling like I was underwater and trying to find the surface.

"Summer."

I pried my eyes open. "Luke. What are *you* doing here?"

"What am *I* doin' here? What the hell are you doing passed out in your truck?"

"I needed a nap."

"Why didn't you just go home?"

God, sometimes I hated when I was right.

"Luke," Dixie said in a breezy voice, opening the passenger door, "I see you found Summer."

"What in the everlovin' hell's goin' on here, Dixie? Why didn't you take her home?"

"Because we're gonna have a meeting with one of the cameramen at Maybelline's. We're waiting for him to show up, and Summer wanted to take a nap."

"She needs to be home. *In bed.*"

"You could just take her home to yours," Dixie said with a wink.

"Dixie!" I croaked out as I struggled to sit up.

Luke gently grabbed my arm and helped me to a sitting position. That was when I realized he was dressed in jeans and a T-shirt. It was the first time I'd seen him in street clothes since my return to Sweet Briar, and while he looked mighty fine in his uniform, he looked downright sinful in his light-blue T-shirt.

But he was oblivious to my perusal.

"Go home." Then his eyes widened. "Jesus, you aren't drivin', are you?"

"No. Dixie is. And I can't go home. Not yet."

"Why are you meetin' with a cameraman?"

"We're workin' on a plan to get even with Lauren," Dixie said. "Bill's gonna help us."

Luke searched my face. "Don't you think you have other things to worry about?"

I knew what he was referring to—I risked losing the money to help pay off the banknote. "In this instance, it all works toward the same purpose." But I wasn't so sure about that. Lauren didn't want the show to be canceled, but she might very well murder us if she found out we were investigating behind her back.

"It's not safe for you to be sleepin' in your truck while it's parked on the street, not to mention you scared the shit out of me. *Again.*"

"Sorry I scared you, but Sweet Briar's one of the safest places on earth." Then I remembered everything that was going on. "Usually."

"That's right. *Usually.* I've got two dead men, a mystery man, and a break-in at your house—and *every single thing* ties to you somehow. You need a damn bodyguard."

"Are you volunteering?" Dixie asked sweetly.

"Dixie!" I protested, but Luke didn't say a word. "I don't need a doggone bodyguard. I'm fine."

Luke still didn't say anything.

"I have Teddy out at the farm," I said. "And whenever I'm in town, I'm with someone almost every minute. I'll be fine."

He didn't look convinced. "I'm headin' into Maybelline's now to grab some dinner. Why don't you ladies join me while you wait for the cameraman?" He pinned his gaze on me. "And I know for a fact you hardly ate anything at lunch.

Let me make it up to you. I'll buy both of your dinners. Or if you want to sleep more, I'll take you to my office."

"Sounds like a plan to me," Dixie said.

"Which one?" he asked.

She grinned. "Either."

I groaned and pushed Dixie out of the way. "I hate you both," I grumbled, but the words didn't carry any heat. How was I supposed to explain any of this to Luke?

If Maybelline had information about the mystery man, he needed to know. And yet I couldn't deny that I wanted to prove I could solve a real case. I wasn't a real PI—I was only playing one for TV, just like I'd done before—but I couldn't deny that I *liked* questioning people for real. I *liked* looking for clues. My gut told me I could be good at this, that for the first time in my life I could do something that helped people and made me feel good about myself. I wanted to really give investigating a chance.

Right or wrong, I wanted to dig into what had happened to Otto Olson, and the odds were five to one that Luke would do everything he could to put a stop to that.

But did I really want to withhold information from Luke?

Maybe I'd just play it by ear.

Dixie already had a table. She sat on one side of the booth, then gestured to the other. "I want to sit by Bill, so you two sit over there."

While I was beginning to believe she really did like Bill, I didn't buy *that* as her reason for making us sit together.

Luke motioned to the seat, and I slid in first, letting Luke play his alpha-male game. I wanted to roll my eyes, but I couldn't deny that part of me liked it.

The part of me that couldn't be trusted.

His jeans-clad thigh brushed the bare skin of mine where my dress had hiked up, sending a wave of heat and lust through me.

I grabbed Dixie's water and took a big gulp.

"Help yourself," Dixie said with a laugh.

Luke lifted a hand and flagged down a pretty waitress who looked like she was still in high school. Her face lit up when she realized he was calling her.

"What can I do for you, Luke?" Her weight shifted to one side, and she batted her eyelashes, although I was positive it was all an involuntary reaction on her part.

"Hey, Rachel, can we get a couple of waters and a refill on this one." He turned to us. "Do you need more time to order?"

"I know what I want," Dixie said. "Shepherd's pie and cornbread."

I waved my hand. "Just bread. Nothin' else sounds good."

Luke gave me a questioning glance, then addressed the waitress, "Bring a meat-loaf plate and country-fried steak with green beans. And bring out some cornbread and Maybelline's dinner rolls right away."

"Sure thing, Luke," she said. Her face flushed, and she practically ran into the kitchen.

"That girl has a thing for you," I murmured, surprised that I was a tiny bit jealous.

"Rachel? She's a kid," he said as though that dismissed the whole thing. "I want to know why you ordered bread. I know you didn't do it because you're on a diet, otherwise you would have ordered a salad."

"My stomach's not right."

"Are you still nauseated?"

"Off and on."

He leaned closer and lowered his voice. "You need to let your head heal, Summer. Remember when I got that concussion the fall of my senior year in the homecoming football game?"

I had been back in California at the time, filming *Gotcha!*, but the news had terrified me. "Yeah. How could I forget?"

"I spent the weekend sleeping, then missed several days of school. You're pushing yourself too hard. If you don't rest, it's gonna take longer for you to heal."

While he was undoubtedly right, my circumstances didn't allow for such luxuries. "I'll be fine."

He looked like he wanted to argue, but he wisely kept his mouth shut.

Bill walked in the back door a few minutes after that, carrying his camera case, but when he saw Luke sitting next to me, he did a double take. Then he tried to hide the huge case behind his back.

"Summer," Luke said in a dry tone, "why's your cameraman bringin' his camera to your meeting?"

Well, shit.

CHAPTER TWENTY-SIX

"It's like this," Dixie started to say, but Luke held up his hand in warning.

"I want Summer to explain this one, Ms. Smooth Talker."

I glanced from Dixie to Bill and then finally back to Luke, whose eyebrows had risen in anticipation of my answer.

Double shit.

My brain was still addled, and that's probably what he was counting on. But then he'd known we were out at the lake looking for information about Otto—he didn't have to be a rocket scientist to figure out what was going on.

Dammit.

Nevertheless, I gave him a saucy look and said, "I'd tell you, but then I'd have to kill you."

"Really?" he asked, looking amused. "I know you're off your game, but I expected something better than that."

I blew out a breath. "I'm not sure we should talk about it here."

"If you weren't gonna talk about it here, what were you goin' to do?"

"Interview someone."

"Summer!" Dixie protested.

Bill hadn't finished his approach to our table, and he looked liable to turn and run back out the door.

"Have a seat, Bill," Luke said in a tone that brooked no argument.

Bill set his case on the floor and slid into the seat, shooting Dixie an irritated look. "Officer Montgomery, I . . ."

Luke leaned over the table and lowered his voice. "I'm not dressed in my uniform, so call me Luke."

Bill looked no less wary.

Luke glanced around before turning back to the table. "I know what you're up to."

Dixie and Bill glanced at each other.

"Look," Luke said, still speaking quietly enough that no one else could hear him, "as much as I hate to admit this, I approve of this"—he held up a hand and gave us a warning look—"within reason."

Dixie narrowed her eyes. "Are you talking about what I think you're talking about?"

"I know you all were out at the lake because Summer was trying to figure out what had happened to Otto, and part of the reason was that y'all want to actually solve a case. So now you have a chance to do that and help Summer in the process."

They stared at him like he'd just proclaimed the second coming of Jesus was tonight.

"I can't take part. After our trip to the church this afternoon, I was reprimanded by the sheriff for interfering with their investigation. But a private investigator isn't bound by their rules. You can investigate anything you want. All you need is a license . . . which you happen to have hanging on your office wall." Despite having given me his blessing, he didn't sound very happy about the aforementioned license.

Dixie was the first one to speak, and she summed up my feelings quite well. "You've gotta be shittin' me. This is a joke, right?"

"I wish it were, and under any other circumstances, I would flat-out be against this. But Summer's life is on the line. However . . ." He paused to make sure we were listening. "The key is that only a PI can do this or it could be construed as interfering. Since Summer's the one who has the license, she has to take the lead on all the investigating."

"So?" Dixie asked.

"So? She's about to pass out at the table from head trauma. We're talking about working eight-to ten-hour days for the show and then investigatin' on the side. I'm not sure she's up to it."

"Excuse me?" I demanded.

A grim smile twisted his lips. "Let me rephrase that. Just because she's stubborn enough to find the stamina to do this, it doesn't mean she *should*. She's only prolonging her recovery." He sighed. "But unfortunately, you're racing a ticking clock. You've only got a few days, to the end of the week, tops."

"No pressure," Bill finally said.

Rachel brought the food out, and when Bill started to order, I pushed my plate toward him. "Here, I'm not gonna eat this."

"Summer," Dixie scolded.

"I'm fine."

Luke glanced up at the young waitress. "Rachel, can I trouble you to bring a bowl of mashed potatoes and gravy? And another set of silverware."

"Sure thing, Luke."

"So you have some leads?" Luke asked. "You said you were about to interview someone."

None of us answered.

"No offense, Luke," Dixie said. "But we don't trust you for shit."

He sat up. "Hey. I've been nothing but supportive."

"Yeah, and it's freakin' me out."

Rachel took that exact moment to show up with the mashed potatoes.

"Thanks, Rachel," Luke said, taking the small bowl from her and sliding it in front of me. "You need to eat something other than bread if you're gonna do this. But you need to eat some protein, so if you think of something you want, I'll order it for you."

"Thank you, *Dr. Montgomery*," I said, picking up the spoon the waitress had left.

"There's only one doctor in my family."

"Hey, how is Levi, by the way?" Dixie asked. "I haven't seen him in ages. I bet he looks great in his lab coat. Does he have his name embroidered on it?"

"Fine. He's still in residency at LSU," Luke said. "And y'all are good at this distraction game, but not good enough. Who are you interviewin'?"

I glanced at my two cohorts and then said to Luke, "I think we need to do this on our own."

"*Why?*" He leaned forward again. "I can help."

"But you just said you can't," Dixie said. "And I think we all agree that it's safer if you stay out of it."

"Two people are dead, Dixie," he said in frustration. "Someone nearly killed Summer after purposely sending her into the woods, and last night they tried to break into her room. *None of this* is safe." He sat back in his seat, looking like he wanted to take a couple of moments, then said, "Look, I get that you don't trust me because of my job, but I'm here as Summer's friend, and y'all are gonna be in over your heads."

"You just said we should do it!" Dixie protested.

"With my supervision!" he bellowed.

Dixie shot him a glare, and he cringed when he realized several people were looking over at us. "Sorry. I just want to know what you're doin' and when you're doin' it so I can come after you if things go south." He set down his fork and shook his head. "On second thought, this is a bad idea. No. I can't let you do it."

Dixie gasped. "*Let* us?"

All of this arguing was adding to my headache. "Maybelline. We're gonna talk to Maybelline."

"Summer!" Dixie snapped, and Bill gave me a disapproving frown.

"What? He's right. We're about to start diggin' deeper, and we don't know what we'll find. Besides, you know she'll end up putting whatever she tells us on her page. We'll be lucky to get a twenty-four-hour head start."

Dixie stabbed the food on her plate like it was Luke's head. Or mine.

"So just to be clear," I said to him, holding his gaze, "we tell you what we're doing, and you don't interfere at all."

"Unless I think it's too dangerous."

I wasn't planning to rush into danger, but I suspected Luke's threshold would be lower than ours. "We'll decide whether to tell you on a clue-by-clue basis."

He didn't look happy with that answer. "I can help you, Summer."

"And yet you *can't* help us. See our dilemma?"

I took his nonresponse as agreement.

"We'll let you watch us interview Maybelline," I said, ignoring the death stares from my partners in crime. "That's all I can promise."

He stared to answer, stopped, then said, "Fine."

"Good."

We all finished eating with little conversation, and when we were done, Dixie pushed Bill out of the way and headed back to the kitchen.

Bill was busy avoiding Luke's gaze.

But I understood Bill's hesitation, and I worried he was about to back out of the deal, especially since, according to Dixie, this had been his master plan.

Dixie hurried back and told us that Maybelline was ready whenever we were, and Bill picked up his camera case and followed.

"Bill doesn't trust me," Luke said, watching him head into the kitchen.

"In all fairness to him, *I'm* having a hard time trusting you."

"Summer."

I shook my head. "Look, my distrust over this is different than his. I think he's worried you're gonna arrest us for investigating. I know you're not stupid enough to face the wrath of two Baumgartner women, and there's no telling what Teddy would do to you. My concern is that you're setting us up to do this just to pull the rug out from underneath us. But I'm trusting you for now."

His mouth pursed, but he gave a slight nod. "I can live with that."

Rachel brought the check, and after Luke handed her some cash, we followed Bill and Dixie to the kitchen. Bill had brought two mikes, and he hooked one up on Maybelline and one on me. He told Dixie to stay close to me so he could pick her up on my mike. Five minutes later, we were filming. Luke stood behind Bill, leaning against the wall with his arms crossed over his broad chest.

"Maybelline," I said, "Dixie says you may have information about Otto."

"A few weeks ago, Otto was talkin' about gettin' a job. Said he had a friend who was gonna help him be rollin' in money."

"Really?" Dixie asked. "I've known Otto for several years now, and I never once heard him talk about money. Or having a job."

Maybelline didn't seem offended by Dixie's contradiction. "That was the thing. He never had before, so it struck me as odd too."

"Did he mention how he was going to get rich? Or anything about his friend?" I asked.

"Supposedly, his friend—who told him to keep the whole thing secret— wanted to hire Otto for some kind of courier service, and he was gonna pay him good money. I'd never seen Otto so excited . . . well, not since what happened to his family. He told me not to tell anyone, so I didn't." She gave Dixie an indignant look. "What? I can keep a secret."

Dixie's eyebrows shot high enough to almost touch her hairline.

Maybelline ignored her. "In any case, Otto never mentioned it again, so I figured nothing had come of it. But then last week I took out the trash, and I saw Otto by the dumpster. That didn't necessarily mean anything—sometimes Otto would dumpster dive, and I never told no one."

She shot a sly grin at Dixie. "You'd be surprised by all the secrets I keep stored in my head." She tapped her temple. "Anyway, I didn't think much of Otto digging through the trash, but he was talkin' to someone while he did it. More like havin' an argument. I couldn't tell what it was about, but I sure tried."

Dixie gave me a sly glance. "I bet you did."

"Did you know who he was talking to?"

Her grin fell. "Teddy."

"My brother Teddy?" Dixie asked in disbelief.

I shot Dixie a worried look, then turned back to Maybelline. "And you're sure you didn't hear what they were talking about?"

"No, but I did hear mention of a bike. Teddy tried to hand Otto a piece of paper, but when he saw me, he said goodbye to us and took off. Otto seemed shaken up, so I asked him if everything was okay. He said yep, right as rain. I remember him sayin' it clear as day. Then he said he needed to go think for a spell." She sniffed and dug a tissue out of her pocket. "That's the last thing he ever said to me."

"Do you remember what day this was?" I asked, trying to ignore that Dixie had gone stock-still.

"A week ago Friday."

"Have you ever seen Teddy and Otto talk before?" I asked. "Even in a friendlier manner?"

"No. Can't say I have."

"And Otto never mentioned bein' friends with Teddy?"

"Nope. Other than Gretchen, I never heard him talk about no one other than his mystery guy. Not even those two old farts he usually hangs out with . . . I guess that should be past tense, huh?" She paused as tears filled her eyes. Then she sniffed and gave a nod. "And I saw Otto every Monday unless he was at his thinking place. Monday's meat-loaf day, and I always gave him a meal in exchange for moppin' my floors after closin'. Only he never came in this past Monday."

I could tell terrible things were racing through Dixie's head—they were sure running through mine—but I needed to stay professional. "Is there anything else you can think of to add?"

Maybelline shook her head. "Nope. Nothing, but I sure hope you find out what happened to Otto. He was a good man, despite what people say."

I waited a couple of seconds and called out "Cut." Glancing over my shoulder, I saw Luke had his gaze pinned on me. The look in his eyes worried me, and I regretted letting him sit in on this. "Is there something else I should ask?"

Surprise washed over his face, and he dropped his arms to his sides. "Me?"

"You're standin' there watching, so I might as well utilize you."

"No. I can't think of anything."

"Thanks."

I unhooked Maybelline's mike. "We'd like to keep the fact that Luke was here a secret."

"Say no more, sugar. I can keep my mouth shut."

After we packed everything up, we went out to my truck, none of us saying anything. Dixie climbed into the driver's seat and closed the door, and I finally broke the silence. "Just because he was talkin' to Teddy . . ." I glanced up at Luke. "That doesn't mean anything."

He watched me with solemn eyes.

I grabbed his arm and dragged him toward the building. "Luke. You have to say something to reassure Dixie. She's freaking out."

He gave me a sympathetic look. "Summer, I can't."

Anger rushed through me. "You can't or you *won't*?"

He remained silent.

The truth hit me like a sucker punch. "Are you investigatin' Teddy?"

He put his hand on my shoulder. "Summer . . ."

I jerked away from him. "You lied to me! You said you weren't investigatin' Otto's death."

He pushed out a heavy sigh as he glanced over at the truck. "I'm not. I swear to you. Boy Wonder is handling it. But I was investigatin' something else before all of this went down, only I had no idea Otto had anything to do with it."

"What is it?"

"Drugs."

"But hearin' Teddy's name wasn't a shock?"

His mouth turned down.

I gasped, then shook my head. "No. I can't believe Teddy has anything to do with drugs." But Teddy had known Ryker was wrapped up in them. How would he have known that if Dixie really hadn't known?

"Summer, I want to tell you what's goin' on, but I can't. He's your cousin, and he's Dixie's brother. Do you know why Dixie broke up with Ryker?"

I opened my mouth to tell him, then immediately clamped it shut. "I'm not telling you anything, Luke Montgomery. You totally misrepresented why you wanted to tag along, and now you're plannin' on usin' what you found out against my cousin."

"No. Not entirely. I'm worried about you, and whatever's going on is wrapped up in the sheriff's investigation. You know I can't touch that part of it. But if you keep me apprised of what you're doin', I can at least help keep you safe."

"So any information about Teddy is a bonus?"

When he didn't deny it, my anger ratcheted up several notches. "Stay away from me! Stay away from my family!"

His eyes hardened. "I can't do that, Summer."

"Why? Because you want to spy on me more? Well, fool me once, shame on you, but there won't be a fool me twice."

I started to walk to the truck, but Luke grabbed my arm and tugged me back hard enough for my chest to hit his. He snaked an arm around my back and held me in place. "You're still in danger, Summer Baumgartner, whether you want to believe it or not, and I aim to make sure you're protected."

"From my own cousin?" I hissed, trying to break out of his grasp. "Are you insane?"

"I suspect Teddy would sooner sacrifice himself rather than hurt you, but let's not forget someone sent you into the woods to find Otto's body. I don't believe for one second that was Teddy. There's more than one force in play here, and you need to be careful." I tried to break free, but his hold tightened. "Summer. Will you stop fightin' and listen to me?"

Stop fighting? He was fooling himself if he thought I was just going to play the good girl and do what he told me. *That* was something I was very happy to have left behind with seventeen-year-old Summer. I'd only just begun to fight for my family, and I wasn't about to stop.

Luke's arms were like bands of steel, holding me against him, and in any other situation, I probably would have melted right into him, but right now I was filled up with righteous indignation. I lifted my foot and stomped on the inside of his ankle with as much force as I could muster—which wasn't much. I'd exerted most of my energy trying to look alert for Maybelline's interview. But it must have been enough because Luke grunted in pain and dropped his arms.

I leaped back as though I was on fire and said in a shaky voice, "I meant what I said. Stay away from me and my family, Luke." Then I spun around and nearly passed out from the onslaught of dizziness. I blinked to push away the black edges of my vision and stumbled toward the passenger door of the truck.

"Drive," I said once I was inside.

"What happened?" Dixie asked as she pulled away from the curb. "What did Luke say?"

What should I tell her? She had enough troubles without knowing that Luke suspected Teddy of something. But I'd sure keep that in mind while we continued with our investigation, if for no other reason than to prove Luke wrong.

"Nothing. Same old I'm-a-weak-woman-and-need-a-big-strong-man-to-protect-me bullshit."

"What did he say about Teddy?"

"Nothing." Which was pretty much true. But what he hadn't said spoke volumes. "I didn't see Bill leave."

"He took the equipment back to the office. He could tell that you and Luke were about to have a knock-down, drag-out fight and wanted to get far away from Ground Zero. Besides, that guy standing down the street was giving us the creeps."

"What guy down the street?"

"Just some guy. He was watching you talk to Luke. He had a camera."

I shuddered. "Damn paparazzi. I'm surprised it's taken 'em so long to show up, given all the crap on those gossip sites. Investigatin' Otto's disappearance will be next to impossible if they start following me around." And Lord only knew how many photographs he'd snapped of me and Luke. *Dammit.*

"Lauren will probably love it," she said.

"True. More buzz, better ratings." I really hadn't missed this part of the showbiz life.

Dixie was quiet for several seconds. "Teddy would never hurt anyone."

"Dixie, *I* know that. No need to convince *me.*"

"But what about Luke?"

"If he doesn't see the truth for the trees, then he's an idiot. I'm sure there's an explanation for why Teddy was talkin' to Otto. We'll just ask him."

"Yeah," she murmured. "So what's our plan next?"

We needed to find out what Otto was up to before he died, and I picked the most logical place to find out.

"Otto's apartment."

CHAPTER TWENTY-SEVEN

"We need to go there tomorrow," I said to Dixie. "Do you think Bill's still on board?"

"Luke didn't scare him off. He said he'd go with us wherever we need to go at lunch tomorrow and after we quit for the day."

"Thank goodness," I said, then thought of something else. "I wonder what he's doin' with all the video. I was led to believe they dump it every night and the video editors go through it all the next day and pick out the usable footage."

"I was worried Lauren would figure it out, so I kind of asked him the same thing. He said he's been saving our stuff to an external hard drive, but he's worried because it takes a lot of memory. He said something about saving it on a cloud."

That made sense. I leaned back on the seat and closed my eyes. My head hurt from thinking too much.

"What are y'all planning to do with this secret footage?" Dixie asked. "Are you gonna replace Lauren's show?"

"Not replace . . ." I hedged. "Supplement." One more thing to worry about. But not tonight. "For now, let's plan on going to Otto's apartment tomorrow at lunch. I'll call Gretchen and make sure she's okay with us using the key we still have."

When we got to the farm, Teddy's truck was parked in front of the open barn doors with its hood open. I could see Teddy working on the engine.

I summoned the energy to get out and talk to him while Dixie went inside to check on Meemaw.

"Don't you dare talk about anything important until I get out there," she whispered to me.

I smiled but didn't agree, hurrying as fast as I could, which wasn't very fast. Teddy looked up when he saw me, but he didn't stop working the wrench in his hand.

"You should have been home and in bed a long time ago," he said with a scowl.

"That's one thing you and Luke Montgomery agree upon."

His frown deepened as he glanced down at his engine again. "You've been talkin' to Luke? I thought you two were still at odds."

"Yeah, well . . . I guess some things never change," I said wistfully.

He was silent for a few seconds before he said, "I remember that summer . . . the two of you were like fire and ice."

"Which one of us was ice?" I asked with an ornery grin.

He looked up with a twinkle in his eye. "Maybe it was more like fire and fire."

That sounded about right. But that was part of why we worked. We had lots of peaceful moments, but the fire—in passion and in anger—was intense.

"The thing is, when you two were gettin' along, you were happy, Summy, but the rest of the time you were miserable."

"We got along until the end . . ."

"Yeah, when the asshole couldn't handle that the world didn't revolve around him."

When I had to go back to California. "We were kids."

His gaze held mine. "Luke Montgomery still likes gettin' his way. That part of him hasn't changed one bit."

I could see the truth in that. "Did he talk badly about me after we broke up?" I wasn't sure why I had asked. If he had, knowing it would only hurt me.

His mouth pursed. "No." It looked like it pained him to admit it. "He spent a long time gettin' over you." He leaned over his engine again. "I'm not sure he ever did, truth be told."

"Well, he blew it tonight, so no worries there."

He was silent for a moment. "You still love him, Summer. But you're right. You were kids, so it's not the same."

Should I warn Teddy that Luke was suspicious of him? Maybe I should start this conversation off with Dixie. "Why didn't you like Dixie dating Ryker?"

His scowl returned, but it was much more intense and fueled by anger, as evidenced by the way he cranked his wrench. "He was a worthless asshole who treated her like shit."

"Why did she put up with it?"

"Because she thinks she deserves it." He set the wrench in his hand on a towel he had set out on the bottom of the windshield. "She thinks she was responsible for that fire, so she believes she deserves every bad thing that ever happens to her. Welcomes it, even. Guys like Ryker see that and take advantage of her."

"She said he broke up with her with no explanation. Did you have something to do with it?"

"Depends on who's askin'. You or Dixie?"

"Me. I won't tell her."

His eyes hardened. "Let's just say we had a come-to-Jesus meetin', and he wasn't near enough ready to meet his maker."

But Ryker had met his maker anyway. Even though Teddy looked deadly right now, I still couldn't believe my cousin would kill someone. "Luke was surprised to hear Dixie had broken up with him. He said he saw Ryker comin' out to our farm last week."

"What the hell was Luke doin' watchin' our farm?" he asked, getting pissed. He lowered the bar holding up the hood and let it drop with a loud bang.

"Do you think Dixie was meetin' him in secret?"

"No."

"Maybe I should ask her."

"Summer." He grimaced, then said, "Ryker was meetin' me."

"*You?* Why?"

"It had nothin' to do with Dixie, and that's all you need to know."

"Teddy!"

He moved closer and looked down at me. "It doesn't concern you, Summer."

"You said Ryker was a drug dealer. Is that how you were gettin' money to help with the farm? Did you get involved in his mess too?"

His eyes were hard, and for a moment I could almost see him as Luke clearly did, but his gaze softened, and he gave me a bittersweet smile. "Listen to me. You need to stay out of this. Don't worry so much. I've got it covered."

"That's not an answer, Teddy."

"It's the best I can do."

Tears of frustration swam in my eyes.

His voice softened. "Summer. I'm askin' you to trust me. When I have things taken care of, I promise to tell you everything, but in the meantime, I'd feel a lot better if you steered clear of Luke."

"I'm not gonna tell him anything about what we discussed," I said. "Your secrets are safe with me."

He leaned over and kissed my forehead. "I know, otherwise I wouldn't have told you, but I think it would be safer for you to just avoid him for a while."

"What does that mean?"

He hesitated, then said, "Something's brewin', and I don't want you to get caught in the middle of it." Then he put his arm around my shoulders. "It's nearly eight thirty, and you're about to turn into a pumpkin. Go in and get to bed."

"Aren't you comin' in?"

He opened his truck door. "I've got some business to take care of." Then he hopped in and turned over the engine.

Dixie came out of the back door as I made my way toward it.

"Where's Teddy goin'?"

"He said he had business to take care of."

"We need to tell him about what Maybelline said."

Should I confess that I'd already quizzed him? I made a split-second decision. "You and I both know Teddy wouldn't have anything to do with any nonsense."

She watched him drive off, lifting her hand in a wave. He gave her a wave back, and I prayed that I was right. Dixie couldn't deal with another loss. Neither could I.

When I woke up the next morning, I felt like a heavy blanket had been lifted off my head. Everything was clearer, and my headache had tuned down to a dull ache. I even had a bit of an appetite.

I hadn't brought very many dresses, so I dug through Dixie's closet, grateful she had a few church outfits that could double as fancy detective wear. "This is ridiculous," I muttered. "What PI gets all dressed up to investigate cases?"

"We'll make it work," Dixie said.

I was glad one of us was optimistic.

We spent the morning canvasing the Hintons' neighborhood, looking for the dog who had dared to impregnate little Fifi, although we were striking out since it was Sunday morning and most people were at church.

"I have an idea," Dixie said after one of the few neighbors at home slammed a door in our faces. "Why doesn't Mallory Hinton just wait until her dog has her puppies and then see what they look like?"

"Or have one of those DNA tests," I said as we walked toward the next house.

"DNA test for a dog?"

"They're all the rage in LA," I said. "You can find out your dog's breed and if they have any hereditary issues."

"Do they make those dogs have DNA tests before they get married?"

"What?"

"I've seen videos of dogs gettin' married out there. Didn't one of your dogs get married? I bet you got her a cake made of dog bones and decorated your house with water fountains in the shape of fire hydrants. Did you wear a mother-of-the-bride dress? Or was it a groom?"

I looked at her like an alien had just popped out of her chest. Was my head injury causing me to hallucinate? "What? No, I never did. And I would hope my dog wouldn't get married before me."

"I want to have a little purse puppy. Maybe two of 'em. I'll have them get married, but not when they're puppies because that would be gross. They have to be old enough to consent." She glanced over at me. "How's that dog-age thing work? One people year to four dog years?"

What was she doing? "Uh . . . I think it's seven."

"Huh," she said, looking lost in thought. "Maybe I'll wait until they turn two, then they can get married when they're fourteen. You know, like they used to do it in the olden days."

"Yeah . . . ," I murmured. There was a twinkle in her eye, and I suddenly realized she was trying to give this stupid show some sort of entertainment value. So far, everything we'd done seemed dull as dirt.

We finally found someone who was willing to talk . . . or, based on the way Lauren seemed prepared when we rang the doorbell, someone who had been prepped to talk to us. A woman answered the door with a dachshund at her heels who seemed pretty frisky for looking like a bratwurst. She said he'd gotten out about a month ago—and confirmed that he did indeed seem to have a thing for the Yorkie down the street.

We filmed the neighbor opening the door five or six times because Lauren wanted the dog to walk up behind her, but the dog wasn't following any cues. (Go figure.) On one of the takes, Lauren suggested we break the news to the woman that she was expecting grandpuppies.

We started a new take with Dixie and me on the porch, looking extra serious—as directed by Lauren. The woman stood in the front door with the barking dog at her feet.

"Mrs. Fisk," Dixie said, clasping her hands in front of her, "I'm afraid we have some good news and some bad news."

My gaze drifted to the end of the street out of boredom, but the white van parked there caught my attention. At first glance, it looked like it was parked on the street, but someone was sitting inside the vehicle. It looked like a man, and he was watching us.

I might have ignored it, but I remembered seeing a white van the afternoon I'd found that money in the parking lot. Oh! And then it hit me—I'd seen it leaving the parking lot after I'd been attacked at the lake. Was he a paparazzo? The way he was watching us sent shivers down my back.

I pulled out my phone while Dixie was delivering the bad news. "Ms. Hinton would like you to share the cost of Fifi's medical bills as well as provide puppy support."

I pulled up Luke's name, but Teddy had just asked me to steer clear of him. After a moment's consideration, I decided that while I didn't trust Luke to treat Teddy fairly, I did trust that he'd protect *me*. I started to send him a text.

"Puppy support? Is that like giving them toys?" Mrs. Fisk asked in confusion as the dog continued to yap at her feet.

"More like provide a monthly payment to help with the cost of raising them."

"What?" the woman gasped while Dixie handed her the paper Mallory had provided that broke down the various monthly costs. I'd seen the total at the bottom, and I had a sneaking suspicion the amount equaled the lease payment on their brand-new Lexus.

I finished typing my text.

We're filming on Monaco and Troost. There's a van parked at the curb, and the man inside is watching us. I think I saw the van at the lake after I was attacked.

Lauren called "Cut," then leveled a furious look at me. "Summer? Care to join us, or is what's happening on your phone too important?"

"Sorry." But I could see that Luke was typing something, so I didn't put it away.

"Summer!"

The text appeared on the screen.

Stay put but keep out of danger. If you feel threatened, do what you need to do to stay safe. I'm on my way.

"Sorry," I said again, stuffing the phone into my dress pocket.

Five minutes later, a police cruiser turned the corner.

We were still filming, but I was doing a good job of staying focused as I took my turn at breaking the bad news to Mrs. Fisk, which took some effort since the dog was now barking in earnest. His owner kept moving her legs to keep him inside.

Mrs. Fisk was the one who stopped midsentence and stepped out onto the porch. She lifted her hand to her forehead to shield her eyes from the sun. "What's Luke doin' down there with that van?"

Lauren whipped around as Luke walked up to the van parked on the street. After motioning for the cameras to turn around to film the new action, Lauren pointed to her mouth and opened and closed it. She was telling me to narrate.

Luke was likely to hate this.

But Dixie was quick to pick up on the cue. "Would you look at that hot policeman . . ."

"Looks like he's gonna arrest that man," Mrs. Fisk said, her sole focus now on Luke. "Would you look at the way he fills out that uniform shirt? I hear he works out at the yoga fitness place downtown."

Dixie's eyes danced with mischief as she smirked at me. "I'd love to see *his* downward dog."

"Dixie!" I admonished.

Mrs. Fisk looked at me in a new light. "You used to date him, didn't you?"

"A long, long time ago . . ."

"Not that long," Dixie added.

A knowing smile spread across Mrs. Fisk's face, but at that moment, her dog decided to make his move.

He bolted between our legs and nearly tumbled down the steps, but he reached the bottom safely and began waddling across the yard like one of those cheap wind-up toys.

"Mr. Hot Stuff!" Mrs. Fisk shouted, pushing us out of the way to go after him.

"Mr. Hot Stuff?" Dixie said. "Are you kidding me?"

Lauren gave us a look that suggested she was pissed and motioned for us to follow.

I held back a groan as I tromped down the steps, but Dixie felt no such compulsion.

"Next thing you know," she grumbled, "we'll be traipsing across fields, lookin' for lost dogs."

Good Lord, I hoped not.

But now that Mr. Hot Stuff had escaped, he was not turning back. He ignored the cries of his owner and did his hobble-sprint straight for Luke, who appeared to be looking at the driver's license of the creepy guy in the van.

"What are you doin', Summer?" Dixie asked with an impish grin. "Aren't you gonna call after it? I bet he responds to his name. It's gonna look like you don't care about that poor little dog."

"Poor little dog, my eye."

Mrs. Fisk was doing her own jog-run, and her knees suddenly buckled. She fell to her side like the wind had blown her over.

"Mrs. Fisk!" I said when I caught up and squatted next to her. "Are you okay?"

"I just twisted my ankle." She waved her hand toward Luke. "Go get Mr. Hot Stuff before he takes off down the street. I heard the Murphys' collie is in heat."

Oh, good Lord.

But Dixie was chuckling. "Go get Mr. Hot Stuff before he ends up on one of those trashy afternoon talk shows." She pitched her voice lower, trying to sound like a talk-show host. "'Mr. Hot Stuff, you are the father of two litters of puppies, born at the same time.'"

The Murphys' collie was currently safe, however, because the randy dog was now attached to Luke's pant leg, and Luke was glaring at the animal like he was trying to decide what to do with it.

"Mr. Hot Stuff!" I called out. "You stop that right now!"

Luke glanced up with a mixture of amusement and irritation, as though he couldn't decide how he felt, but he quickly settled on irritation when he saw the cameras and microphone boom in my entourage. "Did you just call me Mr. Hot Stuff?"

"*Seriously?*" I asked, torn between moving closer to get the dog and edging away from the possible threat.

"Summer, go wait at the corner." He pointed to the street sign to emphasize his point. The guy's driver's license was still in his hand.

I could tell he didn't want me near the guy in the van—and I didn't want to be anywhere near him either—but Mr. Hot Stuff had dug in his heels, and I was worried he'd be distracting enough to put Luke in danger.

"Don't you want me to get Mr. Hot Stuff?" I asked, cringing as I said it.

Dixie was still just halfway down the street, letting me take point on this one.

Luke lifted his leg slightly off the ground, and the dog's front legs lifted with him.

The van door opened, and a thirty-something man got out with an expensive-looking camera in his hand.

So he *was* a paparazzo? I wasn't sure whether to be relieved or annoyed.

But my answer came quickly enough—neither.

"*Summer?*" the guy said. His eyes were wide, and his jaw had gone slack. He took several steps toward me, putting his free hand on his chest. "It's me. Sebastian." When I didn't answer, he added, "Sebastian Jenkins."

I shook my head. "I'm sorry. I don't know you."

"I told you she wouldn't know you," Luke said in a firm voice, still trying to gently shake the dog loose. "Now get back in your vehicle, Mr. Jenkins."

"No," the man said, taking several steps closer. "You *do* know me. We met at a shopping mall in Atlanta eleven years ago. You wrote me a note!"

I shook my head. "At an event?" The network used to send us to shopping malls for mini-events, and afterward we'd do autographs. We'd meet hundreds of fans, but we signed our photographs so quickly there was no way I'd remember one of them individually.

He nodded and moved closer as excitement lit up his eyes. "I *knew* you would remember me. I forgot to give you my last name, so you had no way to find me."

I took a step back, feeling majorly uncomfortable. "No. I just remember going to the Atlanta mall."

Luke's face had hardened, and I was sure he was pissed that the dog was still firmly attached to him. He touched a button on his shirt and said, "Willy, I need backup at Troost and Monaco. I have a 10–66 with civilians present."

"A 10–66?" Willy's voice cracked over the intercom. "Is that a vicious animal?"

"*A suspicious person*, Willy. I need you stat."

Although Willy wasn't too far off, there was a tenacious animal still clinging to Luke's pant leg.

Sebastian shot a glare at Luke. His body shook with anger. "I am *not* a suspicious person. I already told you I know Summer!"

"Then why don't you get back in your vehicle while we sort this out?" Luke asked calmly. "You can talk with Ms. Butler's people about setting something up."

His eyes turned wild. "I've been trying to set something up with her people for years! That's why I'm here. I heard she was in Sweet Briar, and I wanted to see her again."

Luke looked torn between dealing with the dog and tackling Sebastian Jenkins.

The creepy guy took a step forward, and Luke blocked his path.

"Summer," Luke said in a direct tone, his full attention on the angry man in front of him, "go back to your truck."

"No!" Sebastian said with wild eyes. "I'm not hurting anyone! I only want to talk to her!"

My heart was racing, and I struggled to not sound breathless when I held up my hands and said, "Sebastian, calm down. You're talkin' to me now, right?"

"Summer!" Luke barked with his back still to me.

Sebastian pointed his finger at Luke. "That cop is trying to make me leave."

"He's only tryin' to do his job, which is to make sure everyone's safe—that includes me *and* you."

"Why would he think you're unsafe? I don't want to hurt you. I only wanted to see you again. Maybe spend some time together so you can see how perfect we are for each other. I can buy you lunch."

"That is a really sweet offer," I said, forcing myself to smile. "But I'm a little busy right now." I pointed with my thumb to the cameras behind me. "See? I'm filmin' my new show."

"I know you are!" Anger filled his eyes again. "You think I don't know? I know what you're doing. I pay attention like any good boyfriend. And I know you dated this asshole." He glanced at Luke's chest. "Officer Montgomery."

He knew about Luke? My publicist had tried to hide our relationship as much as possible, but it had leaked to a couple of gossip sites.

"Summer." Luke's voice was tight. *"Go to your truck."*

And leave him to deal with this lunatic on his own? If I just talked to the guy, he might calm down.

"I'm telling you, Summer," Sebastian said in frustration, "I know you. And I'll treat you better than this jerk"—he flung his hand to Luke—"or those stupid actors you date. Aiden Clay? What were you thinking with that guy?"

I took a step back. This guy was obsessed. "You were the one callin' my house last week. Only you always hung up after you said my name."

"I was shy," he pleaded. "But I've been here, working up the courage to say something to you."

"Today?"

"Since you got into town."

Sebastian took another step forward, and I backed up a few more paces.

"Summer," Luke said, backing up so that he was practically in front of me, dragging Mr. Hot Stuff with him. "For the last time, go get in your truck."

Suddenly sirens filled the air, coming closer, and panic filled Sebastian's eyes. He ran back to his van, slammed the door shut, and tore away from the curb.

"Dammit!" Luke shouted, still trying to remove the dog.

Luke was close enough that I could bend down and pry the dog loose, but Mr. Hot Stuff wasn't ready to let go yet. He obviously wasn't going to respond to force, so I reached underneath him and began to scratch his belly. The dog let go of Luke's now-ripped pants and began to lick my hand.

Luke pointed a finger at me while shooting me a glare. "You and I need to talk later."

I didn't respond—not that I had time to—because Luke took off running for his car, already barking orders at poor Willy through his intercom.

"You saved Mr. Hot Stuff!" Mrs. Fisk cried out as she ran around the production crew to get her troublemaking dog.

"Cut!" Lauren shouted as a smile stretched across her face. She punched her hand into the air. "That, my friends, is how reality TV is done!"

But knowing that Lauren's version of reality was almost entirely staged, I had to wonder if she had something to do with Sebastian Jenkins's appearance.

CHAPTER TWENTY-EIGHT

Everyone was a little shaken up after the incident, but Dixie took it upon herself to play mother hen.

"I'm fine, Dixie," I insisted. "Things like that used to happen fairly often when I was on *Gotcha!*" What I didn't say was that I'd always been surrounded by security back then. They'd been left to deal with fans like Sebastian while I was swept away to another event or party or filming.

We shot a few more scenes, trying to find more cooperative neighbors with dogs so it wouldn't look like we'd found Fifi's boy toy so quickly, but most of the neighbors who were home had seen the incident and kept wanting to talk about it on camera. Finally, Lauren threw up her hands and declared it was lunchtime.

"Already?" someone said. "It's only eleven."

"This isn't about food or eating!" Lauren shouted. "This is about everyone getting their shit together before we pick up the next case. Be over at 351 Oak Street at twelve."

"The haunted house?" Tony asked.

"That's the one. Summer's got a psychic showing up at one, so I'll need you all to be ready."

Dixie gasped. "A psychic?"

I lifted my hands. "I didn't have anything to do with that." *What a circus.*

But we didn't waste any time heading to the truck. Bill told Lauren that he was taking his camera with him so he'd be ready to get B-roll of the haunted house.

I still hadn't called Gretchen, so I placed a call to her after we got into the truck. "Gretchen, I'm so sorry I haven't called you sooner, but Chief Montgomery told me that he talked to you and let you know that I . . . found Otto."

"And he told me you were injured. I'm so sorry."

"No," I said. "I wish I'd found him alive."

"I know you do, girl."

"There's still a lot of questions about what happened to Otto, and I want to keep looking into it. Someone moved his body, and I'd like to find out who and why."

"I thought the sheriff was looking into it," she said, sounding confused.

I wondered how much I should tell her, but then decided she deserved the truth. "I think you should know that the sheriff's department thinks *I* moved his body."

"Why on earth would they think that?"

"For the show."

She was quiet for a moment, and I was starting to worry she would hang up when she said, "That's the most ridiculous thing I've ever heard. All anyone has to do is look into your eyes to know you're incapable of such a thing."

Her statement caught me by surprise. I kept hearing it was a ridiculous proposition due to my size, but she was the first person to have based her opinion solely on my character.

"I want to keep digging," I said, "but I want to keep this quiet, even from my producer. She doesn't want me to do this, so we're doin' it on our time off."

"Why would you do that?"

"I'll be honest; we're still filming while we search. We want to show the truth on camera. But even if we weren't filming, I'd still be lookin' into his death. And not just to clear my name. I promised you I'd find out what happened to him, and I take that seriously."

Gretchen's voice broke. "You have no idea what that means to me."

"I'd like your permission to go inside Otto's apartment. You gave us a key, but that was when we thought Otto was alive. I just wanted to make sure it was still okay. I promise we'll be respectful of Otto's things."

Gretchen was silent again, and her voice sounded strained and teary when she finally spoke. "Thank you. I can't bring myself to go over there yet, so feel free to go in."

I glanced over at Dixie after hanging up. "We're good." It was then that I realized Dixie had turned on the video camera.

"Do you think Luke caught that creeper?" Dixie asked.

"Knowing Luke, yeah." I called Luke's cell next, then dialed the police station when there was no answer.

"Hey, Amber," I said in response to the receptionist's greeting, "it's Summer. Is Luke handy?"

"He's in the interrogation room, but let me check in on him. He told me to let him know if you called."

"Do you know if he caught my . . . fan?"

"Oh, yeah," she said. "He caught him, and you'll never believe what the guy had with him."

"What?"

"Nope. Luke made me swear not to tell you. Let me go get him."

"Okay." I shot Dixie a confused glance. "Luke got him, but Amber says he had something with him."

"Probably a rag soaked in chloroform."

"Dixie!"

"Just sayin'. He wasn't driving a pedophile van for nothin'."

"Dixie!" Only there was a chance she might be right.

Luke came on the line. "Summer? Can you take your lunch break later this afternoon so you can come by the station?"

I shot another glance at Dixie. "We're on our lunch break now."

"Are you planning on investigatin' Otto's case?"

After last night, I almost told him that it was none of his business, but he had just come to my rescue, so I said, "Maybe."

"Well, you may not need to do that."

"Why?"

"We found Otto's bike in Sebastian Jenkins's van."

I sat stock-still.

"Summer?"

"Yeah. I'm here. I'm just shocked. That's the last thing I expected you to say." But a memory of that afternoon tickled my brain. What was it?

"And it was the last thing I expected to find. The sheriff's department headed over to look at his van, and I'm trying to wrap things up here so I can join them."

"Where is the van now?"

"It's impounded."

"So how did he get it?"

"Surprisingly, he's spilling his guts. He says he followed you out to the lake and took the bike after you ran off in the woods."

"Was he the one who chased me into the woods?"

"He swears he isn't, but I'm not so sure. There's something else, Summer." He paused. "He knows where your farm is located and even knows which room is yours. He had a hand-drawn picture of it in his van. I think he might be the one who broke into the farmhouse."

I shuddered. "That's a good thing, right?" Even if it was beyond creepy.

"Yeah." He paused. "You're sure this guy isn't the one you talked to at the church?"

"No. He doesn't look anything like him."

"I know, but I was hopin' anyway, because if he's not, then the mystery guy is still out there."

"None of this makes sense," I said.

"Tell me about it."

Then the missing memory finally hit me. "Luke, there were two people out there. *Two* people were chasing me."

"*What?* Are you sure? Why didn't you tell me earlier?"

"I just now remembered. My head was screwed up."

There was a commotion in the background. "Shit, I've got to go. Willy's camped out with the van, and he says deputies from the sheriff's department have shown up."

"Okay, thanks, Luke."

"I still need to see you later."

"Okay."

I hung up and relayed all the information I'd gotten from Luke to Dixie.

"Do you still want to go by Otto's?" she asked.

"Yeah. We still don't know why he was scared last Sunday, and I doubt he was scared of Sebastian Jenkins."

We were only a minute away by that point. When Dixie turned into a run-down apartment complex, I wasn't surprised by the condition of the place, but I was sad that Otto had lived that way. The parking lot was full of older beat-up and rusted cars, and the frame of a swing set with no swings stood to the left side of the small complex.

Bill was already waiting for us with his camera out of its case.

"Luke caught the creeper," Dixie told him when we reached him. "And he found a surprise."

"Really?"

"Otto's bike."

His eyes widened in surprise. *"What?"*

"He said he followed Summer out to the lake and took the bike."

Bill blinked and shook his head. "That's wild. I never saw him. Do you think he's the guy who chased you?"

I shrugged. "I don't know, but I remembered there were *two* people chasing me, so Sebastian could have been one of them."

"He has to be," Dixie said. "And this proves you weren't lying."

"Maybe." Still, there was a tangled mess of questions in my head. But we had a limited amount of time, and we needed to make the most of it. "Let's get started."

"Okay."

Bill started rolling and I addressed the camera. "We're outside of Otto's apartment building, and so far, things aren't adding up." I laid out a few of the details, then said, "But Otto's sister still wants us on the case, which makes checking out his apartment the next logical step. I'd also like to talk to a few neighbors."

I only realized my mistake as Bill took footage of us walking up to the building. "Oh, crap. I forgot the key in my desk drawer."

Dixie stared at me for a moment, possibly calculating how bad it would be for us to pick the lock in broad daylight, then flashed a smile. "No problem. Why don't you and Bill work on talkin' to the neighbors, and I'll go get the key."

"Sorry, Dixie."

"No worries."

As Dixie drove off, Bill and I started knocking on doors. The complex was full of older residents, and most were home from church. Unfortunately, most of them didn't know anything.

"He kept to himself," an older man who lived in the apartment next to Otto's said. "He was usually quiet, but sometimes I'd hear sounds through the walls I couldn't make out, kind of like cryin'." He shrugged. "Maybe it was the TV."

That broke my heart, and I took a second to ask, "Have you seen any strangers lately? Anyone snooping around?"

He laughed. "I'm talkin' to y'all right now."

"Good point," I conceded. "No one other than us?" When he shook his head, I said, "I know Otto had a bike. Do you know where he kept it?"

"Yeah, down under the stairs." He gestured toward the staircase, and Bill's camera turned slightly to capture the movement.

"Do you usually notice when it's there?"

He hesitated. "I do, but only because it's so colorful with all that red and blue. I'm not nosy."

"You're just observant," I said reassuringly. "There's a difference."

"I ain't seen it since Sunday morning. That lady from the church came by looking for Otto, and I pointed out that if his bike was gone, he was gone."

"And you never saw Otto or his bike again?"

"Nope."

"Did Otto have many visitors?"

He laughed again. "Otto? Nah. He was usually leavin', not entertainin'."

"Did he seem scared?"

"Nah. Just sad."

"If you think of anything else, could you give me a call?" I asked, pulling one of my business cards from my purse. "We're tryin' to figure out what happened to him."

He took the card and looked it over. "Yeah. Sure."

Dixie was pulling into the parking lot as he shut the door. I wished we could talk to more neighbors, but our lunch break was more than halfway done, and I needed to change before we showed up at the haunted house.

Bill lowered the camera as Dixie came hurrying up the walkway with the keys in hand. "Sorry! Lauren was at the office, so I had to be careful about gettin' them."

I made a face. "Sorry."

"Well, it turned out to be good timing. She got a call while I was there. I think she found out that your creeper got arrested, and she wasn't too happy about it."

"What? Are you sure?"

"Yeah, she turned a little pale and asked, 'Are you sure they found it with him?' Then she asked where he was now, and *then* she told Karen she'd be back. She took off alone."

"That's pretty generic. She could have been talking about anything."

"True. But the timing is coincidental."

She had a point. Plus, I didn't trust Lauren as far as I could move a grown man's body. Still . . . "We know that Lauren's all about sensationalizing anything that's not part of her dog and pony show. I suspect she was hopin' to draw it out over more episodes."

"I sure hope so," Dixie said. "Because thinking she either brought your creeper here to stalk you for the sake of this show and/or that she might have actually moved Otto's body is freakin' me out."

"Yeah, me too." Eager to change the subject, I filled Dixie in on what little I'd learned from the neighbors.

Dixie said, "So, based on the whereabouts of Otto's bike and what his friends said, we know that he disappeared on Sunday. But we still don't know what scared him?"

Traitor that I was, I found myself thinking about Teddy and Otto arguing in that alley a couple of days before the latter had disappeared.

Teddy would never hurt anyone.

"I don't know," I said. "I sure hope we find out something inside to help us figure it out."

She handed me the keys, and we walked down to Otto's apartment. The curtains were all pulled, and his doormat looked like it was original to when the apartment complex had been built fifty-some-odd years ago.

The smell hit me as soon as I unlocked the door and pushed it open.

Bill held the camera up to his face, but I could see him cringing behind it.

"Oh, sweet baby Jesus," Dixie said, waving a hand in front of her face. "What *is* that?"

"It smells like something dead." I waved my hand in front of my face. "Did Otto have any pets?"

"I don't know," Dixie said, pinching her nose. "He never mentioned any. Maybe he left out some food, and it spoiled. This is rank."

Maybe so. But I had a very bad feeling. "Don't touch anything until we've looked around. We don't want to leave fingerprints."

"But Gretchen gave us permission to be here."

"I have my reasons."

Her eyes widened with fear.

Something inside me told me to call Luke, but I knew he had his hands full with my stalker. I almost called Cale, but I knew he was working on the murder investigation. Bottom line: I hated to bother either of them if this turned out to be nothing. "Let's just make a quick pass through the apartment and see if we can figure out what's causing the stink." I was hoping we'd need to call animal services instead of 911.

The living room was furnished with older, mismatched furniture; and there were piles of plates, takeout containers, and wrappers strewn everywhere.

"Do you think that's the source of the smell?" I asked, already guessing the answer.

"Nah, this smells like the time the barn cat died in the loft in July."

Oh, Lord.

We peeked into the tiny kitchen. I had half hoped to find a maggot-infested hamburger on the counter, an absolutely disgusting thought but much better than where my imagination was running.

I headed down the hall. "Did Otto live with anyone?"

"Not that I know of. And Gretchen didn't mention it."

"True." I stopped next to a partially closed door. The smell was leaking through the cracks. The room was dark so I couldn't see what was inside. "The stink is comin' from in here. You think this is the bathroom?"

"The bedroom's down there." She gestured to an open door with the foot of a bed showing through the opening. "And this door looks like a closet." She pointed to a slim door closer to the bedroom before looking back up at me. "I think it has to be."

"We can't turn on the light and risk touching the light switch," I said, digging my phone out and turning on the flashlight. "I'll have to use this until we figure out what's goin' on in there."

"Or what *went* on in there. Past tense," Dixie said in a small voice.

My stomach did a flip. She had a point. But I still stood in front of the door, scared to see what was on the other side.

Finally, I sucked in a breath . . . and instantly regretted it since I pulled in a lungful of something putrid. I started coughing and Dixie groaned.

"Let's just get this over with." She pushed the door with her foot, and it halfway swung into the room before it met resistance.

Crap.

Pinching my nose, I held up my phone and shone the light into the space. A pair of jeans-clad legs was blocking the door.

"Oh, God," Dixie gasped.

My heart took off like a race car. I knew I should get the hell out and call Luke, but I suspected I might know who it was—and I had to find out for sure.

I took a small step into the room, trying to control my nausea, when the smell got even worse. I shined the light around the door, illuminating the man's blue T-shirt and then the bullet hole in his forehead. From the way his face was bloated, it was obvious this hadn't just happened.

A wave of dizziness washed through me that had nothing to do with my concussion.

Sometimes I really hated when I was right.

"Well," I said, "we just found our mystery man."

CHAPTER TWENTY-NINE

We stumbled out to the living room while my fingers fumbled to call the police station.

"Amber, this is Summer. Is Luke still there?"

"He's over at the impound lot with Deputy Dixon."

Dammit. "Okay. Thanks. I'll call his cell."

"Why didn't you tell her?" Dixie asked as I hung up the call.

"Because that guy's been dead for a while—probably since soon after I saw him, based on the fact he's still wearing what he had on at the church and . . . his face. And Luke's looking at the van with Deputy Dixon."

"We could call Cale or Willy," Dixie said.

"Luke would be furious. He's going to want to see this himself."

"You should wait," Bill said. "This gives you a chance to look around." He'd lowered his camera and obviously wasn't filming.

"But if we look around, we'll be tampering with a crime scene."

Beads of sweat dotted his upper lip. "So we're careful. We can erase the last part of you finding the body and head back to his bedroom to snoop around. Then I'll film you finding the body. If we play it this way, you're not knowingly tampering with a crime scene. It's all about intent."

"He has a good point," Dixie said.

He did, but it still felt wrong.

"That guy was in Otto's apartment for a reason," Bill said. "He was looking for something. Maybe we can find it."

"And somebody found him in here and killed him. They probably found it themselves."

Bill looked away, but not before I saw the conflict waging in his eyes. I was facing the same war.

"Look," he finally said when he turned back to me, "I didn't want to tell you this, but I think you have a right to know."

My back stiffened. "What?"

"Lauren's totally sabotaging this show. She's making you and Dixie look like first-class idiots." Once he started spouting off, he quickly picked up steam. "On top of that, she's buying the sheriff's version of what happened in the woods. Why do you think she got upset that your stalker had Otto's bike? It doesn't fit with her narrative. She doesn't want you to find out the truth. She wants the other version to stand. Better ratings."

My jaw dropped.

We were silent for a few moments before Dixie said, "We have to look, Summer."

"No, we don't." Now that I was trying to reason this through, I was rethinking the idea of involving Luke. This was clearly wrapped up in the whole mess of Otto and Ryker—and Luke clearly thought Teddy had something to do with that. "I'm calling Cale. He's investigatin' Ryker's murder, and I suspect this one's related to his."

Dixie headed for the bathroom door. "I'm gonna take a peek at him. There's a chance I might recognize him."

"Dixie . . . ," I warned. "Prepare yourself. It's bad."

She glanced back at me with a grim look, then stepped into the small opening to peer around the door. After a couple of seconds, she came back out, her face pale.

"You know who it is?" I asked, even though it was obvious that she did.

"It's Ed."

"Ryker's friend and partner Ed?"

She nodded. "He cut all his hair off—it used to be several inches longer—but it's him."

That settled that. I found Cale's number and called him.

"Summer," he said when he answered, "you doin' okay? You sound kind of shaky."

"Oh . . . yeah." I'd momentarily forgotten about my stalker. "I found another dead body."

He paused. "By the lake again?"

"No, in Otto's apartment."

"*Shit.*" He paused for several seconds. "Do you happen to know who it is?"

"Dixie says it's Ed."

"*Ed Reynolds?* In Otto's apartment?"

"Yeah."

"Are you still there?"

"Yeah."

"I need you and Dixie to go outside and wait for me, okay? I'll be there in a few minutes." Then he hung up.

I glanced up at Dixie and Bill, but Bill was filming again.

"Cale told us to wait outside."

Bill followed us to the front door. I grabbed the hem of my dress and carefully turned the door handle, hoping I didn't rub off any potential fingerprints.

We didn't have to wait long. We'd barely had time to huddle into a small circle outside of the apartment, all of us shaken, before Cale's cruiser sped into the parking lot. After he parked, he walked quickly toward us. He cast a glance from me to the partially open door.

"How'd you get in Otto's apartment?"

"His sister gave us a key."

He frowned. "I thought the sheriff's deputy told her to stay out of it until they had a chance to come by."

"I called her earlier to get permission, and she never mentioned it."

"What did you touch inside?" he asked in a deadpan voice.

"Nothing," I said. "Except for the door handle to get out. I grabbed it as lightly as possible with the hem of my dress."

"Did you disturb the body at all?"

I cringed. "No. He's behind the bathroom door. The door only partially opens."

"And you think it's Ed Reynolds?"

I glanced at Dixie.

She nodded. "Yeah."

"This is important," Cale said, holding my gaze. "Did you take anything out of the apartment?"

"No," I said in surprise. "We smelled something dead as soon as we opened the front door, and I knew right away we shouldn't touch anything."

"And why didn't you call me then?" he asked, getting irritated. "What on earth possessed you to go inside?"

"Because Luke was tied up with Deputy Dixon, and I know you've got your hands full with Ryker's murder investigation. For all we knew, it was a dead cat. We would have called animal control for that."

"Why were you here *at all*?" he asked, working up a snit.

I lifted my shoulders and stared him in the eye. "I'm investigatin' a case, Cale Malone."

"You're not a real private investigator, Summer. Leave the investigatin' to the professionals."

I gasped in outrage. Sure, he was right, but he didn't have to be so blunt about it. Besides, there was no denying I did have my license . . . qualified or not.

"How is it that Luke is lettin' you do this anyway?" he asked.

That one loosened my tongue. "*Excuse me?* What in the hell makes you think Luke Montgomery has any say in what I do?"

He groaned and took a step to the side. "Oh, come on, Summer. It's obvious to everyone you two still have a thing for each other, and he's bein' extra vigilant with anything to do with you. I'm surprised he's not sittin' in the parking lot, watchin' you even as we speak. Why'd you call me instead of him? Did you two have another fight?"

"Because he's meetin' Deputy Dixon to look at my stalker's van."

Bewilderment filled his eyes. "*What?*"

"You haven't talked to him?"

He looked unsettled. "No. What stalker?"

"He probably didn't have time to call you," I said as my anger faded slightly. "It all just happened over the last hour or so." I gave him a quick explanation.

He shook his head. "Jesus. You sure do have a way of courtin' trouble."

"Gee . . . thanks."

"Say, I wanted to apologize for asking you to keep that secret for me. I know you told Luke, and I want you to know that I'm not holding a grudge."

"Cale . . . I'm sorry. It seemed kind of important."

"No big deal."

Bill shifted his weight, looking anxious. "If we're gonna get to our location on time, we need to get going."

"Can we go, Cale?" Dixie asked, looking only slightly better.

"Yeah," Cale said, motioning toward the parking lot. "If I have any questions, I know where to find you."

When we got to the parking lot, Bill put his camera into his car. "Who do you think killed all these guys? Three dead men in a matter of days. This town seems pretty small for that many deaths."

I thought about my conversation with Teddy the night before. "Teddy told me to be careful. That something was brewing." I hesitated, then added, "He told me to stay away from Luke."

"Why?" Bill asked.

"Teddy and Luke haven't gotten along since Summer left town," Dixie said. "But now Teddy hates Luke after . . . the fire."

"What fire?" Bill asked.

"Nothing," I said. "But I think this is more than bad blood between the two." I caught Dixie's gaze. "I think it has something to do with Ryker."

Dixie's eyes flew open. "Ryker?"

"I don't know what. All I know is that he's nervous."

Dixie's breath came in short pants.

"This doesn't leave this group, understood?" I asked.

"Yeah," Bill said. "I'm not telling anyone."

"Dixie?"

"Yeah," she said absently.

"Okay, then, let's go. We still need to change." I glanced up at Otto's apartment, surprised to see Cale still watching us. He gave a wave then went inside.

Did he think I had something to with Ed's murder? Why had he been so intent on asking if we'd taken anything out of the apartment?

It only took Luke two hours to turn up at the haunted house.

Dixie and I were filming a scene with a paranormal investigator Lauren had brought in from Asheville, North Carolina.

"Lauren couldn't find a closer one?" Dixie had asked after we were introduced. "Sissy Trotta claims to see ghosts all the time."

Karen leaned in and whispered, "But Piper Lancaster has a one hundred percent success rate. Plus, she's young and pretty. People would rather see her than some eighty-year-old bag of bones." She paused. "*And* she's doing it for next to nothing."

"Hmm . . . ," I murmured.

Piper seemed too normal to be a ghost hunter. I would have expected Lauren to go for someone more flamboyant. And maybe Lauren had expected her to be that way, because she started giving Piper a pep talk after our second take, telling her to show more energy and demonstrating with big, sweeping hand gestures.

Out of the corner of my eye, I caught sight of Luke standing in the doorway. We'd just finished shooting the scene, so I had no idea how long he'd been standing there, but the expression on his face suggested he was vacillating between concern and irritation.

Obviously he'd heard about us finding Ed Reynolds.

Watching him now, I couldn't believe Luke could be as dangerous to me as Teddy had insinuated. But I also couldn't believe Teddy was linked in any way to Ryker's or Otto's deaths.

So were both men wrong, or was one of them right?

"Summer."

"Luke." I wanted to do more than just walk over to him, but we were surrounded by the crew and under Dixie's watchful eye. Besides, I wasn't sure whether his irritation or his concern would win out.

"Why didn't you call me about finding Ed Reynolds in Otto's apartment?" Irritation it was. I crossed my arms over my chest. "You were busy."

"You should have called me anyway."

"I called Cale."

Hurt filled his eyes, making me feel even worse.

"I stopped by the apartment and . . ." His eyes softened. "Finding two dead bodies within a matter of days. Are you okay?"

His concern had won out, and my heart melted just a little. "I'm fine. Mostly."

"How are you feeling physically? You look better today."

"I am."

He glanced down at the ground and pushed out a breath. "Deputy Dixon and I looked at the van together. Sebastian Jenkins had his own little shrine to you in that van, and based on photos on his phone and his camera—and one we think is yours—he really has been watching you since you came to town." He paused and looked up at me. "Summer, he was out at your farm. There are photos of you standing on the farmhouse front porch from the first night you got back into town."

"How do you know it's from the first night?"

His voice lowered. "I remember what you were wearin'. The blue in your shirt made your eyes look even bluer."

I stared at him, dumbfounded that he remembered.

"We don't have much to hold him on other than stealing Otto's bike and your camera and refusing to pull over after he ran off. Jenkins lawyered up, and I'm certain he's gonna get sprung at his arraignment tomorrow."

My heart leaped into my throat. "You mean he gets to go free?"

"He'll have a trial, but I'm positive the judge will let him post bail. The charges aren't serious enough for him to withhold it."

"So he can follow me again?"

"Not if you file a restraining order. Judge Waldo says he'll see you today in his chambers and issue it tomorrow at the arraignment." He paused. "You'll be safe in Sweet Briar, Summer. He'll be forced to stay a hundred feet away from you, but only in town. Once you leave the city limits, he's free to do what he wants. And the judge says he'll make sure Jenkins is aware your farm is also within city limits."

"He's comin' in on a Sunday?"

"He thinks this is important enough to warrant it."

"Okay," I said, feeling nervous. Would Sebastian Jenkins really obey a restraining order?

"You need to go to the courthouse to see Judge Waldo at five. After this morning, I suspect Lauren will be eager to add more drama, so be sure to play it up to get her to let you go."

"Good thinking. Thanks."

He turned to leave, then spun back around, his jaw clenched. "Oh, and one more thing your investigation into Otto Olson is done."

"Say what?"

"Another dead man? You're done. It's too dangerous." Then he turned around and walked to his car.

Seriously? He thought he could issue an order and I'd just obey?

"Can we bother you to join us, Summer?" Lauren asked from the doorway. "Or will you let us know when filming fits in with your schedule?"

I couldn't wait until this show was finished.

I walked toward her. "Chief Montgomery came to tell me I need to go speak to Judge Waldo at five."

"What in God's name for?"

"I need to file a restraining order against Sebastian Jenkins, the guy who showed up this morning. Turns out he's been following me since Karen brought me into town."

Her eyes lit up with excitement.

I added, "He followed me out to the lake too. He was the one who took Otto's bike."

"Karen," Lauren said, looking behind her, "you need to rearrange the shooting schedule for this afternoon. We'll wrap up here with Piper, then we'll all go by the courthouse."

This was going to be a circus.

We shot the scene again, and Piper tried to play it more over the top, but she seemed to be more of the touchy-feely type than the woo-woo type. She told the owner she felt something disturbing in the house, but she couldn't be sure if it was the spirit of a deceased person or the energy of her soon-to-be-ex-husband. Lauren shot several takes of Piper smudging the house with burning sage, and then Dixie and I promised to check on the owner's husband.

We headed downtown after we finished.

The courthouse was uneventful—much to Lauren's dismay. The judge refused both her request to film in his chambers and her request to interview him on camera, so Lauren made me sit outside the courthouse while she asked me questions about my stalker and what I knew about him.

"Are you living in fear?" Lauren asked.

"While it's concerning that a troubled individual will possibly be in the area," I said, "I trust the Sweet Briar police to take care of any adverse situations that might arise."

"What the hell kind of answer is that?" Lauren snapped.

"What exactly do you want me to say, Lauren?" I asked with forced patience.

"Oh, I don't know, Summer. Perhaps show a little emotion? Act a little scared? Be thankful that your boyfriend's there to take care of you?"

"You want me to say I'm scared? Sure, I'm freaked out, especially since the guy's getting out tomorrow. They gave me a restraining order, but how many times do those get broken? All the same, I don't expect the Sweet Briar police to babysit me."

"Do you think your boyfriend will insist on personally taking care of you?"

"If you're referring to the police chief, we dated when we were in high school. We were kids. We're adults now, and we're not together."

"Then why is he so interested in your well-being? He came to the hospital while you were still in the ER."

"I'm sure Chief Montgomery would be concerned about any other citizen in his town." I wasn't going to admit to her that he was still interested in me.

"Then why does he keep showing up and checking on you?"

"I guess you'll have to ask him."

Lauren leaned forward and gave me pleading look. "You have to give me something, Summer. Tell me how it feels to come home and find out that your high school sweetheart still cares about you."

I wanted to come back with some snappy retort, but instead my cheeks flushed.

Lauren smiled and mouthed, *Perfect.* Then she yelled "Cut" and told everyone to head back to the office. "Summer," she added, "can I have a word."

"Of course," I said, bracing myself for her sharp tongue.

We moved a few feet away from everyone else. "Summer, I'm going to be frank," she said with a grim face. "This show is crap."

"Well, it's no wonder," I blurted out before I could stop myself. "It's totally fake."

Her brow lowered. "I don't think you appreciate the situation. We're in big trouble. If the first few episodes are awful and the ratings suck, they'll cancel the rest. Then you won't get paid the full amount, and I won't get to move on."

Well. Crap.

CHAPTER THIRTY

The next morning was more of the same made-up cases. We investigated the ex-husband of the haunted-house woman by following him as he drove from his house to work at the local bank. (Nothing happened.) We went to the city park and met an older woman who was sure someone was trying to steal her cat. (She brought her cat on a leash. And, of course, we took her case.)

But I was nervous. Sebastian Jenkins was supposed to get out of jail this morning, and I had no idea if he'd start following me again. I should have felt better when I saw Willy Hawkins pull up to the curb in the park while we were filming to watch for a bit, but it only confirmed that Luke was worried too.

When Lauren called for a lunch break, Dixie, Bill, and I didn't waste any time before heading out to the Dollar General. We'd stopped by the strip mall the previous evening to talk to Otto's friends, but neither of them had been there. Not knowing what else to do, Dixie and I had gone home for dinner with Meemaw. Teddy hadn't come back until late, long after we'd gone to bed—something both Dixie and I had noticed but hadn't discussed.

But now we were on our way back to the Dollar General with Bill in tow in his own car. I pulled into the parking lot and heaved a sigh of relief when we saw the two guys sitting at the table.

A goofy grin spread across Fred's face, and he broke into a raunchy song about "goin' down south on Dixie" when he saw us.

"Hello, *gentlemen*," Dixie said as we got out of the truck and walked toward them, Bill following us with the camera. "And I use the term loosely."

"*Ladies,*" Al said with a wink.

"You guys weren't around late yesterday afternoon," I said. "I hear that's unusual. Where were you?"

"We ain't got to tell you nuthin," Al grunted, taking a sip from his paper-covered bottle.

"We stayed at home," Fred mumbled.

"Together?" Dixie asked.

Fred nodded.

Dixie sat down next to Fred. "What scared you?"

His face jerked up. "Nothin' scared us."

Dixie frowned. "Okay, sorry. I can see you're tough guys who don't get scared. So why'd you stay home?"

Al grimaced, then said in a lowered voice, "We heard they found that guy in Otto's apartment."

"Why do you think he was there?" I asked. "Do you think he was lookin' for something?"

Both men gave a noncommittal shrug.

"We want to find the guy who scared Otto," I said. "Do you think he really drank himself to death?"

Both men shook their heads. "Otto never got drunk off his ass," Fred said. "Never."

"When Summer found him, he had a bottle of Jim Beam," Dixie said.

Again, they shook their heads. "Nope," Al said. "He wouldn't have drunk that."

"Not even with his extra cash," Fred said.

"Where did he get the extra cash?" I asked. "What was Otto mixed up in?"

Both men were quiet for several seconds, then Fred glanced up at us. "He was running errands for this guy. He carted things to the dry-cleaning business, then back. 'Easy money,' he called it."

"The rules were he couldn't look in the bag," Al added. "But week before last, he did."

"What did he see?" I asked.

"Money. Lots of money." Al said.

Fred shot a glance at Al, then turned back to us. "And drugs. He told us not to tell anyone, and we didn't. That's why we didn't tell you when you was here before, on account of we thought Otto was still alive, but now he's dead. I'll bet anything it's because he looked in the bag."

"How would anyone know he'd looked?" Dixie asked.

"Dunno," Al said.

And who was the "anyone"? I couldn't get it out of my head that Maybelline had seen Otto talking to Teddy the Friday before his disappearance.

No. Teddy was *not* involved in this.

"Do you know if there was a schedule?" I asked. "Did he usually drop the money off at the same time or different times?"

Fred shot Al a look, then said, "A few times he left on his bike and told us he was meeting some guy in an alley."

Dixie stiffened next to me.

"Which alley?" I asked as I tried to control my rapid breathing. *No. No. No.* Teddy couldn't be involved in this.

"Dunno," Al said.

"But other than that, no schedule?"

Both men shook their heads. "But it was usually during the day and on weekdays."

"When the dry cleaner's was open," I said.

"Yeah, I guess so."

I tried to collect my wits to think of what else to ask, but I was so thrown by the apparent connection to Teddy that I was struggling to concentrate.

Oh, God. What if the reason my cousin had told me to stay out of the Otto investigation wasn't just because he wanted to protect us? What if he didn't want us making the connection?

"Thank you," I told them, and waited a few seconds before saying "Cut."

We headed back to the truck and Bill's car, and once we had some privacy, I brought up the point none of us wanted to address. "We need to look at the two incidents in the alley. The one I saw with Mayor Sterling and Ryker, and the other one Maybelline saw with Teddy and Otto."

"Teddy didn't do this, Summer!" Dixie protested.

I took a deep breath and tried to swallow the lump in my throat. "We have to be objective, Dixie."

"Surely you don't believe Teddy had anything to do with those murders or Otto's death!"

"I don't," I said in defeat as I sagged into the side of the truck. "I can't. So let's focus on Mayor Sterling and Ryker."

"I find it hard to believe the mayor's mixed up in drugs," Dixie said. "Mayor Sterling is as straight as they come."

"Then why was he talking to Ryker? We can't forget that Ryker dropped a bag of money outside the dry-cleaning business . . . or that he was later found dead." I tried to say that softly, or at least as softly as someone can when talking about a murder victim.

"Good point," Bill said.

Why was *Teddy* seen talking to a man who turned up dead?

I turned to Dixie with wide eyes, and she stared back with an equal amount of horror in hers. Was her mind wandering to the same places mine was?

"Dixie . . . Teddy . . ."

"We need to focus on Mayor Sterling and Ryker right now," she said in a brisk tone.

I glanced over at Bill. The sheepish look on his face suggested he thought we shouldn't dismiss Teddy's possible involvement either.

"Okay," I said. "We need to go to that dry-cleaning business."

Dixie gave me a half grin/half grimace. "We need to get rid of your tail first."

I glanced back over my shoulder to see Luke halfway across the parking lot, leaning against his police car with his arms folded over his chest.

Dammit.

"He's obviously here to see you," Dixie said. "What are you gonna tell him?"

I frowned as I watched him. He didn't look happy. "I don't think withholding information from the police chief is a good idea."

"He's not investigating Otto's death."

"But he *is* investigating a murder that I'm pretty doggone sure is connected."

"No, *Cale* is investigating the murders."

"It's not a huge department. I'm sure they work cases together."

Bill didn't say anything for several seconds. "Look, I hate to be the one to bring this up, but are you really sure he's not using you? Lauren's been pretty generous when it comes to doling out stuff to benefit the community. Maybe Chief Montgomery got in line."

I shook my head. "The Luke I know wouldn't do that."

"You knew that guy ten or twelve years ago, right?" he asked. When he saw my look of surprise, he added. "It's a small town. People talk."

Luke was still waiting and was starting to look irritated.

"People grow," Bill said. "They change. Sometimes you don't even recognize them anymore."

He looked like he was speaking from personal experience.

"I'll meet you at the dry cleaner's," I said. "Dixie and I will be there shortly."

"Make sure he doesn't follow."

I walked over to Luke, feeling that familiar warmth when he watched me walk toward him, his gaze dropping to my legs since I was wearing a dress again. I needed to keep reminding myself this was strictly business.

"You need something?" I asked when I was about six feet away.

"You look good in that dress," he said, lifting his gaze to my face. "I thought you wearin' a dress yesterday was a fluke. This must be Lauren's doin'."

"Are you here to discuss my clothing choices, or do you have another purpose?"

His attitude shifted. "What are you doin' talkin' to Al and Fred? I thought I told you to leave this case alone."

"Excuse me?" I asked. "I'm a registered PI in the state of Alabama with a client who hired me to look into her missing brother's whereabouts. Now she's asked me to look into the circumstances of his death. What I'm doin' is perfectly legal, Officer."

His eyebrows rose. "Officer? We're back to formal now?"

"Are you here on official business?"

"Yeah, I'm here to tell you to stop this nonsense, Summer. You're treadin' on dangerous ground. Are you doin' this to piss me off?"

"What? No! Do you really think the world revolves around you? Well, I'm not some half-witted woman who's enamored with you. I'm trying to save my family farm, Luke, and this stupid show is crap. The only way to save my family is to figure this out. And even if Lauren canceled the show tomorrow, I'd still want to look into it because I promised Gretchen."

He leaned his head closer to mine. "It's not worth losin' your life over, Summer."

"I'm not so sure of that." I turned away and started toward the truck, but he grabbed my arm and spun me around to face him.

"What does that mean?"

"It means I'm an insignificant nobody despite my name and my past. And no, I don't have a death wish, and I definitely don't plan on doing anything reckless, but I'm still doing this. I'm giving Gretchen closure. And I'm saving the farm, because other than that summer with you and my cousins, my life has been a string of insignificant experiences that don't even add up to a pile of dog shit." I took a breath. "So I'm doin' this one good thing, Luke. One good thing that benefits somebody else. And you can't stop me."

Anger and shock covered his face. "You truly believe that?"

I studied his face. "Yeah. I do."

"Summer."

His grip loosened, and I tugged my arm free. "I'm not lookin' for your sympathy. And I'm not lookin' for you to save me. I don't want you to. I need to do this myself."

"Sebastian Jenkins is free on bail, and there's a murderer out there who is connected to Otto Olson—I just don't know how yet. You're flittin' around like this is some kind of game, but it's not, Summer!" he said in frustration. "There's something dangerous goin' on in this town, and you're puttin' yourself smack-dab in the middle of it. Yeah, you have a legal right to do this, but it's dangerous. That plot of land isn't worth your life."

"Maybe it's the perfect price."

He put his hand on my upper arm and tugged me closer, close enough that my chest almost touched his. "I'm worried about you."

"Why do I think you're talkin' about Teddy now and not Otto's case?"

"I'm not going to deny it. You're right. I think Teddy's tied up in something bad. He seemed pretty angry the night I was out at the farm. Has he been prone to losin' his temper since you came back?"

"What? No!"

I started to back up, but Luke's hold tightened slightly. "I don't want to keep anything from you. I . . . I'm goin' to tell you something so you're not caught off guard."

My heart slammed into my rib cage. "What are you talkin' about?"

"Teddy's a person of interest in Ed Reynolds's murder."

I gasped. "Why?"

"Summer, we have evidence tying it to him."

"What kind of evidence?"

"The murder weapon. It was next to Ed's body, and it was covered in Teddy's prints."

I shook my head and mouthed a silent *no*. But I also couldn't believe he was sharing something like that with me. Wasn't this the kind of information police officers kept to themselves?

"I know this is a shock," Luke said as he held my gaze with soft eyes, "but I need you to tell Teddy that I want to help him. If he cooperates, maybe we can get the DA to lessen the charges."

"How?" I asked, trying to gather my wits about me. He gently rubbed my arm, but it did nothing to ease my tension. "Murder is murder."

"If he gives the DA information about the operation, I'm sure he'll work with Teddy. Will you talk to him?"

"What operation?"

"Drugs."

I wanted to protest that Teddy would never have anything to do with drugs or a murder—or the two together—but I couldn't seem to find my voice. I had my own doubts. Desperate men were capable of terrible acts, but surely this was too much for Teddy.

"I think Otto is connected to all of this," Luke said. "Which is why you need to stop investigatin.'"

"So you've already become Teddy's judge and jury?" I asked in horror. I took a couple of steps back. "Just like you were Dixie's?"

His mouth parted in surprise. "What are you talkin' about?"

"Teddy told me you arrested Dixie. How could you?"

His face hardened. "I was doin' my job, Summer."

"You berated me for doin' my job," I shouted, "but your job ruined my cousins' lives! My job never hurt anyone!"

He was angry now. He pushed way from his car. "You so damn sure about that?"

"What the hell does that mean?"

"Your job hurt *me*, Summer. Don't I count for anything?"

"With all due respect, Luke," I said, "arresting my cousins and putting them in jail is a hell of a lot different than bein' separated by a freaking job!"

I spun around and stomped to the truck, half expecting him to stop me.

Dixie was behind the driver's wheel, so I slid into the passenger seat.

"Everything okay?" she asked.

"No. Let's go."

We were quiet for a minute before Dixie said, "I heard part of what you said."

"Which part?"

She grimaced. "Almost all of it." She turned to me. "What's goin' on with the farm?"

Crap. Crap. Crap. How could I be a PI if I couldn't keep a damn secret? But I told her everything. I was finishing up as she pulled into the parking lot of the dry cleaner's.

"Does Teddy know?"

"Yeah. I told him a couple of days ago."

"But not me?" The hurt in her voice sliced through my heart.

"Dixie. What was the point? I only told Teddy because I wanted to know how much new trouble the farm was in—and what *he* was planning to do about it."

"What did he tell you?"

"Not a damn thing other than that he has it covered."

She pushed out a heavy sigh. "That's what he tells me too." Then she added in a quiet voice, "Are we gonna lose the farm?"

"I'm not gonna let that happen," I said. "I'm gonna fix this. I promise you."

She glanced over, her face pale and her eyes filled with tears. "Okay."

"This is why I didn't want to tell you. I don't want you to be worried."

"You haven't been back for years. Why do you even care?"

"I didn't come back before because I was ashamed. But my heart has always been here. I won't let you lose the land."

"Us," she whispered.

"What?"

"Us. *We* won't let us lose the land."

It felt good to be back in the Baumgartner kids' club again.

"Teddy hates Luke for arresting me," she said in a small voice. "But he was right to do it. I was to blame."

"He arrested you for an accident. Teddy was right to be pissed."

"That's not the whole story," Dixie said. "You need to give Luke a break. He was doin' his job."

My mouth parted. "I can't believe you're saying that! Your arrest devastated Teddy. Gutted him. And now Luke's wanting to arrest *him*!"

Her lips pressed together in grim determination. "Then we have even more reason to find out the truth. To help clear Teddy's name."

"Yeah."

But those doubts wouldn't lay themselves to rest. I was such a traitor.

I grabbed my phone and sent Teddy a text.

I need to talk to you. It's important. Text me.

We were silent for the next couple of minutes until Dixie pulled into the parking lot. "Bill's already here. Let's find out what's goin' on."

We got out and went over to Bill's car. He rolled down his window.

"This looks incredibly obvious," I said. "Us walking up with a camera. They're not gonna talk this way. Besides, they could potentially be dangerous. If they think we're trying to record anything, we could get hurt or worse."

"Which is why I'm going to film you from outside and pick everything up from the mike. Dixie," he said, "I think you need to stay with me for this one. What if they recognize you?"

"They're more likely to know Summer."

"But they might be more willing to talk to Summer since she's wrapped up in this."

It seemed unlikely—why would they talk to someone they knew was playing detective? But I wasn't about to send in Dixie alone.

"I should be the one to go in," Dixie said in a firm voice. "I was Ryker's girlfriend. It makes more sense I'd show up askin' questions."

Bill gave me a grim look. "She has a point."

"I'm the licensed PI," I said. "Luke said that for this to be legal, I have to take the lead on the questions."

Bill glanced up and held my gaze. "You're right. It has to be you."

I nodded. "Are you ready?"

"Give me a second . . ." He lifted his camera and aimed it at the dry cleaner's. "Ready."

I took a breath and walked over to the store. My pulse pounded in my ears as I opened the door. Racks of clothes looped from the front to the back, and a young woman walked up to greet me.

"Can I help you?" she asked. She looked like she'd had a hard life. Her clothes were worn and faded, and her eyes were dilated, even though the reception area was bright with the noonday sun.

She was high.

"Hi," I said. "I think my friend left some dry cleaning here, and I wanted to pick it up for him."

"Sorry," she said in a bored tone. "You can only pick them up if you have the ticket."

"Maybe it would help if you knew who my friends are," I said. I put a five-dollar bill and three ones on the counter. I was pretty sure it would have been more effective with a twenty, but when you're broke, you're broke. "I'm lookin' for a good time."

Her eyes widened. "That's not gonna get you much."

"There's more where that came from." I rested my hand on the counter and paused for several seconds. "This town is just as boring as I remember it bein', and I'm dyin' . . . you know?"

She gave me a look of disbelief. "*You* want to party?"

"What?" I asked. "You think I don't like to party?"

Her answer was to look me up and down.

Okay, so Dixie's church dress didn't exactly lend itself to the Sweet Briar party scene.

"Look, I know who you are," she said. "And I know you've got a squeaky-clean image."

"The wonders of a good publicist," I said sardonically. "Didn't you hear that I punched that guy? I was stoned out of my gourd. Why do you think I'm here now? They're trying to get me to detox *au naturel*," I said, using air quotes around the phrase. "But I snuck a small stash with me, and now it's gone and I'm desperate . . . What's your name?"

She couldn't have telegraphed her distrust better if *she'd* been the actress, but she answered anyway. "Christina."

"I'm desperate, Christina." I grabbed the sides of my head. "I'm under all this pressure from this stupid show and everything else, and I'm *dyin'* to unwind. So can you hook me up or not?"

Her mouth twisted to the side. "I'm not sure I trust you. You're filmin' that PI show."

"Do you see any cameras with me now? Besides, everyone in town knows the show is fake. Are you gonna help me or not?"

She still hesitated.

"You don't even have to sell it to me. Just give me a name of someone I can contact. Surely there's no harm in *that*."

She sighed and rested her hip against the counter's edge. "What are you lookin' for?"

"Beggars can't be choosers, right?" I asked. "I prefer coke, but I'm open to a substitution."

"Supplies are kind of low right now," she said, and instantly looked like she regretted it. "There's a turf war goin' on, and I hear a shipment never reached its rightful owner. But I know a guy who's got some Oxy. Maybe some Xanax. I bet he'd be willing to sell you some." She gave me a sneer. "Just bat those pretty blue eyes and he'll give it to you for pretty cheap."

"Who?"

"Tommy Kilpatrick."

I did a really good job of hiding my initial surprise, but then I realized he'd told me about the Oxy. I'd just presumed he'd gotten a scrip from his doctor. Maybe he'd give me his source. "Do you have his number?"

"Yeah. What's yours?"

I wasn't exactly thrilled about giving her my number, but there was no way around it.

She typed it into her phone, and seconds later, my phone dinged. Sure enough, Tommy's contact information was on my screen.

"Thanks, Christina." I started for the door.

"Say," she said.

I stopped and turned back to her.

"Do you think I could be on that show?"

I dug a business card out of my pocket and handed it to her. "Call the office, and maybe we can make something up for you."

I headed out into the parking lot, studiously ignoring Bill's car, and climbed into the truck. Bill followed me as I drove down the street and then pulled into a church parking lot. As soon as we got out, Dixie ran over and pulled me into a hug.

"That was amazing!" she said.

"I know a way we can butter up Tommy," I said. "We need to get one of those photos we took blown up. I'll sign it, and we can tell him we want to drop by with it."

"Oh! Good idea."

I only hoped it produced results.

CHAPTER THIRTY-ONE

When we wrapped up for the day, Dixie drove up to Eufaula to pick up the photo. Although we had a working printer in the office, we didn't have any photo paper. So she sent several photos to the Walgreens in Eufaula and left as soon as she could get away . . . which was sooner than I could. Lauren had insisted on keeping me late to show me some of the footage they'd been sending to LA to use for the show.

It didn't take long to realize it was a joke. It ranged from boring to downright campy.

"I had to up our promotion game," Lauren said, her mouth turned down. "I thought it best to give you warning . . . and show you why."

My heart fluttered with fear. "What does that mean?"

She didn't answer, only shook her head and walked away, but I saw what looked like worry in her eyes.

Oh, God. What had she done?

She'd sent Bill off to get B-roll of several of the places we'd gone, so I headed to Maybelline's Café while I waited for Dixie to come back with the truck.

I slid into a booth and pulled a small notebook out of my purse to organize my thoughts. I'd already written down several points when I heard a man say, "Are you really investigatin' Otto's death?"

I looked up into Mayor Sterling's worried face.

I nonchalantly moved my hand over what I'd written. "Mayor Sterling! What a wonderful surprise. How're you doin?"

Maybelline appeared at the table with a glass of tea in her hand. "Good evenin', Mayor. You're not usually in here for dinner."

"Myra's not feelin' well, so I thought I'd pick something up and take it home. Why don't you give me two of your meat-loaf specials?"

"Sure thing," Maybelline said with a grin. "And what about you, little miss? Your usual?"

I couldn't stop my grin. She'd always called me little miss when I was a kid. "As tempted as I am to say yes, I'm gonna have to go with your house salad. Too much good food is making all my dresses snug." I patted my waist to prove my point.

She laughed. "Then I'm doin' my job. You're too damn skinny. I'll have it right out."

As she walked away, I realized the mayor was still standing next to me. I could definitely use this opportunity to talk with him. "Mayor, would you like to sit with me while you wait?"

He looked surprised. "Yes, thank you." He sat across from me, and seconds later, Rachel, the young waitress from a couple of days ago, brought him a glass of water.

I was scrambling to figure out how to ask my questions, but he said, "Tomorrow night's the parade. Are you excited?"

I'd completely forgotten about the parade. "Of course!"

"It starts at five sharp, but we'll need you at your float by four thirty. Your float will be the last one, of course." He grinned, but it was shaky. "The best for last."

"Mayor Sterling? Is everything okay?"

He reached for his water, but when we both saw his quivering hand, he shoved it under the table. Then he looked up at me. "Are you really lookin' into Otto's death?" he asked again.

I wasn't sure how to answer, but there was really no point in lying. People talked in this town. "I'm askin' some questions for Gretchen."

He nodded, his mouth pressed into a grim line. "I'm sure she appreciates that."

"Did you know Otto very well?"

He looked surprised. "We all knew Otto, but I don't think anyone really knew him. He was a troubled man."

"Sounds like he got a new job before he died."

His eyes widened. "Otto?"

"He told Maybelline he was a courier."

His head jutted back, and he gave it a slight shake. "Otto didn't drive."

"On his bike."

He blinked and picked up his glass, his hand tremor free. "Well, good for him. I always told him he needed a purpose." He took a sip of water before lowering the glass. "We all do, don't you think?"

"Yeah."

"What's your purpose, Summer? What do you want deep down?"

I wasn't planning to bare my soul to this man, especially since I didn't trust him. I flashed a grin. "Isn't that the eternal question everyone asks themselves?"

He frowned. "Such a California answer. Maybe there's nothin' left of Sweet Briar in you."

I gasped at his bluntness.

His gaze held mine. "Are you involved with Luke?"

I bristled. "I don't see how that's any of your business."

"There's no doubt he's still very interested in you. It's all over Maybelline's Facebook page."

I shook my head. "I haven't seen her post anything new about it."

"Not Maybelline. The posts the townsfolk have been putting up."

Crap. I hadn't thought to look at those.

"Just be careful," he said.

"What's that mean?" I asked. Was he threatening me?

"Yeah," Luke said, sliding into the booth next to me. "What *does* that mean?"

His question felt ominous.

How much had he heard?

The mayor looked flustered. "Nothin'. We'd just hate for her to get injured again. She gave us all quite a scare." Then he slid out of his seat. "If Maybelline shows up with my food, could you tell her I had to go to the restroom?" With that, he disappeared down the hall.

I turned to look at Luke, trying not to gawk. He was dressed in snug-fitting jeans and a T-shirt that clung to every muscle of his upper arms, shoulders, and chest. Damned if the bad-boy look didn't suit him every bit as much as his uniform.

Rachel was openly gaping at him. *Poor girl.*

Fighting my own urge to throw myself at him, I said, "What are you doin'? Why are you here?"

"Getting dinner. Of course." He didn't seem phased by me in the least, but he cast a suspicious look at the mayor.

My temper was rising. "Why are you sitting next to me?"

He grinned, that sexy grin that had always made me melt, and just like Pavlov's stupid dogs, I was practically a puddle. "I can't believe you," I said in a whisper-shout, refocusing all that heat to my anger. "You accuse Teddy of murder, then you think you can just sit next to me and pretend like everything is okay?"

But it also reminded me that I still hadn't talked to Teddy. He'd texted earlier and said he was tied up and would call me later. I was still waiting.

Luke lowered his head next to mine. "I never accused him of murder, Summer. I said he was a person of interest, and I needed to talk to him. Did you tell him?"

"Why are you here?"

"I want to tag along with you and your film guy."

I snorted. "No. *No way.*"

"Come on. This way I can make sure you're safe and suggest any follow-up questions."

"Really?" I asked, turning in the seat to face him. "So you can take what I find and twist it into something you can use against Teddy?"

"Summer." He said my name in a husky voice that sent a shiver down to my toes. "Did you ever stop to think maybe I really do want to help Teddy?"

I wanted to believe that, but I wasn't sure I could take the chance. Even if I did, there was no way I could bring the chief of police with me to buy a Schedule II controlled substance. But I decided to change the subject in the interest of avoiding an argument.

"Do you have a house in town?"

He grinned. "You wantin' an invitation to see it?"

"Maybe," I answered honestly, to my chagrin. *Dammit.* I could *not* start something with Luke Montgomery. But I'd always found him so hard to resist. "So, do you?"

"Yeah. I like bein' closer to the police station."

"How long have you been chief?"

"A couple of years."

"You, Cale, Willy . . . none of you are much older than thirty. That seems . . ."

"Strange? It's no wonder. The job doesn't pay much. Hard to raise a family on our salary. All three of us have to find ways to supplement it."

That sobered me. While all the money I'd made hadn't defined me, I'd never been a fan of scraping by. "Especially if you insist on your wife stayin' home to raise your kids," I said with a hint of attitude.

He looked surprised, then laughed. "Jesus. I knew that conversation would come back to haunt me."

"You remember that conversation?"

"How could I not?" he asked, his gaze firmly on my mouth. "That was the night I first kissed you."

A wave of lust washed through me.

He paused. "Wait. You don't think I still believe that?"

"Why wouldn't I?"

"Because I was a seventeen-year-old idiot trying to impress you. Hell, you'd just confessed to how much you hated living in LA, but you said you had to do it to earn money for your momma. I was trying to prove that you wouldn't have to keep working out there if you were with me."

I gave him a dubious look. "You seriously expect me to believe that?"

"Okay . . ." He grinned. "So maybe I *did* believe it, but my momma stayed home, and my dad was damn proud of it. You know most families around here scrape by on *two* incomes. So saying my wife would never work was my way of trying to show I could take care of you."

I shook my head. I was treading on dangerous ground.

Maybelline appeared with a big bowl and a white bag. "What happened to Mayor Sterling?"

"He said he had to go to the restroom. He'll be right out." But I had to admit he'd been back there awhile. Luke looked like he was thinking the same thing.

"Huh." She set the bowl in front of me. "I made a batch of shrimp and grits tonight. I remembered how much you loved 'em, so I couldn't bring you a salad. But I'll bring the salad if you try 'em and don't want them." She turned to head back into the kitchen before I could stop her.

Luke laughed. "Maybelline."

"She didn't take your order."

"I suspect she'll be bringing me a bowl in a minute. She knows how much I love 'em too."

I picked up my spoon.

"So who are you planning on interviewing next?" he asked.

I snorted. "Do you really think I'm gonna tell you?"

My phone vibrated on the table next to me, and I picked it up when I saw Dixie was calling. I considered letting it go to voice mail since Luke was sitting next to me, but I knew she'd worry.

"Did you get it?" I asked.

"And a few extra copies . . . just in case."

"I'm scared to death to see which one you picked."

She laughed. "It's not like I had a ton of options. Are you still eatin'?"

"I'm almost done. Do you want me to get you something?"

"I picked up Popeyes in Eufala. How about I text you when I get there?"

"Perfect." That meant I'd have a chance to ditch Luke.

"Dixie?" he asked as I set the phone down. "What did she pick up?"

Rather than answer, I scooped up a spoonful of grits and a shrimp, took a bite, and moaned.

Luke lowered his mouth to my ear, whispering, "You used to moan like that for another reason." His warm breath on my neck sent a shiver through me.

I blushed. "We were underage minors, so I'm not sure you should be talkin' about that. Especially in public."

"I was talkin' about when you used to eat Momma's peach cobbler. Get your mind out of the gutter, Summer Baumgartner."

Just for that, I scooped up another spoonful and placed the tip of the spoon on my lip, licking the edge of it. "Mmm . . ." Just like I'd done for a yogurt commercial promoting good bowel health about two years ago. But Luke didn't seem to make the connection. Okay, so maybe I'd put a little bit more innuendo into this performance. Or a lot more.

His eyes darkened as his gaze fell to my mouth.

I slowly slid the spoon into my mouth and released a slightly louder moan. Luke's breath turned shallow.

Leaning closer, I pulled the spoon out. "I bet you want some now."

He shifted in his seat, but his gaze didn't stray from my mouth. "You have *no* idea."

I knew he wasn't talking about the grits. He started to lean toward me, and I was sure he was about to kiss me when Maybelline came back out with his plate. "Here you go, Luke. Gotta keep you big and strong." Then she winked at me as though to tell me, *Congrats on snagging your man again.*

"We're not together," I called after her, but she lifted her hand and waved it in dismissal.

"Is it such a terrible idea?" Luke asked as he picked up his spoon.

"Luke . . ." My heart skipped a beat, and my body flushed. Part of me was fully on board with this idea.

"I'm serious."

"We're not the same people. You just said so yourself."

"But from what I can see, we're not all that different either."

"Luke."

"I know you're goin' back to California, so I'm not lookin' for something long term here," he said, ignoring the food in front of him. "Aren't you curious to see if we still have chemistry? From where I'm sitting, we have enough to provide the Fourth of July fireworks show."

I couldn't believe what I was hearing. How many times had I fantasized about getting back together with Luke, moving back to Sweet Briar, and trying again? So to hear him say it like that—to cheapen it like all the other guys who'd wanted a fling with Summer Butler just to say they had—made me sick to my stomach.

I scooted closer to the wall in disgust. "Let me get this straight—you're looking for . . . what? A one-night stand?"

"Summer," he said defensively, "it's not like that. More like a fling. You know, until you leave."

"So a meaningless fling?" I said, devoid of emotion.

Luke was missing my reaction, instead forging on to convince me. "We'd avoid the mistakes we made before, and there'd be no hurt feelings when you leave again."

I grabbed my now-lukewarm bowl of grits and dumped it on his head.

He stared at me in shock while the grits dripped down his face. "I take it that's a no."

"That's a hell no. A no-fucking-way no." I gave him a shove. "Get the hell away from me."

"Summer."

Willy Hawkins walked into the restaurant, and surprise covered his face when he realized his boss was wearing a bowl on his head.

The whole reason I was back in Sweet Briar was because of my bad behavior in a restaurant, and here I was again. Maybe I needed to start eating in more often.

"Officer Hawkins," I called out to him, "can I file a complaint with you about someone in your department?"

I gave Luke another shove, but he still refused to budge. He took the bowl off his head and put it on the table, but grits clung to his hair and dripped down onto his shoulders. "Summer, wait. That came out all wrong."

"You're only saying that now because you didn't get the reaction you were hopin' for." I glanced up at Willy. "Officer Hawkins, this man is harassing me."

"*Summer.*"

Willy looked torn but said, "Chief, the lady wants you to move out of her booth."

"Summer," Luke pleaded.

Willy's expression looked so conflicted I almost felt sorry for involving him, but he gave Luke a stern reprimand. "*Chief.*"

Luke started to slide out of the seat, but he stopped and said, "Summer, I don't want you leavin' like this."

"You had your chance."

He stood next to the table. "Are you talkin' to anyone else tonight?"

I scooted across the seat, thankful he hadn't dripped grits onto the vinyl. "Where I go and what I do is none of your business."

"You're in danger."

"Then you should have thought of that before you insulted me with your proposition."

"Summer, I swear to you. I didn't mean it as an insult."

I leaned closer and looked up at him. "You said we're basically the same people, so let me ask you this: Would the Summer you knew before have settled for a fling?"

His face fell. "No."

"Well, there you go, you moron."

I glanced past him and saw Maybelline standing in the doorway to the kitchen, watching us in disbelief. "Maybelline, Chief Montgomery has graciously offered to pay for my dinner."

"You hardly ate any of it," she protested.

I gave Luke a hard glare. "I suddenly lost my appetite."

I half expected him to protest when I walked out. Instead, I heard him grunt and looked back to see Maybelline pull back her hand from slapping him on the back of the head.

CHAPTER THIRTY-TWO

Dixie and I met Bill in front of Tommy Kilpatrick's house a few minutes after seven. Tommy was under the impression we were coming over to bring his photo to him and film his reaction to it. He was eager for his fifteen minutes of fame.

Little did he know, he already had it.

When we knocked on the front door, Tommy yelled out, "Come on in!"

We found him in his worn La-Z-Boy recliner watching a baseball game on TV.

"Hey, Tommy," I said. Bill was already filming the scene from the doorway. "I brought you that photo for your sister. In fact"—I glanced back at Dixie, and her lips twitched with a grin as she gave me an encouraging nod—"I brought one for you too."

"No shit!" he said, reaching for it. "That's a damn good photo. I'm looking pretty buff."

I cringed but said, "You definitely are!"

In the photo we'd selected, I was flung over his shoulder with my butt looking as wide as an 18-wheeler due to the angle, but he was wearing a goofy grin. Whatever it took.

I still doubted I would get him to sell me anything on camera, but Bill said he thought he could work around it. Our ploy was to play up the photo first.

"I signed the one for your sister," I said, plopping down on the sofa next to him without an invitation, "but I waited to see if you wanted anything special on yours."

Dixie sat down beside me while Bill kept filming.

"Oh," Tommy said, looking up. "How about 'To Tommy: You're a muscleman rock star. Love, Summer'? Then you can add those *X*s and *O* things."

Dixie leaned into my ear. "He's starting to remind me of your stalker."

I shot her a grimace. *No kidding.* But I uncapped the black marker in my hand and signed the message he'd requested. When I handed it over to him, I said, "Hey, you got any beers, Tommy?"

He gave me a hesitant look. "Yeah. In the fridge."

"Mind if I get one?"

"Sure," he said, his eyes widening, surprised that we were staying. "Your friend can have one too."

I stood and glanced at Dixie, but she shook head. "Nothing for me."

I left the room and went into the kitchen, which was separated from the living room by a three-foot opening. I started opening cabinet doors, looking for any drugs that might be tucked away, prepared to use the excuse that I'd decided to get Dixie a glass of water. I found a shelf full of pill bottles, but most seemed benign enough—over-the-counter pain relievers, antacids, a box of Band-Aids, and a nearly empty pill bottle for Tylenol with codeine. No OxyContin and no Xanax. Either Christina had sent me on a wild-goose chase, or Tommy kept the good stuff somewhere else. I opened the refrigerator and called out, "Tommy, you want one?"

"Yeah, sure!" was his excited response.

I grabbed two cans of Pabst Blue Ribbon (God help my taste buds), filled a glass with water, then picked up all three drinks and headed back to the living room. I handed Dixie her water first—she gave me a weird look since she hadn't asked for it—then gave Tommy one of the beers.

Tommy pointed to Bill. "I'm glad you're getting this on tape because no one's gonna believe Summer Butler just got me a beer."

I plastered a cheesy grin on my face. "I bet."

We drank our beers while he watched the Braves play the Pirates in near silence. Talk about a fun date. Still, I couldn't just jump into the next part. I had to butter him up first, although this seemed like a questionable way of buttering *anyone* up.

"Say, Tommy," I finally said out of desperation, "what do y'all do for fun here nowadays?"

"Christina texted and said you were gonna drop by to get some Oxy."

I sat in stunned silence for a few seconds. I'd sat through fifteen minutes of utter boredom for no reason—all I'd had to do was ask.

"Do you have any?"

"Yeah. Those muscle relaxers Dr. Livingston gave me ain't enough to cut the pain, so I got some to help out. She said you might want some Xanax too. I've only got one of those."

And here was my shot.

"Really? I was hopin' you'd have more. This show has me on edge. My prescription's out, and I'm out of my other recreational pharmaceuticals. Do you think you could hook me up with your source, so I could get it directly from him?"

"I don't know," he said with a grimace. "I used to get it from Ed Reynolds, and I'm not sure if you've heard, but he's . . ." He made a slashing motion across his throat, complete with a weird sound effect.

"So what do you do now?" Dixie asked.

"I got a text from the new supplier this morning. He said to text him if I needed anything."

If I could ID Tommy's new supplier, then I might have a chance of cracking this whole thing wide-open.

"Do you think you could give me his number?" I asked. "Do you have his name?"

"No name. Just a number." He pulled out his phone, tinkered with it for a few seconds, and then rattled off a number. I entered it and read it back to him to make sure I'd gotten it right. I really didn't want to come back.

My phone rang, and I saw Luke's name on the screen. I hit "Ignore" and looked back up at him. "You know, Tommy, that was a call from our next appointment. Maybe we can come back some other time and hang out."

"Don't you want the pills?"

"It sounds like you need them more than I do. I'll try to get some from your new supplier."

"Okay," he said, his gaze firmly fixed on the TV.

I gave him a small wave. "Thanks for the beer. And the number."

"Yeah," he said with a grin.

Dixie, Bill, and I all walked out onto street, and once we were clear of the house, Dixie said, "I can't believe he just gave you that number. And on camera."

Bill shrugged. "People forget and say all kinds of things you don't think they'll say."

Dixie turned to me. "Do you think the number is a setup?"

I thought for a moment. "I doubt Tommy's capable of much deception. He seems like a typical stoner, don't you think? Kind of absentminded but chill."

"I guess."

I pulled out my phone even though my hands were shaking with nerves. "I think I'll send a request for ten Xanax and ask how much."

Bill and Dixie both stared at me.

"What? Too much? Too little?"

Bill shook his head. "This is getting dangerous, Summer."

"We knew that going in."

"Maybe we should reconsider."

"No." I shook my head. "I need this show to succeed, and if we can solve this case, the show's guaranteed to be a success with all the video we've got." Not to mention that I had to prove Teddy wasn't part of this—and I desperately needed to give Lauren a reason not to pull out Dixie's arrest.

"But, Summer . . ." Dixie's voice trailed off as I quickly typed out a text.

I need ten Xanax, and I hear you're the new source. Can we work out a deal?

299

I hit "Send" before I could change my mind. "Too late to protest now."

We spent the next full minute staring at my phone. All of us jumped when it started to ring,

"Oh, God," Dixie said, stumbling back into the trunk of Bill's car.

I looked at the screen and felt slightly relieved. "It's Teddy."

I answered, walking toward the front of the truck to put some distance between Dixie and me. "What's goin' on, Teddy?" I asked in a direct voice. "What are you mixed up in?"

"What are you talking about?"

"I'm not stupid, and I'm starting to piece things together."

"Again, what are you talking about?"

"Luke wants to see you. He says you're a person of interest in Ed Reynolds's murder."

"He told you that?"

"He says they found the murder weapon, and your fingerprints are all over it."

"They have my gun."

"What? How did they get it? Does it have anything to do with the break-in?"

He didn't answer.

"Teddy!"

"Do you think I killed Ed Reynolds?" he asked in a low voice.

"No! But I'm waiting to hear your explanation."

"So you think it's a possibility?"

"No. I think you're being framed, but I want to know what's goin' on." It was the only explanation that made sense to me, and having recently been framed myself, I knew how easy it could be to make someone look guilty.

He didn't respond.

"Teddy!"

"I can't tell you, Summy. Not yet."

"When?"

"A few days. And please, for the love of all that's holy, I need you to stay away from Luke."

"Why? I'm not gonna tell him anything. But maybe you should talk to him."

"No. God, no. I don't trust him, and he's using you to try to get to me. Please, make me feel better and promise you'll stay away from him."

"You're scaring me, Teddy. Who's framing you?"

"I'm not sure yet, but I'm soon to find out." I heard several voices behind him, but the sound was too muffled for me to make out any words. "I've got to go. I won't be home until late. Lock all the doors, and tell Dixie to make sure her gun is loaded."

Then he hung up.

I was surprised that Dixie was still standing by Bill's car, wearing a serious expression.

My phone buzzed with a text from the number I'd texted.

Call and leave a message.

My face must have betrayed how I felt.

"What?" Dixie asked. I showed her and Bill the message—and then called the number before they could stop me. Bill had pulled out his camera again and was filming before I got the computer-generated voice-mail message.

"Hi," I said, thankful my voice wasn't as shaky as my hand. "I'm calling about the transaction I texted about." It didn't seem smart to leave a voice mail asking for Xanax. "I've run out of my personal stash, so I'll pay extra if I can get it tonight." Then, unsure of what else to say, I added, "Thanks."

After I hung up, I glanced at Dixie and Bill. Dixie had an I-can't-believe-you-did-that expression. Bill looked grim as he lowered the camera.

"I don't think you should do this, Summer," Dixie said, wringing her hands. "He's bound to know who you are and that you're filming a show. The last thing these people will want is publicity. Three men are dead. I don't want you to be next."

Bill didn't say anything, but the fear in his eyes confirmed he felt the same way.

"Too late now," I said, more flippantly than I felt. "It's already done." But I wasn't feeling so brave either, so I added, "He might not even call or text me back." I felt like a traitor for hoping that was the case.

We stood around for ten more minutes waiting for a response, and when I hadn't heard anything, I finally called it. "We'll try to come up with another lead tomorrow. Maybe we can figure out where Otto used to hide out for days at a time. Gretchen mentioned he used to go fishing at a creek. I can call her and find out where he went."

"Good idea," Bill said with a big yawn. "I need to dump all the video anyway. See you girls tomorrow."

Dixie and I headed back to the farm, and we caught an earful from Meemaw for failing to inform her we'd be late.

"I just washed all the table linens for spring cleaning," Meemaw said with frown. "So you girls can iron them all." She pointed to an overflowing basket of white tablecloths and napkins.

Dixie gritted her teeth and gave me a look that suggested she really wanted to tell Meemaw no, but we both realized this was our punishment. Better to just get it over with while we watched TV.

We were halfway through the basket—me ironing and Dixie folding—when my phone rang.

I started and dropped my iron on the ironing board. *Crap.* I was completely unprepared to chat with a drug dealer/possible murderer, but my heart sped up when I saw Luke's name on the screen. After how he'd behaved, I absolutely should not be this excited to talk with him.

I answered. "Did you get all those grits washed out of your hair, Luke?"

The worried expression on Dixie's face turned to a grin. She was going to want *that* story later. Of course, it was probably all over that Facebook page.

"Turns out grits are a pretty good conditioner," he said with a smile in his voice. "I know it's late, but can I come out to the farm to talk to you?"

My traitorous heart skipped a beat. "I guess it depends on why you're plannin' on comin'."

"I don't like how we left things. I didn't express my real intentions well."

I knew I should tell him no, but my heart ached just from talking to him. Still, I couldn't forget that he was trying to pin a murder on my cousin. "I don't think that's a good idea."

"Please."

"Okay." God, I was so weak.

"I'll be there in about ten minutes." He hung up quickly, as if he knew I was already questioning my decision.

"I have ten minutes before Luke's gonna show up to talk to me, so we need to get as much ironing done as possible."

Dixie just gave me a knowing grin. About five minutes later, my phone dinged with a text. I expected it to be Luke, but it was from my mystery number.

Be at the Jackhammer in fifteen minutes. Come alone.

Oh, shit. This was happening.

"Dixie." I held out the phone to her. "How long will it take to get out there?"

"Fifteen minutes."

"Crap." I picked up my purse. "I've gotta go."

"Not without me," she protested.

"The text says come alone. I'm not risking you, or the chance to find out what's goin' on."

"What about Bill?"

"No. I'll use my phone." I headed out the front door toward the truck.

"But Luke's coming to the farm!"

Dammit. "Tell him I decided I didn't want to see him." I hopped in the truck, wasting no time driving out to the county road. Thankfully, I didn't pass Luke. He definitely would have followed. I glanced at the time on my phone—9:55 p.m.

I'd never been to the Jackhammer before, but I wasn't surprised to see the parking lot full of pickup trucks and older cars. I was really going to stick out here in my dress—Meemaw hadn't let me change before saddling Dixie and me with our endless chore. Maybe that was for the best. There'd be more witnesses paying attention to me if the mystery texter tried anything.

I pulled up my recording app and turned it on. I had no idea what was going to happen, but I wanted to have some sort of record of it. If things went south, I'd ditch my phone and hopefully someone would find it.

I walked in, surprised and pleased to see how many women were here. The banner declaring it **LADIES NIGHT $1 DRAFTS** explained it. I walked straight up to the bar, found an empty stool, and took my perch so I could scan the room. I had no idea whom I was looking for, but it didn't hurt to check. There was no one sinister-looking here, just a bunch of hardworking people letting off steam.

"What can I get you?" the bartender asked.

I flashed him a smile. "A draft beer, of course."

"Hey," he said, "I know you. You're Summer Butler. Can you do that thing?"

I resisted the urge to groan, and instead cocked my head. "What thing?"

"You know. The *Gotcha!* thing."

I felt someone walk up behind me, and a male voice said, "Come on, Austin. The lady's takin' a night off. Get her beer and let her enjoy it in peace."

The bartender frowned and walked off to get my drink while the man behind me slid in between me and the guy next to me. He looked to be close to my age—late twenties or early thirties. He was tall and filled out the T-shirt he was wearing quite nicely.

"Thanks," I said, my palms turning clammy. Was this my *date*? If so, he wasn't anything like I'd expected. The grin on his face was downright playful.

"You here alone?" he asked, looking around. He lowered his gaze to my chest before lifting it to my face. "No friends with you?"

Okay, so maybe he wasn't as nice as I'd initially thought.

"I'm here to enjoy my night off," I said, throwing his words back at him. "Just like everyone else."

His grin stretched a little wider. "Darlin', you are *nothin'* like everyone else here."

The bartender placed the glass in front me. "That'll be a dollar."

I reached into my purse to get my wallet, but my new friend was already putting money on the counter. "I'm paying for the lady, Austin, and get me another."

"I thought you were goin' home, Rebel."

Rebel continued grinning like an idiot. "I just changed my mind."

It was becoming increasingly clear he wasn't the man I'd arranged to meet, so I gave him a sassy look as I slapped several ones down on the counter. "Don't go changin' your plans on my account."

Austin the bartender laughed, but Rebel looked less amused.

I picked up my glass and moved to a stool farther down the bar, hoping Rebel would get the hint and leave me alone. I needed to be unencumbered so the mystery texter could approach me. I took a sip of the beer to ease my nerves. I was terrified the texter would follow through, and terrified he wouldn't. I checked my phone to see if he'd sent another message. Nothing.

"I can appreciate a girl who plays hard to get," Rebel said, sidling up to me again. "I can be persistent."

I looked up into his face. "Look, I want to be nice, but you're makin' that difficult. I've had a really bad day, and I'd like to sit here alone and enjoy my beer."

He leaned his elbow on the counter. "I can make it a whole lot better."

I sighed. "Let me make this perfectly clear," I said in a firm voice. "I'm not interested."

An ugly expression washed over his face. "You think you're too good for me, bitch?"

I'd been through this more times than I could count, and while it could be humiliating and sometimes downright scary, I knew the best way to deal with a guy like Rebel was to stay calm. And if that didn't work, the pepper spray in my purse would do the trick. The only thorn in this plan was my current bad attitude.

Looking him in the eye, I said with plenty of attitude, "It doesn't matter what I think. All you need to hear is the word no and then go on about your business."

"You're just a washed-up TV-show-actress-turned-slut. You should be lucky I'm even interested in you."

"If I'm so nasty, why did you approach me in the first place?" I shot back against my better judgment. "What does that say about *your* standards?"

It was pretty mild as far as insults went, so I wasn't expecting it when he lifted his hand to hit me, leaving me little time to grab my pepper spray. I'd just gotten ahold of it when I saw a hand seize Rebel's wrist from behind and jerk him backward.

Luke spun him around and shoved him toward the door. "Get the hell out of here, Rebel, before I beat your ass!"

"Your badge doesn't work here, Montgomery," Rebel sneered, his hands balled into fists.

"Which is why I'm free to beat the shit out of you. So either leave now or I'm calling the sheriff."

"Word has it you and the sheriff's department aren't the best of friends."

"My relationship with the sheriff's department has no bearing on the fact I stopped you from physically assaulting one of Rudy's clients."

"She's not worth my time. Since when were you interested in my leftovers, Montgomery? But hey, you're welcome to that dried-up piece of—"

Rebel didn't finish his sentence because Luke punched him in the jaw hard enough to send him reeling backward.

Rebel regained his footing and launched himself at Luke, landing punches on his face and in his gut.

Luke got in another swing before a big man stepped out from around the bar, carrying a baseball bat, although the size of him was impressive enough. "Knock it off." His voice boomed through the entire bar, and everyone fell silent.

The man turned to Rebel. "Were you about to hit a woman?"

That ugly look stole over Rebel's face again. "The bitch thinks she's too good for me."

Rudy shot a quick glance at me, then shifted his gaze back to Rebel. "That's because she is, you asshole. Now get the hell out before I put a knot on your head the size of a baseball."

Rebel spun around and stormed out the door as Rudy turned his attention to Luke. "And what's your excuse? You're the one I count on to keep a level head."

"He insulted Summer."

Rudy's mouth quirked into a grin as he got a better look at me. "Summer Butler?" He waved a hand. "Rebel's lucky he still has all his teeth. Go get cleaned up."

I gasped, still in shock, when Luke pushed past me. He had a bloody nose. "Luke." I reached for him, but he continued on toward the bathroom. Before he slipped out of sight, he twisted around and pointed at me, grunting, "Don't you dare leave!"

I almost told him off, but the sight of his bloody face stopped me.

"That boy's got it bad for you," Rudy said, standing next to me and watching Luke duck into the bathroom.

"Luke?"

Rudy laughed and shook his head. "I've known that boy since I coached him on the middle-school football team. I've only ever seen him get into three fights, and all of them were over you."

"Wait," I said, looking up at him. "This was the only time I ever saw him get into a fight."

He simply grinned.

"When? In high school?"

"One of 'em."

"When was the other?"

"About a year ago."

"Over what?"

"Someone besmirchin' your reputation."

"He told me he only wanted a fling," I said. Not the sort of thing I'd normally share with a stranger, but I was totally caught off guard. Luke had acted like he straight-up hated me a few days ago.

Rudy laughed. "That's a good one." Then he scanned the crowd. "Fight's over. Get back to drinkin.'"

Luke came back out a minute later. His face was cleaned up, but his left eye was swelling. Anger washed over his face as he stopped in front of me and glared down at me. "Do you cause trouble everywhere you go? Why did you leave Sweet Briar?"

"I had my reasons." Which surely had been blown to smithereens by now. My presence had led to a bar fight and the appearance of a police officer. There was no way the mystery texter was showing himself.

"Here I thought I was protecting you from Sebastian Jenkins, not Rebel Lancing."

"I could have handled it. I have pepper spray."

"Like that was gonna stop Rebel Lancing." He grabbed my elbow. "Let's go."

"What?" I took a step backward. "You punch a guy for me and suddenly you're my keeper? How about a *please*?"

He shook his head. "Dammit, Summer. Will you please leave with me now?"

"Fine, but I want you to know that I planned to leave anyway."

He opened his mouth to say something, then closed it. He followed me into the parking lot and walked me to my truck.

"Who were you planning to meet?" he asked.

"I told you—I just wanted a drink."

"That's bullshit, and we both know it. And why did you park your truck practically behind the building? You could have been attacked."

"Again . . . I have pepper spray."

He opened my truck door. "Pepper spray's no match for bullets, Summer."

"No one's gonna shoot me." I hoped so anyway. There was no denying I was on the trail of a murderer who'd killed at least two people with a gun.

His face softened, and he lifted his hand to my face. "You scared the shit out of me again."

"And here I thought you were in the bathroom cleaning up your bloody nose."

"I'm serious."

He ran his fingers down my cheek and the slope of my chin, spreading a trail of warmth, and the tension shifted between us, going from anger to desire.

"I'm fine. I'm safe," I whispered as I rested my palm on his chest and stared up into his troubled eyes. "I'm here."

I was here, and I wanted him. Why was I fighting this? Despite what he'd said, it was obvious neither of us wanted a one-night stand.

I stood on my tiptoes and kissed him—gentle at first, just my lips brushing his. He was so still I started to worry I'd read him wrong, but then it was like I'd roused a sleeping lion. Within seconds, he took over, pushing my back against the side of the truck as his mouth ravaged mine. I wrapped a hand behind his head, pulling him closer as our tongues tangled.

His hand slid down to my bottom, and he lifted me up and onto the truck seat. His mouth skimmed my neck and made a trail of kisses down to the scooped neckline of my dress while his hand slid under the fabric and traced the outside of my thigh.

A shiver ran through me as his hand inched higher.

I reached for his shirt and pulled it over his head, then gasped when I saw his bare chest. Luke had always looked impressive without a shirt, but he'd definitely filled out since we were teenagers. I leaned over and kissed him with twelve years' worth of restrained passion. His hand found the edge of my panties, and I groaned as my body came alive.

But just as quickly, he took two steps back. "Summer, we have to stop."

I gawked at him, trying to come to my senses.

"This might be the back of the parking lot, but we can't do this here. *I* can't do this here. I'm the damned chief of police. I can't get arrested for indecent exposure and lewd acts, and you *definitely* can't. Not to mention cameras."

He was right, of course, but that didn't quell my disappointment.

"Come home with me."

"Now?"

He laughed. "I'm not inviting you over for dinner, although on second thought, maybe I should feed you since I interrupted your meal earlier." Then he moved closer and kissed me again. "Come home with me."

"You're not playing fair. I have to be at work at eight," I murmured as his mouth skimmed down my neck, setting me on fire again.

"You don't have to spend the night."

I leaned back and shoved on his chest. "So this *is* just a booty call?" I asked, getting pissed all over again.

He snaked an arm around my back, keeping me close. "This is whatever you want it to be. You can spend the night. You can leave. This can last as long as you want, because you're in control. I just want what I can get."

He kissed me again, making me lose all reason.

The vibration of my cell phone caught my attention. I broke away to check the screen. "It's Dixie. I have to get it."

"I'm sorry," she said as soon as I answered. "He made me tell him."

So *that* was how Luke had found me. Stupid me—I hadn't even considered why he'd shown up. "I'm fine. I'll be home soon."

"Okay."

"You're goin' home," Luke said softly as I put my phone on the seat.

"I want this, Luke. I do. Maybe a little too much."

"What's that supposed to mean?"

"It means I'm scared to get hurt again. And I'm scared of hurting you. I'm not sure what I'm doin' when this show is done filmin'."

"So you want to forget this happened?"

"No, I just want to slow it down. We are different people from who we were before—we've both done some growin' up. I want to get to know the Luke you've grown into." I gave him an apologetic smile. "Are you mad? I kind of started all of this by kissin' you."

A warm smile spread across his face. "Mad? Why would I be mad, Summer? You're giving us a shot. You set the rules, I'll follow your lead."

"Thanks."

He kissed me again, then pushed my legs into the truck. "I'm gonna follow you home."

Part of me was glad. What if my mystery texter had followed me home instead?

CHAPTER THIRTY-THREE

The supplier didn't send another message, and I wasn't sure whether to write back. What would I say? Sorry a guy hit on me and then there was a bar fight? It seemed better to say nothing.

But I'd put plenty of thought into Otto's special place, and I was pretty sure I was onto something. Whenever I was overwhelmed and sad, I went home to the farm. Sure, not for real—at least not over the last decade—but in my head. I would relive the happier times I'd spent with Mccmaw and Pawpaw, Teddy and Dixie, and Luke. It made sense that Otto would do the same, which meant the place *he* had likely gone to was the land he'd owned with his family.

On the way to our location the next morning, I called Gretchen to see if she could give me directions. "Do you happen to know who's living there now?" I asked.

"No one," she said in a sad voice. "Otto still owned it."

"Do you mind if we check it out?"

"No. You do what you need to do to find out what happened. I'll text you the directions."

This morning, we interviewed our new client at her house instead of our office, presumably to save time. Lauren sent us into this one cold, so I was more than a little worried about what she had in store for us.

"What would you like us to help with, Mrs. Stoneybrook?" I asked the middle-aged woman who was wearing leopard-print leggings and a sparkly gold tank top.

"I want you to prove that my neighbor is peeing on my hydrangea plants."

"You mean his dog?"

"No," she said, getting grumpy. "I mean *Ned*, the old fart next door."

I glanced at Dixie, then asked, "What makes you think *anyone* is peeing on your hydrangeas?"

"Because my hydrangeas are pink!"

I shook my head in confusion. "I don't follow."

"Hydrangea colors are determined by pH, and I know that rat bastard takes medication that raises his pH. A high pH produces pink flowers. If it were his dog, the flowers would probably be a bluish purple. Plus, Ned hates me, and he wants me to lose the upcoming garden contest. What better way? The pink flowers clash with my pink begonias."

We filmed the interview several times, then walked around her yard, scoped out the neighbor's yard, and came up with a plan to set up a nanny cam on her flower bed.

It was nearly noon when we finished up, and Lauren was happier than I'd ever seen her.

"Congrats, Summer!" she said. "You've made the gossip sites again. I can only presume your mystery man is the chief of police." She tapped her chin. "That might actually come in handy."

Oh, God. What was she talking about?

She looked around at the crew standing on Mrs. Stoneybrook's front yard. "Okay, everyone. Time for lunch. You have off until four. The Boll Weevil parade starts at five. We'll need to get set up downtown beforehand, not to mention Tony needs to stick with Summer to get footage of her preparing to get on that float."

I maneuvered closer to Bill while Lauren finished up her orders.

"I know where we're going," I whispered. "I found out the location of Otto's family's fire. We have permission to look around. I bet it's where Otto used to disappear to for days, and I suspect if he was gonna hide something, that would be the place."

Bill's face lit up. "Who said you weren't good at this? That's great news!"

"Who said I'm not good at it?"

He suddenly looked unsure as he glanced over at the crew, then back to me. "Uh . . . no one."

The crew could say whatever they liked. I was about to prove them all wrong.

As soon as we got into the truck, I made Dixie look up the gossip sites.

"Oh!" she gasped in excitement.

"What?" I asked. "What did you find?"

"Well, I had no idea Luke was so buff."

I cringed.

"And, damn, girl. You need to start wearing shorter dresses or maybe shorts. Your legs are sex-y."

I pulled up to a stop sign and grabbed the phone out of her hand. There were several photos of Luke and me from last night. One was of the two of us kissing next to my open truck door, both of us fully clothed. Then next one was Luke standing shirtless next to the truck, my bare leg hooked around his hip. Even though he was wearing jeans, it looked like we were having sex in the parking lot.

"Oh. No. Luke's gonna be furious."

"Why? He looks *hot*."

"He's the chief of police, Dixie. He can't do things like that."

"Have sex?"

"In public!"

"You never told me you had sex with Luke," she said in a pout.

"We didn't. It just looks that way."

I handed her the phone and grabbed my own to call Luke. When he didn't answer his cell, I called the station.

"Hey, Amber, it's Summer. Is Luke in his office?"

"He's in a meeting with the mayor and the city council."

Oh, God. My heart sank to my toes. "Can you tell him I called?"

"Sure thing."

Fifteen minutes later, I turned into the Olson family farm. The fields were overgrown and had long since been abandoned. I was surprised Otto hadn't rented out the land or at least had neighboring farmers cut the fields for hay, but he clearly hadn't cared about such practicalities. Why would he?

I pulled to a stop in front of a pile of charred wood and brick, which had obviously been a house at one time. Dixie had been chatty until we turned onto the property, but she'd clammed up. I reached over and grabbed her hand. "You okay?"

She nodded.

She was so not okay.

I almost hadn't brought her, but she'd insisted, and I sure wasn't gonna tell her no. "Why don't you wait in the truck while I look around the house?"

"Not a chance," she said as she opened the door and hopped out.

We started walking along the perimeter of the house while Bill pulled up in his car. He got out his camera and started filming, walking away from us.

Dixie looked shaken, so I grabbed her hand and linked our fingers, squeezing tight while she wiped away a tear.

"It was awful, Summer."

"What was?" I asked quietly.

"That night. The fire." I knew she wasn't talking about Otto's.

"I wish I'd been here for you, Dixie. I'm so, so sorry I wasn't."

"Even if you'd come back, you wouldn't have been here that night. The night they died."

We continued walking. Dixie seemed like she wanted to talk about it, but it was as if the words had left her.

"I know it happened at night," I prompted her.

She nodded.

"Was it late? Early?"

"Later. Around ten."

"Where were you when it happened?"

She released a bitter laugh. "In the overseer's house with Trent Dunbar. We were high. Trent's older brother had a hookup, so Trent brought some over to party with me.

"You could see the fire from there?"

"I'd gone in the barn earlier to clean the horse stalls. Momma came and checked on my work and told me that I'd done a bad job and I couldn't leave the barn until it was done right. I was pissed because I had plans with Trent. So I snuck out the back and met him at the house. We were out there for at least an hour and a half before I heard the sirens. I saw the flames. When we got up there, the whole thing was engulfed, and Meemaw and Teddy were crying and screaming that Momma and Daddy and Pawpaw were inside." She glanced over at me. "Teddy told me Momma said she'd found my jacket. They thought I was inside. They went back in to save me."

I let go of her hand and wrapped my arms around her. "Oh, Dixie."

"I killed them."

"No, you didn't. It was an accident."

"You know that's not true. The fire was arson, Summer."

"You were down at the overseer's house. A quarter mile away."

"Trent and I had taken Xanax, then drank. I couldn't remember at least forty-five minutes of that night. And when I *did* become aware of where I was, I was in a field between the barn and the overseer's house."

My head got fuzzy. "That doesn't mean anything, Dixie."

"I was furious with Momma. I was talkin' about how unfair it was for her to make me clean out the barn."

"That doesn't prove anything, Dixie."

"My clothes reeked of gasoline."

I couldn't catch my breath.

"Teddy tried to cover it up, but Luke smelled it as soon as he got close to me." She held my gaze. "Teddy blames Luke for arrestin' me, but he had no choice, and I didn't fight him on it. He tried to make it as easy for me as possible. He even got me an attorney."

I started to cry. "No one told me. Oh, Dixie. I should have been here for you." The story I'd heard was boiled down and vague—most of this was new to me.

"What could you have done?"

"I could have been here for you."

"I didn't want anyone. I refused to talk to Teddy, and like I told you the other day, Meemaw didn't want to have anything to do with me after I pled guilty. I just wanted to die."

"Dixie." My voice broke.

"Luke talked to the prosecuting attorney and made sure they charged me as a juvenile. I got out in two years, but I was in bad shape. But Luke was there when I got out. He helped me through things."

"What do you mean, helped you through things?"

"When something got too bad to handle, he made me promise to call him. He would listen and offer advice."

"Why didn't you tell Teddy?"

"He was freaked out when I came home. Worried I'd start using drugs again. And I understand, but Luke was easier to talk to. You know?"

"Yeah." I remembered all the hours we'd logged on the phone while he was waiting for me to come home.

Bill waved at us. "I've got enough B-roll. You ready to check out the barns?"

I glanced over at Dixie, but she was already breaking away from me and heading toward Bill.

We went into the smaller barn first, Bill filming our every move. The barn doors faced south, letting in plenty of light in addition to the light streaming in from the holes in the wooden walls. "First, we're going to see if we can find anything to suggest that Otto actually came out here," I said. "Because so far, it's all a guess."

Dixie and I walked around, kicking dirt and leftover straw that stunk to high heaven. Ten minutes passed without us finding anything.

"Let's check the other one," I said, grateful for an extended lunch break.

Dixie nodded her agreement.

This barn was in better shape than the smaller one, and the doors faced east. We opened them wide, and I turned on the flashlight on my phone to give us a better view. We only searched a few minutes before we found something.

"I found a blanket," Dixie said.

I hurried over, Bill following us with the camera. We squatted down next to a pile of hay to look at it. "It's not that dirty," Dixie said. "It could have been Otto's. Let's keep looking."

We sifted through the hay until I found a small wooden box. I pulled it out and looked it over. It was nothing fancy, like something you'd likely find in a thrift store. I opened the lid and gasped. "I think I found what they were lookin' for."

Dixie leaned over to get a look. "Holy mother of contraband."

Bill leaned over to film the plastic bag stuffed full of pills.

"We have to call Luke," Dixie said.

"Luke's in a meeting with the mayor and the city council members."

Her mouth dropped open. "Over those photos?"

My stomach turned cartwheels with nerves. "I don't know," I said. I couldn't stand the thought of him losing his job because of me. "I told Amber to have him call me the moment he's free, and he hasn't called yet." I grabbed my phone and pulled up Cale's number. It seemed like the murders were mostly his cases, so he was probably the right person for us to bring in anyway.

"Hey, Cale," I said when he answered, "Dixie and I stumbled upon something I think you'll be interested in."

"I'm all ears," he said.

"We're out at Otto Olson's old farm, and we found a bag of pills."

He was silent for a second, then he laughed. "Damn, we should put you two on the force."

I got more satisfaction out of the compliment than I probably should have. "I opened the box they were in, but other than that, we haven't touched it, so you should be good for prints."

"See? You two are naturals. I take it you're there right now?"

"And our cameraman, Bill."

"Your cameraman?"

"He's filming all of this so we can expose the murderer on the show."

He paused. "I thought the show was a bunch of fake cases."

"That's what the producer thinks. We're doin' this on our own."

"Pretty smart," he said. "Okay, you all hang tight out there. I'll be there shortly. Don't leave."

"Okay," I said. "We don't have to be back until four to get ready for the parade."

Dixie and Bill had gotten the gist of the conversation.

"So Otto stole the drugs and hid them?" Dixie asked.

"And the person he stole them from kidnapped him to tell them where they were," I finished. "Or so I would guess."

Bill cringed. "I hate to be like Lauren, but could you two repeat that on camera?"

"Sure," I said. "That's a great idea."

We decided to sit by the box with the bag. Dixie said her line and I repeated mine.

"But who could it be? Luke said Otto and Ryker died within hours of each other, so maybe the same person killed them both."

"But they died in two totally different ways," Dixie said.

"I think it's safe to assume that Ryker and Ed were partners." I looked at Dixie for confirmation, and she nodded. "What if Ryker tried to get the information out of Otto—maybe by making him drink Jim Beam—and then he died from alcohol poisoning. Ed could have gotten pissed and killed Ryker."

Dixie nodded. "Yeah."

"But who killed Ed? Seems like it could only be the supplier who contacted Tommy." And where did that leave Teddy in this situation? Because I was sure he was involved.

"The one you were supposed to meet last night," Dixie said.

"Maybe I should text and apologize," I said. "We still need to figure out who he is."

"I think we should tell Cale," Dixie said. "It's his case. We've done a lot of the legwork for him. He can take it over from here."

I wasn't sure that would be good enough for the show, but I wasn't selfish and stupid enough not to tell him. "Okay. Good idea."

I heard a car engine outside, getting closer. "Cale must be here already. I'm gonna go out and meet him."

I walked to the barn door and glanced down the long driveway. The vehicle at the end of it looked familiar, but not how I'd hoped.

"Oh, crap. It's a white van."

"Like your stalker was driving on Sunday?" Dixie asked in disbelief.

"*Exactly* like the van from Sunday."

Dixie pulled out her phone. "How did this guy find you? I'm calling Cale to see how close he is." She shoved me out the door and toward the truck. "We need to go."

"Cale said not to leave the pills," I protested.

"Leave them. This guy's more interested in getting you than a bunch of pills."

We hadn't quite made it to the truck when the van sped past it and pulled to a halt, blocking our way out.

"Summer . . . ," Dixie warned.

"Stay back and call 911."

Sebastian got out, and he looked pissed. "I'm very disappointed in you, Summer."

"I'm sorry to hear that, Sebastian."

"You know my name now," he said with a sneer. "I guess you had to learn it to file your restraining order."

"That wasn't my doin'," I said. "That was the police chief's."

"I know you're screwing him."

"*What?*"

"I thought you were a good girl, Summer. Turns out you're just a slut."

319

I saw Dixie coming toward me. Why hadn't she stayed in the barn?

But Sebastian didn't seem to notice. "I saw you at that bar last night. Screwing him in the front seat of your truck."

"We didn't have sex!" Not that it was any of his business.

"It sure looked like it to me," Sebastian said. "He didn't have his shirt on. I guess you go for guys with lots of muscles like that."

"Duh!" Dixie exclaimed. "Who doesn't?"

"Not helping, Dixie," I muttered.

She made a face. "Oh. Yeah, I guess not."

"What were you doing at the bar, Sebastian?" I asked.

"Trying to see you."

"Did you take photos?" I asked. "Did you sell them to those websites?"

"No!" he said in disgust. "I don't want your nasty pictures out there for the world to see." His mouth pressed together. "He doesn't love you. He would never disgrace you like that if he did."

"Why are you here now?" I asked. "You're supposed to be a hundred feet away from me."

He started to pace. "That's in town, Summer. But we're out of town now, so that police chief can't stop us."

"He's sure gonna be surprised," Dixie muttered under her breath.

I didn't want to give him a head's-up. I needed to keep him talking. "Luke can't stop us from what?"

He stopped and his face turned red. "Being together! Keep up!"

I held up my hands. "I'm sorry if I'm actin' slow. I had a head injury a few days ago. If you were in town, you probably knew."

He took a step closer, and his eyes pleaded with me. "I was there."

"Where?"

Some of his anger faded. "In your hospital room. While you were sleeping. You were so beautiful. I left you a rose."

"That was from you?" *Where is Cale?*

Dixie grabbed my arm and whispered, "I'm officially creeped out, Summer."

I was a few steps ahead of her. How ironic that I had a stalker now, years after I stopped being actually famous.

"Okay, Sebastian," I said. "You're here. I'm here. What do you want?"

My question seemed to stump him.

"This is between you and me, right?"

"Yeah."

"I want to send Dixie away. So it will be just the two of us."

"Summer!" Dixie shouted. "No!"

"Dixie. Trust me." I turned to Sebastian. "That's a good idea, don't you think? Then we can be alone."

"I want the guy with the camera gone too."

I turned around and realized that Bill was still filming us from the open barn door.

"Bill," I said, "come on out. Why don't you both head toward the truck?"

"Summer," Bill called out as he walked toward me, "I don't think we should leave you."

I heard a car engine approaching, and apparently Sebastian did too. "You bitch!"

So much for being my number-one fan.

Dixie and Bill took off running for the truck.

Sebastian lunged at me and tried to make a grab for my arm, but I jerked out of his reach and started running toward the truck too. I didn't stop until I reached Dixie and Bill. When I turned around to see if Sebastian was still following, I didn't see him anywhere.

A police car pulled up behind us, and Cale climbed out. "Summer. What's goin' on?"

"My stalker showed up," I said, trying to catch my breath.

"He ran into the barn," Dixie said.

Cale's eyes widened, and he was instantly on full alert. "Does he have a weapon?"

"No," I said. "I didn't see one, but he's acting agitated and then some."

"You guys stay back here." Cale made his way toward the barn, casting a couple of glances back at us as he approached. "Sebastian, come on out so we can discuss this."

Sebastian didn't answer.

"Cale," I called out to him, "the pills are in there."

He gave a sharp nod and pulled out his gun.

Dixie let out a squeak, and she, Bill, and I squatted down next to the truck.

"Sebastian, just come on out. Hidin' in the barn's not gonna solve anything."

"I'm outside of the city limits," Sebastian called out from inside the barn. "I didn't do anything wrong. I just wanted to see her."

"Summer?"

"Yeah. If she just spent some time with me, she'd see we're perfect for each other. I don't care that she slept with the police chief."

"Whoa, whoa, whoa," Cale said. "One thing at time. If you want to see her, then you're gonna have to come out."

"No."

Cale continued trying to coax Sebastian out of the barn, but my stalker had quit talking. After a couple of minutes, Cale told Sebastian he was coming in.

I held my breath when Cale disappeared inside the darkness, but he returned alone after a minute or so. "He's gone," he said, shaking his head. "He slipped out a back door. And I think he took the pills with him."

"What?" Dixie asked.

I wrapped my arms across my chest. It had felt like we were so close to ending this thing . . . and now we were further away than ever. "We should have taken the pills, but you said not to move them, and he showed up so fast . . ."

Cale moved toward us. "Summer, you didn't do anything wrong. It's okay."

"What are you gonna do?" I asked. "Are you gonna go after him?"

"We don't have the manpower, and even though he took off with the pills, you said he didn't have a weapon. We don't consider him dangerous to the town." He paused. "However, he's escalating with you. You should cancel your appearance in the parade."

Even though I wasn't excited about riding on a float down Main Street, I'd made a commitment. "No. I promised I'd do it. People are counting on me."

"It's not worth risking your life so you can wave to the crowd, Summer. I'm sure that Luke will pitch a fit." He gave me a grim smile. "But that's between you and him. I'm more interested in how you three knew to come out here."

I shrugged. "I just thought about where Otto used to be happy. It made sense he'd come here whenever he was feeling down. But we think we might have figured out what happened."

Surprise washed over his face. "Oh? What?"

I told him our theory about the deaths. "If Ed killed the other two, the real question is who killed Ed."

"And why," Cale said.

"We figured that part out too." I gave Dixie an apologetic grimace. "I have the phone number of the new supplier."

Cale did a double take. "Say what? How'd you get that?"

"I'd rather not say, but I was supposed to meet him last night out at the Jackhammer; however, things got a little out of hand, and I'm pretty sure it scared him off."

"What does Luke think about all of this?"

"We haven't told him," I said. "We just reasoned most of it out while we were waiting for you."

"But he knew why you were at the bar last night, right?"

"No. He followed me there to protect me from Sebastian. I never told him about the number, and then we had a fight . . ."

He gave me a wry smile. "Some fight."

I grimaced. So he'd seen the photos too.

Cale's smile spread. "Isn't this the part in your show when you'd say *Gotcha!*?"

"I'm not sayin' it, Cale."

"Aw . . . come on."

I put a hand on my hip and gave him stern glare. "Not a chance in hell."

Still grinning, Cale turned to Bill. "You've been filming it all?"

"Yeah. I think we've nearly got enough to make this effective," he said.

"And who else knows about it? You three?"

I wasn't sure Luke wanted Cale to know about his involvement, so I kept it to myself. "Yeah."

"And where's the video?" Cale asked. "Any chance your producer can stumble upon it?"

"No," Bill said. "It's in my motel room."

Cale nodded his head, looking grim. "Okay. How about we all go into the barn, and you can show me where the drugs were."

Bill thumbed toward his car. "I'm gonna put my camera away and go get some of the B-roll I was supposed to get while we were investigating."

"Actually . . . Bill, is it?"

"Yeah."

"I think it would be helpful if you came too."

"All three of us?" I asked. "Dixie and I were the ones to find it."

Cale started to say something, but my phone vibrated with a call. I dug it out of my pocket and answered when I saw Luke's name.

"Luke," I said when I answered, "I heard about your meeting. They didn't fire you, did they?"

"Why would they fire me?"

"The photos."

"What photos?"

Oh, crap. "Then what was your meeting about?"

"The damn Boll Weevil Parade. What photos?"

"Don't freak out, but someone got photos of us last night, and they're plastered on some gossip sites. But they don't have your name. They just call you my mystery man."

"Your mystery man," Luke said in a husky voice. "I like the sound of that."

"You're not pissed?"

"If you're asking if I'm thrilled, the answer is no. But if you're asking if I'm upset over it, that answer is no too. It's part of datin' you. It's a small price to pay."

"Datin'?" I asked in surprise.

"I plan to woo you, Summer Baumgartner, which I hope leads to datin', and we'll see where that leads to."

My face flushed, and Cale watched me with open annoyance. "I better go. Cale's gettin' ticked off. I'm supposed to bring him into Otto's barn to show him where we found the drugs."

"*What?*"

"I have a lot to tell you."

Cale motioned toward me. "Let me tell him."

I handed Cale my phone and listened to him tell Luke that my stalker had shown up and escaped. Then he told him about the missing drugs and our theory about who had killed whom, but noticeably absent was the fact I'd had an appointment with the new supplier last night.

Cale handed me back the phone, covering the mouthpiece. "Don't tell him about the meeting last night. It's only gonna worry him. Let's tell him after the parade."

While I didn't want to keep any secrets from Luke in this situation, I had to agree that might be a good idea. I took the phone back. "Hey."

"As soon as you finish there, you come straight to the station until the parade."

"You plan to babysit me?" I asked in dismay.

"Just until we catch this guy. I didn't just get you back in my life to lose you."

CHAPTER THIRTY-FOUR

A few hours later, I stared in astonishment at the float I was supposed to ride on. It was covered with fake cotton plants that looked like they were planted in a field. Giant bugs were plastered all over the side of the float and on some of the fake plants.

"Is it too late to change my mind?"

Luke laughed, and I shot him a warning look.

Mayor Sterling walked by looking flustered and shouting orders to everyone. He seemed irritated that I wasn't on the float yet.

"Did I ever mention I was in Macy's Thanksgiving Day Parade?" I asked Luke as I continued to stare down the bugmobile. It could have doubled as a float representing pest control. "Twice."

Luke grabbed my hand, and a grin quivered on his lips. "I believe you may have mentioned it in passing."

How the mighty had fallen.

There was a set of steps next to the trailer, and I started to climb up while Luke still claimed my hand.

"There's nothing precarious about climbing up these steps," I said, leveling a look at him.

He flashed a mischievous grin. "Maybe I'm just lookin' for an excuse to hold your hand."

"Don't you have a job to do?"

"It just so happens I'm doin' it."

I shot him an exasperated look. He'd been hovering over me all afternoon. "I'm one citizen in this town, Chief Montgomery. Surely you should be protecting the rest of them too."

"Citizen?" he asked. "You mean temporary?"

I gave him a sassy smile. "I'm thinking about stickin' around." Then I hastily added, "And before you get a big head about it, it's because I miss my cousins." And because I was losing my house in California and had nowhere else to go, but I wasn't going to tell him that part. But the more time I spent here, the more it felt like home, and something in me was desperate for home.

The smile that spread across his face filled me with happiness. "But maybe I can see you sometimes when you're not hangin' out with Teddy and Dixie?"

I smirked. "We might be able to work something out."

Bill approached with his camera, looking unscathed by our afternoon.

"I thought Tony was in charge of filming me," I called down to him.

He shrugged. "We switched. Lauren made a last-minute change." Then he grinned. "I think Tony's afraid your stalker's going to try something, and he'll get caught in the middle of it."

Based on Luke's behavior all afternoon, it was a legitimate concern.

Luke studied Bill for a moment before he cast a glance out at the growing crowd half a block down the street. "Now that your cameraman is here, I'll get goin'. If you see anything that concerns you, just motion to me. I'll be watching you and the crowd."

"Okay," I said, suddenly feeling like something was off. But I had no idea what, and no reason to base it on other than a niggling feeling at the base of my spine. I'd look like a baby if I called him back for some nothing reason like that.

Less than a minute after Luke walked away, Mayor Sterling walked over from another float. He looked less frantic than before, but still agitated. "Now, remember to wave to the crowd," he said. "And to smile."

I almost reminded him about all the pageants and parades I'd been in, but he'd already moved on.

Cale walked over with an anxious look on his face. "How're you doin?" he asked, then cast a glance to Bill. "I'm surprised Luke's not hovering."

"He said he had to do some crowd control. There might be a small chance he deputized Bill."

Both men laughed, and Bill said, "Which would fulfill a childhood fantasy . . . and maybe a few X-rated adult ones too."

I shook my head with a grin as I scanned the crowd. "TMI, Bill." But I was getting nervous. "Where's Dixie? I haven't seen her since Luke made me come to the police station for the afternoon. She told me she was headed out to the farm to see Teddy."

"She's here," Cale said. "But she's closer to the end of the route."

"Really?" I asked. "For some reason, I thought she'd want to be part of all of this." I motioned to the float.

"I think Luke wanted her at the end," Cale said. Then he looked up into my eyes. "You spent all afternoon with Luke. Did you mention having that contact number?"

I blinked in surprise. I still wasn't sure why Cale was wanting to keep it so secret. "No. But I plan to tell him soon after the parade."

Cale nodded. "That's fine. As long as Mayor Sterling gets his parade, you can tell Luke anything you want."

He moved to the next float, and I had to admit that I was surprised Cale was so invested in the success of the parade. It didn't seem like something that would overly concern him.

"I'm worried about Dixie," I said to Bill. "It seems like she should be here." I pulled my phone out of my pocket. "I'm gonna text her and see where she is." Why hadn't I thought of that sooner?

Where are you? Haven't seen you all afternoon, and I'm worried.

The marching band started playing in the front, making it nearly impossible to hear, and I could see movement at the beginning of our small procession.

"Summer!" shouted Mayor's Sterling's assistant, practically skipping toward the float. I'd met Annie Lee about a half hour earlier, and I had a hard time trusting someone that perky and energetic. "We nearly forgot your partner."

"My partner?" Were they having Dixie ride on the float with me?

If only. Someone in a giant bug costume strutted out of the pharmacy next door.

I cringed. "Why is that giant tick heading over here?"

"It's not a giant tick," the mayor's assistant said, way too jolly for the situation. "It's a boll weevil. You have no idea how hard it is to find one."

"I can see why."

The first float in the parade—a wagon pulled by a bicycle—started down the street.

"We couldn't find the guy who was supposed to play the boll weevil, but we found a replacement, and we're all set!"

"A replacement?" I asked.

Annie Lee helped the seven-foot bug up onto the float. "Mayor Sterling told you the route, correct?"

"No, he didn't tell me anything."

"What is goin' on with him?" she asked. "He's been out of sorts today. All this murder and mayhem is throwing him off."

No wonder. No doubt it was bad for tourism.

"Okay," she said, shouting to be heard. "The parade's going two blocks down Main Street, then turning right at the corner on Buttercup, then going two short blocks, then turning left on Henry. Right in front of the police station. Your job is to stand there and wave to everyone. Easy enough?" she asked.

I nodded. My stomach tightened into a ball. That sensation washed over me again—something was off in a big way, but I couldn't put my finger on what or why. I checked my phone again to see if I'd heard from Dixie. Nothing.

"Okay," Annie Lee said. "Showtime! I've got to hurry to my spot at the microphone."

The marching band had begun to move, so I took my place on the spot marked with a giant X.

Up ahead, I heard the mayor's assistant's perky voice on a microphone that was broadcasting through several speakers set up around downtown. "And welcome to the third annual Sweet Briar Boll Weevil Parade! We're here to celebrate the anticipation of healthy and fruitful cotton plants! First up, we have Edgar Snitt pulling a small float sponsored by his accounting firm. If you look closely, you can see Barbie and Ken figures inside tending to a roaring fire. It's meant to represent farmers burning their crops back in 1914."

I peered around the float in front of us, and sure enough, there was a tiny fire in the back that had begun to consume the white butcher's paper decorating the sides of the wagon.

"Oh, dear," the assistant said, then tsked. "Edgar's town's on fire. Wrong parade, Edgar! That's in July, when we celebrate half the town burning down!"

The crowd clapped and cheered.

"Next up," Annie Lee said, "we have the cheerleaders from Sweet Briar High School representing the Sweet Briar Suffragettes. Since there were only two suffragettes in Sweet Briar and we have six cheerleaders, the other four have taken up the roles of the other women who drove them out of town."

What?

She announced several more equally bad floats and marchers, and then our float began to move. As it did, the giant boll weevil started walking toward me.

"And next we have the very loud Sweet Briar High School marching band," Annie Lee announced, "playing a song written by our very own Sweet Briar High School band director, Woody Briar the seventh. Titled 'Our Farm Is Now Bankrupt from Boll Weevils So I Might as Well Enlist to Fight the Germans in the Great World War before I Die from the Spanish Influenza' . . . Oh, my," she said as an aside, "that's a long title. In any case, it was inspired by the fate of his uncle who was a descendant of one of our town's founding fathers, Woody Briar the second."

I hadn't heard from Teddy since morning, and now that I hadn't heard from Dixie too, I was well and truly worried. I still hadn't figured out his part in all of this. Part of me was scared that he might be the new supplier, but I just couldn't believe it. Teddy hated drugs and what they had done to Dixie.

I scanned the crowd, looking for the members of the Sweet Briar police force. I could see Luke farther down the street, standing on the corner where we would turn, and Willy was standing at the edge of the crowd about halfway down the street, but I didn't see Cale, and I definitely didn't see Dixie.

The thirty-five-member band was attempting to form the shape of a cotton plant while they marched down the street playing an off-key song that sounded like ragtime jazz.

Bill was walking beside the float, filming everything—me, Annie Lee's monologue, the other floats. I wondered if he felt something was off too, but he seemed fine. Grinning, even. I could only imagine this would be gold for the reality show . . . Speaking of which, I saw Lauren and Karen half a block up standing with the rest of the crew.

Where was Dixie?

The float jerked as it picked up a little speed, and the racket of the band got louder again, probably to represent something terrible happening in the life of the band director's uncle. The suffragettes began to do the jitterbug while other cheerleaders chased after them down the street.

I started to wave to the crowd as we drove down Main Street, and the boll weevil inched closer still, stumbling on the cotton plants.

"I think you're supposed to be waving," I said.

But the boll weevil seemed more interested in reaching me.

I sidestepped a cotton plant and shifted toward the back of the float, still waving to the crowed.

The boll weevil kept advancing.

I sidestepped to the other side, not breaking form.

"And here's the float for our guest of honor, Summer Butler, former teen star of *Gotcha!*, now a washed-up and bitter actress starring in a reality TV show filmed in our own Sweet Briar!"

I was proud of not reacting to being called washed up and bitter.

"Summer is portraying her ancestor Minny Baumgartner in her valiant yet hugely unsuccessful attempt to save her farm from boll weevils by running around trying to scare them away with her pockmarked face, the result of a smallpox epidemic that swept through the town five years earlier."

Say what?

"But instead of running away, the boll weevils turned on her and consumed all the flesh on her body."

The boll weevil seemed intent on catching me, and I realized this was part of "the show." Annie Lee had forgotten to tell me.

I glanced down at Bill in bewilderment, preparing to tell him that boll weevils didn't consume human flesh, when several giant boll weevils emerged from the doors of local businesses and ran through the crowds and into the street. The crowd shouted and laughed, and several small children began to scream and cry hysterically. The giant bugs threw out candy from the buckets slung over their arms.

The parade progressed down the two blocks, and I continued waving and evading the boll weevil, who had started to act frustrated. Then it occurred to me that maybe he *was*. She'd said Minny had been surrounded and then consumed by boll weevils. So I stood still as our float got to the end of the street before it started to turn the corner. (Thematically, it seemed the right time. The children didn't need to see the whole flesh-consuming thing.)

The boll weevil grabbed my arm and held tight. "Once this float stops, you're coming with me," it said, and I realized it had Sebastian Jenkins's voice.

I frantically searched the crowd for Luke, but he was busy breaking up an argument between two women on the sidewalk.

I supposed it was up to me to find a way out.

The float leaned as it turned the corner, and I took advantage of the opportunity. Jerking free from Sebastian's hold, I elbowed him in the stomach and gave him a hard push off the float, the momentum nearly making me fall off with him.

"Oh!" Annie Lee's voice echoed downtown. "Minny's puttin' up a fight!"

Sebastian fell to the ground, rolling around like a roly-poly, then got to his feet and took off running.

"Luke!" I shouted. *"Luke!"*

I finally caught his attention.

"The boll weevil is Sebastian Jenkins!"

But the other boll weevils had all followed.

"And all the boll weevils were chased out of town," Annie Lee said as though she were finishing a bedtime story.

Luke took off running, and Willy joined him as they began to chase the boll weevils, who were heading in the opposite direction down Buttercup. It occurred to me that although I'd shoved Sebastian off the float, all the boll weevils had fallen in ranks around him, making it difficult to immediately see which one was Sebastian.

Which meant Sebastian had help. From who?

Mayor Sterling? He was in charge of the program, which made him the most likely culprit.

The parade continued despite the ruckus. I could see that Luke had tackled a boll weevil a half block down, and Willy had grabbed another before we turned onto Henry and headed past the police station.

"Would you look at Sweet Briar's finest subduing the boll weevils?" Annie Lee asked with admiration in her voice. "I'm sure if Luke Montgomery had been the police chief back then, the Sweet Briar crops would have been saved!"

Several women catcalled.

The float came to a halt, and Bill reached up a hand, laughing. "Lauren's bound to be pissed as hell we can't reshoot the boll weevil falling off."

I scanned the crowd again, taking advantage of the height, before I climbed down. "Cale said Dixie was down here, but I don't see her anywhere."

My phone vibrated in my hand, and I saw she'd just sent a text.

Found something for the case. Bring Bill to the Sweet Briar Cotton Mill. This is big. Don't bring Luke. He's in on the whole thing.

What? I couldn't believe that.

I hopped off the float and showed the text to Bill.

His gaze jerked to mine. "Where's the cotton mill?"

I pointed to the abandoned cotton mill halfway down the street and set back from the road.

Everyone in the parade in front of us had gone running back to Main Street to watch the giant Boll Weevil Crushing, which Annie Lee was now describing over the microphone. Apparently the crowd had joined the hunt, and there was quite a melee in progress.

"What do you want to do?" Bill asked. "Do you really think Luke's part of it?"

"No."

"You don't sound sure."

"Why would Dixie say he was otherwise?" But part of me couldn't help wondering if the text was really from my cousin.

"What do you want to do?" Bill asked.

I was torn. If Dixie hadn't sent the text, then someone had her phone, and likely had *her*. But if Bill and I just showed up, we'd probably be walking into a trap. "Maybe we should wait for Luke."

But even as I said the words, a new text arrived.

If you want to see Dixie alive, you and Bill come now. Come alone. The cotton mill.

The text was from the supplier's number.

"Shit," Bill said when he saw the text. "I bet you want to go."

"You can stay behind and warn Luke."

He gave me a shaky smile. "Think of the ratings."

"Yeah," I said, feeling like I was going to barf. "The ratings."

Dixie's text had said not to tell Luke, but I forwarded the text to Luke anyway as I started walking down the street to the mill, with Bill following behind me.

We walked across the overgrown lot toward the storage building about two hundred yards from the road, traipsing across the overgrown gravel parking. No one would think to look for us here. He'd chosen well.

I glanced down at my phone, surprised Luke hadn't answered yet. Why hadn't he answered yet?

The door to the building was ajar, and Bill and I hesitated in the opening before walking into the darkness. Dixie was counting on me. I had no doubt she'd come looking for me if our positions were reversed.

My eyes adjusted, and I saw a faint light at the end of the interior, coming from a partially open door.

"My camera won't pick up anything in here," Bill whispered.

"I'm going to turn on the video on my phone."

"But if you get a text or call, you won't be able to see it or respond."

"I doubt our mystery person will let me make calls anyway." I quickly had the video rolling.

We walked across the massive space, my heels clicking softly on the broken concrete. So much for surprising our host. When we reached the partially open door, I took a breath, then walked in, big as I pleased, torn between hoping I'd see Dixie and hoping I wouldn't.

My heart sank.

Dixie sat in a rickety-looking wooden chair, with a handgun pointed at her head.

I gasped in horror, not only because my cousin was being held at gunpoint, but because Cale Malone was the man holding the weapon.

Chapter Thirty-Five

"Summer, Bill," Cale said. "Come on in."

My feet froze in place. "What are you doin', Cale?"

"Come on now, Summer," he said good-naturedly, but his hand shook a little. "You've been pretty smart up until now. In fact, that's why the three of you are here. You've put so much together already. Surely you can figure out the rest."

When I didn't move, he motioned with his other hand. "Come on in. If you don't, I'll just shoot Dixie in the forehead."

Tears streamed down her face. "Run! Both of you, run!"

Cale gave her shoulder a hard shake. "Shut up, Dixie."

I remembered I had the phone in my hand, recording all this. I was going to get him to admit to as much as I could. I walked into the room, and Bill followed. "I'm not leaving you, Dixie. Never again."

Cale made a face, but I could tell he wasn't as cavalier about this as he was trying to act.

"Summer," he said, "I'm gonna need you to toss that phone on the floor. Can't have you trying to sneak a call or a text."

I saw no reason to fight him. My phone could capture his voice just as easily on the ground, so I squatted and set it down on the concrete. "It's new," I said. "And I didn't buy insurance."

"*Always* buy the insurance," Bill said.

"I know . . ."

Cale stared at us in disbelief, then motioned to Bill. "Drop the camera."

"This camera cost thousands of dollars, and I can't set it on the ground. How about I just hold it under my arm."

Cale's mouth sagged.

Bill tucked it under his arm, snugged against his hip. "See?"

Cale shook his head. "Whatever. Just come in and move away from the door."

"So are you gonna shoot us just like you did Ed?" I asked, forcing the words past the lump in my throat. "That's why you were so surprised we found his body. You said you hadn't checked his apartment yet. You were saving it. Why?"

He grinned, but it didn't quite reach his eyes. "You tell me."

"I don't know." I looked down at Dixie. She wasn't tied to that chair with anything but her fear. If I rushed Cale and distracted him, Dixie and Bill could make a run for it. "Were you the one who convinced Ed to tell me about Otto's bike?"

He just continued grinning.

"I'm going to take that as a smug yes. Did *you* move Otto's body?"

"Summer, you're smart, but you're still not thinking like someone who's trying to cover their tracks. The trick is to find someone else to do your dirty work so you have as little connection to the crimes as possible."

I'd already suspected that Cale had no intention of letting us out of this room alive, but that just confirmed it. "Ed moved the body," I said. "Then you told him to find me at the church and tell me about the bike. Why?"

"Who came running when you ended up in the ER?" he asked.

"Luke." How had I not made the connection? My stomach knotted. "You were handling Ryker's murder, and you didn't want Luke paying too much attention."

"I knew he'd be distracted if he believed you were in danger. The sheriff's department is nosing in on the murders too, but they're too wrapped up in their investigation into the dirty cop in Sweet Briar to pay much attention."

I shook my head. "Dirty cop?" Then it hit me. "You set up Luke to look dirty with the sheriff's department." That helped explain why Luke was having so many issues with Deputy Dixon—and why Teddy had been so anxious for me to stay away from him. But where did my cousin fit in? "You bastard. Luke's your friend."

"I didn't want to do it, Summer, trust me. He's been my friend since we were kids, but I'm in too damn deep now, and I'm not going to jail. Not as a cop."

"So you'd sentence him to it instead? On what charges? Murder? Moving Otto's body? Drug trafficking? Why kill Ed and Ryker?"

"Dixie knows about Ryker," Cale said. "She used to date him. She knew he was a dealer."

She shook her head, her eyes wide. "No. I didn't. I knew he used, but not that he sold it. He knew Luke and I were close, so he never fully trusted me."

"Well, I didn't know he dealt until about a year ago. When I pulled him over for driving under the influence, I quickly figured out he wasn't under the influence of alcohol. I searched his car and found his stash, but I didn't confiscate it. I told him that I'd let him off if he paid me a percentage of the profits. This town doesn't pay shit, and I was tired of scraping by. I was making good money and looking the other way so Ryker could build his business. Everything was goin' fine until he got too big for his britches. He decided to end our arrangement, but he knew I was watching, so he started using Otto to run as a courier for him."

"Why did you kill Otto?" Dixie asked, fresh tears filling her eyes. "He never hurt anybody. How could you, Cale?"

"I didn't mean to, Dixie," Cale said in a deceptively calm voice. "My temper got the better of me. I knew he was runnin' for Ryker, so I told him to keep the next delivery for me . . . or else."

"But he hid the stash in the barn," I said.

Cale tilted his head. "I knew he hid it. I just didn't know where. Thank you for findin' it," he said. "I told you that you were good."

"So how'd you kill poor Otto?" I asked. "They said he died from alcohol poisoning."

"I made him keep drinkin', thinkin' he'd get drunk enough to tell me. But the damn fool held out and never did."

Dixie shot him a glare. "So he died, then you had Ed move him. How'd you get him to do that? He was Ryker's partner."

"After I killed Ryker, Ed realized he'd be better off workin' with me. At least at first. He went to Otto's apartment to search for the stash, and when he called to say he couldn't find it, he said he was gonna turn me in. I was a block away, so I went over and caught him as he was leavin'. I made him go into the bathroom, and I shot him. I'd already gotten what was left of Ryker's stash, and with Ed dead in Otto's apartment, I figured I had several days to find Ed's. I had enough to get started. I had Ryker's phone, so I started goin' through his contacts, sendin' them messages with a burner phone and lettin' them know a new sheriff was in town." He grinned at his almost-pun. "And then *you* sent me a message, Summer."

"Were you really gonna meet me last night?" I asked as a cold sweat broke out all over my body.

"I was there," he said. "Lurkin' in the back. But you were a popular girl, and I couldn't get to you. I followed you and Luke outside. You both confirmed Luke's continued interest in you, so I took some photos and sold them to that gossip site."

"Another distraction," I said.

"I'm meetin' my supplier," he said. "I needed to keep Luke busy. Like trackin' down your stalker after you left Otto's farm and convincin' him to wear that stupid bug suit. I knew Mayor Sterling planned for all the other bugs to run around, but when you knocked Jenkins off the float and he took off . . ." He grinned. "Some things just can't be planned."

"Why are you doin' this?" I asked. "Why lure me here?"

"You'd already figured too much out, Summer. I had to put an end to this before you figured out the rest. I was goin' to do it this afternoon out at Otto's farm, but then you answered Luke's call and linked me to y'all. No one else knew I was there at the barn."

I couldn't believe he was talking about killing us so matter-of-factly, but then he'd already killed three people. What were three more?

"So why not just shoot us?" I asked, the words tumbling out of my mouth. "Why keep us here? Aren't we going to be in the way?"

"I thought so at first, but when God gives you lemons, make lemonade. The supplier will be here any minute, and I'm gonna use you three as an example of what happens to people who get in my way."

"Well, that sounds fun . . . ," Dixie said in a sarcastic voice. I was glad to see she was more like herself, for however long that would be.

Cale grabbed his phone and checked the screen. "He's comin' in." He motioned to the corner with his gun. "You all stand over there away from the door. Dixie, you get up and join 'em."

She got out of her chair. I wrapped an arm around her back and practically dragged her to the corner. Where was Luke? Why wasn't he here already?

We heard footsteps in the outer warehouse space. Cale pointed his gun at us and lifted his finger to his lips to tell us to be quiet. I wasn't sure it was wise of us to obey. A quick glance at Bill suggested he was wondering the same.

I decided I was going to rush Cale the moment the door opened. I had no hopes of disarming him, but if I could distract him and the supplier, Dixie and Bill could escape.

I pulled Dixie into a hug, then whispered in her ear, "When I make my move, run out of here and go find Luke."

"What?" she gasped.

I had my back to Cale and mouthed to Bill, *Take Dixie and run.*

The door swung open, but my intention to make a run toward Cale was shattered when I saw the man in the doorway.

My cousin Teddy was the supplier.

CHAPTER THIRTY-SIX

"Teddy?" Dixie called out.

Teddy's gaze turned toward us, and the self-assured look on his face instantly faded. "Dixie? Summer? What the hell are you doin' here?"

"What are *you* doin' here, Teddy?" Dixie asked, but the dismay in her voice gave away her fear. "You're selling *drugs?*"

Cale started to laugh. "Teddy Baumgartner. I never would have expected it. I guess that explains the extra cash you've been spending on your farm."

His eyes hardened. "Gotta do what I gotta to do to take care of my family."

Cale's eyebrows rose. "Funny you should mention that."

"Why's my family here, Cale?"

"They're far too nosy."

Disappointment filled Teddy's eyes. "I told you to leave it alone, Summer. Why the fuck didn't you listen to me?"

"Why the fuck are you supplyin' drugs to lowlifes like Cale Malone and Ryker Pelletier?" Dixie asked in disgust.

Teddy pointed to the door. "I want them gone, Malone."

"Not gonna happen, Baumgartner. They know too much, and I don't trust your cousin one iota."

"Then no deal."

"Dixie won't talk," I said. "She's used to keepin' secrets. Keep me, let her and Bill go."

Cale's face hardened. "Everybody stays."

Teddy looked like he was about argue, then said, "Fine. Let's get this deal ironed out."

Cale nodded. "Now we're talkin'."

Teddy turned all business. "I head up to Atlanta twice a month to get a new shipment. I'll give it to you at the same price I offered Pelletier."

"I'll pay five percent less," Cale said.

"Five percent and we send Dixie out of here right now."

Cale grinned. "Ten percent less and you've got yourself a deal."

Teddy gave me an apologetic grimace. "Done."

"What?" Dixie wailed. *"No!"*

I grabbed her arm and gave her a shove toward the door through which we'd entered. "Dixie, go."

Cale moved in front of her, blocking her path. "You will keep everything that happened here to yourself. If anyone walks in through that door, I'm shootin' your brother and then your cousin," he said, aiming the gun at me while he spoke. "Have I made myself perfectly clear?"

She nodded as tears streamed down her face. "I hate you, Cale. If you hurt them—"

"Don't piss me off with meaningless threats, Dixie. I suggest you get out of here before I change my mind."

She looked back at me with guilt-filled eyes.

"I'll be okay," I lied. "I'll see you in a few minutes. Go." I expected Luke to show up any minute, but now I worried what would happen if he did.

I pushed out a sigh of relief when Dixie walked out the door, and Teddy's face relaxed a bit.

"Summer." Teddy reached out his hand to me, and I started to walk toward him.

"She stays where she is," Cale said in a cold voice.

I lifted my hands in surrender. "I'm fine here. Just get your deal done." I cast a glance back at Bill, who looked like he was about to crap his pants. I understood why he was worried. He didn't have anyone fighting for him.

Teddy and Cale discussed delivery dates and how the shipments were never the same, but always a mix of prescription drugs that included Adderall, Xanax, and Oxy. When they reached an agreement, Teddy looked Cale in the eye. "I have a shipment I planned to sell to Ryker right outside this door. I'm ready to make a deal right now. You got the cash?"

Cale grinned. "Eager, huh?"

Teddy didn't respond.

"Okay," Cale said. "I'm ready to do this now. Summer, go get his supply. And you better come back or Teddy's a dead man."

I'd never hated anyone like I hated him right now. "Unlike you, Cale Malone, I believe in loyalty."

"Save the lectures, Summer," Cale said as though exhausted, "and get the drugs."

I cast Teddy a worried look, but part of me was so pissed at him I wanted to kill him myself if we survived this mess.

I walked out the door into the dark room and nearly screamed when I bumped right into Luke.

He covered my mouth with my hand, then pulled me into his arms and leaned in to my ear. "Are you okay?"

I nodded.

"Jesus, Summer." His hold tightened.

"What's takin' so long?" Cale called out from the room.

I pushed Luke's hand away and said in a loud voice, "I'm lookin' for it."

"It should be to your right," Teddy shouted.

I stared into Luke's terrified eyes, fighting the urge to cry, then whispered, "Teddy's makin' a drug deal with Cale."

"I know." He sounded defeated, and I realized he was holding a small black bag in his hand. "You have a choice, Summer," he whispered, but his tone sounded ominous.

"What are you talking about?"

"Teddy's workin' with the sheriff as an informant—I didn't know until about five minutes ago—but he needs this deal to go through to nail Cale."

The relief I felt was palpable. My cousin wasn't a bad guy. I'd been right to believe in him. "I have to go back in there."

Luke grabbed my upper arms and held me in place. "No. You don't."

"Yeah. I do," I said more calmly than I felt. "I have to. For Teddy and for me."

"This is dangerous, Summer."

It was, and Teddy would do it for me. In a heartbeat. "I know." I snatched the bag from him, then turned around and went inside.

Cale looked furious. "Where the hell were you, Summer?"

"I couldn't find it. I think Dixie must have kicked it on her way out."

Cale reached for it, but I had no idea how this was supposed to work, so I shoved it at Teddy.

Bill was still in the corner, his camera tucked under his arm. He looked like a statue.

Teddy unzipped the bag and dumped the contents on the chair. Two bags full of pills landed on the seat.

"The goin' price is two thousand," Teddy said.

"Eighteen hundred with my discount for not killin' your sister."

"What about my cousin?"

Cale held his gaze. "Eighteen hundred."

Teddy put out his arm and pushed me behind him, but I stood to the side so I could see. "Fine. Where's the money?"

Cale reached into the top pocket of his shirt and pulled out a folded-over envelope that looked all too familiar. The last time I'd seen it was in a brown paper bag.

"That doesn't look thick enough to be carryin' eighteen hundred dollars," Teddy said.

"That's because it's not. It's a deposit of five hundred. I'll get you the rest once I make a few sales."

He held out the envelope, and Teddy snatched it from him. "I look forward to doing business with you."

Cale gave Teddy a questioning look, suspicion covering his face. "No argument?"

"I just want to make sure Summer's safe." Then he glanced over at Bill. "And him too. No one needs to get hurt here. We're all adults. We know how to keep our mouths shut."

Cale shook his head. "You know that'll never work. Dixie's good at secrets. She never told a soul who sold her boyfriend those drugs, but him . . ." He turned his gun and attention on Bill. "I don't know shit about him."

My heart jolted when I heard a gunshot, quickly followed by another. Everything was happening too fast for me to follow.

Bill fell to the floor, his camera banging on the concrete. He lay sprawled on his side, not moving.

I screamed as Teddy shoved me to the ground and then fell on top of me.

There was movement behind us, and I realized Luke was in the room, holding a gun on Cale.

Cale's left arm was bleeding, but he was holding a gun on Luke.

My heart leaped into my throat, and I felt like I was going to throw up. *Oh, please let Luke be okay.* I couldn't lose him again—not like this.

"Cale," Luke said. His voice was calm, but I saw the tension on his face. "Just put the gun down."

"No. No way. If I put this gun down, it's all over for me." Cale pivoted and pointed the gun at me and Teddy, his arm shaking. "I'll shoot her, Luke. I'll empty this gun into the both of them to make sure I kill her."

"And you know I'll kill you, Cale. Before you even get off the last shot."

A bitter smile lit up Cale's face. "That's a chance I'm willing to take. Are you?"

Luke's eyes filled with indecision.

Bill moaned in the back corner, but Luke kept his gaze on Cale. "Why are you doin' this, Cale? You're a good man."

"If there's one thing I've learned, it's that being a good man doesn't mean shit. And we both know we can't make squat in this town."

"Then move to Birmingham. Or Atlanta. Don't start supplying drugs to addicts."

Cale released a sharp laugh. "Hey, job security, right? Besides, you and I both know that addicts will get drugs no matter what. I might as well be the one makin' money off it."

"And killin' people?"

"An unfortunate consequence."

"An unfortunate consequence," Luke repeated in disgust, then straightened his arm with a new determination hardening his eyes. "Don't make yourself another unfortunate consequence, Cale."

He grinned. "Funny, I was just thinking the same thing about Summer."

The two men held their guns on each other for two more seconds.

Bill released another moan, and Luke said, "I'm willing to let you walk, but you can't hurt anyone else. You just take your drugs and get the fuck out of here."

Triumph filled Cale's eyes, but he looked down at the bag, then back at me. "Summer's gonna put this back in the bag."

"No fucking way," Luke grunted.

But I was already trying to shove Teddy off me. "Let me up, Teddy."

"No."

I elbowed him hard in the stomach, then took advantage of his momentary shock to scramble out from under him.

Luke started to protest, but I held up my hands and slowly walked toward the chair. "Let me do this and we can send Cale on his way."

Luke swallowed, his Adam's apple bobbing, as he watched me reach for the first bag of pills. I stuffed it into the larger bag and then did the same with the second. After I zipped up the bigger bag, I held it up, facing Cale. "Is this what you want? Was this bag full of pills worth three people's lives?"

An ugly grin spread across his pale face. His arm was covered in blood, and a small puddle had collected on the floor beneath him. "We're gonna take a walk to my car, and then I'll let you go."

"You think I believe *that*?" I asked, outrage overriding my fear. "You just stood there a few minutes ago and told me I was smart."

"I guess that's the chance you'll have to take," he said, but I could see he was starting to wobble.

He was standing about three feet from me, his gun pointed at my chest. I knew in my gut if I went with him, he'd shoot me just to hurt Luke. He'd already killed three people and injured another. What was one more?

I took a step toward him, holding the bag of drugs in my clenched fist. "You want this bag, Cale?" I said, as my anger continued to build. "Here's your fucking bag!" Then I swung the bag upward, putting my whole body into the move as I aimed for his arm.

The gun went off, and I ducked on instinct, but the ricocheting sound told me the bullet must have hit a metal beam above us. Cale lost his balance and stumbled as his gun went flying into the air.

"Son of a bitch!" Luke yelled and rushed past me to tackle Cale to the floor.

Seconds later, several sheriff's deputies ran into the room with guns raised, but Luke already had Cale pinned to the ground.

Adrenaline flowed through my veins, and I stomped closer to Cale, ignoring the hatred in his eyes. I put a hand on my hip and pointed my finger at him. "*Gotcha!,* you asshole."

Luke glanced up at me with an expression that vacillated between relief, admiration, and anger. But admiration won out, and he grinned. "Yeah, you did."

CHAPTER THIRTY-SEVEN

The next morning Dixie and I were at the Darling Investigation office two hours before our call time. News had broken that I'd helped bring down a dirty Sweet Briar policeman due to my PI work, and my manager, Justin, had set me up with several morning news programs to talk about it. I had agreed as long as Dixie was allowed to sit with me. Since we already had a film crew, it was decided that they would hook their cameras up to the live feed and handle it themselves.

When we walked in, the crew was already there waiting for us, with the exception of Bill and Lauren.

Bill was currently in the Sweet Briar Hospital recovering from a gunshot wound to his chest, but thankfully the bullet hadn't hit anything vital, and he was expected to make a full recovery.

I hadn't spoken to Lauren since the night before, but during all the questioning with the sheriff's department, it had come to light that Bill had taken a lot of video of our side investigation, including the showdown in the back room of the cotton mill. Bill had left his camera running the whole time. The footage wasn't the best, but Bill, bless his heart, had held the camera at an angle that had gotten most of Cale in the shot. Even after being shot, he'd still made sure the camera was capturing the standoff, and me taking Cale down. Surely he deserved some sort of award for that. And they had my phone as a backup recording.

The crew started clapping as Dixie and I walked in, and someone shouted, "Thanks for pulling this show out of the shitter."

I grinned. "Never doubt that I fully commit to my work." Then I looked around. "Where's Lauren?"

Tony grimaced. "Schapiro flew in last night. She's got a morning meeting with him."

I wondered what that might be about, but I didn't care. With all the interest over our investigation of Otto's death and the footage—even if it was bad—of Cale's takedown, we were guaranteed to have good enough ratings to make sure I got paid my salary, and possibly the bonus too. The farm was safe.

"Our first interview is in less than ten minutes," Karen said. "I thought we'd have you and Dixie sit in the client chairs." She'd angled them so the name of our investigation company was directly behind us, even if it read backward.

"Good idea," I said, giving her a smile.

She smiled back, then turned to the crew to work out a few logistics.

I snuck a glance at Dixie while Chuck hooked up our mikes. "Are you still doin' okay?"

She grinned. "As good as can be expected after leavin' my brother and cousin and friend at the mercy of a man I'd always trusted."

"Everyone trusted him, Dixie. Even Luke."

Her grin turned mischievous as she glanced at the door. "Speak of the devil."

Luke stood in the doorway in his police uniform, staring at me with an intensity that sucked my breath away. He and Teddy had spent most of the night with the sheriff's deputies. Turned out Teddy had discovered Ryker was a drug dealer a couple of months before, and after the last time Dixie had gotten mixed up with a guy and drugs, he'd approached the sheriff's department about becoming an informant to bring him down. Teddy had spoken with Otto in that alley, but only to try and convince him to help out. Otto had refused to tell him when he was making his next courier run (by then Cale had already waylaid him) and had hidden the drugs in his barn instead.

The sheriff's office had started suspecting there was a dirty cop in Sweet Briar, and Teddy had found out from them. Soon after, Cale had started feeding them false information about Luke, which had only made Teddy more suspicious of him. Mayor Sterling had caught wind of the rumors, which had given him a major case of buyer's remorse about welcoming us to town with open arms. Cameras were everywhere, after all, ready to catch the slightest bit of tension, and besides, some of our "cases" had encouraged small-scale feuds. Becky MacDonald had lit Nettie Peabody's rose bushes on fire. And as for why he'd met Ryker behind the café my first day in town—Luke had been right. Mayor Sterling said he'd been discussing a zoning issue over Ryker's bike shop.

Teddy still had no love for Luke, but earlier that morning, my cousin had admitted that not only was Luke clean, but it was obvious he still cared about me.

And now Luke was here, watching me as though we were the only two people in the room. He strode toward me with purpose before he gathered me in his arms and kissed me in front of everyone.

I kissed him back, clinging to his neck and showing him how scared I'd been over possibly losing him, and it occurred to me that he was showing me the same.

Several people catcalled and clapped, but for once I didn't care.

Luke lifted his head and cupped my cheek with his hand. "I'm sorry I'm just now seein' you. We didn't finish until early in the mornin', and I—"

I reached up and gave him a soft kiss to quiet him. "It's okay. You don't need to explain."

"You have to know that I wanted to be with you, Summer, makin' sure you were really okay. I wanted to be the one reassurin' you."

"I know."

He breathed in as he searched my face, his hand lightly caressing my cheek. "You scared the shit out of me."

"You scared the shit out of me too."

"But it's my job."

"Apparently it's mine too."

He scowled at that. "At least until you finish shooting."

I didn't answer.

Dixie and I had talked about my options until early in the morning. According to Justin, this exposure was like a shot of adrenaline to my dying career.

Staring into Luke's warm brown eyes, I knew he deserved to know the truth. "I've got some possible jobs lined up for when we finish shooting next week. A movie, even. My manager says it's like my whole career just got a reboot."

He tried to look excited. "That's great. No more money problems, then, right?"

"Yeah," I said.

"Is that what you want, Summer?" he asked softly.

"I need you in your chairs, ladies," Karen said, grabbing my arm and tugging. "You've messed up your lipstick."

I let her guide me to the chair, my gaze still on Luke.

What *did* I want? When was the last time someone had asked me that? When was the last time anyone had cared about the answer?

Karen handed me a mirror, and sure enough my lipstick was smudged, but I glanced up at Luke.

Sorry, he mouthed.

I'm not, I mouthed back with a grin.

Dixie handed me my lipstick tube. I quickly repaired the damage, then handed the mirror and lipstick to someone as Chuck checked our sound levels. Someone had set up a monitor next to Tony's stationary camera, allowing Dixie and me to see the person interviewing us.

Karen counted down, and a popular national morning host's face appeared on the monitor. His voice came through my earpiece as he introduced our segment. The host smiled and said, "Summer, welcome to our show. You've had a busy week there in Sweet Briar, Alabama. Is it usually that crazy?"

"Thanks for having us, Matt, and no, Sweet Briar is usually a calm, friendly town. I suspect that Mayor Sterling sees me as a tornado that swept into town and exposed the town's secrets."

The host took on a serious expression. "You're there to film a reality TV show with you acting as a private investigator, and yet you found yourself investigating a real case."

I pulled out my Southern charm and said, "Not *acting* as a private investigator, Matt. I *am* a private investigator. I even have a license to prove it." Then I gave him a huge smile.

"You really consider yourself a PI?" he asked in disbelief. "The only experience you have is portraying your teen character, Isabella Holmes."

"And taking down a dirty cop," I said, still smiling but injecting a hint of attitude into my voice. "Along with solving three murders."

"She *literally* took him down herself," Dixie said. "Stared down the barrel of a gun and knocked it out of his hand."

"All in a day's work," I said with a laugh as I turned to her. She winked as though to say, *I've got your back.*

And I knew she did. Just like I had hers.

Movement by the door caught my eye, and I realized Lauren had just walked in. She made her way over to Karen.

The host continued. "So you're in your hometown, filming this reality show, and suddenly your face is everywhere. *Everyone* is talking about Summer Butler. What do you plan to do once you get this wrapped up? What projects do you have lined up?"

I glanced past the camera at Luke.

He offered me a smile of encouragement, and I knew he'd changed. He wasn't threatened by my career. He wouldn't like it if I left, but he wouldn't pressure me to stay. It made my answer so much easier.

"Well, Matt, I plan on staying right here in Sweet Briar for a while," I said. Surprise washed over Luke's face, quickly followed by joy.

"And what will you be doing in your small hometown?" the host asked.

Lauren held up a piece of paper, and a mixture of relief and dread washed through me. I'd revel in the first feeling and deal with the second later.

"Why, I'll be continuing my new career as a private investigator," I said, then read the sign again.

WE GOT PICKED UP FOR A SECOND SEASON.
REAL CASES THIS TIME.

"Darling Investigations is open for business. And who knows," I drawled with a broad smile, "if you hire us, *your* case just might be on season two."

Acknowledgments

Summer Butler was born on a hot June day in 2016.

I was looking ahead to wrapping up my Magnolia Steele series and was starting to think about a replacement. So while I was driving from Orlando, Florida, to Jacksonville, with four of my kids in the car, my developmental editor, Angela Polidoro, and I spent an hour brainstorming. We'd both agreed to think of ideas to discuss, but when she called, I had nothing. (I'd just spent two days pitching my book *One Paris Summer* to librarians at ALA.) But it worked out because Angela had two ideas—one, that the protagonist was a PI in a reality TV show, and the second was that the protagonist was also a former teen star. Since I'd just binged two seasons of *UnReal*, I was intrigued. We discussed several other ideas and ended the call with several potential plots. Since I was headed to the beach for a vacation with my kids, I told her I'd send her a synopsis soon.

I suspect she didn't expect one the next day.

But once the wheels started spinning, I was dying to write them down.

In less than a week, I had a completed, ready-to-turn-in synopsis and proposal, and thankfully Alison Dasho saw the potential Angela and I had seen and soon made an offer. Alison had been my developmental editor for several of my indie books as well as my 47North book *The Curse Keepers*, before she deserted me (not that I'm bitter) and took a job as an editor for Thomas & Mercer. So I was thrilled with the opportunity to work with Alison again.

I visited Amazon a few years ago and ran into Alison in the Thomas & Mercer department. She told her coworker that I was great at revisions. I sure hoped she believed that after I turned in the first draft of this manuscript, because this book saw some major changes.

I turned in the first draft and knew it was bad. Bad enough that I pushed "Send," opened a bottle of wine, and called my oldest son and said, "I need you to help me plot a crime." Perhaps I should have been more worried when he said, "No problem."

Trace and I spent the next hour coming up with a crime and motives . . . then I changed half of it when I started revising, because just like Baby in *Dirty Dancing*, turns out my brain doesn't like being put in a corner. So my apologies to the patrons who were present at Buffalo Wild Wings in Independence, Missouri, on the night when Trace asked me at a family dinner how my revision was going, and I confessed I'd changed his murderer.

Oops.

Thank you to Angela for always having my back and dealing with my recent missed deadlines with a sunny attitude and multiple pep talks. It's a blessing when your editor truly gets you—both on the page and off.

Thank you to Alison for taking a chance on me. Especially thanks for not demanding back your advance after reading the first version.

Thank you to my son, Trace, for helping me brainstorm crimes. Please save your criminal mastermind for my plots.

Thank you to my children who deal with a frazzled mother who feeds them fast food for dinner way too many times when she's on (or behind) deadline. At least we still eat together at the kitchen table. (Hey, I'm taking my Mother of the Year points wherever I can get them.)

And thank you, dear readers, who chose to read my book out of the millions available. I never take you for granted.

About the Author

Denise Grover Swank is the *New York Times*, *Wall Street Journal*, and *USA Today* bestselling author of the Rose Gardner Mystery Series, the Magnolia Steele Mystery Series, The Wedding Pact Series, The Curse Keepers Series, and others. She was born in Kansas City, Missouri, and lived in the area until she was nineteen. Then she became a nomad, living in five cities, four states, and ten houses over the course of ten years before moving back to her roots. Her hobbies include witty Facebook comments (in her own mind) and dancing in her kitchen with her children (quite badly, if you believe her offspring).

Hidden talents include the gift of justification and the ability to drink massive amounts of caffeine and still fall asleep within two minutes. Her lack of the sense of smell allows her to perform many unspeakable tasks. She has six children and hasn't lost her sanity—or so she leads you to believe. For more information about Denise, please visit her at www.denisegroverswank.com.